A CHICAGOLAND VAMPIRES NOVEL

WILD THINGS

✠

CHLOE NEILL

NAL NEW AMERICAN LIBRARY

New American Library
Published by the Penguin Group
Penguin Group (USA) LLC, 375 Hudson Street,
New York, New York 10014

Ⓟ

USA | Canada | UK | Ireland | Australia | New Zealand | India | South Africa | China
penguin.com
A Penguin Random House Company

First published by New American Library,
a division of Penguin Group (USA) LLC

First Printing, February 2014

LIBRARY OF CONGRESS CATALOGING-IN-PUBLICATION DATA:

Neill, Chloe.
Wild things: a Chicagoland vampires novel/Chloe Neill.
pages cm
ISBN 978-0-451-41519-6 (pbk.)
1. Merit (Fictitious character: Neill)—Fiction. 2. Vampires—Fiction. 3. Chicago (Ill.)—
Fiction. I. Title.
PS3614.E4432W55 2014
813'.6—dc23   2013038459

Printed in the United States of America
1 3 5 7 9 10 8 6 4 2

Set in Caslon 540

PUBLISHER'S NOTE
This is a work of fiction. Names, characters, places, and incidents either are the product of the author's imagination or are used fictitiously, and any resemblance to actual persons, living or dead, business establishments, events, or locales is entirely coincidental.

continued . . .

ACKNOWLEDGMENTS

Thanks, as always, to the usual crew of fantastic Novitiates who assist in the development of these books, including my editor, Jessica Wade, my agent, Lucienne Diver, and my continuity editor and assistant, Krista McNamara.

Very special thanks to Jesse Feldman, who offered valuable editing advice, and to Penguin's fantastic publicity and marketing staff, including Jessica Butler and Jodi Rosoff, without whom no one would know these books existed.

Keely Buesing and Debi Murray provided very helpful advice on medical matters, and Nicole Peeler taught me an outlining trick that kept this book miraculously on track.

To the other fantastic romance and fantasy authors I've had the good fortune to meet at conferences over the last year, it has been an absolute pleasure, and I look forward to future shenanigans.

The heartiest of thanks to SHB, who has the unfortunate job of putting up with me when I'm days away from a deadline or sweating the small stuff. You're the best.

Such as we are made of, such we be.

—*William Shakespeare*

WILD THINGS

✠

CHAPTER ONE

MIDNIGHT RIDER

Mid-February
Chicago, Illinois

Within the last ten months, I'd become a vampire, joined Chicago's Cadogan House, and become its Sentinel. I'd learned how to wield a sword, how to bluff a monster, how to fall, and how to get back up.

Perhaps most of all, I'd learned about loyalty. And based on the magic that was pouring through the House's first-floor hallway, I hadn't been the only one who'd taken that particular quality to heart.

Dozens of Cadogan's vampires stood in the hallway outside the office of our Master, Ethan Sullivan, waiting for a call, for a word, for a plan. We stood in our requisite Cadogan black with our katanas at our sides because Ethan—our Liege and my lover—was preparing to run.

"Out of one fire and right into another," said the attractive blond vampire beside me. Lindsey was a member of Cadogan's guard corps and a skilled and capable fighter, but tonight she looked, as usual, more like a fashionista than a century-old vampire guard. She'd left her suit jacket downstairs and had matched her satin-striped black tuxedo pants with a white button-down and four-inch stiletto heels.

"Do they actually think we'd just let them take him?" she asked. "That we'd let them arrest him—our *Master*—right there in front of the House?"

An hour ago, a Chicago Police Department detective—fortunately, one of our allies—had come calling, advising us that the city's prosecutor had obtained a warrant for Ethan's arrest.

Ethan had killed Harold Monmonth, a powerful vampire from Europe who'd murdered two human guards before turning his sword on us. Ethan had acted in obvious self-defense, but violence had recently rocked the Windy City. Its citizens were afraid, and its mayor, Diane Kowalcyzk, was looking for someone to blame. She'd apparently managed to bring the prosecutor to her side.

That's why Ethan was sequestered in his office with Luc, the captain of Cadogan's guards, and Malik, the House's second in command, making a plan.

Detective Jacobs suggested Ethan seek refuge with the Breckenridges, a family of shape-shifters who lived in Loring Park, a suburb outside Chicago. That meant he'd also be outside the mayor's jurisdiction. The Brecks were über-wealthy, well connected, and politically influential. That was a powerful combination and enough, we hoped, to keep the mayor from using him as a sacrificial lamb.

Papa Breck, the family patriarch, was a friend of my father, Chicago real estate mogul Joshua Merit. I'd gone to school with some of the Breckenridge boys and had even dated one of them. But the Brecks had no love for vampires, which was part of the reason for the closed-door negotiations.

Ethan was the other reason. He was nearly four centuries old, and he had the stubbornness to match his age. Going gently into that good night wasn't his style, but Luc and Malik wanted him safely away. It had been a long winter for the House—including Ethan's premature demise and resurrection—and we didn't need any more drama. We certainly didn't trust Kowalcyzk and feared turning Ethan over to a justice system that seemed to be rigged against us.

The door had been closed for an hour. Voices had been raised, and the disagreement between Ethan and his soldiers spilled tense magic into the hallway. That was my particular point of contention. I was Cadogan's Sentinel, but I hadn't been allowed in the office. The words "plausible deniability" had been thrown around—right before the door had been shut in my face.

"The mayor knew there'd be trouble," I said. "The CPD already said Ethan acted in self-defense. And we just handed McKetrick to them on a silver platter. The city has absolutely nothing to complain about where we're concerned."

The detective's warning had come only hours after we'd managed to prove McKetrick, the city's now former supernatural liaison, was the source of the riots that had spread violence, destruction, and fire around the city. You'd think that would have put us in the mayor's good graces. Alas, no.

"They won't stay away forever," I said. "Jacobs wouldn't have warned us if he didn't think they were serious. And that doesn't give us many options. Ethan flees, or we have to fight."

"Whatever their next move, the House will be ready," Lindsey said. "We just have to scoot Ethan out of here." She checked a delicate gold watch. "Not much time before sunrise. This is going to be close."

"Papa Breck could still say no," I pointed out, wrapping my arms around my knees. He and Ethan were different sups, but equally stubborn.

But Lindsey shook her head. "Not if he's smart. Arresting a vampire for a bullshit reason isn't far from arresting a shifter for a bullshit reason. If Papa Breck doesn't take a stand now, he'll put the Pack at risk. But if he does take a stand?" She clucked her tongue. "Then he wins, double or nothing. We'll owe him a favor, *and* he'll have stood up to Kowalcyzk. That reinforces his power, and it's just—"

Before she could finish, the office door opened.

Luc and Malik emerged, Ethan behind them. All three were tall and bore the toughened shoulders of men in charge, but the physical similarities ended there.

Luc had tousled blond-brown hair and preferred snug jeans and well-worn boots to Ethan's and Malik's exquisite suits. Since Ethan's welfare fell under his jurisdiction, Luc's ruggedly handsome features were tight with concern.

Malik had cocoa skin, closely cropped hair, and pale green eyes that thoughtfully took in the hallway of vampires. Malik was reserved, careful, and unquestionably respected by the House. But like Luc, he also didn't look thrilled with the circumstances.

And then there was Ethan.

He was built like an athlete—long and lean, with taut muscles and a body that fit perfectly into his trim black suit. His hair was straight, shoulder length, and golden, framing a face so gorgeous it might have been sculpted by a master artist. Straight nose, honed cheekbones, lush mouth, and eyes as sharp and green as flawless emeralds. Ethan was as alpha as they came, protective and pretentious, intelligent and strategic, and stubborn enough to match me well.

We'd had our false starts, but we'd finally found a clear path to each other. That might have been the biggest miracle of all.

Ethan's forehead was pinched in concern, but his eyes gave

away nothing. He was the Master of our House; he didn't have the luxury of self-doubt.

A dozen vampires jumped to their feet.

"I'll be traveling to the Breckenridge estate," Ethan announced. "Cadogan vampires do not run. We do not hide. We do not scurry into the dark. We face our problems—head-on. But this House has been through much of late. I have been asked, for the sake of the House, to consider making myself scarce. I have agreed to do so—as a temporary measure."

The tension in my chest eased, but not by much. He clearly wasn't thrilled with the plan.

"In the meantime, we'll try to put this ugly business to bed. The House's lawyers will address the warrant. Malik has a friend in the governor's office, and he'll reach out to determine if the governor can encourage Mayor Kowalcyzk to act reasonably."

That was news to me, but then again, Malik was the quiet sort. And I didn't think he was the type to call in a political favor unless absolutely necessary.

"You'll take Merit to the Brecks'?" Lindsey asked.

"Assuming she can fit it into her schedule," he said.

Drama or not, there was always time for snark in Cadogan House.

"I'll manage," I assured him, "although I hate to leave my grandfather here."

My grandfather was Chicago's former supernatural liaison—emphasis on the "former"—but he and his employees, Catcher Bell and Jeff Christopher, still helped the CPD with supernatural issues. Because he'd helped us investigate the riots, McKetrick had targeted him. Grandpa's house had been firebombed, and he'd been caught in the explosion. He was recovering, but he was still in the hospital. He'd been more of a father to me than my actual father, and although he had people to protect him, I felt guilty leaving while he was out of service.

"I'll check in on him," Luc promised. "Give you updates."

"In that case," Ethan said, "we'll leave shortly. Malik has the House. And as you know, he makes a very capable Master when I'm . . . indisposed."

There were appreciative chuckles in the crowd. It wasn't Malik's first rodeo as Master; he'd held the job when Ethan hadn't been among the living.

"I will be honest. This may not work. We are betting that Diane Kowalcyzk is politically ambitious enough to not cross the Breckenridge family. That gambit could prove incorrect. Either way, our relationship with the city of Chicago could get worse before it gets better. But we are, and we will remain, Cadogan vampires."

He arched an eyebrow, a habit he used frequently and usually with good effect. "Of course, those Cadogan vampires should be at work right now, not eavesdropping outside their Master's office."

Smiling and appropriately chastised, the vampires dispersed, offering good-byes to their Liege as they passed. Margot, the House's brilliant chef, squeezed my hand, then headed down the hallway toward the kitchen.

Malik, Luc, Lindsey, and I stepped inside Ethan's office. He looked over his staff.

"We have a brief reprieve," Ethan said, "but the city may come knocking again."

"The House is ready," Luc said. "Lakshmi, however, is still on her way. We couldn't convince her to delay."

That was another sticky situation. Cadogan was no longer a member of the Greenwich Presidium, the organization that ruled

North American and Western European vampire houses. Mon-month had been one of its members. The GP was no friend of Cadogan House, and they apparently weren't willing to ignore the fact that we were now responsible for the deaths of two of their members. While we were no longer concerned about their opinion of us, they made powerful and dangerous enemies.

Lakshmi, one of the remaining GP members, was traveling to Chicago to render its verdict. It probably helped that she was one of the more commonsensical members of the GP, but it was odd that she was traveling while Darius West, the GP head, stayed under the radar in London. He'd been a political nonentity since an attack by a vampire assassin relieved him of his confidence, or so we surmised.

As it turned out, Lakshmi also was a friend to the Red Guard, the secret organization that kept watch on the Houses and their Masters. I was a new member, partnered with the guard captain from Grey House, Jonah. Lakshmi had provided insider information about GP shenanigans; in return for her help, I'd offered an unspecified favor. It was inevitable she'd attempt to collect; vampires were particular that way.

"Keep her out of the House," Ethan said. "We aren't members of the GP, and she has no business in our domain. She may have a legitimate claim to reparations, but that can be dealt with when we've dealt with the city."

"I spoke with Lakshmi's majordomo," Luc said, "tried to winnow information out of her. She wouldn't budge."

"We'll deal with it when we deal with it," Ethan said. "This entire situation is fraught with hazard."

Malik nodded. "It all comes down to who blinks first."

Ethan's eyes flattened. "Whatever happens, Cadogan House will not blink first."

We lived in Chicago, which meant off-street parking spots were hard to come by and the objects of envy. The House's coveted underground parking lot was accessible through the basement, so we headed downstairs. Ethan keyed the security pad at the door and stepped inside the basement but, when the heavy door closed behind us, dropped his duffel and grabbed my hand.

"Come here," he said, voice heavy with desire. He didn't wait for my response, but caught me by surprise, his mouth on mine, his hands at my waist, suddenly insistent.

I was nearly out of breath when he finally released me.

"What was that?" I barely managed to ask.

Ethan brushed a lock of hair behind my ear. "I had need of you, Sentinel."

"You've got me," I assured him with a smile. "But at the moment, we have need of speed."

"Not your best work," he cannily said, but he put a hand on my cheek and gazed into my eyes as if he might discover the world's secrets there. "What's wrong?"

"I'm nervous about leaving," I admitted.

"You're worried about your grandfather."

I nodded. "He was asleep when I called. He'll understand—he always does. I just wish I didn't have to ask him to be understanding."

Ethan kissed my brow. "You are a good granddaughter, Caroline Evelyn Merit."

"I'm not sure about that. But I'm trying." Sometimes, that was the best a girl could do.

I gestured toward the gleaming silver bullet that sat in the House's visitor spot, the antique Mercedes roadster Ethan had bought for me from the Pack leader himself. She was sweet and perfectly restored, and I called her Moneypenny. She was also still registered in Gabriel's name, which seemed a better transportation option than taking Ethan's car. But since he had decades' more driving experience than me—and we were in a hurry—I held out the keys.

"Shall we?"

Ethan's eyes widened with delight. He'd been attempting to buy Moneypenny for years and had probably wanted to slide behind the wheel for even longer.

"If we're going to run," he said, taking the keys from me, a spark jumping across our fingertips as they brushed, "we might as well escape in style."

Sometimes that was the best a vampire could do.

CHAPTER TWO

✦

UPSTAIRS, DOWNSTAIRS

That the Breckenridges had money was undeniable when one was facing down their palatial estate in Loring Park. Chicago was a metropolis bounded by water on one side and farmland on the other. Loring Park managed to fit itself just outside the latter, a fancy suburb of rolling green hills a simple train ride away from the hustle of the Second City.

Loring Park itself was a small and tidy town, with a central square and pretty shopping centers, the area newly developed and decorated with dark iron streetlights and lots of landscaping. A winter carnival had even set up shop in a parking lot, and residents undoubtedly sick of winter were trundling around amid the games and handful of rides. It would be months before green would peek through the flattened brown grass, but the snow was nearly gone. It had been a strange winter in northeastern Illinois—the weather veering back and forth between frigidly cold and practically balmy.

The estate was located a few miles outside the city center on the crest of a long, rolling hill. The house, with turrets and windows and several wings of rooms, was modeled after Biltmore and was surrounded by rolling hills of neatly manicured grass; the back lawn sloped gently down into a forest.

As hidey-holes went, it wasn't a bad option.

We pulled the car up to the door, covered by a stone arch, and got out, gravel crunching beneath our feet. The night was dark and moonless; the air was thick with wood smoke and magic.

"Is that what you think?" A tall, dark-haired man burst through the door, and a wave of prickly, irritated magic followed him like a cresting wave. He was broad shouldered, and he came out with arm raised, pointing an accusing finger at us. "You want to let those bloodsuckers stay here? In our home?"

The accusing gaze and shoulders belonged to Michael Breckenridge, Jr., the oldest of Papa Breck's sons. He was in his thirties now, but he'd been a football player in his youth, and he hadn't lost the muscle, or apparently the testosterone. He was the expected heir of Breckenridge Industries and the family fortune, and he evidently had a temper. Papa Breck was going to need to keep an eye on that.

Michael Breckenridge, Jr., I silently told Ethan, using the telepathic connection between us.

Charming, was his reply. He was even sarcastic telepathically.

"Be polite to the guests," said another voice in the doorway.

The man who stood there was tall and lean, with dark hair that waved over his forehead and a glint in his steely eyes. This was Finley Breckenridge, the second oldest of the Breck boys. There were two others—Nick, the one I'd dated, now a journalist, and Jamie, the youngest.

I guessed Finley and Michael had been in the middle of a disagreement regarding their father's decision to let us stay.

"Go back inside, Finn," Michael said. "This doesn't concern you."

Finley took another step outside, hands tucked casually into the pockets of his trousers, but his eyes were cool, his body taut, ready for action.

"It concerns the family," Finley said. "And it concerns Pop, who's already made his position clear."

Michael stalked toward us. Being good security, I shifted to block his path to Ethan. He stopped, glared down at me. "Get out of my way."

His tone was laced with hatred, and the magic that spilled off his body was downright contemptuous. The threat began to speed my blood, but I kept my voice calm. We were guests, after all. Welcome or otherwise.

"I'm afraid I can't do that," I said, forcing a light smile. "It's good to see you again, Michael."

His jaw twitched, but he took a step back. "Fine," he said, lifting his hands in the air like a cornered criminal. "But when they fuck up everything, I won't hear a word from you."

He stepped around me and stalked off around the house, leaving the scent of expensive cologne in his wake.

Ethan glanced back at Finley, brow raised.

"Apologies," Finley said, walking forward with a hand outstretched, ready to play peacemaker. He and Ethan shook hands, both of them obviously appraising the other.

"Finley Breckenridge."

"Ethan Sullivan."

"The vampire who made Merit," Finley said. The statement was a challenge, poorly disguised by curiosity and a smile that didn't quite reach his eyes.

"I initiated the change," Ethan confirmed. "I saved her from an attack, and I made her immortal. I find she has no complaints." His tone was mild, his expression unperturbed. If he was irritated by the question, he wasn't going to let Finley see it.

Finn flicked a glance at me. "It's good to see you, Merit. If not under these circumstances."

I nodded, the most I was willing to offer considering the attitudes. "I take it Michael's not thrilled we're staying here?"

"Michael and the old man disagree on various things," Finn said, gaze falling on the point where Michael had disappeared into the darkness. "Including having vampires in residence."

Their timing impeccable, liveried staff in dark pants and short jackets emerged silently from the house, took our bags and keys, and whisked Moneypenny down the driveway.

How very upstairs/downstairs, Ethan said.

My father would be jealous, I agreed. Although my grandfather had been a cop, my father was obsessed with money. Perhaps not surprisingly, he was very good friends with Papa Breck.

"Where will we be staying?" I asked.

"The carriage house. You got permission from the big man to stay, but he drew the line at your being in the house." Finn gestured toward the gravel walk, which led around the house to a series of secondary buildings.

Ethan looked unimpressed with our demotion from the main house, which did ring of supernatural pettiness. But we were here because we didn't have a better option. I thought it was best not to look that particular gift horse (shifter?) in the mouth.

The carriage house was a small brick building, its sides marked by dark green shutters around the windows that had once been doors for cars or carriages. The building was just behind the main house, completely invisible from the road and the driveway. The carriage house might have felt like an insult to Ethan, but it would be a secure location to spend a few quiet nights on the lam.

Finn pushed a key into the lock and opened the door. "Please come in."

The invitation wasn't strictly necessary—that particular bit of vampire myth was actually myth—but we preferred not to trespass.

The carriage house had been outfitted like a small apartment, with hardwood floors, colorful furnishings and décor, and a ceiling striped by large oak beams. There was a sitting area and a small kitchenette, and a door that led to what I guessed was a bedroom. The Brecks hadn't spared any expense on the décor. Books and orchids were arranged just so on a coffee table, knickknacks placed here and there, one wall covered in a mix of line drawings and paintings in gilded frames.

"Pop uses the place for visiting board members," Finn said, stepping inside and surveying the living room, hands on his hips. "Kitchen's stocked with blood and food, so you should find everything you need here."

He pointed to a keypad beside the door. "The entire house is rigged to the security system, which is hooked up to the main house. There's also an intercom in case you run into trouble."

I glanced around, didn't see a back door. "Is this the only door in and out?"

Finn smirked. "Yes. And I see Nick wasn't kidding—you really are a vampire fighter now."

"All night long," I said, gesturing toward the windows. "What about those?"

"Ah." Finn pressed a button on the keypad. Segmented plates descended across the windows, covering them completely. With those guards in place, we'd be safe from sunlight and marauders.

"Thank you, Finley," Ethan said. "We appreciate your family's thoughtfulness."

"It was Nick's idea."

"In that case," Ethan tightly said, "we appreciate his thoughtfulness. And with all due respect, as we have amply demonstrated, your family has no reason to be hostile toward us."

Finn's eyes narrowed. "I'm not hostile toward Merit. I'm hostile toward you. I don't know you, except that you've embroiled her in a world that's worrying her father and put her grandfather in the hospital."

The attitude was irritating, as the facts were wrong. My grandfather had been Ombudsman before I'd become a vampire, and I wouldn't have become a vampire without my father's meddling. Not that Finley needed the details.

"We all make our own choices," Ethan said, his smile thin and dangerous.

"So we do. A suggestion?"

Ethan lifted his brows, as Finley slid his glance to the sheathed katanas in our hands.

"You might want to leave the weapons here. They don't exactly scream 'friendship.'"

He walked back to me, concern in his eyes. He held out the set of keys, which I took, our fingers brushing. He might have played polite, but he was as angry as Michael. He spilled magic into the air, sending an electric thrill across my fingers.

"Be careful," he said.

I nodded, not sure what to say.

With that, he opened the door and disappeared into the night.

"Well, they are just delightful," Ethan said.

I snorted, then walked over and locked the front door. I was responsible for Ethan's safety, after all. Not that a dead bolt would do much good against a sustained attack. I didn't think SWAT teams, paranormal or otherwise, would drop down on us during the daylight, but I suppose that was a risk we'd have to take.

"Has Michael always been that aggressive?"

I glanced back at Ethan, who'd pulled off his suit coat and draped it on the back of a nearby chair. "Actually, yes. When we were younger and I spent summers here, Nick and I, sometimes Finn, would play together in the woods. Michael never played at anything. I mean, he participated in football, but it wasn't a *game* to him. It was a battle. He's always had a very serious demeanor. And it doesn't seem like he's loosening up with old age."

"Times are challenging for everyone," Ethan said. "But it's taken some supernaturals longer than others to realize and accept that. It's easier, I think, for them to name us enemies rather than consider the possibility they're surrounded by millions of humans who'd easily wish them dead."

I grimaced. "That's not exactly a comforting thought. Especially since it's undoubtedly true." I was sure we had human allies—those who didn't judge, those who were fascinated by our differentness, those who longed for our fame. But we'd been coming face-to-face with mostly the haters recently.

Ethan glanced around the apartment, gestured toward the open doorway. "Bedroom?"

"I actually have no idea." I'd spent a lot of time at the Breck estate as a child, but I'd never ventured into the carriage house. Why bother, when there was an entire mansion to explore?

I followed him through the door, found he was right. It was a small bedroom, with tall, exposed-brick walls. A bed covered in white linens and a buffet of pillows in shades of blue and green sat in the middle of the room, the head covered by a canopy of wispy tulle that draped romantically over the sides.

"Like the world's weirdest bed and breakfast," I muttered, dropping my bag onto the bed. There was an old-fashioned alarm clock on the bedside table and a copy of *Cosmo*. I hoped it had been left by a former guest and not a member of the Breck family who hoped to give me and Ethan a particularly exciting evening.

There was a small bathroom on the other side of the room. Pedestal sink, black-and-white-checkered floor, shower large enough for three. Very pretty, down to the monogrammed guest towels.

When I peeked back into the bedroom, Ethan stood with one hand on his hip, the other holding his phone as he reviewed his messages with a narrowed gaze. He looked more like the head of a Fortune 500 company than a Master vampire on the lam, but I wasn't complaining. Ethan might have been cunning, funny, brave, and generous . . . but he was also undeniably eye candy.

Tall, lean, and imperious, he'd been my enemy, and he was the opposite of the man I'd thought I'd grow to love. I'd expected to fall for a dreamer, a thinker, an artist. Someone I'd meet in the coffeehouse on a weekend with a satchel full of books, a pair of hipster glasses, and a tendency to quote Fitzgerald.

Ethan preferred Italian suits, vintage wine, and expensive cars. He also knew how to wield a sword, or two of them. He Mastered the House, and he'd killed vampires by his own hand. He was infinitely more complex and difficult than anyone I might have imagined.

And I was more in love with him than I'd imagined was possible. Not just infatuation. Not just lust. But love—complex and awe inspiring and utterly frustrating.

Nearly a year ago, I thought my life was over. In reality, it was just beginning.

Ethan looked up at me, frustration fading to curiosity. "Sentinel?" he asked.

I smiled at him. "Go back to your domineering. I'm just thinking."

"I hardly domineer."

"You made several lifetimes of domineering." I gestured toward his phone. "Any news from Chicago?"

"All is quiet on the eastern front," he said. "Let's hope it stays that way."

We could hope all we wanted. Unfortunately, hope rarely deterred humans with a grudge against vampires.

Much like he had in the rest of the building, Papa Breck hadn't spared any expense in the bedroom. The bed was soft and undoubtedly expensive. The linens were silk soft—and probably just as expensive. Not that a twin-sized bed in a cold room was bad when you got to fall asleep beside a very sexy blond vampire.

We unpacked and undressed and prepared for the day ahead. I ensured the windows were covered, then messaged Catcher to check my grandfather's condition.

ASLEEP, Catcher responded. AND WELL CARED FOR. YOUR FATHER SPARED NO EXPENSE.

He rarely did. If I couldn't be with my grandfather, at least I knew he was getting the care he needed.

I also messaged Jonah, my RG partner, to let him know we'd made it safely to the Brecks' house.

YOU'RE RUINING ALL OUR RG FUN BY HANDLING THESE THINGS.

IT'S NOT BY CHOICE, I assured him. DRAMA FINDS CADOGAN HOUSE.

SO I SEE.

I made him promise to tag me if there was trouble.

YOU'LL BE IN THE FIRST FIVE, he cheekily promised.

"Business?" Ethan asked, as I sat on the edge of the bed, one leg curled beneath me, the phone in hand.

"Jonah," I said, fingers finishing my equally snarky good-bye.

Ethan growled, a manly display meant to remind me he still wasn't thrilled about my ties to the tall, auburn-haired, and handsome guard captain.

"He's my partner," I reminded him. "And you've already consented to that."

"I'm aware of what he is, Sentinel. Just as I'm aware of what you are to me."

The sun peeked above the horizon only seconds before Ethan's hands were on me, stripping me of clothing and inciting my body to flame. His mouth enveloped mine, then my neck, my breasts, my bare stomach, before he extended the length of his body over mine and chained my wrists above my head with his hands.

"You are mine," he said, with a wicked spark in his eyes that sent a thrill down my spine.

"You don't own me," I reminded him, arcing my body just enough to prove the point.

"No," he agreed, his lips so soft, playing at the edges of my breast. "We own each other. I am your Master. And you are my Sentinel."

He wasted no time; I hadn't needed any. "Mine," he said, plunging inside me, plundering my body, demanding everything I had to offer, and then more.

"Mine," he growled, as pleasure bloomed across my body like a living thing, as cold as ice and as hot as fire, emptying my mind and soul of anything but Ethan. His mind, his soul, his body, and the word he murmured over and over again.

"Mine," he said, each word a promise, a declaration, a thrust. "Mine," he said through gritted teeth, passion riding him as it had me.

"*Mine,*" he said, kissing me with such ferocity I tasted blood, the magic rising between us as he thrust fiercely and groaned like an animal as pleasure swamped him.

"Mine," he said, softly now, and pulled my body into his. The sun rose, and there in the darkness of a borrowed room, we slept.

We awoke to riotous noise—pounding on the front door that had both of us shooting upright. The sun had only just dipped below the horizon again, but not quite far enough along to pull us from sleep.

"What in God's name?" Ethan asked, his voice still slumber slurred, his hair more surfer than moderately pretentious Master vampire.

The pounding sounded again. Someone was in a hurry.

Ethan moved to climb off the bed, but I stopped him with a hand. "Get dressed. I'll see who's there first. Luc will kick my ass if I let yours get kicked." I had a bad feeling this was going to be one of those nights on which I really, really wished I could sleep in and defer being an adult for a few more hours.

I pulled on Ethan's shirt from the night before and buttoned it up. It wouldn't do as protective armor, but there weren't enemies at the door, at least not of the CPD variety. I'd tempered my own katana with blood and magic, which left me sensitive to the presence of steel and guns. I didn't sense any outside.

Now draped in tailored and expensive menswear—only the best for our Master—I trundled back into the living room. Ethan's katana was propped beside the door; I'd taken mine to bed, just in case. I picked it up and took a cautionary peek through the peephole . . . and found a shifter on our stoop.

"Open up, Kitten. I know you're there."

I opened the door; a cold breeze lifted goose bumps on my bare legs.

He stood in the doorway, six feet and some-odd inches, all muscle and wolfish energy. His hair was tawny and gold tipped, and it reached his shoulders in shaggy waves. His eyes were amber colored and, at the moment, swirled with amusement.

"Kitten," said Gabriel Keene, the Apex of the North American Pack. He gave me an up-and-down perusal. "I trust I'm not interrupting anything?"

"Sleeping," I managed, crossing my arms over my chest. "We were sleeping."

Ethan stepped behind me, chest bare, buttoning jeans. "I'm fairly certain you know precisely what you were interrupting."

Gabe smiled broadly, revealing straight, white teeth. "Doesn't matter now, since you're both awake. Get your asses dressed. We've got business to attend to."

Ethan arched an eyebrow, his favorite move. "What business? What are you doing here?"

"I'm here for the Pack, just as you are."

Ethan grunted. "We're here because Papa Breck made us pay for the privilege."

I slid Ethan a glance. He hadn't mentioned a payment to the Brecks. And that information would have been good to know before we put our fate—before I put *his* fate—in their hands.

"He made you pay," Gabriel said, "but not for the privilege you think. That money was an admission fee."

"For what?" Ethan asked.

"For the Greatest Show on Earth," Gabriel said with a smile that could only be described as wolfish. "It's the first night of Lupercalia."

"What's Lupercalia?" I asked, in spite of myself. I should have been ducking back inside, but I found the name—and Gabe's appearance at our door—intriguing.

"Our annual NAC festival," Gabe said, "and has been since Rome's founding. Three nights in late winter to call spring to rise, to celebrate our animals, our connections to the woods, to the world."

That explains Michael's animus, Ethan silently said. *He wouldn't want us here for that.*

Part of it, maybe. But I'd bet Michael hadn't cared for vampires before we'd arrived, and wouldn't like us any more when the festival was over.

"Tonight," Gabe said, "you're our guests. Among others." He stepped aside, revealing two sorcerers and a shifter behind him. The sorcerers were my best friend, Mallory Carmichael, and Catcher, her boyfriend. Mallory had been disgraced by bad deeds, but Gabe had adopted her for rehabilitation.

Mallory and Catcher were bundled against the cold in jeans and boots. Hers were fawn colored and knee high over skinny jeans. Her blue hair, darker at the tips, lay straight on her shoulders.

Catcher stood beside her, wearing his typically dour expression. His hair was shaved, his eyes sparkling green, his mouth lush. He was partial to snarky T-shirts, but I couldn't tell if he wore one beneath his coat.

Jeff was the final member of the trio, my grandfather's employee and favorite white-hat hacker. Granted, he was the only computer hacker I actually knew in person, but I'm pretty sure he'd have been my favorite anyway. Tonight he'd traded in his usual uniform—khakis and a button-down shirt—for jeans, boots, and a rugged outdoor jacket. His light brown hair was tucked behind his ears, and he wore his usual smile—friendly, with touches of bashful and goofball.

"Sullivan," Catcher said with a bob of the head, then answered Ethan's unspoken question. "We're here for Lupercalia."

"I'm here to participate," Jeff said, a blush in his cheeks as he dutifully managed not to stare at my legs.

It was great to see them, but if they were here, my grandfather was down two guardians.

They must have seen the worry in my eyes. "Your mother and father limited your grandfather's visitors today," Catcher said. "They want him to rest. So we're out of a job there."

Jeff wiggled his phone. "Although we did manage to sneak in a panic button, just in case. He can reach us immediately if there's any problem."

"Good idea," I said with a smile, relieved that they'd thought of it.

Of course, I was still standing half naked in the doorway of a shifter's carriage house, my hair undoubtedly ruffled by sleep and sex. Throw in a college math class I'd somehow forgotten to attend, and I was revisiting my recurring nightmare.

"And what are you doing here?" I asked Mallory, smoothing a hand down the front of Ethan's shirt to ensure no important parts were leaked to the public.

"I'm here to practice," Mallory said.

Part of Mal's rehab was figuring out how she could use magic productively. A little more Luke, a little less Anakin. She'd made progress during our anti-McKetrick brigade, and it looked like the Pack was giving her another opportunity to try.

"She's expanding her understanding of magic," Gabriel added. "What it is, what it isn't, what it can be."

Mallory smiled prettily and held up two bottles of Blood4You, the bottled blood that most vampires drank for convenience, and a bag from Dirigible Donuts, one of my favorite Chicago food-stuffs. (To be fair, it was a long and distinguished list.) "I have a consolation prize for your humiliation." She gave me an up-

and-down look. "I'd say two to three raspberry-filled donuts should do it."

I stood there for a moment, cheeks flushed in embarrassment, toes freezing from exposure to the cold, my friends confident I'd be mollified with nothing more than a bag of jelly donuts.

"Just give me the damn thing," I said, bowing to their expectations and snatching breakfast. But I gave them all a deadly look before stalking back to the bedroom.

"And now that we've satisfied your bodyguard," Gabe said to Ethan behind me, "we'll just come in and make ourselves comfortable."

As it turned out, raspberry-filled donuts were an exceptional way to soothe humiliation.

I'd emptied a bottle of blood and devoured two of the donuts before Ethan came back inside, a bundle of red fabric in hand.

"I don't suppose you saved one of those for me?" he asked.

"I better have," I said. "She bought a dozen."

"I stand by what I said."

"You won't get any with that attitude. What's that?" I asked, gesturing toward the fabric.

"Apparently someone in the Pack decided they wanted swag," Ethan said, unrolling two T-shirts, cardinal red with what looked like a retro ad for a bar called Lupercalia, the name in old-fashioned letters above two wolves toasting with beer steins at a pub table.

"They actually made T-shirts," I said. "Gabriel okayed that? It seems very . . . public." The public knew shape-shifters existed, but the Packs still tended to keep to themselves.

"I'd guess this was a do-it-and-apologize-after-the-fact scenario," Ethan said. "These are for us to wear. Gifts from the Pack."

"Chilly for February."

"I'm sure they'll allow you to layer, Sentinel." He held out a hand for the bag of donuts, but I didn't budge.

"Were you going to tell me we had to pay the Brecks?"

His gaze flattened. "I'm perfectly capable of managing the House's financial affairs, Sentinel."

"I didn't suggest you weren't. But I also don't like being blindsided."

"It was a business transaction."

"It was protection money," I insisted, and from the flash in his eyes, he knew it, too.

"And I don't care to advertise that fact, Sentinel. But I'd have told you."

He must have seen the doubt in my eyes, because he stepped forward. "I'd have told you," he said again. "When we had a moment to discuss it. As you'll recall"—he tugged gently at the first button on the shirt I wore—"you were very distracting last night."

Ethan was still shirtless, and he stood at the edge of the bed, washboard abs and a trail of blond fuzz peeking above his jeans' top button. Heat rushed me as he moved in for a kiss, and my eyes drifted shut.

But he sidestepped me, grabbed the bag, and pulled out a donut.

"Distracting?" I asked him, offering a dubious look.

"All's fair in love and pastry," he said, swiping a drop of raspberry jam from the edge of his mouth. The urge to lick it away nearly silvered my eyes.

He rolled down the top of the bag and placed it on a side table, then pulled on his Lupercalia T-shirt. The flat plane of his abdomen rippled as he moved, and I didn't even bother to pretend not to look.

When he was done dressing, he cocked an eyebrow at me.

"Oh, don't mind me. I'm just enjoying the show."

He snorted, snatched up the second T-shirt, and swatted me with it. "Go get dressed, or Catcher, Jeff, Mallory, and Gabe are going to suspect more than dressing is going on in here. Again." He put his hands on the bed on each side of my body and leaned in. "And although I have definitive plans for you, Sentinel, they do not involve the lascivious imaginations of the sorcerers and shifters presently outside that door."

He touched his mouth to mine—soft and promising, his lips berry sweet.

Ten minutes later, I was dressed in my Lupercalia T-shirt, a long-sleeved T-shirt beneath it for warmth. I wore two pair of socks against the cold, boots, and jeans, and put my long, dark hair into a high ponytail. I pulled on my leather jacket, a gift from Ethan to replace the one torched in the fire that injured my grandfather, and tucked a small and sleek dagger into my boot. The Pack wasn't likely to appreciate my bringing a katana to a shifter festival, so I'd have to rely on the dagger if anything went amiss. And since I was heading out with a refugee vampire, two rogue sorcerers, and a family of shifters who hated vampires, I presumed "amiss" was pretty likely.

I was dressed and ready for action. But before I turned my attention to the Pack, I had one final bit of business. I'd missed checking in on my grandfather yesterday, so I dialed the hospital and requested his room.

"This is Chuck," he answered.

I smiled just from the sound of his voice. "Hey, Grandpa."

"Baby girl! It's good to hear your voice. I understand you're in a bit of a pinch."

Relief swamped me. I hadn't realized how much I'd wanted to

talk to him—or how much guilt had settled in when I hadn't been able to make it happen.

"A misunderstanding. I'm sure Mayor Kowalcyzk will come around eventually." And if she didn't, hopefully Malik could convince the governor to intervene. "How are you feeling?"

"Broken. I'm not as young as I used to be."

"I don't believe that," I cheerily said, but I had to push back the memory of my grandfather huddled beneath debris. I made sure my voice was steady before I spoke again. "I'm sorry I can't be there."

"You know, I always thought you'd be a teacher. You love books and knowledge. Always did. And then your life changed, and you became part of something bigger. That's your job, Merit. That something bigger. And it's okay that you have to do it."

"I love you, Grandpa."

"I love you, baby girl."

There was mumbling in the background. "It's time for what they generously refer to as 'dinner' around here," he said after a moment. "Call me when you've got things in hand. Because I know you'll get there eventually."

I found the crew in the living room, chatting collegially.

"Merit," Catcher said, sitting beside Mallory on the couch, an arm around her shoulders. Their relationship had hit the rocks when Mallory turned to the dark side, so the casual affection was a pleasant development. "It's nice to see you clothed again."

"And now that she is," Gabriel said, standing, "we should get moving."

"Where are we going, exactly?" Catcher asked.

"To a land beyond space and time," Jeff said drawing an arc in the air. "Where the rules of mortals have no meaning."

Gabriel looked up at the ceiling as if he might find patience there. "We're going to the Brecks' backyard. Into the woods, right here in Illinois, where most of us are quite mortal."

"Illi-*noise*," Jeff said with cheeky enthusiasm. "Because the wolves will howl."

Gabriel shook his head but clapped Jeff on the back good-naturedly. "Settle yourself, whelp. We haven't even gotten started yet."

I had a sense they weren't going to settle themselves anytime soon. And since I was playing bodyguard, I took it upon myself to act like one. If we'd be staying on the Brecks' property, we'd be as safe (as we'd ever been) from Mayor Kowalcyzk's troops. But that didn't necessarily mean we'd be safe around the Pack. Not if they shared the Brecks' attitude.

"Does the Brecks' protection extend to the woods? And the rest of the shifters?"

Gabriel smiled at me. Keenly. "If you're here, Kitten, you're safe. That goes for both of you. Frankly, most Pack members don't give a rat's ass about politics in Chicago. And even if they did, they aren't going to choose a bullying politician over friends of the Pack."

"And I've got your back, Mer," Jeff said with a wink, earning a dark look from Ethan.

The shifters and sorcerers filed into the night, but Ethan stopped me with a hand. "Dagger?" he quietly asked.

"In my boot," I said. Vampires usually preferred not to employ hidden weapons, but these were special circumstances. "You don't share Gabe's confidence?"

"Gabe knows what he has planned. I do not. We have allies, certainly. Him, Jeff, Nick. A Pack member would have to be, as you might say, wicked ballsy to commit treachery under Gabriel's nose." We'd seen it before, and with unpleasant consequences. "But clearly many of the shifters aren't fans of vampires, and like Michael, they won't be glad to see us here."

"I would never say 'wicked ballsy.' But I take your point." And I hoped we hadn't escaped Diane Kowalcyzk only to fall into a new kind of drama. But in case we did: "You're armed, too?"

Ethan nodded. "A blade, like yours. A matched set," he added with a smile, tugging on the end of my ponytail. "And we'll see what we'll see."

He slipped his hand into mine but, when we started toward the door, glanced down at my booted feet.

"Color me surprised, Sentinel. Your shoes appear to be appropriate."

I rolled my eyes. "It was icy that night, so I wore galoshes."

"With couture. Very expensive couture."

"It was Chicago in February. I made a practical decision. And I pulled it off."

Only to have him carry me to my parents' threshold and fake a marriage proposal on one knee. So I'd managed to avoid falling in stilettos—but had still nearly had a heart attack.

"Children," Mallory said, peeking into the doorway. "I believe we're waiting on you."

"Sorry," I said, stepping outside as Ethan followed behind me. "Just debating the finer points of fashion."

"Only vampires," Gabriel muttered, and moved forward into the darkness.

CHAPTER THREE

LONE WOLF

The night was cold but uncommonly still. No wind at all, which was a blessing in Chicago in February.

With Gabriel in front, the frozen ground crunching beneath our feet, we played follow the leader around the house and toward the estate's back lawn. It dipped down to the woods, which made a dark curtain at the edge of the visible world, a black sea beneath a blanket of stars. They twinkled above us, cold and unfeeling, and a sudden ominous shiver went through me.

Sentinel? Ethan silently asked, taking my hand.

I squeezed in response and dismissed my fear. I wasn't a child; I was a vampire. A predator, and with allies around.

"Dark out here," Mallory said with a nervous laugh ahead of us, hand in hand with Catcher.

"Could be worse," Catcher said. "You could be a vampire on the lam."

"Yeah, I don't recommend it," I said. "Although it certainly does make for interesting bedfellows."

"I'd better be your only bedfellow, Sentinel."

"Who could possibly replace you?" I asked, grinning when Mallory looked back and winked. A twinge of nostalgia went through me. That was the camaraderie I'd missed, something we'd begun to lose when the supernatural drama had grown between us.

As we descended the hill toward the tree line, a breeze blew toward us, and there was magic in it. Fresh and peppery and hinting of animals.

We stepped onto the dirt path that led into the woods, ground that I'd trod many times before. The trail where Nick and I had played as children had been cleared and widened, allowing access for adults.

There was movement to the left. Nick Breckenridge emerged from a side trail in front of Mallory and Catcher, a woman behind him, their hands linked together. He was dark and tall, with closely cropped hair and rugged features. With his snug shirt, cargo pants, and strong jaw, he looked every bit the journalist, albeit one more used to war zones and exotic locations than tramping through the woods of a multimillion-dollar estate.

The woman didn't look familiar. I knew Nick was dating someone—or at least that a woman had answered his phone a few nights ago—but I didn't know if she was the one. She had the self-assured bearing of a shifter, but if she had magic, she hid it well.

"Merit," he said.

"Nick."

"I don't think you've met Yvette."

Yvette nodded.

"Merit and I went to high school together," Nick said.

"Nice to meet you," she said, and they disappeared into the darkness ahead of us.

Mallory moved back to me and linked an arm in mine, displacing Ethan as my hiking partner.

"I think you just got jealous," she whispered.

"I'm not jealous. But I am more than 'a girl he went to high school with.'"

She snorted. "What did you want him to say? That you're the girl he's pined over since he made the regretful decision to break up with you in high school? Which was ten years ago, I'll point out."

"*No,*" I said, drawing out the word to emphasize just how silly that thought was. "But maybe something along the lines of, 'This is Merit, sentinel of Cadogan House, protector of the weak, defender of the innocent'?"

"Yeah. Let me know when the Avengers come calling. In the meantime, while he does have a very curvy Yvette, you have an Ethan Sullivan."

"I hate it when you have a point."

"I'm wise beyond my years."

The trail narrowed, and we fell into a silent, single-file line, the skeleton trees standing sentinel around us. The woods were draped in winter silence, the native creatures sleeping, hibernating, or deliberately avoiding the train of predators. The woods were deep, and I'd been back as far as a hedge maze that I thought was somewhere to my right. But it was dark and the trail was pitched, and I wasn't entirely sure of my direction.

We followed the trail for ten or fifteen more minutes, until the woods opened, revealing a large meadow surrounded by glowing torches.

The clearing was at least the size of a football field, and in the middle stood a twenty-foot-tall totem, animals carved in a trunk at least four feet thick. Tents, campfires, and folding chairs were sprinkled here and there. And everywhere, shifters milled, most in the official black leather jackets of the North American Central.

Scents filled the air. The fur and musk of animals, charcoal, roasting meat, earth. There was life here. Renewal and rebirth, even though spring was still weeks away.

I guessed that was why the Brecks hadn't wanted us here. Shifters could take care of themselves, certainly, but there were a lot of families in the open space, and tents wouldn't be easy to defend. On the other hand, they were, like us, on private property held by one of the most powerful families in Chicago. That was a point in their favor.

Gabriel left us at the edge of the wood, walking to his wife, Tanya, who stood in the clearing with their infant son in her arms. Tanya was a lovely brunette, a woman with smiling eyes and pink cheeks, her softness a contrast to Gabe's tawny ferocity. Gabe put a paternal hand on Connor's head and pressed a kiss to Tanya's lips. She beamed up at him, the love between them comfortable and obvious.

Jeff found Fallon, Gabriel's younger sister. They'd been on-again, off-again for a time, but considering the warmth of their embrace, I guessed they'd made "on" a little more permanent. Fallon was petite, with a sturdy, athletic body and wavy hair the same sun-kissed color as Gabe's. She preferred black clothing and tonight wore knee-high motorcycle-style boots, a short skirt, and an NAC leather jacket.

I didn't know Fallon very well, but I knew Jeff, and there weren't many I respected as much as him. If he loved her—and the look in his eyes made clear that he did—then she was good people.

"Ready?" Catcher asked.

"Now or never," Ethan said, taking my hand as we stepped forward into the meadow and into the fray.

Shifters chatted in camp chairs, watching cautiously as we passed. Others hurried around us with steaming food or boxes of gear. Someone nudged my elbow, and I turned to find a squatty woman with freshly bleached hair standing behind me, a foil-wrapped bundle in her hands. It was as large as a newborn baby and smelled of meat and chilies.

She looked me over, shook her head in disappointment, and thrust the package at me.

I nearly grunted under the weight. It was as heavy as a newborn baby, too.

"Hello, Berna," I said.

Berna was a shifter, a relative of the Keene family, and the bartender at Little Red, the Pack watering hole in Chicago's Ukrainian Village neighborhood. She was convinced I didn't eat enough and enjoyed plying me with food. Since I enjoyed eating, we'd managed to stay friends of a sort.

She looked at Ethan and winged up her pencil-drawn eyebrows suggestively. "Hello, man," she said in her sturdy Eastern European accent.

"Berna," Ethan said politely, eyeing what I guessed was a baby-sized burrito. "Nothing for me?"

Without even blinking, Berna yanked the package from my hands and offered it to Ethan.

"Is family recipe. You will eat. You"—she looked him over, from blond hair to booted feet—"should remain strong. Handsome."

I think I just won Berna, he silently said, and nodded gravely at her. "Thank you, Berna. I'm sure this will be delicious."

She sniffed, as if offended by the mere possibility it wouldn't be delicious, but her eyelashes stayed batty, and her gaze didn't stray much from his face.

"I guess we aren't getting anything," Catcher muttered behind us.

"So these are the vampires?"

A shifter stepped beside Berna—a woman who was taller and thinner, with a short shock of platinum blond hair. She was muscled and rugged, her features better described as handsome than pretty. And she all but vibrated with irritated magic.

"Twilight," Berna confirmed, pointing at me and Ethan. "Grumpy," she said, pointing around me at Catcher.

She looked at Mallory for a few seconds before offering judgment. "Magic," she finally said with the smallest of smiles, and it was obvious she meant the word as a compliment.

Mallory beamed, but Berna's friend was not impressed.

"You shouldn't be here," she said, pointing at each of us in turn and flinging magic with each movement. It left a sting like tiny insects. "This isn't any of your business, and it isn't for you." She stuck her nose into the air, slid Berna a narrowed look. "And you shouldn't carouse with them."

"We were invited here," Mallory said. I think she might have put an arm around Berna, except that Berna had already puffed out her chest and was nearly buzzing with irritation.

"Go," she said, flicking her hands at the woman. "Go elsewhere. Too negative."

But Berna's dismissal only seemed to encourage the woman.

"Mark my words," she said, that finger pointed again. "This is all doomed because we didn't go home when we could have. We should have left Chicago months ago, and we certainly shouldn't be here now. The Keene family should have been removed a long time ago. They are leading us right into disaster." Her eyes flashed with self-righteous anger. That emotion seemed to be in unusually strong supply among shifters lately.

She walked away before Berna could respond to the slight,

joining up with two other women who gave us suspicious looks. But Berna's balled fists made it clear she'd had words in the hopper.

"I see you've met Aline." Gabriel joined us, made a point of putting a hand on Ethan's shoulder. Aline and her troop of friends didn't seem impressed.

"She's a charmer," Ethan dryly said.

"Where have you been keeping her locked away?" Mallory asked.

"She keeps herself locked away," Gabriel said. "She and my father butted heads and she's transferred that hatred onto our generation."

Berna patted his arm collegially. "You are not popular, but you are doing right."

"Maybe," Gabriel said, "but I'd prefer to be both." He towered over Berna and glanced down at her from his couple of extra feet. "We ready?"

She made a sound that made clear exactly how ridiculous she thought the question. Berna, apparently, was always ready.

Gabriel smiled. "My fanged friends, you're about to be witness to a very special treat. Tonight, you get to hear us roar."

He lifted his head and unleashed a howl that sent shivers down my spine—and invoked the rest of the chorus. Not all shifters were wolves, and the Pack's sounds were just as varied and cacophonous. Howls, screeches, feline roars, and screams that might have been from birds of prey. Together, as the shifters formed a circle around the totem in the middle of the meadow, they lifted their voices and sang into the night, the very sound magic.

Goose bumps lifted on my arms. Ethan slipped his hand into mine as we shared the sight and sound of it. After a moment, the howls quieted, now a backbeat instead of a melody.

Gabriel looked at Mallory appraisingly. "You ready?"

She blew out a breath with pursed lips, then loosened her shoulders and nodded, this time confidently. And although nervousness still fluttered in the air around her, it was a good kind of nervousness. Excited anticipation—not the resigned dread I'd sensed before.

Side by side, they walked forward into the circle and stood in front of the totem. A hush fell over the crowd.

I glanced at Catcher. His expression was blank, but his eyes fixed on Mal and the shifter at her side. If he was nervous for her, he wasn't showing it.

His hair pushed behind his ears, Gabriel looked more like a biker or boxer than Pack Apex, the king of his people, but there was no doubt in the set of his shoulders and grave expression that he stood as leader of them all.

"Tonight," he said, hands on his hips, "we celebrate the Pack, the mothers, the sires. We celebrate our founding, our brothers, Romulus and Remus, and our future. We celebrate the wild things. We have voted to remain in the realm of humans and vampires. That decision was not unanimous, but it was a decision to stay, to join, to bind together with our brothers and sisters and become stronger in the binding."

He looked at Mallory. "There are those among us who have erred, deeply and significantly. Who have wounded the world and broken themselves. The worst of them lose themselves in their errors. The best of them crawl back, one foot at a time, and seek to amend their breaches. That is the way of the brave."

Gabe looked back at the crowd. "This woman knows only of the magic of sorcerers and vampires. Tonight, we sing to her of the rest of it. Of the truth of it. Of the magic the earth has to offer."

Gabriel reached out his hand. After sucking in a breath, Mallory linked her fingers with his. She closed her eyes as magic began to spill out and through the shifters again. I closed my eyes and savored the hot rush of raw, unmitigated power. It was the life force of the earth, called up by the predators who gathered together to celebrate their community.

And then it transformed.

Mallory must have unlocked some magical gate of her own, because a new stream of magic—younger, greener, brighter—began to mix with the magic of the Pack. Her hair lifted like an indigo halo, and her lips curled into a smile of satisfaction and contentment. Of relief.

Together, the magicks swirled and danced around us, invisible but tangible, like an electric breeze. This wasn't defensive or offensive magic. It wasn't used to gather information, for strategy or diplomacy, or to fight a war against a supernatural enemy.

It simply *was*.

It was fundamental, inexorable. It was nothing and everything, infinity and oblivion, from the magnificent furnace of a star to the electrons that hummed in an atom. It was life and death and everything in between, the urge to fight and grow and swim and fly. It was the cascade of water across boulders, the slow-moving advance of mountain glaciers, the march of time.

The shifters moved around the circle, grabbing our hands and pulling us in, connecting us to the magic. Magic flowed between us like we were transistors in a circuit, connecting the shifters to one another and us to them. We moved in concentric circles around the center totem, heat rising until the air was as warm as a summer's day, until sweat beaded on my forehead.

This magic was lustful, almost drowsy with sensuality, and I felt my eyes silver and my fangs descend in an answering call. This was the magic of feasting and fucking, of savoring the blood of a kill and calling the Pack to dine.

Mallory's eyes were open now, her hair damp with sweat, her body shaking with power, but her hand was still linked to Gabriel's, and she smiled with more contentment than I'd seen from her in months.

A year ago, I'd assumed my relationship with Mallory would continue just as it always had—that we'd be friends who shared silly inside jokes, griped about our jobs, dreamt about our futures.

And then I became a vampire, and she discovered she was a sorceress.

Our lives were never going to be the same. They would never be as simple, as predictable, as they had been those years before. Instead, they'd be overlain by our responsibilities, by our strengths, and by the burdens we undertook because of them.

For the first time, I realized that was okay.

Our friendship wasn't limited to habits, to circumstances, to neighborhoods. We were friends because we were connected together, because something in our souls called to each other, understood each other. That connection, that spark between us, would remain even if our lives had changed completely. I hadn't accepted that before.

I could accept it now.

I searched for her in the circle so I could let her know that I finally understood, that I'd come to terms with it. But I moved so quickly, my feet dancing to keep up with the shifters beside me, that I couldn't get my bearings, couldn't find her in the crowd.

Something strange flitted in my chest. A pinprick, sharp and uncomfortable. Not tangible, but a hidden note of magic. A bit of the current that wasn't meant to soothe or celebrate but to incite.

I tried to ignore it, thinking I was just being paranoid, that the quantity of magic was triggering some protective instinct.

But I feared that wasn't right. I'd felt magic before—many varieties, many flavors—even mixed into the current tonight. This was different. Panic began to bloom like dark roses.

The hand on mine tightened, as if the shifter at my side had felt my wavering fear.

I looked for Ethan, found him five yards away, eyes closed as he swayed in time with the shifters around him.

I pulled my hands free, breaking the circle and pushing through bodies to get closer, to put him in reach in case my fear was real.

Ethan, I told him. *Stay where you are. I'm coming for you.*

Sentinel, he said, obviously surprised. *What's wrong?*

I didn't have time to answer, because I'd been regrettably correct.

The sky blackened as a thick, dark cloud began to spin above us, angry with sound and magic. The shifters stopped, the furious dance coming to a stumbling halt as they, too, cast their gazes on the threatening sky.

"A storm?" someone near me asked.

I moved forward until I reached Ethan, grabbed his wrist. But he didn't even look at me. He stared at the sky as it broke open, revealing the truth of the cloud.

It wasn't the forerunner of a storm, but an attack.

All hell broke loose.

CHAPTER FOUR

GHASTLY, GRIM, AND ANCIENT

They looked like the harpies of Greek and Roman mythology. Bodies of pale, thin women. Massive wings, the feathers so deeply black they gleamed like velvet. They were naked but for their long hair—straight and black, with thin braids tied throughout—and their silver, crested helmets. Supernatural battle armor, I feared, as they spun above us like a supernatural tornado, blotting out the stars, the magic that accompanied them fierce and unfriendly.

"Ethan," I yelled over the rising din, adrenaline beginning to rush through me. "Nobody told me harpies existed!"

"I imagine nobody knew it until today," he said, pulling a dagger from his boot and gesturing for me to do the same.

When the dagger was in hand, I looked for Gabriel. He stood a few yards away, shouting orders and sending his own sentinels in various directions. He and Mallory exchanged a glance, and I saw him weigh the choices, the decision.

He made the call and nodded at her and, I guessed, authorized her use of that magic he'd been so careful to train up. Catcher had no such hesitation. He'd gone to Mallory, grabbed her hand, was already pointing into the air, discussing what looked like strategy.

Gabriel unleashed a bloodcurdling yell, a call to arms. Light erupted across the clearing as shifters changed into their animal forms, the transition as stirringly magical as their ceremony had been. Changing into animal form was rough on clothes, so some shifters disrobed before they shifted, leaving shirts and pants in piles on the ground, ready and waiting for when it was time to shift back.

The smaller creatures, pairs of sleek red foxes and coyotes, ran quickly for the shelter of the woods. The larger animals prepared to fight: the Brecks—big cats; the Keenes—big wolves. I recognized Gabriel's great gray form as he sprung into existence.

Jeff, a shockingly large white tiger with deep gray stripes, appeared beside him and roared with fury enough to raise the hair on the back of my neck. Fallon stayed in human form, a hand on Jeff's back, perhaps to remind both of them that they fought together.

Ethan was beside me, dagger in hand, poised for action. I had the urge to drag him into the trees to keep him safe. But he tossed the dagger back and forth in his hands, his history as a soldier peeking through his eyes, which were fixed on the harpies and flat with concentration. He wasn't leaving now.

The swarm of creatures descended, growing larger as it sunk toward us. I watched them fly for a moment, circling around the meadow but avoiding the trees—and the torches that lined them.

Suddenly, they let out a horrific scream as sharp as nails on a chalkboard and dive-bombed the clearing like dogfighting World War II planes.

What had been a celebration . . . became an unexpected battle-field.

The shifters who remained on the field weren't afraid of battle, and many of them leaped, meeting the harpies in the air. The human portions of their bodies might have been thin, but harpies were strong. Some overbalanced, hitting the ground in a tumble of fur and feathers that shook the earth; others batted away the shifters with a dip of wings that sent wolves flying.

A harpy spied us, the only vampires on the field, dropped her head, and dove toward us.

"I'm open to suggestions," I yelled to Ethan over the din.

"Stay alive!" he offered back, blading his body toward the harpy, limiting her access to vital organs. I did the same, moving closer beside him so we were a combined vampiric weapon, immortal and strong, although my heart raced like life was a delicate and fragile thing.

And wasn't it?

"I don't suppose you know anything about harpy anatomy?"

"Not a lick, Sentinel. But they look like ladies to me!"

A lot of help he was.

The sound was ferocious now, the beat of her wings as loud as a jet plane, sending gusts of air across the field. She was close enough that I could have seen the whites of her eyes, if she'd had any. Her eyes were solid black; regardless the shape of her body, they carried no visible trace of thought or humanity.

She extended her arms and scratched out her claws, their tips aimed at our necks. We dropped to the ground, her smell— pungent and sour—streaming past as she flew above us.

"She did not get perfume for Valentine's Day," Ethan surmised, spinning to watch her bank and turn back for a second shot. The width of the harpies' wingspan helped them rise and fall quickly, but their turn radius was substantial. It took seconds for her to spin back in our direction, but only a moment for her to dip again. She'd learned the mistake of her first effort and, instead of swiping at us on the move, came straight for us and didn't veer.

We hit the ground, rolling away in different directions to avoid the claws on her feet, which were as black and sharp as those on her hands.

She decided to follow me. I was on the ground, a few feet away from the spot where she'd fallen to earth, and it wasn't far enough. She followed and scratched, talons raking at my arms and abdomen with vicious effectiveness.

The claws had looked pointy and sharp, but they were jagged like serrated knives, and they tore at flesh instead of slicing through it. They were weapons of destruction. She scraped my face, and the skin burned like fire beneath her nails.

Fear turned to fury, but it took me a moment to remember the dagger in my hand, and I thrust it upward again and again, the knife bouncing off bones I couldn't see, hitting no true target but causing enough of a painful nuisance that she backed off.

"Here!" Ethan yelled, pivoting back and forth behind her to let me get to my feet.

I stood, adrenaline numbing the cuts I'd already received, and wiped the dagger's handle, slippery with the harpy's wine-dark blood, on my pants. The smell of it was just as pungent as the rest of her body, more like vinegar than the penny scent of human blood. Even for a vampire, there was nothing appealing about it.

She turned on Ethan and flapped forward only a few feet off the ground.

That, I thought, was my chance. If flying was her advantage, I'd have to take it away from her. And I only needed gravity for that.

Distract her! I silently told Ethan. He obeyed, weaving back and forth as she tried to follow him, her wings too large for quick maneuvers.

While she focused on him, I dropped . . . and lunged for her ankles.

She screamed out, bobbing in the air as she fought off my weight, kicking at the vampire who'd become her uninvited (and literal) hanger-on. But I held tight, sinking my face into the curl of my arm to avoid the barbs at the tips of her wings, which were as jagged and sharp as her nails.

Gravity won, and the harpy pitched forward, taking me with her. I hit the ground, rolling quickly to avoid her frantically beating wings, but she kicked out and hit me square on the left cheekbone, which cracked and sang with pain strong enough to bring tears to my eyes.

As she rose again, I uttered a curse that would have had my prickly mother swatting my bottom in horror, and tried to climb to my feet but found the ground swayed a little. I made it to my knees, nearly retching from the sudden vertigo.

The harpy slammed to the ground beside me, her black eyes open, a thin line of blood trickling from the corner of her mouth, and a bloody wound across her neck, pale sinew and bone peeking through skin.

The sight didn't help my dizziness, and I sat firmly on the ground again. I looked up to find Ethan standing over her, hands and dagger bloodied, eyes green and fierce. There were streaks of blood and scratches across his face, and worse across his shirt.

He crouched in front of me, looked over my face. "You're all right, Sentinel?"

I blinked. "I'll be fine. She got my cheek."

"The bruise is already showing," he said, offering a hand and helping me to my feet. "You'll heal."

"That's what they say. But it doesn't make the punch feel any better."

A voice rose behind us. "Little help here!"

We glanced across the meadow, found Catcher and Mallory twenty feet away, lobbing blue orbs of light at a pair of harpies who easily avoided them, swiping at their heads as they bobbed overhead. The sorcerers looked tired; their font of magic wasn't endless, but required recharging. They both looked wan and sweaty, like they'd need the recharging soon.

"I'll help," Ethan said. "Stay here until you're balanced again."

I'd have argued if I could have, but he was already on his way to Mallory and Catcher.

Before I could join him, a wolf was beside me, nudging my leg. I glanced down. It was Gabriel, his wolf form enormous, his haunches nearly reaching my waist. And although he was undeniably animal—from thick fur to the tang of musk—there was something very human in his eyes.

Fear.

He nudged my hand again. Odd, because it wasn't like Gabriel to turn his back on a fight. And why would he be afraid?

The thought struck me with cold dread. Tanya, also a wolf, could have shifted. But Connor was only an infant; I wasn't entirely sure if infants could shift. And in any case, she'd have to carry him away.

"Tanya and Connor," I said, and he yipped in agreement.

We ducked to avoid the tips of claws and wings.

"I'll get them out of here and into the woods," I promised. "Keep Ethan out of trouble."

I'm going to find Tanya and Connor, I warned Ethan, who'd already reached Mallory and Catcher and was joining his dagger to their efforts. *Please keep yourself safe.*

I . . . intend . . . to, he haltingly responded, between his own evasive maneuvers.

I ducked and ran to the highest point in the meadow, a spot near the tree line on what I guessed was the southern side of the field, in order to scan the battlefield. Most of the shifters had actually shifted, but there were still some who I guessed found it easier to fight this particular enemy in human form. Tents were crumpled to the ground and fluttering wings obscured the view. If I was going to find them, I was going to have to run for it.

It was like an obstacle course, but instead of paintballs, giant naked women dropped from the sky with daggerlike claws. That wasn't nearly as romantic as it sounded. I darted from one tent to the next, looking for any sign of the queen of the Pack and the heir to the throne. But I found nothing.

I made it to a tree stump, dropped beside it as I scanned the part of the field closest to me. I saw nothing but fighting, harpies apparently intent on wiping out the Pack in one fell swoop. And I'd traversed only a third of the meadow.

"This isn't working," I murmured, cupping my hands around my mouth and screaming into the night, "Tanya!"

I strained to hear a response but heard only the yips of injured shifters and the squeals of pissed-off harpies.

"Tanya!" I tried again. And this time, I heard an answering call.

"Merit!"

The cry was too low to be close, but it was enough to signal her direction. I ran to the next obstacle, then the next, and finally found her crouched on the ground beside the totem, which now lay on its side in the middle of the clearing, sheltering her son with her body.

There was no fear in the magic that swirled around her, just a sense of determination. She was a mother, and she would protect her son, regardless the cost.

I ran toward her, put the dagger back in my boot, and extended a hand. "Long time no see."

She smiled just a little. "I don't think this is quite the party Gabriel had in mind."

"I would hope not," I said, "or he's a horrible planner. Are you okay?"

"I think I twisted my ankle. Tripped over something in the field."

I nodded. "I'll help you get to the woods. The harpies can't fly through the trees."

Tanya nestled Connor in the crook of one arm, nodded, and grabbed my hand with her free one to pull herself upright. She bobbled a bit on her left foot but stayed upright.

My arm around her back, I scanned the sky, gauged the distance between the shelter and the trees, and prepared to run. If I could just wait for them to begin the rotation away from the woods, we'd have a few seconds to make a run for it.

A metallic screech rang out above us. We crouched as a harpy flew only a foot above our heads, sending Connor into a fit of tears.

"Ready," I told her, trying to drown out the noise and the fire and the scent of blood and the snow of molted black feathers that fell from the sky.

The harpy banked and turned and gave us our chance.

"Run!" I yelled, and we took off at our stumbling pace.

She made it ten awkward yards before stumbling forward, nearly pulling me down with her. But I managed to stay on my feet and keep an iron grip on her waist. I kept her upright and she found her balance again, but her ankle wobbled beneath her. Shifting into her wolf form would allow her to heal, but we didn't have time for that.

The piercing scream rose behind us, and I risked a glance over our shoulders. The harpy had seen us, and she'd turned our way.

Tanya tried to release my grip. "Take Connor. Run for the woods. Keep him safe."

A nervous laugh bubbled up. "Are you kidding me? I'm not going to leave you here for the world's angriest chickens. We do this together." I pulled her free arm around my shoulder and put my arm back around her waist, tilting my body to take more of the weight off her ankle. Together, the sound of *thwush*ing wings behind us growing louder with each step we took, we hobbled to the tree line.

The hair rose on the back of my neck. *Gods, but this is going to be close.*

"Faster!" I said, sucking in oxygen as we raced the last twenty yards, then ten, pulling her toward the trees with all the strength I could muster.

The harpy dipped, and time seemed to slow. Visions passed before my eyes, of friendships, of my nieces and nephews, of Ethan, and of the green-eyed child Gabriel had once hinted was in my future. Green eyes I wouldn't get a chance to see if we didn't make it.

I pushed harder, calling up every spare ounce of effort I could find, that same determination that had driven me through all-nighters in grad school and endless hours of ballet practice. It didn't feel good, but that was irrelevant. *You don't stop until the job is done,* my father was fond of saying.

Tanya wasn't yet safe; my job wasn't done.

We reached the stand of winter-bare trees, and the harpy banked, wings swatting the trees on the edge of the wood, black feathers ripped out by branches floating to the ground.

I helped Tanya sit down on a fallen tree, Connor now crying

fitfully. Other shifters who'd taken shelter in the woods turned back into their human forms and looked out on the battle with horror.

I knelt down in front of Tanya, who tried to calm her son.

"What's this about?" I asked, when her gaze met mine.

She shook her head, her eyes still wide with shock. "I don't know. I don't even—what are they?"

"Harpies, I think. Is this a fight with the Pack? Did the Pack piss someone off?" *Perhaps by inviting vampires to his woods?* I silently wondered, hoping this wasn't because of us.

"I'm sorry, but I don't know. This is so horrible, Merit. So awful."

The bare limbs above us shook as harpies circled overhead, looking for a place to dive into the undergrowth. I pulled the dagger from my boot and stood up again.

"You're going back."

I nodded. "The Pack still needs help, and Ethan's still out there. I don't quit until he's safe."

There was bravado in my voice—the kind of bluffing I actually could manage—and it masked the fear. My allies were engaged in battles of their own, and I had only a slim and slender dagger to take down a woman-bird with an attitude problem.

But Tanya smiled at me like I'd seen Gabriel smile before. Knowingly. Wisely. And with utter calm. "You can do this, Merit of House Cadogan. Go save your man."

I nodded, somehow buoyed by the sentiment, and left Tanya and her subjects in the trees. Flipping the dagger nervously in my hand, I walked back to the tree line and peered into the darkness.

She dropped to the ground in front of me, torchlight flickering across her naked body.

She seemed, somehow, even larger on the ground. At least six feet tall, with a twenty-foot wingspan. Her eyes were solidly black, hair blowing wildly in the wind, revealing small breasts and a web of battle scars across her abdomen.

She tucked her wings behind her and moved forward, knees bent, the motion bouncy and unnatural. Harpies clearly weren't meant to run; they were meant to fly.

She opened her mouth and screamed. I winced at the aural assault and resorted to my standard defense mechanism. Sarcasm.

"You are not going to Hollywood with pitch like that," I advised her.

Her dark eyes flicked back and forth like a bird's, but it didn't appear she actually understood what I'd said. Maybe she didn't understand English. Or finely grained sarcasm.

Regardless, she understood battle. She attacked, vaulting forward, teeth bared.

For a moment, I was too transfixed to move. She looked like a creature from an ancient time, a warrior from an era when gods and goddesses reigned in gauzy robes and gold laurel crowns. If *The Ride of the Valkyries* had begun to play, I wouldn't have been surprised.

I kicked, trying like I had before to get her off her feet. She avoided the shot by taking to the air, then gave back better than I had, kicking forward and hitting me square in the chest, sending me flying.

I hit the ground on my back, knocking the wind out of me. I clutched at the grass at my sides, gasping for air, as the ground rumbled beneath my feet.

"Up, Merit!" yelled Tanya behind me, and I reared back, then hopped to my feet, as if her words had been an order instead of a frightened suggestion. I was tiring, still healing and dizzy from my last round, adrenaline beginning to fade, and I was beginning to react on autopilot. Fortunately, I'd been trained to fight beyond fear, beyond exhaustion.

Standing again, I bounced on my feet. The harpy's eyes narrowed and she moved forward again. I looked for a target, recalled how ineffective my dagger had been against the other harpy's abdomen, and picked a new target.

If I couldn't beat the human, I'd go for the bird.

I beckoned her forward, and she windmilled her claws as she moved toward me again, looking for purchase and a soft bit of flesh to tear. I swerved to the left, and she followed. Her legs moved awkwardly, and her wings provided just enough drag to make me faster than her. I dodged back to the right, and she moved back again, but slower this time . . . giving me just enough time to make my move.

Her wing brushed me as she sought to move again, and I grabbed the top of it, a long rib beneath a covering of slick and oily feathers, and stuck with my dagger.

She screamed in distress, reared back, and swung at me, but I leaped backward, flipping to avoid the shot. Her wing hung limply on one side, and I was struck with pity. I'd winged my enemy but hadn't brought her down.

And she was pissed.

Faster than she'd moved before, she bent her knees and jumped forward. She was on me before I could move, heavy and awkward, her mouth wide and pointed teeth aimed for my face, apparently intent on taking a bite.

"Ethan will not like that," I muttered, humor my last weapon against fear and exhaustion. I watched for the right moment and, when her head darted up to strike, pushed the dagger through her neck.

She arched back, screaming, hands at her throat, and pulled

out the dagger, which hit the ground some feet away. I watched it roll, afraid she'd come back for a second round and I'd have no recourse, no protection. But blood and worse gushed from her wound, and she staggered and fell, shaking the earth beneath.

I wiped fresh traces of blood from my face, thinking, just as I'd promised Ethan, that I'd heal. The harpy, unfortunately, would have no such luck.

When I'd gotten to my feet again, grabbed up my dagger, and scrubbed off blood and dirt, I took a look at the rest of the battle. Harpies still circled the sky—a dozen maybe—but the attack was clearly on the wane. And it would leave death and destruction in its wake.

Some shifters fought; others lay on the ground, unmoving, the scents of untimely deaths moving across the field, thrown into the air by the flap of wings. Shifters could heal themselves, but only if they shifted, and they had to be awake and conscious to do that. For some of them, it was clearly too late.

So much death, I thought, staring blankly at the carnage, trying to process it. I'd fought battles before, and seen death. But rarely this much, and never all at once.

"Merit."

I looked over, found Ethan a few feet away. He was dirty and blood smeared, but all limbs were intact. I nearly sagged with relief.

"Tanya and Connor?" he asked, moving quickly nearer and looking me over.

"The woods," I said. "I got them to the woods, then dealt with her." I gestured to the harpy, who looked scrawny and pitiful there on the ground, her wings folded in death.

"This is a miserable thing," he said, no little pity in his voice. "Let's get back in there."

We walked back into the clearing as Gabriel finished off a harpy with a vicious bite to the neck, and we ran to his position at the edge of the battle.

Light exploded, and Gabriel burst back into human form, naked as the day he was born. There were a few scratches on his body, a result of the weird magic of shape-shifting. Although changing from human to shifter would heal injuries received as a human, it didn't work in reverse.

"Everyone is tiring," Ethan said.

Gabriel nodded. Jeff ran up, hastily clothed, pointing at Catcher and Mallory.

"They think this is a magical attack," he said, "and they think they know how to finish it with the magic they have left. But it will be big magic."

Catcher and Mallory knelt together on the ground in the center of the meadow, near the fallen totem. They held their left hands together, palms flat, and their right hands flat against the earth, as if testing it for weakness, or pulling strength from it.

"Mallory won't do it without your go-ahead."

Gabriel looked at her for a moment. "Will it hurt the Pack?"

Jeff shook his head. "It will be targeted at the magic itself. It shouldn't touch anyone else."

Gabriel wet his lips, nodded. "If they think they can end it, they should. Just tell us what to do."

"Get down," he said, then cupped his hands around his mouth. "Go!" he yelled across the clearing.

As Catcher nodded at Mallory, Ethan grabbed my hand and pulled me down into a crouch.

I couldn't see the magic around Catcher and Mallory, not with my eyes, but I could feel it ramping up, like the supercharged atmosphere before a storm, the air suddenly heavy and smelling of ozone.

A bubble of magic emerged from the earth, quickly encompassing the two of them, growing until it was ten feet tall, and then suddenly exploding, pulsing, like a wave through the sky.

The magic hit the birds like a bomb. They exploded into swirls of acrid black smoke. Like it was a living thing, the smoke rose into a giant, swirling column over the clearing, a cyclone of magic. It screamed with noise—like the squeals of a thousand harpies together—and blew tents and leaves and the rest of the bonfire to the ground in an explosion of noise.

It spun faster and faster, debris winding around and around like a children's toy, narrowing and rising farther and farther into the sky until, with a final scream of sound that made me clap my hands over my ears, the column broke apart, sending black tentacles of smoke into the sky.

The night went silent, and the smoke began to dissipate, revealing the stars once again.

We all rose again. Gabriel looked at Ethan. "Get back to the house. And Catcher and Mallory, as well."

"Back to the house?" Ethan asked, his magic and body suddenly tense, making all my spidey senses tingle uncomfortably.

"We were just attacked, and you're the odd ones out."

We weren't shifters, he meant.

We were different.

We were suspects.

CHAPTER FIVE

BLOOD WILL TELL

They'd undoubtedly been attacked before. They'd had intra-Pack struggles, and they'd overcome them. But to-night they'd been attacked, without warning, by crea-tures that weren't supposed to exist.

This had shocked them. Unfortunately, we were on the wrong side of that shock.

We followed Gabriel silently back to the house, where Finn directed us to the kitchen.

It was large, with white cabinets and sleek black countertops, and a large kitchen island with an expensive stove and several stools for casual meals. The Breckenridges' kitchen staff, dressed in their formal black-and-white uniforms, watched us from one corner as Mallory, Catcher, Ethan, and I were directed to the center island.

"Sit," Finn said, then disappeared from the room. The house staff, also shifters, but apparently on duty during the festival, stood together, arms crossed, whispering and regarding us with obvious hostility.

Ethan sat beside me, his hand protectively at my back. Catcher and Mallory took seats across from us, and the strain in her face was clear. They'd interned us in the house while they grieved together, reminding us just how separate our worlds still were.

"What will they do now?" Mallory asked.

"Clean up. Mourn. Heal," Catcher said, running a hand over his shorn scalp.

Mallory looked worried and guilty, and she nibbled nervously on the edge of her thumb. I could read the fear in her face: She was the witch, the woman who'd used black magic, the one they'd taken in.

She'd come here, and she'd brought death with her.

As if reading my mind, she looked up at me and met my gaze, and the weight of her emotions made my chest clench.

I knew her again. As well as I'd known her before, but now as a sorceress, tested by magic and come through the other side. I might not ever forget the past, what she'd done. I wasn't a child, or naive. But I could forgive her, and we could move on and try to build something better, something stronger, than what had been before.

But still, no one spoke. I could deal with comfortable silence, but this silence was not comfortable. I broke through it, clearing my throat. Ethan, Mallory, and Catcher frankly looked relieved by the intrusion.

"Harpies don't exist," Mallory said. "They aren't supposed to exist."

"I'm not certain they do exist," Ethan said, glancing at Catcher. "I presume from their disappearing act they were magic?"

"A manifestation of some kind," Catcher agreed. "They weren't real."

"They killed," I said. "They fought and wounded. They were real."

"They were *tangible*," Catcher said. "But they weren't real.

Not real harpies, anyway," he added at my questioning look. "They were magic—power shaped and molded into something three-dimensional and solid."

Ethan glanced warily at the kitchen staff, then leaned forward. "That's how you thought to use magic to destroy them at the end."

Catcher nodded, glancing at Mallory. "She figured it out. They fought like real animals, fiercely, drawing blood, killing when they could. But their magical signature was wrong. The look in their eyes was wrong."

"Blank," I offered.

Mallory looked at me and nodded. "Exactly. More automaton than actual monster. So we unwound them."

"You unwound them?" I asked. "What does that mean? And use nongeeky, layman's terms."

"There's a formulaic element to magic," Catcher said. "It can be a chant. A charm. A spell. Some start with that but deepen it. They layer it. Charms atop charms atop charms." He glanced at me. "We took those layers, unfolded them, stripped them back to their elemental magic, and dispersed them. That spell wouldn't have worked if they'd been real."

"But this wasn't just a monster," Ethan said. "It was dozens of harpies, acting individually. Not just a walk and slap, but something with the look of a coordinated attack, and on shifter territory."

"Walk and slap?" Mallory asked.

"An old European custom," Ethan said. "Before the houses existed, certain feuding vampire covens engaged in petty slights, back and forth, to air their grievances."

"Aristocratic vampire slap fights? With period costumes?" Mallory asked, looking at me with obvious delight. "I am all over that and the graphic novel it inspires."

"Coordinated attacks," Catcher said, returning to the point. "The magical layering is doable, but it would have required someone powerful and very talented."

Ethan looked at Catcher for a minute. "You could have done it."

Catcher's jaw twitched at the insinuation. "With enough time, yes. Mallory, too."

"There's Paige, Simon, and Baumgartner," Ethan said. "Could they do it?"

Paige was a magician formerly stationed in Nebraska and now in Chicago. She didn't live in Cadogan House, but she was dating the House librarian, which was close enough. Baumgartner was head of the sorcerers' union, which Catcher had been kicked out of, and Simon was Mallory's former and utterly incompetent magical tutor.

Catcher drummed his fingers on the countertop, considering the question.

"Baumgartner has the magical capacity, but he wouldn't have a reason to do it. It would upset his apple cart. Simon doesn't have the mojo."

"Paige?" Ethan asked.

"Maybe, but she doesn't seem like the type. She's interested in the mathematics of magic, the history. Not so much the execution, and certainly not wholesale destruction."

Ethan sat back, drawing the attention of the kitchen staff, whose eyes narrowed suspiciously. Did they think he was plotting a revolt right here in the Brecks' kitchen? I considered flashing my fangs but guessed it wouldn't be easy to intimidate the staff of a shape-shifting family.

After a moment of silence, he glanced at Catcher. "If we're going to tell the Pack we think this was a magical attack, we're going to have to prove it, one way or the other. Talk to the sorcerers, confirm their whereabouts. If they are, as we suspect, not involved, find out who they think might have done it."

"We aren't errand boys," Catcher testily said, lip curled.

But Ethan wasn't fazed. "No, you aren't. But we're in Pack territory, surrounded by shifters who are angry and grieving. And they have us separated and under guard. Until we prove otherwise, we're their suspects." He glanced at Mallory, and my stomach curled. "And I imagine Mallory is suspect number one."

We were summoned an hour later, still filthy and scarred from the battle. A man in a trim suit sent us to Papa Breck's study, which had been one of my favorite rooms in the house as a child. Nick and I had stolen several summer days there, poring over antique books, inspecting mementos of Papa Breck's travels, and nabbing lemon drops from a crystal dish he kept on his desk.

Tonight, the room was dark, cigar smoke swirling in the air. Gabe sat in a leather armchair, the Keene and Breck brothers surrounding him like men at arms. Papa Breck, silver haired and barrel-chested, sat behind his desk, a cigar between his teeth.

"Three dead," Papa Breck said, ashing his cigar and beginning the inquest. "Three dead. Two missing. Fourteen injured."

Ethan clasped his hands in front of him, met Gabe's eyes. "We're sorry for your losses."

Michael sniffed. "I notice you aren't injured."

Ethan slid his gaze to Michael but didn't alter his tone. "We incurred our share of injuries, but we heal. We fought alongside you, and as you may recall, Catcher and Mallory destroyed what remained of the harpies." He glanced at Gabriel. "We also took care of your queen."

"You showed up at our house," Papa Breck said, "and all hell broke loose."

"Again, we are sorry about tonight's tragedy. But you should look elsewhere for the blame, as we had nothing to do with it. Merit and I are your guests because of circumstances in Chicago. Mallory and Catcher are your guests because she is a student of Gabriel's. We fought with you against the harpies. We did not create them, nor did we lure them here."

Papa Breck shook his head, looked away. He'd already decided we were guilty, and rational arguments weren't going to sway him now.

Ethan looked at Gabriel. "I'll ask the obvious question: Has the Pack made any new enemies lately? Or incited any old ones?"

"We always have enemies," Gabe said. "And I don't know of any new ones."

"Then what about old ones?" Michael asked, looking at Mallory. "How did you know to use magic?"

I didn't think sorcerers and shifters had been enemies, but Michael didn't seem the type to be concerned with fact.

Still, Mallory stepped forward, shoulders squared against the doubt in their eyes and the fear in the room. I liked this Mallory.

"Their magic was too uniform," she said. "Not even a hint of personality or distinctiveness. And their eyes were blank. Empty. We guessed—correctly as it turned out—that someone wound the magic to create them. Layered magic to create the harpies," she said, when the shifters looked confused. "We unwound it. That's what blew them apart."

Gabriel bobbed his head, considering. "That was good work."

But Michael snorted. "If they knew how to stop it, why didn't they stop it earlier?"

"Are you kidding?" All eyes turned to Catcher, whose loathing was barely masked. "Are you seriously suggesting we knew what was going on and just let it continue?"

"Does it matter?" Michael asked, pleading with Gabe. It wouldn't have surprised me to see him drop to his knees in supplication. "This was magic, and they have magic."

"So what?" Gabriel challenged, leaning forward, elbows on his knees. "What, precisely, would you have me do, Michael? String them up for coincidentally having magic? And even if they didn't stop it soon enough, would you have me kill them for that? As far as I'm aware, you didn't fight at all."

Michael paled. "I was protecting the house."

"You were protecting your own ass," Gabe said, giving him a dismissive look and his father a warning one. "The two who are missing—who are they?"

Papa Breck's eyes fairly bulged with shock. "You can't possibly think they were involved."

"What I think is irrelevant. What matters is the truth. Who's missing?"

"Rowan and Aline," Nick said.

Ethan's eyebrows perked with interest. "Aline, who doesn't like your father or your siblings?"

"The very same," Gabriel said. The look in his eyes made it clear he wasn't dismissing the coincidence.

"Shifters wouldn't do this," Papa Breck spat. But his voice was quiet. He disagreed with the Apex, but he wasn't going to be overly loud about it.

"Frankly, we don't know anything about who did this, except that they used complicated magic." He offered Ethan an appraising glance. "Fortunately, we have right in our presence a group that's pretty good at figuring those things out."

Ethan's magic spiked alarmingly, but he stayed silent.

"The vampires and sorcerers maintain they're not responsible for what happened here. Considering their unique skills, they should be able to identify who is."

"And if they can't uncover who did this?" Papa Breck asked, as if we weren't in the room and couldn't hear the doubt that stained his voice.

Gabriel steepled his fingers, gazed at us through hooded eyes. "Then we'll just continue to wonder."

The sun would soon be on the rise. Gabriel dismissed us, and three shifters I didn't recognize escorted us back to the carriage house like prisoners returning to their cells. Considering the implicit threat in his final words, maybe we were.

We'd come to Loring Park to avoid prison; instead, we'd found a different one.

Since we were still dirty from battle, the four of us agreed to take turns in the shower. Mallory, then Catcher, then me, and Ethan was last. They hadn't planned to stay at the Brecks' and hadn't packed bags, so I let Mallory borrow clothes, and Ethan offered replacements for Catcher.

I emerged from my turn in the bath wrapped in a towel, my skin blissfully clean of gore and dirt and probably worse, hair damp around my shoulders.

Ethan stood in the bedroom, naked from the waist up, bare toes peeking beneath his jeans. His hand was on his hip, his dirty hair framing his face. His phone was in his free hand, brow furrowed. That expression was easy enough for me to read.

"What's wrong?"

He glanced up at me, male appreciation in his eyes as he took in the towel. But exhaustion quickly replaced interest. I didn't take it personally; it had been a long night.

"I advised Luc of tonight's events and asked him about the CPD. He said there's been no contact, either from the CPD or Kowalcyzk."

I moved to my duffel bag to pick out sleepwear. "Maybe

that's a good thing. Maybe she's realized how ridiculous she's being."

"Maybe," he said. "Luc has given her a copy of the House's security tapes, which quite clearly show the intrusion and Monmonth's threats."

I glanced back at him. I wasn't normally one to play the optimist, but we'd already gone on the lam. There wasn't much else to do but wait and hope.

"That could have been enough. Maybe Detective Jacobs convinced her that pursuing you would be completely illogical."

"As much as I appreciate Detective Jacobs, your premise requires her to use rational thought and logic. I'm not certain she's capable."

I found a tank and pajama bottoms, zipped up the duffel again. "Well, if she intends to push, she isn't showing it now. We'll just have to wait until she relents or our other plans work. What about my grandfather? Any word from Luc?"

"He's stable," Ethan said with a smile. "And he despises hospital food. You have the appetite in common."

My grandmother had been an amazing cook—a whiz with vegetables and salt pork—and she'd undoubtedly sparked the appreciation of it in both of us.

"Good." I frowned. "I'm not sure if it's better or worse to tell him what went on tonight. He won't need the stress."

"Then you must give him constant fits."

"Your material is usually better than that, Sullivan."

"Perhaps you'd like to see just how good my material is." Ethan put the phone on a bureau and moved toward me, arms outstretched for a hug and a grin on his face.

But he was filthy, so I hustled out of reach and pointed a warning finger at him.

"You're still disgusting, and for the first time in hours, I'm not. Shower first. Then affection."

"You're a cruel mistress," he said, but disappeared into the bathroom.

I dressed while Ethan showered, grateful for a few minutes of privacy and silence. I checked in with Jonah, advised him what was up, and wasn't at all surprised by the cursing that followed.

LEADS? he asked when he'd exhausted his phone's symbol keys.

NOT YET, I advised, BUT GABE HAS ASSIGNED US TO INVESTIGATE. WE FIND ATTACKERS, OR WE ARE ATTACKERS.

YOU GET ALL THE FUN JOBS, he advised. CALL IF YOU NEED HELP.

ROGER THAT. KEEP CHICAGO SAFE.

THAT WILL BE EASY, he messaged. ALL THE TROUBLEMAKERS ARE IN LORING PARK TONIGHT.

I couldn't argue much with that.

Ethan had emerged from the bathroom—clad only in perfectly fitting jeans and scrubbing a towel through his hair—when the carriage house's front door opened and closed.

My gaze on Ethan's chest, it took me a moment to recognize the sound and turn my head toward the shuffling in the other room.

"I'll just check that out," I said, moving toward it while Ethan searched for a T-shirt.

Gabriel stood in the living room in front of the coffee table, arms crossed, watching as Berna and several shifters, her apparent helpers, carried in aluminum trays of food. My stomach, empty and roiling, rejoiced.

"I have brought dinner," Berna pronounced, eyeing me nastily, as if there was a chance I'd decline free food. My patience for shifters was growing shorter by the moment.

"Honestly, Berna, when have you ever known me not to eat?"

She didn't seem entirely satisfied with the answer, but I was saved by distraction.

Ethan walked into the room, hair still damp but fully dressed. Berna's eyes lit with feminine appreciation.

"Berna brought us dinner," I said.

"That was very thoughtful of you, Berna," Ethan said.

"Is for health," she said, squeezing her knotted fingers around Ethan's biceps. "For muscles and teeth. Good, strong muscle. Strong. Good."

"I think they've got it." Gabriel smirked.

She humphed and herded her crew back to the door, but not before snapping a towel in his direction.

"I'll meet you outside," Gabriel said, closing the door when he was the only shifter left in the room.

"Chow time for the prisoners?" Ethan asked. His voice was low, threatening, and very, very alpha.

Gabriel grunted and headed for the kitchen. While Ethan, Mallory, Catcher, and I exchanged glances, the refrigerator door opened and closed again, and the *clink* of glass sounded.

He walked back in with a bottle of beer in hand and looked, I realized for the first time, utterly exhausted. He'd probably been playing Apex all evening, and for the festival he'd planned for. Here, finally, he was with people who weren't his subjects. For a brief moment—a rare moment—he shook off the mantle of power and sprawled onto the couch.

"The Pack is pissed," he said, taking a drink of the beer. "No," he amended, gesturing with the bottle. "They're scared. And that's infinitely worse."

Ethan considered the admission for a moment, then took a seat on the couch across from Gabe. If you hadn't known they were Apex and Master, you might have thought them athletes re-laxing after a game. Or A-list actors between scenes on a movie set. There was just something about the supernatural that brought out the best in male genetics.

Taking cues from the alphas, Mallory and I took seats as well, and Catcher followed. I sat beside Ethan, comforted by the closeness of his body and the smell of his cologne, the familiar things that brought comfort in unusual times.

That, I thought, was one of the best parts of being in a rela-tionship. No matter how foreign the world, the landmarks, the customs, I'd never be a stranger beside Ethan. Love bred the best kind of familiarity.

If, down the road, Ethan was leaving dirty socks on the floor, I might not find the familiarity so charming. But for now, it soothed with a depth that surprised me.

"We are not their enemy," Ethan said.

"No," Gabe said, taking another drink, the bottle slung be-tween two fingers. "But trouble arrived shortly after you did. That coincidence isn't going unnoticed." He looked up, smiled wolf-ishly. "It would go a long way toward mending fences if you could figure out what happened."

"You haven't given us much choice," Ethan said. "You've made it sound like we're guilty if we *don't* figure it out."

"Added incentive," Gabriel said with a smile.

I didn't smile back. I, for one, was sick of being manipulated by shape-shifters. In addition to being slammed in the face. At the moment, those two things were at the top of my shit list.

Gabe sat forward. "Look. You're not cops, and you're certainly not on the Pack payroll. It's not your job to solve our problems. I get that. But you know how to do this." He glanced at me. "You and your team have a way of figuring these things out. You're

better at it than I am, even if I had the time. But I've got colleagues to mourn, a Pack to watch over." He paused. "I need the
help, Sullivan. And I'm asking for it."

Ethan watched him silently, jaw clenched. He didn't like
being manipulated. But he was a vampire and a Master at that,
and honor was everything to him.

"All right," Ethan said, resignation in his voice. "But we'll
need information, starting with your theory about who orches-
trated this attack."

"I don't know of anyone with the skills to build a hoard of
harpies," Gabriel said.

"Magic can be bought," Catcher said. "But animosity like we
saw tonight grows naturally."

"Our enemy list hasn't grown any deeper recently," Gabriel
said. "Yes, there are people who don't like the family, don't like
the Pack, don't like shifters. But there haven't been any catalysts—
nothing that would have set off a night like this."

"What about Aline?" I asked. "You said she butted heads with
your father. What's the story there?"

Gabe nodded, glanced at me. "She had relatives—cousins—in
the Atlantic Pack. They got into trouble—got drunk, roughed up
a clerk at a bodega, and stole some money. Afterward, they wanted
shelter and turned to us. Aline was in favor of it, said the kids were
set up. But my father didn't buy it and wouldn't allow it. He didn't
want to shelter troublemakers. He told Aline about his decision,
and they had a very public disagreement. She backed down, but
she didn't forgive him."

"And the cousins?" Ethan asked.

"Killed," Gabe said. "The robbery wasn't the first time they got
into trouble, and it wasn't the last. They tried grift, a short con, and
got caught. The vic wasn't amused, and made an example of them."

I grimaced. "That couldn't have engendered any better feelings in Aline."

"It didn't," Gabriel said. "When my father died, she rallied for another alpha to take over the Pack." He smiled, with teeth. "That particular whelp was not successful."

"And now Aline is missing," Catcher said.

"Or she left," I said. "It sounds like her anger's been simmering for a long time."

Gabriel nodded. "I think that's accurate. But I wouldn't say there's been anything recently. And I don't know of any connections she'd have to magic like this."

"What about Rowan?" Mallory asked.

"He's a good man," Gabe said, with obvious regret. "Employed by the Brecks, works on the property. Keeps to himself, is a hard worker. I don't know of any reason he'd organize something this violent." He rubbed his jaw contemplatively. "All that said, they're still missing. If they don't return by sunset—or we don't find evidence they were victims—I'll have to question them myself."

There seemed little doubt the Apex of the North American Central Pack would find the answers.

"What will you do about the rest of Lupercalia?" Mallory asked.

"That's a rock and a hard place," Gabe admitted. "We cancel, we show weakness. We continue, we put shifters at risk of round two of whatever this is." He looked at Ethan. "I imagine you've faced similar dilemmas."

Ethan nodded. "To stand or to protect. It is the perennial dilemma of the Master of any house."

Gabe nodded. "Truth. I'm mulling over our options, but I'm leaning toward letting the party continue. When the mourning's done, the Pack will need a release."

"And what about us?" Catcher asked.

Gabriel's eyebrows lifted. "You're part of the mystery-solving gang, aren't you?"

Catcher muttered something unflattering, and Mallory nudged him. "I presume you want us to stay here tonight?" she asked.

"It would make things easier," Gabe said.

"So we'll sleep on the couch," Catcher said, "like we're twelve-year-olds at a slumber party."

"In fairness," Ethan said, "we don't *all* have to sleep on the couch."

"In fairness," Catcher said, "you can kiss my ass."

"Ladies," Mallory said. "Let's put on our big-girl panties. Merit and Ethan are already sleeping in the bedroom, and there's no point in making them move. Catcher and I can take the couch. The shifters will feel better if we make this work, and it's no great loss to any of us."

We all stared at her for a moment, at her implacable tone and reasonable words. If this was Mallory 2.0, I thoroughly approved.

"She's right," I said. "We can make this work."

"We're going to run out of clothes, though," she said.

Gabriel nodded, looked over the sorcerers. "I'll talk to Fallon, Nick. They should be about your size, might have something to offer." He grimaced. "And there will be plenty of Lupercalia shirts to go around. I doubt most will want the souvenirs."

"We'd appreciate whatever you can find."

"I actually have a small request," I said, and Gabriel angled his head toward me.

"Yes, Kitten?"

"We didn't have our swords tonight. Finley basically told us not to wear them, that they'd piss off the family. But if we're looking for monsters—especially monsters with magic—I want steel."

He chuckled, sharing an appreciative glance with Ethan. "I'll talk to them."

Gabriel then gestured toward the food still untouched on the coffee table. "Sun will be up soon. I'll let you eat and get some rest."

I was seated closest to the door, so I rose, too, intending to fix the locks after he'd gone. But when we met at the door, Gabriel stopped to turn his gaze on me. His eyes, the color of warm amber, swirled like tempests.

"Thank you for saving them."

I nodded, smiled. "You're welcome. I was glad to help."

But his expression stayed serious, his eyes deep and fathomless, the sight of them enough to raise goose bumps on my arms.

"As in much of life," he quietly said, "it could have gone the other way."

My chest tightened. Like sorcerers, shifters had the gift of prophecy. Did he mean Tanya might have died? That he might have lost her and Connor in the battle?

A bolt of something ran through my chest, a feeling on the precipice between gratitude and grief. I was glad his family was safe, and troubled that things might so easily have ended in tragedy. I didn't know how to give voice to the feeling or how to respond.

"I don't predict the future," Gabriel said, answering one of my unspoken questions. "But I know the weight of things. There is a gravity about her now, about Connor, that suggests things might have gone the other way. That their roads might have diverged from mine. They didn't, and I'm grateful."

"I'm grateful, too."

He smiled. "That's why I like you, Kitten. You're good people." He leaned in and pressed a kiss to my cheek, and the flush rose from the tips of my toes to the top of my head.

"Thank you," I said, and before I could ask my own questions—about the other prophecies he'd made—he slipped outside and into the darkness. There never seemed to be time for that particular future.

Gabriel gone, and a long night of warring behind us, we looked back at the food. It smelled porky, but when Mallory pulled back the aluminum foil, she revealed a tray of unidentifiable grayish chunks, some of which were tubular and looked distastefully intestinal.

Ethan slanted his head as he looked at it. "Is Berna trying to feed us or kill us?"

"I suspect the Brecks put in their two cents about what we should be eating," Catcher said, who nevertheless forked a pile of the meaty chunks, flecked with fat and sinew, onto one of the paper plates she'd provided.

"You aren't digging in, Sentinel," Ethan said.

"I think I'll stick to blood," I said, the meat not even slightly appealing despite my obvious hunger. "What ever happened to that package Berna gave you?"

"Lost in the battle," Ethan said. "And isn't that a disappointment?"

I grabbed bottles of Blood4You for Ethan and me and sat down on the couch beside him again, exhaustion sinking heavy into my bones.

"What a miserable night," I said, handing over a bottle.

"Seconded," Catcher added. "Unfortunately, I doubt we've seen the end of the trouble." He lifted a long, spiral bit of pork from his plate.

My stomach—usually so hearty—twisted nastily. But I'd need my strength, so I made myself finish the blood and then grabbed a yeast roll from the other tray Berna had brought. The meat might have been questionable, but there was no faulting the warm and buttery bread.

"You think they'll attack again?" Mallory asked.

"I think it would be unusual to bring the amount of fight and magic we saw tonight and assume that was the end of it. But I doubt they'll attack overnight."

"Why?" Ethan asked.

"Because the harpies were as much show as substance," Catcher said. "You attack when everyone's asleep, you don't get the show."

Ethan walked to one of the large windows and pushed aside the curtain. "In the event there is an attack, there are two guards. One on each side of the door." He hit the button that dropped the window guards into place and turned back to face Mal and Catcher.

"Perhaps, to be on the safe side, you could add a layer of magic?" Ethan asked. "A ward in case Gabe's colleagues decide their loyalties aren't entirely firm?"

Catcher nodded, chewed. "Already discussed it. A little buzz along the doors and windows to signal a trespass, and a second layer to make trespassers think twice."

Ethan nodded and returned to the couch, but instead of sitting beside me, he stretched out along its length, his head in my lap. He didn't relax easily, and certainly not with an audience. Exhaustion must have worn him down. I ran my fingers through the golden silk of his hair, watched his eyes close in relief. It had been a long night; I was thankful we'd come through it mostly unscathed.

Something made me glance up. I found Mallory watching me, surprise in her expression. She'd been with me when I met Ethan for the first time, and while we'd battled each other. Ethan and I had grown closer when Mallory and I had grown apart; maybe she was still getting used to seeing us as a couple. Hell, I was still getting used to it. I made a mean Sentinel now, but at the time of my making I'd preferred books to most everything else, and he'd chosen me. That still awed me on occasion.

"Sun's nearly up," Catcher said, patting Mallory's knee. "Why don't you two get to bed, and we'll get things fixed up in here?"

Ethan nodded, rose from the couch, and held out a hand, his gaze beckoning. "Come, Sentinel. Let us away and leave them to their magic."

Here, in the midst of Pack territory, I didn't think it would be easy to escape.

I woke once during the day, the bedroom still dark. We weren't meant to wake when the sun was above the horizon, so my mind was thick and fogged. But I heard a wolf baying, the sound long and mournful. More voices joined in, the animals obviously grief stricken and wailing for their dead.

They'd have their own rituals, their own ways of mourning. This was their funeral, their dirge beneath the cold, cruel sun.

I drifted back to sleep, Ethan warm and quiet beside me, and dreamt of amaranth.

CHAPTER SIX

GAME, SET, VAMPIRE

I woke with a start just after sunset. Ethan lay at my side, his eyes closed in sleep, an arm over his head. His long legs were tangled in the pale sheets, his silk pajama bottoms riding temptingly low on his hips.

He opened one eye, smiled invitingly. "Good evening, Sentinel."

"Sullivan," I said, leaning over to press a kiss to his lips.

There was a knock at the bedroom door. Catcher opened it without waiting for a response. I sat up straight again, grateful I'd slept in pajamas and wasn't staring him down half naked.

"You're awake," he said. He wore his typically dour expression and a T-shirt with NOPE! across the front in bold, white letters.

Ethan flipped the blanket over my body like a matador, covering even the pajamaed parts. "I don't recall inviting you in."

"I'm a sorcerer, not a vampire. I don't need an invite. And now that we've discussed our supernatural predilections, we need to get going. Gabriel wants to talk."

Mallory stepped into the doorway, a bowl of cereal in hand, mouth busy with a spoonful. "Good evening, vampires."

It didn't escape me that she took a moment to admire my particular vampire.

"Eyes on your own man candy."

"My man candy's already dressed," she said between bites of what looked like chocolate sludge. "Yours is . . . less so."

And mine was clearly enjoying the attention. He linked his hands behind his head, showing off his well-toned chest.

"Down, boy," I murmured.

"Yes, boy," Catcher said. "Quit flirting with my girlfriend."

Ethan only smiled. "You're the ones darkening my doorway. I'm beginning to see why so many sups don't like sorcerers."

"Oh, he's grumpy at sunset," Mallory said, glancing at me.

"It's not just sunset," Catcher offered. "And we're wasting time on the argument, so get dressed, and let's go." He rapped twice on the doorjamb before he and Mallory shuffled back into the main room.

"Fine friends you have, Sentinel."

"They're your friends, too, Sullivan. You've known Catcher longer than you've known me."

I climbed out of bed, and he swatted me on the bottom.

"I'm not sure that's flattering to either of you."

"Neither am I," I admitted, "but at the moment, we're all stuck with each other."

Ethan grabbed breakfast from the kitchen while I dressed. Thinking I couldn't be too careful, I dressed in my leathers, then settled in with blood and a bagel.

After he'd eaten, Ethan pulled on jeans and a V-neck sweater with a shirt beneath. A lock of blond hair fell across his face as he tucked the shirt into very-well-fitting jeans, looking more like an East Coast blue blood than a midwestern vampire.

His phone rang, and Ethan finished the tuck, pushed his hair behind his ears, and picked it up.

"Luc," Ethan said in greeting. "You're on speaker. We were just about to leave."

"This won't take long. Just wanted to give you an update. The lawyers report Kowalcyzk is apparently trying to convince the prosecutor the House's security tapes were tampered with—that the video of Monmonth arriving at the House and killing Louie and Angelo was doctored."

"And therefore that Ethan didn't act in self-defense," I concluded.

"That's patently ridiculous," Ethan said. "As if we don't have anything better to do than doctor our own security footage."

"Rumor is, the prosecutor has doubts. And he's the one who'd have to take the case to a jury. In any other city, that would probably be enough. But this is Chicago; the mayor's got pull."

God knew, I loved my hometown. But sometimes the Second City needed a good kick to the groin.

"We can prove the tapes weren't doctored," Ethan said. "Forensics run both ways."

"We can," Luc agreed. "And the lawyers are negotiating for that, and billing the House like its going out of style," he mumbled. "Unfortunately, while the lawyers argue, she's attacked on another front."

Ethan's gaze narrowed. "How?"

"Anne Rice–style, as it turns out." Luc waited a beat for us to get the punch line.

"*Interview with the Vampire*," Lindsey put in. Luc must have had us on speakerphone.

"That's my girl," Luc said. "And you win the prize. Jonah

called. The mayor's people picked up Scott Grey fifteen minutes ago for questioning."

Scott Grey was the Master of Grey House, and Jonah's boss.

Magic spiked as Ethan's irritation rose. "I presume Scott's Second arranged for a lawyer?"

"He has. Our guys say she's sharp, but the mayor's muscle isn't letting her near Scott. She apparently was told he doesn't have a right to counsel because the Houses are under suspicion as domestic terrorists."

It took Ethan a moment to respond. And in the seconds that passed, magic rose to a furious crescendo.

"Domestic terrorists?" Each syllable was bitten off.

"Their words. The muscle's from a task force she's set up. All the lawyers are talking. I also called Morgan and gave him a heads-up."

Morgan rounded out the city's three Masters. He became Master of Navarre after the former Master, Celina Desaulniers, was accused of murder. Morgan and I had briefly dated when I'd first become a vampire, but the relationship, such as it was, hadn't lasted long.

"I'm surprised he answered the phone considering the blacklist."

When we left the GP, the organization had responded by forbidding Navarre and Grey from communicating with us. That hadn't stopped Grey House, at least not in the long run, but Navarre played by the GP's rules.

"He wasn't thrilled. I'd call it denial with an arrogance chaser."

"I don't know what you saw in him," Lindsey said.

I glanced at Ethan. "My Master demanded I date him for the benefit of the House."

"Not one of my better decisions," Ethan admitted. "Kowalcyzk can call us domestic terrorists if she wants, but she won't be able to make that stick. There's no evidence of anything but the opposite—that we help the city at every turn. What about the governor?"

"No dice so far," Luc said. "Malik's spoken with her, but she's loath to get involved in an investigation. She's calling it comity and federalism and blah-blah political mumbo jumbo I don't care about. In any event, we'll let you know if there's any movement."

Ethan nodded, and silence descended for a moment.

"You're exactly where you're supposed to be right now," Luc said, responding to Ethan's unspoken complaint. "And we have a plan. It just may not come together as soon as we'd like."

"Well, we're here for the duration in any event," Ethan said.

"Shifter arrest is better than human arrest?" Luc cheekily asked. "Oh, and one more thing while I'm checking off my list of craptastic news. Lakshmi's arrived. She's in a suite at the Peninsula." The Peninsula was one of Chicago's swankiest hotels, located a few blocks east of Michigan Avenue.

Nerves jangled at the edges of my consciousness, but I pushed them back. Worrying about when she'd call in her favor would have to wait; my plate was full.

"She's made arrangements to speak to Malik?"

"Nope. She said she'd wait to talk to you."

I looked at Ethan. "That seems like good news. If they were going to go ballistic, they wouldn't care if you were there or not."

"Or their price is stiff and meant just for me."

That ominous prediction settled uncomfortably in the room.

"We have to go," Ethan said. "The Pack is awaiting our arrival. Keep us posted."

They said their good-byes and ended the call, and Ethan slanted a worried glance at me. He'd pulled his hair back today, framing rugged cheekbones and his emerald eyes, which were clouded with worry.

"Is this one of those times I'm supposed to be supportive and tell you everything will work out perfectly?"

Ethan made a vague grunt of amusement. "Only if you can say it honestly."

"So I'll just keep my mouth shut."

Ethan smiled, but it didn't reach his eyes. He pulled me into an embrace, his warmth and clean cologne enveloping us both. "I don't want others to bear the burdens of my choices."

So Scott's situation concerned him, I thought.

"She's just interviewing him," I pointed out. "We've all been through worse than an interview. And frankly, this may not be retribution against you. If she's got a task force, it could just be her usual brand of paranoia."

He kissed the top of my head. "You're a good and comforting Sentinel."

"I'd prefer to be the Sentinel that talks some damned sense into the mayor, but that opportunity hasn't yet arisen."

I texted Jonah, let him know we were aware of Scott's interrogation and were monitoring. Unfortunately, there wasn't much else we could do from Loring Park.

Vampiric business concluded, we met Catcher and Mallory in the front room.

"Took you long enough," Catcher said, taking a final drink from a mug before putting it down on the table.

"Scott Grey is now in Kowalcyzk's custody," Ethan said.

Catcher looked up, surprised. "Really."

Ethan nodded, just once. "Suspected of domestic terrorism, according to our rather creative mayor."

"That lady is off her rocker," Mallory said, adjusting her knit cap, from beneath which peeked two ombré braids.

"She is something," Ethan said. "Any leads in the sorcery area?"

Catcher shook his head. "Baumgartner's on vacation in Tucson with his wife and grandkids. And even if he'd been here, he's not exactly a think-outside-the-box type of guy. We haven't reached Simon yet. Paige and the librarian have been in a hotel room in the Loop for a belated Valentine's Day. Their minds are on other things."

"So Paige and Baumgartner are out, if they weren't already. And once again, we have nothing."

"For now," I said, squeezing Ethan's hand. "We always find something."

The issue was finding it soon enough.

We pulled on coats and gloves, belted on our katanas, and headed outside. The shifters who awaited us didn't even spare them a glance, so I presumed Gabriel had approved our wearing them.

The night was cold, the sky covered by a bank of clouds that glowed orange on the horizon, lit by the pollution of a million sodium lights in Chicago. But I was jumpy and couldn't stop glancing into the darkness, waiting for a new squadron of monsters to emerge.

We walked silently back to the house, hands in pockets and collars lifted against the wind, the shifters forming a guard in front of and behind us. They were all men, all wearing NAC jackets. They didn't bother to look at us, which I found I preferred. Disinterest, in my book, was better than barely concealed loathing.

One of the shifters in front held open a door, and we entered a spare and utilitarian hallway. This part of the house was for the staff, allowing them to serve the Brecks inconspicuously.

We were marched into the main portion of the house, and then into a formal living room, where Gabriel held court again. The same crew was here again tonight—the Keenes, the Brecks, and a dozen other shifters, including Jeff.

Once again, the room was mostly men, but tonight there were exceptions. Fallon sat on an immaculately tailored couch beside her brother, and Tanya sat on his other side, Connor in her arms. Another female shifter sat on the floor at Tanya's feet, a petite brunette who had Tanya's big eyes and sweet features. I guessed she was in her early twenties and probably a younger sister of Tanya's. She was a lovely girl, with bee-stung lips and pink cheeks, her brown hair pulled up in a messy knot.

The energy in the room was different than it had been last night. Still cautious, grieving. But tonight there was something else, a new softness running through the weft and warp. I presumed Tanya and her sister had brought that to the party.

Tanya glanced at me, nodded her head in acknowledgment as she brushed a hand across the fuzz on Connor's head, comforting him—and probably her—at the same time.

"Guests," Gabriel said, nodding mildly at us. He wore a long-sleeved T-shirt with a complicated pattern, jeans, and boots with traces of mud on the bottom. The faint scents of dirt and blood lay beneath fresh flowers and the cologne of the various men in the room. They'd been outside, probably walking the earth where their comrades had died.

Gabe caught my gaze, and I looked up at him. "I trust you slept well."

"As well as possible, considering."

"Any developments regarding the attack?" Ethan asked.

"Not yet." Gabe glanced at the large grandfather clock that ticked ominously across the room. "But that report should come any moment now."

"And the festival?" Ethan asked.

"We do not give up easily," Gabriel said. "We've managed to get the grounds back into shape, the tents prepared again." That explained the mud on his boots. "Lupercalia will continue tonight."

Volleys of magic filled the air as the shifters in the room reacted to the announcement. Some were relieved, some nervous, some angry.

I felt Ethan's jolt of surprise, understood it. But we were vampires, and the violation hadn't been against us. Perhaps they needed to prove to the world—and themselves—that they could battle back.

"We wish you the best," Ethan said. "And obviously we're happy to assist as we can."

The clock struck six with a sound like church bells, and the door creaked open.

The shifter who stood in the doorway was tall and rangy, with black hair that reached his shoulders and a shadow's worth of stubble. His skin was honeyed, and his eyes were chocolate brown and deep set, offsetting honed cheekbones and a generous mouth. He wore the NAC jacket over jeans and boots, and a series of tangled cords and wraps on his right wrist.

As manly appreciation wasn't appropriate under the circumstances—and considering the stink eye from Ethan's direction—I muted my expression. But as I looked away, I happened to catch the wide-eyed interest in Tanya's sister's face. I'd seen that look before—I'd *had* that look before—and it was immediately recognizable, as was the way she seemed to shrink back into her own body, as if willing herself to disappear. She was interested in this new shifter but hadn't yet confessed her feelings. It was the look of every shy teenager who'd come face-to-face with a high school crush, of every coed who'd decided the object of her affection was out of her league.

All the while, the shifter stood statue still before his Apex, oblivious to the wanting in her eyes, waiting for instructions.

"Damien Garza," Gabriel said, gesturing to him. "A member of the Pack." Gabe gestured to us. "Merit, of Cadogan House. Ethan Sullivan, of Cadogan House. And you know Catcher and Mallory."

Ethan nodded, and Damien acknowledged us with a small dip of his chin, his face devoid of expression.

"Damien is here to report on our missing mates," Gabe said, signaling Damien to begin.

"There is no sign of Aline," Damien said, his accent melodic. "But Rowan's body has been found. Just inside the tree line on the south side of the meadow."

His expression was as neutral as it had been before, but the magic in the room dipped sadly, becoming low and melancholic. Gabe closed his eyes and leaned back against the couch, shoulders slumping in grief.

"We are sorry for your loss," Ethan gravely said. We'd had to say that too many times since our arrival in Loring Park.

Gabe nodded, rubbing his forehead with his palm as if to soothe the tension there. "Is Aline gone by choice or coercion?"

"I do not know," Damien said. "But she is not on the estate. And I have looked well."

"Surely she's just gone home," Finley said, glancing at his fellow shifters. "Left the premises because of the drama."

"All those years she didn't leave," Fallon said. "Why would she leave now?"

"Because you brought sorcerers and vampires into your sanctuary."

All eyes looked to Mallory, who'd spoken the words. She glanced across the room, making eye contact with each shifter, the act an apology and a reckoning.

"It's the truth, right out of her mouth," Mallory said. "Maybe it was the final straw for her."

"Regardless of the reason," Gabe said, "the timing is suspect. She left precisely when the night brought tragedy to our people, and I don't believe in coincidences."

He looked up at Damien. "Go to her home. Learn what you can." Then he looked at Ethan. "As you've offered your help, I suggest Merit go with Damien to look for Aline. It wouldn't be wise for you to leave the estate, all things considered. I suggest you and the sorcerers stay here and help us ensure the safety of the Pack tonight."

Papa Breck scoffed at the notion he needed protecting, and it was clear Ethan didn't like the idea of our splitting up. But as plans went, it wasn't as bad as it might have been. We had agreed to investigate, and Ethan couldn't leave the estate until the coast was clear. Lupercalia was going ahead as planned, so we might as well help the Pack.

"I cannot speak for Catcher or Mallory," Ethan carefully said. "Merit will go with Damien—but Jeff will go as well."

Ethan, ever the strategist, had done the math. Damien was an unknown, but Jeff was an ally. We'd literally walked through fire together.

A thin smile played at Gabriel's lips. "Your terms are acceptable, Sullivan. Damien, Jeff, Merit—go now. And find her."

I didn't want to leave Ethan. I (mostly) trusted his safety to Catcher and Mallory, but they'd still be surrounded by shifters who hadn't decided whether we were friend or foe. And many were leaning toward the latter.

Ethan escorted me to the foyer, where we waited while Jeff and Damien researched Aline's address. I took the opportunity to play Sentinel.

"Make sure you're armed in case there's another attack. Keep your phone on you. And stay in Catcher's line of sight at all times. He'll keep you out of harm's way."

Ethan cocked an eyebrow. "I do not need a sorcerer to keep me safe."

"Let's hope not," I said. "Because that wouldn't do much for your hard-ass vamp cred."

Ethan humphed. "I have *all* the hard-ass vampire cred." The ferocity in his eyes was actually pretty convincing. "You'll stick to Jeff?"

"As close as I can. Do you know anything about Garza?"

"Nothing at all," Ethan said, sliding his gaze to the tall and rangy shifter, who stood against the opposite wall, arms crossed as he looked down at Jeff.

"This was the best bargain you could make," I assured Ethan, squeezing his hand. He didn't look entirely convinced, but I was right; there was no better bargain in the offing.

"Got it," Jeff said, tucking his phone away and moving back toward us. "We're good to go."

"You'll keep an eye on her?" Ethan asked, giving Jeff the same cool look he'd given me.

"I was hoping she'd keep an eye on me," he good-naturedly said. We smiled, looking at Damien pleasantly to invite him into the conversation, but his expression stayed blank.

Realizing the joke hadn't gone far, Jeff grimaced and gestured toward the door. "Let's forget this happened and get in the car."

Wordlessly, they walked to the front door and disappeared outside, letting in a swift breeze that swept across the foyer.

Ethan took my lapels in hand and hauled me against him, his body hard and hot against mine. He kissed me slowly, deeply, madly.

"I love you," he murmured, mouth slipping to my cheek, an electric chill running the length of my body.

I closed my eyes for a moment, letting myself linger against him. "I love you, too."

He kissed me again and released me. "And Sentinel?"

I glanced up at him, fairly drunk from the kiss.

"For the sake of peace between shifters and vampires, do try to avoid staring at Damien Garza." With that advice and a sly smile, he slipped back into the room, just in time to avoid catching the blush on my cheeks.

I hadn't stared.

I'd *admired*. There was a difference.

In his boots, Damien couldn't have been a hair under six feet five. He was long and lean, which made the small electric car he pulled up to the front of the Breckenridge house seem like a clown car by comparison.

"This looks . . . energy efficient," I politely said, as I squeezed into the backseat, katana across my lap.

Jeff climbed into the passenger seat beside Damien, the front of the car small enough that their shoulders nearly touched.

"It is," Damien said, eyes narrowed at me in the rearview mirror. I smiled politely and couldn't help imagining the possibility he'd drive Jeff and me to the middle of a cornfield, take us out, and leave our bodies for the crows.

On the other hand, I thought, as he revved the car's lawn-mower engine, *I could probably run faster than the car.*

"Where are we going?" I asked.

"Into town," Jeff said, glancing back. "Aline's got a house near downtown."

"Any friends or relatives she might have gone to visit?"

"Not here in town," Jeff said. "But she does have a human resources gig at an agricultural company about halfway between here and Chicago."

"Friends?" I asked.

"Unknown," Damien said. "She kept to herself."

"I don't recall seeing her at the battle," I said. "We met her before it started. She made a snarky comment about nonshifters and the downfall of the Pack, and then hustled off into the crowd."

Damien nodded but didn't say another word.

A few minutes later, he pulled the car into the driveway of a small cottage on a quiet residential street. The surrounding houses were small but the yards were tidy, and probably would have been full of pansies had the weather been warm enough.

Jeff helped me out of the car, and I belted on my katana. Damien gave it a quick glance, lifted his gaze to mine.

"You can use that effectively?"

Not appreciating the tone, I decided to meet it head-on. I rested my fingers on the handle, gave him an appraising glance. "Can you shift effectively?"

When he made a dubious sound—something between a snort, a chuckle, and a grunt—I decided I'd made the right play.

Alert for any sign of life, or harpies with hostages, we walked up the sidewalk to the front door. Jeff climbed the stairs, pulled open the metal storm door, and tried the doorknob.

"Locked," Jeff said, glancing back at us.

"Allow me," Damien said, sliding into Jeff's spot, wiggling the knob, and then rapping his knuckles along the edges of the frame, as if testing for weakness.

"Stand back," was the only warning we got, and he barely managed to finish the warning before his foot was up and out and he'd made contact, kicking the door in.

It flew open, slamming back against an interior wall with rattling force. When it swung forward again, still propelled by his momentum, he caught it in a hand, nodded at us.

"Not locked," he simply said.

Quiet was Damien Garza. And effective.

The scent that wafted from the house was strong and not entirely welcoming. It wasn't the smell of death—thank goodness—but of dirt. Old paper. Dust. Musty fabrics. And beneath it all, the acrid scent of animals. Cats, I thought. A few of them, considering the odor.

My eyes adjusted to the darkness. Aline's house was small, dingy, and full of . . . everything. Dust motes floated through the few shafts of light that managed to penetrate the darkness and the tall columns of boxes, magazines, and flea-market finds. Ceramics from the 1970s competed with quilted jackets, and romance novels with bodice-ripping covers were stacked with tangled coat hangers.

"She's a hoarder?" Damien asked.

Jeff nodded. "Apparently so." He glanced around the room and the narrow paths through the stuff, then pointed at the pathway straight ahead. "Merit and I will go that way. You go to the right."

"Roger that," I said, and Damien quickly disappeared behind a towering stack of mismatched encyclopedias. I took a few steps into the other path, and Jeff fell in step behind me.

"So what's the scoop on Damien?" I quietly asked.

"The scoop?"

"I've never seen him around before."

"He stays behind the scenes," Jeff added. I glanced back. He'd found a stack of magazines and papers and was flipping through them. He chuckled, pulled out a magazine, and held it up. *Monthly Disco Review*, read the cover, which featured a couple in flimsy chiffon beneath an enormous disco ball.

"A classic publication," I said. "Better photographs than *Disco Review Monthly* and better articles than *The Disco Month in Review*."

Jeff chuckled, as I'd meant him to.

"You're avoiding the question."

"Not avoiding," Jeff said. "Just being discreet." He slid the magazine back into its stack. "Damien handles the Pack's messier matters. Sensitive matters."

"He's an enforcer?"

"He doesn't have a title," Jeff said. "He's a trusted Pack member, and that's all a nosy vampire needs to know."

I snorted. "If I wasn't nosy, Jeff Christopher, Gabriel wouldn't want me here. It's one of my finer qualities. And speaking of nosy, it looks like you and Fallon are getting along well."

The circumstances might have been grim, but that didn't stop the smile that lifted his lips. "We're officially a couple."

"Congratulations. I'm glad to hear it worked out."

Something ghosted across his face, but he shook it off. "Me, too, Merit. Me, too."

We walked quietly through the labyrinth.

"Looks like she found solace in this stuff," Jeff said. "Or tried to."

I nodded, gently pushing aside the dusty leaves of a silk houseplant as I walked past. The dust looked undisturbed, and there was no sign of life in the house. We continued down the path, the clearing so tight we couldn't see more than a few feet in front of us, and crossed a threshold into a small bedroom. There was a bed, a single window, and piles of clothing and newspapers and knickknacks in every bit of the room that wasn't occupied by the bed. The bed was neatly made, a glass of water on the side table. But a thin layer of dust covered the surface of the water.

"It looks like she hasn't been here in a while," I said.

"That's my thought," Jeff said. "But if she isn't here, where is she?"

As if in answer, something skittered on the other side of the bed, rustling the ruffled curtain. I held up a hand to signal Jeff, pointed to it. He nodded me forward.

I took one step, then another, flipping the thumb guard on my sword as I moved. "Aline? Is that you?"

A stack of sweaters shuddered from the movement of some unseen foe. I swallowed, gripped the handle of my katana, and prepared to unsheathe it. "Jeff," I whispered. "What animal is she?"

"I'm not sure. Gabe didn't say."

There in the dark, with shadows moving across unfamiliar towers of stuff, my brain decided she was a wolverine, teeth bared and claws exposed, pissed off and ready to defend herself.

I did not want a faceful of wolverine.

"Aline? Can you come out? We just want to talk." I took another step forward.

Without warning, as quick as a fox, she attacked, a blur of black fur and teeth and bright green eyes. I let out a howl of surprise, my body jolting with fear, and slashed the air where the animal had attacked.

"Merit!" Jeff yelled out, rushing forward . . . as a small, sleek black cat dropped onto the bed. Oblivious to the commotion it had caused, the cat stuck its bottom into the air and began to knead the blanket.

Jeff howled with laughter.

I tried to slow my racing heart while mortification reddened my face. "You have got to be kidding me."

"You screamed like a kid in a horror movie," Jeff said, now doubled over and wiping tears from his eyes. "That was tremendous."

"Any chance that cat's a shifter?" I asked, hoping to save what remained of my pride.

"It's barely a cat," Jeff said, laughing as Damien emerged from a clearing across the room.

"Everything okay?"

"Merit found a monster," Jeff said, gesturing toward my feline attacker. "And a fierce one."

The cat looked up at Jeff and began to clean its paw.

"Thanks for the help, buddy," I murmured, resheathing my sword and saying good-bye to what was left of my pride.

Damien glanced at me, and for the first time, I caught a glimpse of humor in his eyes. "I don't suppose you actually found anything helpful?"

"Merit has decided she hasn't been here in a while. I'd agree."

"Although she hasn't been gone long enough to bother the cat," I said. Apparently clean enough, he sat on his haunches and looked between us, the picture of health.

"What about magic?" Damien asked.

"I've seen a sorcerer's workshop," I said, thinking of the basement in Mallory's Wicker Park brownstone. "Nothing here looks like she's been mixing spells or magic."

"So no magic," Damien said, "and no Aline. If she's not here, where is she?"

"She has to be somewhere. We just need a clue. I'll check the mailbox," I said, then glanced at Jeff. "Maybe you can find a computer or laptop in this mess? Maybe her Web searches will give us a clue, or there's a receipt that tells us where she's been."

He nodded. "Good thought."

I entered the labyrinth again, only a little nervous when Damien fell into step behind me.

"So, do you live in Chicago?" I said conversationally.

"Curiosity killed the cat."

"The cat's perfectly healthy," I reminded him, "and I'm a vampire."

"Gabriel calls you Kitten. Although since you're scared of them, the moniker seems a little inappropriate."

I was glad Damien was behind me and couldn't see the searing expression on my face. But I changed the subject.

"There was a girl sitting by Tanya at the house. Is that her sister?"

It took him a moment to answer, which only piqued my killing curiosity even more. "Emma," he said. "Her name is Emma."

His voice was softer now, careful, as if speaking her name too loudly would work its own magic.

We reached the front door and I pulled it open, relieved to breathe fresh air again. The neighborhood smelled different than the Breckenridge estate had. There, the air was heavy with the scents of crushed pine needles, animals, pastures. The air on Aline's front porch smelled more like a city—more smoke, more vehicle exhaust, even the scent of food from the carnival down the road.

Aline's mailbox was at the end of the pitted sidewalk in front of her house, the wooden post surrounded by a tangle of vines with long-wilted flowers. I pulled open the door, found a single envelope inside.

I looked at it for a moment, debating whether I'd be jailed for tampering with the mail.

"Problem?" Damien asked, looming behind me. He was tall enough to peer over my shoulder but seemed content to let me do the tampering.

"None at all," I said, sliding the envelope from the box and turning to read the label in the streetlight.

Luck shifted. It was addressed to Aline Norsworthy from Pic-N-Pac Storage, and from the clear window on the front, I guessed it was a bill.

"Aline has a storage unit," I said, handing the envelope to Damien, who ripped it open and pulled out the letter.

"A new storage unit," he said, handing the paper to me. It was a bill for forty-eight dollars, fifteen of which was allocated to a "New Locker Setup Fee," which was processed two days ago.

I whistled, glanced up at Damien. "Our disappeared shifter just rented a storage unit."

I memorized the address, stuffed the letter into the mangled envelope, and put it back where I'd found it.

"I'm pretty sure mail tampering's a felony."

Damien made a gravelly laugh, started back up the sidewalk. "Girl, you're a vampire. This day and age, everything you do is a felony."

———— ≍◈≍ ————

CHAPTER SEVEN

WITHIN AND WITHOUT

We walked back into the house to collect Jeff, found him huddled over a boxy computer that sat on a desk comprised of cardboard boxes and vintage board games.

"Not much for tech, is she?" I asked.

Jeff offered the arrogant grunt of an IT whiz kid. "Not even slightly. And she's stealing wireless from her neighbors. But that's neither here nor there."

Damien stepped forward. "Did you find anything that *is* here or there?"

"As a matter of fact," he said, typing with the heavy, plastic *clack* of ancient keys, "I did."

He pulled up a browser window that showed the pixelated image of a receipt—for a flight to Anchorage that had left at eight o'clock this morning.

My brows lifted in surprise. I hadn't actually expected him to find evidence Aline had skipped town. She seemed the naive and complaining sort, the type to gripe about irritations but not actually attempt to fix them.

I looked back at Jeff. "I presume you fly into Anchorage if you're going to Aurora?" The North American Packs' ancestral home was in Aurora, Alaska. If she was running, she was running back to ground.

"You do," Damien said.

"Leaving town doesn't mean she had anything to do with the attack," I pointed out. "Maybe it was the last straw for her. The last failure of the Keene family."

"The ticket was booked five days ago," Jeff said, pointing to the purchase date on the screen.

I frowned. "So she planned to leave nearly a week ago, but shows up to Lupercalia, waits out the attack, and leaves. If she knew the attack was going down, why show up at all?"

"Maybe she wanted to see it," Jeff said. "Maybe she's angry enough that she wanted to watch it go down. She wanted her revenge."

It was definitely plausible. And it was the best lead we had.

"I've uploaded the hard drive onto a thumb drive," Jeff said, holding up the small stick. "I can dig more at the house. You find anything?"

"She rented a storage unit. Bill was in the mailbox."

"I love the smell of evidence in the morning," Jeff said. He flipped the computer's power toggle and rose again. "I think we're done here. Let's check it out."

"What about the cat?" I asked. "If she's gone to Alaska, we shouldn't leave it here alone."

Damien disappeared for a moment, reappeared a minute later, the kitten blinking drowsily in the crook of his arm. "I'll take him."

Tall, dark, and handsome was hot. Tall, dark, and handsome with nestled kitten? *Atomic.*

"It will need a name," Jeff said.

Damien looked down at the scrimpy kitten in his arms, scratched between his ears, and set the cat purring. "Boo. I'll call him Boo."

And that's how Boo Garza joined the North American Central Pack.

The brain coped with complexity by making shortcuts, by categorizing.

Shifters, to my brain, were a rough-and-tumble sort. So I expected Damien Garza was the type to open a beer bottle with his teeth. I expected he loved a good steak, had specific opinions about football or boxing or hockey. He had the look and the vibe.

I did not expect we'd drive to Pic-N-Pac Storage in his tiny, fuel-efficient car while he held a kitten on his lap, its rumbling purr audible even in the backseat.

Damien Garza was a good reminder that people were rarely what they seemed, that judging a book by its cover was a remarkably inaccurate way of taking its measure.

On the way, Jeff called Aline's work. I checked on Ethan and advised what we'd found.

ALINE MAY HAVE SKIPPED TOWN, I messaged. FOUND TRAVEL RECEIPT TO ALASKA. CHECKING STORAGE UNIT.

It took a few moments for him to answer—a delay that made me worry more about his safety—and I felt a wash of relief when his message came through.

THAT'S A LEAD, he agreed. SORCERERS MAKING GO OF FESTIVAL. MOOD STILL GRIM, BUT BOOZE AND MEAT SOOTHE FEELINGS.

So I'd been right about the meat and beer.

STAY ALERT, he told me, and my phone went silent again.

Communications done, I glanced at Jeff. "Any luck at the office?"

"No answer," he said. "But her voice-mail box was full."

"So people have been trying to reach her?" I wondered.

"That's what it looks like."

We found the Pic-N-Pac on the edge of town, a run-down area far from the wealth of the Breck estate.

The facility, a few rows of low-slung metal storage sheds, was situated between a mobile home park and a closed skating rink, the FOR SALE sign fading and cracked, not unlike everything else we saw.

We pulled through the gate, passing only a couple of pot-bellied guys in a beat-up truck loading very large boxes into storage. They stared at us as we passed, clearly not happy about the company.

"What number?" Damien asked.

"Forty-three," I told him. It was the last locker on the second row, its aluminum sliding door closed with a silver padlock.

We climbed out of the car, waited until Damien had built a bed for Boo on the front seat from his leather jacket. Boo immediately climbed inside, pawed at the leather, and snuggled in.

We glanced at the lock. "I don't suppose either of you has a bolt cutter?" I asked.

"Bolt cutters lack subtlety," Damien said, stepping forward and pulling a couple of small silver implements from his pocket. He inserted them into the key slot while Jeff looked nervously around.

"Might want to do that quickly," Jeff suggested. "In case there's security?"

"Camera's busted," Damien said without looking up. "Check Merit's seven o'clock."

Jeff and I both looked back to the position Damien had indicated, found a small camera perched on the wall between Aline's locker and the next one, its unconnected wires dangling below like tentacles.

Little wonder Gabriel trusted Damien with "sensitive" matters. His attention to detail was impressive.

With a snap, the lock flipped open. Damien replaced his tools and tossed aside the lock.

He put a hand on the lever but looked back at us. "Anybody think anything's in there?"

I lifted the block on my vampire senses, which was usually down so I wouldn't be driven mad by an excess of sensations. But even with my shields down, I sensed nothing at all.

"Not that I can tell," I said, but unsheathed my sword anyway. Better to be safe than sorry. Or leave Boo without a father.

"In that case . . . ," Damien said, pulling up the door with a ratcheting sound. He flipped a penlight from his pocket and shined it into the space.

It was empty except for a cardboard box on the ground, the top flaps woven closed.

"That was anticlimactic," Jeff said as I slid the sword home again.

Damien moved forward and nudged the box with a toe. When nothing happened, he crouched in front of it and pulled open the flaps.

"Looks like trash to me." He stepped back, gesturing for me to take a look.

The box was filled with ephemera. Old photographs and paper scraps, notes and holiday cards. I reached inside, pulled out a black-and-white photograph. It was an old-fashioned Polaroid, a pretty woman kneeling on the ground, each arm around a cute kid.

I turned the picture around. "Chas and Georgie," it read.

I glanced back at Jeff and Damien. "What were the names of the boys Aline wanted the Pack to shelter?"

"Jack?" Jeff asked, looking at Damien. "Something with a 'J'?"

"George," Damien said. "And Charles."

Wordlessly, I handed over the picture, let Jeff and Damien reach their own conclusions.

"I somehow doubt this is a coincidence," Jeff said, dropping the photograph back into the box. "But why would she bother to get a storage unit for one box of stuff?"

"Maybe this stuff was important to her," I said. "The boys certainly were. Maybe she wanted to keep these things separate and safe when she decided to run."

"Or she needed the space for more hoarding," Damien said, rising again. "And this is the first thing she decided to store here."

That was certainly the easier answer. The more obvious answer. But either way, the case against Aline was getting stronger.

Without another immediate lead, Jeff and Damien decided to take a break and work through what we knew about her reason for leaving. They picked a twenty-four-hour chain restaurant not far from the Pic-N-Pac, a diner-style joint at the end of the parking lot where the carnival held court.

It was late, music still blasted from the carnival's speakers, and the Ferris wheel rolled lazily, the spokes outlined in lights that flashed in patterns as it turned. The air smelled deliciously of fried food and sugar. Damien tucked Boo into his nest, and we walked inside, found plenty of quiet booths. While the guys slid into one, arguing about the best way to serve hash browns—plain, or covered with cheese and onions—I stopped at the jukebox inside the door, bosom buddies with a cigarette machine that now held packs of gum. I hadn't seen a jukebox in years, so I scanned the music choices, which ran the gamut from Top 40 to classic country, heavy on the big hair and sequin vests.

My phone rang, and I pulled it from my pocket, found the number blocked.

"Hello?"

"It's Lakshmi," said the prettily accented voice on the other end of the line.

My heart began to pound, and I glanced back at Jeff and Damien, who were looking over laminated menus. I had only a moment to talk.

"Hi," I nervously said. "Are you trying to reach Ethan?"

"I am trying to reach you," she said. "I'd like to discuss our previous arrangement."

I cursed silently. It wasn't as if I hadn't known this was coming, but her timing could hardly have been worse. "You need a favor?"

"I do. But it would be better to discuss in person."

I wouldn't renege on our deal. That would be dishonorable for me, the House, and Jonah, who'd put his ass on the line to get the favor from Lakshmi in the first place. On the other hand, I was rather involved in something at the moment.

"I can't really get away right now."

"Ah, yes. The murder investigation and the shifters," she said, apparently aware of what was going on.

"Yes. I don't suppose you have any pull with Mayor Kowalcyzk? Or know anything about harpies?"

She was silent for a moment. "That's what attacked the Pack? Harpies?"

"Well, a magical manifestation of harpies, anyway."

"And the Pack is holding you hostage?" she asked.

"We're helping them investigate." That was only partly the truth, but enough for her purposes. I wasn't about to incite a war between shifters and vampires by telling the GP we were at their mercy.

"When can we meet?" she asked.

I stood there dumbly for a moment, the phone in hand, debating my next move. I'd have to meet with her, one way or the other. But to do it, I'd have to get away from the shifters, the sorcerers, the house, and Ethan. He knew about my RG membership, but he didn't know Lakshmi was a source. This was going to be tricky.

"I can come to you," she offered. "It's a matter of some urgency. Where can we meet?"

I looked back at the table, and Jeff caught my eye, waved me forward. I was nearly out of time.

"There's a carnival in Loring Park," I said, providing directions to the first place that came to mind. It would be busy—full of sounds and smells and people—and would give us a bit of anonymity.

"One hour," she said, and disconnected the call.

I checked the clock on the wall, ensuring I knew when to make my exit. Now I just had to figure out how to do it.

I rejoined the shifters, sliding into the booth beside Jeff. "Cadogan House," I said. "Just checking in."

"News from home?"

"Not at the moment," I said. "What looks good?"

"Waffles and bacon for me," Jeff said, handing over his menu. "And Damien's looking at crepes."

"I do not eat crepes. Eggs, sausage, toast," he said, when the uniformed waitress walked over, a notepad in hand. "Eggs over hard. Toast buttered."

"Hon?" she asked, glancing at me over glasses with square frames.

"Just orange juice."

She nodded and disappeared through a door that flapped back and forth.

"Just orange juice?" Jeff said with a chuckle, sliding his menu back into place. "Since when do you just have orange juice?"

Since a member of the GP asked for a secret meeting, I thought, my stomach roiling with nerves. But I couldn't exactly tell them that.

"Stress," I said, crossing my arms against the chill. Patrons moved in and out of the diner, which sent blasts of cold air careening across the restaurant.

"Ah," Jeff said, linking his hands on the table. "So Aline. What are we thinking?"

"The receipt says she left town," Damien said. "Although the circumstances are suspect. She left a cat and a single box in a storage locker. She left one day into Lupercalia, when she could have avoided it altogether."

I tilted my head at Damien. "So you think the receipt's bogus?"

He glanced up at me. "I am not sure. But I think it's suspect."

"She could have been set up," Jeff said.

"Do we know of any specific enemies?" I asked. "Other than the Keene family, I mean."

"I do not," Damien said.

The waitress came back bearing drinks, which she passed out with smiles.

"Does she have any friends in the Pack?" I asked, when the waitress disappeared again. "She seemed to know Berna. They talked last night, anyway."

"Good thought," Damien said. "I'll ask her. Other than that, I believe she kept to herself?" He glanced at Jeff for confirmation.

"Far as I know," Jeff said.

"What about people in Aurora?" I asked. "Would she have told anyone she was coming? Made arrangements to stay with a friend? I mean, I don't imagine there are lots of hotels up there." I leaned forward, curious. "Actually, how do you accommodate everyone if the Packs get together up there?"

"Giant puppy piles," Damien dryly said. "Curled up on an old plaid blanket by the fire."

I knew he was joking, but it did make for an interesting mental image.

"There's a resort," Jeff said. "A former resort, anyway. The Meadows. Had its heyday in the fifties and sixties."

I imagined well-heeled men and women playing badminton in long white skirts and pants, staff members carrying watermelons to their bunkhouses, *Dirty Dancing*–style.

"It fell into disrepair," Jeff said. "The Packs got together, bought it, rehabbed it. Now it's private, and it holds a hell of a lot of shifters. Nothing fancy, but it does the job. Plenty of space to act human, plenty of space to roam."

Visiting the Meadows popped up to the top of my bucket list. "How does a vampire get an invitation to such a place?" I wondered.

"They don't," Damien said. "Unless you're volunteering to be kibble."

"I am not," I crisply said, sitting back again. He was joking, but considering the mood at the house, I decided there was still a kernel of truth in it.

"We wouldn't make kibble of you," Jeff said. "We'd serve you up with fava beans and a nice Chianti."

I pointed at him. "You've been hanging out with Luc too much, and you've reached your quota for movie references today."

Jeff grinned. Damien rolled his eyes.

"Even if she skipped town because she's the cause of this, she couldn't have done it herself." Damien looked at me and Jeff, eyebrows knitted over those dark eyes. "Tell me about the sorcerers."

His implication was clear, and it had Jeff shifting in his seat. "They're solid, both of them."

"The girl—Mallory—caused a lot of trouble. Has a lot of power."

"She did and does," I agreed. "And she's making amends, as I'm sure you know." My tone was icy. But if it bothered him, it didn't register in his face.

"They aren't the only ones who can make magic," Damien said.

"They aren't. There are three others in the Chicago metro area." I gave him the details about Simon, Paige, and Baumgartner—and what we'd learned so far.

He looked surprised. I wasn't sure if that was because he didn't figure we'd bother to ask, or because the sorcerers were potentially alibied.

"So who did this? Aline couldn't do it alone."

"No," I agreed. "She couldn't. But we don't have anything that suggests who else was involved."

Damien lifted hopeful eyes to me, and I felt him shift the weight of that hope to my shoulders. "Gabriel thinks that's what you're good at. Finding out who was involved."

"I'm not sure about 'good,'" I said honestly. "But we do tend to get wrapped into things."

"Well, you're wrapped up good and tight in this one," Damien said. "And good luck to you."

The waitress brought our food, offered ketchup and hot sauce, which the guys declined. As they ate and I sipped my orange juice—and ate a piece of bacon Jeff had thoughtfully offered— we came up with a to-do list.

Damien would check with the resort to see if Aline had made arrangements to stay there, and find out if other Pack members had information about her travel plans.

Jeff would continue to check her computer for anything that suggested she was involved in the attack—or offered any clue about her whereabouts; I'd look through the box we'd found in the storage unit.

When the waitress topped off coffee and brought the check, I put a couple of dollars on the table for my orange juice. Damien looked up at me with irritation.

"What?"

"You think I can't cover your orange juice?"

"I have no idea whether you can cover my orange juice," I said. "But I don't expect anyone else to pay my way."

He looked at me for a moment, considering. "I wondered if you'd expect it."

Jeff whistled low in warning, aware of the sensitive spot Damien had poked. My father may have been wealthy, but I'd worked my way through college and grad school, and I'd bled, quite literally, for the pay I'd earned as Sentinel. I had the scars and aching cheekbone to show for it. I wasn't thrilled I had to defend myself against others' assumptions, but such was life as the daughter of a real estate mogul. I'd grown up with enough of an advantage that I could suck it up.

"I make my own way," I quietly said, not taking my eyes from his. If he wanted to confirm the truth, he could read it in my eyes.

"My bad," Damien said, and I nodded back, the momentary build of tension dissipating again.

I cleared my throat, thinking my moment had come while the

guys sipped their coffee. "I need a few minutes to take care of something."

They both looked at me curiously, so I broke out the ultimate weapon, the errand it seemed nearly guaranteed they'd want to avoid.

"I need to run down to the grocery store at the other end of the shopping center. We left Chicago in a hurry, and I need to grab a few things." I cleared my throat. "A few personal items."

Vampire or not, the mention of unspecified "personal items" was uncomfortable enough to send both of them—the tech genius and the rugged shifter—into awkward foot shuffling and throat clearing.

"Maybe we'll drink our coffee and wait for you here," Damien said, raising his mug to his lips.

"Coffee," Jeff agreed, and I left them in the booth, doctoring their drinks with extra attentiveness and trying not to consider what personal items, precisely, I needed.

None, of course. What I needed was at the carnival.

I grabbed my katana from the car, thankfully unlocked, and glanced at my phone. I had ten minutes until the meet. Figuring I'd need evidence when I joined the guys later, I followed the sidewalk across the shopping center to the grocery store, where I bought gum and an energy bar, then wrapped up the bag and stuffed it into my jacket.

Humans in coats still milled around the carnival, holding cheap stuffed animals and knickknacks they'd won on the midway. Some enjoyed cotton candy; others tore pieces of steaming funnel cake from paper plates, their shirts and fingers dotted with a spray of powdered sugar.

I walked down the small midway, barkers begging me to throw

a hoop or a baseball or use a water gun to take down a target, probably weighted, that wouldn't move unless the barker wanted it to.

"You look like you're looking for excitement. I think you've come to the right place."

I glanced over at the woman who'd called out, not to me but to a middle-aged man whose wife looked doubtfully over the entire event.

She was petite, with gray eyes, dimples at both cheeks, and long, wavy, brown hair tucked into a braid that fell over her shoulder. Her bangs fell in a neat trim just above her eyebrows, and a tiny hat was perched coquettishly to one side. She wore a button-up shirt with old-fashioned trousers and suspenders, the pants rolled up to reveal tidy boots with lots of buttons and argyle socks.

She stood in front of the Tunnel of Horrors, where a small car on rails disappeared behind a giant mural depicting a classic Count Dracula character, a mummy, and Frankenstein's monster.

The man, blushing as the barker tucked her arm into his, looked back at his wife. "What do you think, hon? Should we do it?"

"It's only five bucks," said the barker, winking knowingly at the man's wife. "That's cheaper than a cup of coffee these days."

"Honey?"

The wife sighed, then pulled a bill from her jeans pocket and handed it over. The attendant grinned, dimples alight, and pressed a kiss to the man's cheek.

Blushing furiously, he climbed with his wife into the tiny car, which lurched forward, sending them into darkness.

I kept moving before the woman decided I was her next victim, wandering to a quiet spot where I watched a blade-shaped ride flip passengers into the air.

"Merit."

I glanced beside me, found Lakshmi at my side. She was absolutely gorgeous, tall and slender, with dark skin and long, dark hair that waved at the bottom. She wore trousers and heels beneath a slim, taxi-yellow trench coat buttoned and tied at the waist.

"Hello," I said.

"Thank you for meeting me."

I nodded. "I don't know how much time I'll have."

"I understand, and I'll get right to it. We have reached an unusual time, Merit. A precarious time. Two members of the GP are dead." She paused. "And the present leadership is weak." She meant Darius, the current head of the GP.

"So we've heard."

She linked her hands together and rested her forearms on the gate, her gaze on the ride as it rotated. "Leading the GP requires a certain cachet, a certain attitude. Due to recent events, Darius has lost both. It's time for him to step down. And that brings us to the favor."

She looked at me, paused for a moment, and then let loose the request she'd flown nearly four thousand miles to make.

"I want Ethan to challenge Darius for the head of the GP. And I want you to convince him to do it."

CHAPTER EIGHT

DEEP-FRIED TRUTH

My heart and head went numb, shocked by the request. She wanted Ethan to challenge, outright, the head of the GP? I couldn't imagine anybody, much less Darius, would take kindly to the idea. Just by trying to *leave* the GP we'd ended up with murder at our doorstep. We were still dealing with the fallout from that decision, which was why I was at a carnival in Loring Park, Illinois, in the freezing air of February.

And then there was the other issue: The GP was in London. Ethan would have to go there, live there, and work there while I stayed in Chicago, honor bound to serve Cadogan House.

My heart jumped in my throat. "We aren't even part of the GP anymore," I said. That was the only defense I could think of, the only words I could put together.

"Not the GP as it was before," she said, turning to lean back against the railing. There was a glimmer of strategic excitement in her eyes. She and Ethan had that in common.

"The GP as it *could* be. A different kind of organization. A federation of Houses, not a dictatorship. And not led by a vampire who lords himself over the rest of us."

I almost snorted. If she didn't think Ethan would lord himself over the rest of us as head of the GP, perhaps she didn't know Ethan as well as she thought.

"You don't think he'd try to take control?" I asked. "You don't think he'd impose his will on the Houses?"

She tilted her head at me, an expression that reminded me she was a vampire—a predator—of repute. "You would convince me he's ill suited for the job."

"He's stubborn."

"Not so stubborn that you aren't in a relationship with him."

She had a point, so I tried a different tack. "He has enemies, and challenging Darius would only make more."

Lakshmi nodded gravely. "The road would not be easy. Ethan has enemies, certainly. His campaign would be difficult. There would be many to convince, to bring to his side. Travails to overcome."

"What travails, exactly?" The *Canon* had been shady about the process of getting a new king.

"He'd have to demonstrate his worth and fitness for the position. Convince the Prelect's council he is worthy of the task, that he is powerful and strong."

I grimaced. Harold Monmonth had been the Prelect. And we all knew how that had ended up.

"And then the Houses vote," she said.

"That all assumes Darius steps down peacefully."

She nodded, acknowledging that. "There is no point in being coy. Ethan would have opponents from the beginning to the end. But he is worth the battle. He'd bring peace and honor to the GP, which have been lacking of late."

Handy, I thought, that she was a member of the GP. Bringing honor to the organization would help her—raise esteem for her and the rest of them. Bring her power that she'd lost in the recent drama.

But there was power, and then there was power . . .

"Why not run yourself?"

She slipped her hands into the trim pockets of her coat. "Because I'm too young. Because Ethan has more allies—even those who don't have insignia above his door. They know him. They don't know me. And there are . . . skeletons in my closet."

"Skeletons?" I asked without moving, like she was an animal I might frighten away.

But she was wise enough to avoid the trap. "My life is no concern of yours, Novitiate. We all have our secrets to bear." She looked at me for a moment. "You're in love with him. I can hear it in your words, see it in your eyes. The fear of loss."

I waited a beat, unsure of her motives, and nodded. "I am."

Her eyes flattened. There was a different kind of predator in her eyes now. "You aren't the only vampire that needs him. We are endangered, and you must consider whether your needs as an individual are more important than the needs of your House, the Chicago Houses, the American Houses, all the Houses in the GP. Ethan Sullivan, I believe, has the opportunity to become a Master of Masters. And consider this: If Ethan doesn't become the new head of the GP, who will?"

We looked at each other for a moment. "You're in Chicago because the GP wants to extract some price of the House. What is that price?"

She looked at me for a moment, taking my measure. And, I belatedly realized, sending her soft and delicate tendrils of glamour, sweeping curls of it, to test me and my defenses. My endurance.

My stubbornness. Fortunately, I had some immunity to that kind of magic.

"That," she concluded, "is also not for your ears." She put a hand on mine. "This will not be an easy road to travel. I understand that. But it is the right road. I know *you* understand that and will make the right decision."

With that, she tucked her hands back into her pockets and turned toward the exit, her heels clacking on the asphalt with every step. After a moment, she disappeared into the crowd, leaving me in a sea of humans with worry in my heart.

I did the only thing I could think of. I grabbed my phone and dialed up my partner.

"Hello?" Jonah said. "Merit?"

"Lakshmi's here. In Loring Park. She came to talk to me." The words flooded out.

"Wait," he said, "hold on a minute." I heard him speak, murmuring to others around him, and then a door opened and closed.

"Sorry, I was in our ops room," he said after a moment. "What's this about Lakshmi?"

"She came here to talk to me. I owe her a favor because she gave us information about the location of the dragon's egg." The Faberge-style egg had been a gift from fairies to Peter Cadogan, the House's founder. On the GP's orders, Monmonth had stolen it in order to bribe the fairies to war with Cadogan. He'd been successful, which was another mark against him.

"I remember," he said. "And much like the Grim Reaper, she's come to collect. What did she ask for?"

It took me a moment to put the words together, because once I said them aloud, they'd be true. "She wants Ethan to challenge Darius for his spot on the GP. And she wants me to convince him to do it."

There was silence.

"I don't know what I think about that."

I knew what I thought. Both sides of it. "What am I supposed to do? I can't tell her no—I can't piss off our best ally on the GP. But I can't help her." And, most important, I couldn't send Ethan to London.

I sat down on a bench bookended by a dead shrub and a pile of dirty snow, which seemed about right. "He may very well want to do it. But I can't just demand he undertake that kind of risk. And he can't do it right now, anyway. We're stuck here until Chicago comes to its senses."

I sighed. "I don't suppose you'd be willing to go out with her? Sweeten her into giving up that favor?"

"You want me to pimp myself to make your life easier?"

"Now that you mention it, yes. Could you?" I asked, feigning hopefulness.

His voice was flat. "No. And I hate to say it, Mer, but her idea's not bad. Ethan's old, he's powerful, and he's got friends. He's one of the few vampires out there who'd actually use all that power and political capital for good."

I didn't disagree that he'd be good at it, that he'd be good for vampires. But I'd be suborning the overthrow of the GP, a ground-up revolution, with Ethan as Paul Revere and George Washington rolled into one. The last American Revolution had been successful in stripping away England's rule. But I wasn't sure we'd get lucky a second time around. And my job was to keep him safe.

I'd also have to give him up. For the greater good, perhaps, but he'd be gone nonetheless.

"What are you going to do?" Jonah asked after a moment.

"I don't know. How does a person decide something like that?"

"With your very good brain and your very good heart," he said. "Keep me posted."

I promised I would, and hoped I'd have good news to share.

I pulled the prop grocery bag from my pocket and walked back to the restaurant, using the strip mall as a windbreak. Fears flitted through my mind like dancers.

London. Treason. Rebellion.

I remembered the first time I'd been near Ethan, when he knelt behind me, bit my neck, and changed me into a vampire. I remembered the first time I'd really seen him, when Mallory and I had barged into Cadogan House. I remembered the night Celina had thrown an aspen stake at me and he'd stepped forward to intercept it, turning to ash before my eyes. I remembered the night I'd seen him emerge from the smoke and destruction that Mallory had wrought, alive once again.

We'd overcome vampires, monsters, death, and each other. And now I was honor bound to send him to war . . . and to London. Thousands of miles away from Cadogan House.

Thousands of miles away from *us*. I couldn't do that.

On the other hand, how could I not? The GP was tyrannous. Dictatorial and cruel. They'd ignored Celina's antics, blamed the House for everything that went wrong in Chicago. They'd sent a sadist to live in the House and demanded we prove our obedience with blood and fire. They'd extorted money, killed humans, and tried to kill us when we hadn't followed the party line.

Wasn't I obliged not just to encourage him, but to do everything I could to help him actually win? Ethan was honorable, fair, dedicated. He believed humans were more than cattle and that all supernaturals should get a fair shake. He knew how to make alliances, avoided making enemies whenever possible. He was willing to take a stand, but also to compromise. He knew the value of both.

He'd make an inarguably good addition to the GP. And while there was little doubt Malik would make a fantastic Master in Ethan's absence—he was doing it now—I didn't want Ethan to be absent. I wanted him here, with me, being cheeky and jealous and fighting at my side. I wanted his intelligence and snark and sarcasm. I wanted him.

I paused and wondered, just for a moment, what it would be like to snap my fingers and become someone else. Bizarro Merit, the evil or twisted version of myself. Bizarro Merit would have her own agenda. Bizarro Merit wouldn't encourage Ethan to run for the GP, or tell him that Lakshmi had suggested the idea. She'd snap her fingers, send the GP into a parallel universe, and warp space-time so she could spend immortality with Ethan and a book on the deck of a boat on Lake Michigan.

While I stood there, engaged in my fantasy, the hairs on the back of my neck lifted, piqued by something . . . magical?

I ignored the quick punch of fear. Without moving my head, I scanned the area around me. I was facing down the length of the shopping center, but other than the usual traffic in and out of the parking lot, nothing looked unusual.

Looks, I knew, could be deceiving, so I closed my eyes, let the breath flow out of me, and allowed the sensations of the world to drip back into my consciousness.

Sound became a roar—moving cars, the squeak of carnival rides, the slide of the automatic door at the grocery store, the faraway whispers of humans . . . and the nearby *shush* of fabric. And now that I was paying attention, I sensed the faint, tart smell of magic. Fresh, green, vegetal.

Someone was here. And I needed a look.

I closed the barriers again and pulled out my phone, feigning sudden interest in it, but sliding my gaze to the store window beside me.

She was behind me, probably fifteen feet, mostly hidden behind a concrete pillar.

I didn't recognize her, or even what she was. She looked physically similar to the mercenary fairies who'd once guarded the gate at Cadogan House. Tall and slender, with a lean face and hollows beneath her sharp cheekbones. But her chin was more sharply pointed, her eyes larger and rounder, dominated by huge, dark irises. Her hair was dark, closely cropped, forming curled wisps around her face.

She wore a simple dark tunic with a keyhole collar and matching pants, the fabric nubby and homespun. She didn't look like a threat . . . until I turned to face her.

Wheeee.

Whistling like a bottle rocket, a three-foot-long arrow flew into the empty planter on the ledge beside me.

My mouth went as dry as dirt.

The shaft of the arrow, pale and slender, with stripes of gold and teal, ivory feathers slitted into the end, vibrated from the movement.

Slowly, I glanced back over my shoulder.

Now a man stood behind me, also in a dark tunic and with short hair, a four-foot-long recursive bow in hand, an arrow tipped with a shiny silver point already strung and taut. The fingers that held the bow were long and thin, ending in long and equally sharp nails.

Had the circumstances been different, I might have admired the weapon. It was carved of pale wood and beautifully curvy. Unless the shafts were made of aspen, being shot by an arrow wouldn't kill me. But that didn't mean I was looking forward to it.

I glanced back, looking for egress, but they'd been joined by another woman and man. It was four to one, and my allies were still tucked in a restaurant down the road.

The odds were not in my favor, but I put on my fighting face—a haughty expression punctuated by a hell of a lot of feigned bravado.

"I think you'll want to lower your weapon, friends. And explain why you're following me."

The man watched me silently without blinking. I could read nothing in his eyes. They were too dark, too glassy, too shielded. "You have made war against us."

"Excuse me?"

"You have attacked the People. You have breached our trust and our pact. We claim the right of retribution."

Completely flummoxed, I evaluated my chances while trying to ferret out what the hell was going on.

"We haven't attacked anyone. We were attacked last night. A squadron of harpies struck from the air." Keeping my eyes on them, I flipped the thumb guard on my katana.

"Nonsense," came the prim voice of the woman who'd followed me. "Harpies are imaginary creatures."

"They were made of magic. And we lost four in the battle. I'm not sure what happened to you, but it wasn't because of us."

The man's gaze narrowed. He pulled the bow tauter, raising his arms so the arrow pointed directly at my heart. Apparently, he meant to skewer me here and now, in front of—I glanced at the store beside us—Pilchuk Mufflers, which, according to the carefully painted storefront, had four convenient metro locations to serve all your muffler needs.

It would be ignominious to die, I thought, sprawled on the sidewalk in front of Pilchuk Mufflers. So I decided not to.

"Harpies!" I yelled out, shifting their attention just long enough to move. I dropped and punched the bowman in the kneecap, drawing a groan and enough distraction that he let the arrow fly over my head.

I pulled my sword, raked the biting edge against his shins. Blood, thin and shockingly green, spilled through the new slit in his leggings and dripped to the ground. He roared in pain, eyes wide in fury that I'd had the temerity to fight back—and that I'd managed to nick him.

He wouldn't make that mistake again.

Before I could move, he kicked, his boot connecting with my abdomen and sending a wave of pain and nausea. I nearly retched on the sidewalk but managed to roll enough so his second shot just grazed me.

Then I was violently hauled to my feet, dropping my katana in the process. I found myself staring back into the eyes of the man.

His orbed black eyes were wild with fury. I brought up a knee, trying to catch him in the groin, but my aim was off and he blocked the blow with a shift of his knee.

He slapped me. The world wavered, and my mouth filled with blood.

Someone behind me pulled my ponytail, wrenching back my head with a hot flush of pain that spilled down my neck like boiling water. My head upside down, I saw the first woman behind me, a feline smile on her face.

She wrapped her arm around my neck and squeezed. Suddenly, I couldn't breathe, couldn't find air at all. Panic struck, my vision dimming on the edges as my legs kicked backward, as I tried to free myself from her vicious grip and find air again.

This is the way the world ends, I thought, and the world went black.

I woke in darkness, gasping for air. It took moments to realize that I was alive, my head still attached, but my neck sore and probably bruised. My throat ached, and my head felt unusually heavy. I couldn't see anything around me. If I could, I imagined it would be spinning.

But I wasn't dead. Which was completely unexpected.

I also didn't think I was in front of Pilchuk Mufflers. Shapes and faint colors began to emerge in the darkness. I lay on a braided rug on the dirt floor of a small round room. The walls were made of pale birch saplings strapped together, and a conical roof was built above it, rising to a point in the middle of the ceiling. The remains of a fire sat in a depression in the middle of the room, and the entire space vibrated with low and malignant magic.

"Merit?"

It was Jeff's voice, and I nearly wept with relief.

"Yeah," I whispered, but my voice was scratchy, hoarse. I rubbed my throat, swallowed past parched lips, and tried again. "It's me."

Slowly, I pushed myself up on an elbow, looking through the darkness. My hands and feet were bound by large silver manacles and chains tethered to a large metal hook in the dirt floor.

Jeff and Damien sat a few feet beside each other, bound in the same silver chains. Their faces were bruised. Jeff's right eye was cut and swollen, and the air carried the peppery scent of blood. They were hurt, but they were alive.

"You're okay?" I asked. My words were scratchy but clear enough.

"Okay," Damien agreed. But his eyes looked a little woozy and unfocused, which couldn't have been good. "Silver chains.

And silver-tipped arrows." He nodded toward a dark spot of blood near the crux of his left shoulder.

Not all myths about supernaturals were accurate, but it appeared the shape-shifter weakness to silver was right on.

I glanced at Jeff, who nodded. "Glad you're awake," he said with a sheepish grin, which belied the worry in his eyes.

"Where are we?"

"We aren't sure," Damien said. "We were out when they brought us here. Farther from the carnival—I can't smell it."

He was right. The air smelled woody, smoky. "In the forest," I guessed. But there was a lot of forest near Loring Park, so that didn't narrow it down much.

"They got you at the restaurant?"

Damien nodded. "Outside it. We were looking for you. When you didn't come back, we got worried. Where'd they get you?"

"Walking back to the restaurant." I considered Lakshmi's visit to be RG business, which made it none of the Pack's. "They were following me. And when I confronted them, they pounced. How long was I unconscious?"

"It's one in the morning," Damien said.

We'd been gone for a few hours. Ethan would be in a panic. I called his name, tried to activate the link between us, but couldn't reach him. He was too far away.

"What the hell are they?"

"Elves," Jeff said. "At least, that's what they looked like. They're relatives of the fairies—mutated relatives. They look even less human, so they had an even harder time assimilating. They call themselves the People. Believe they are the highest order of sentient beings. Everyone else is Other."

"Early Europeans found them, hunted them down," Damien continued, looking around, wincing when the move strained his shoulder. "They were believed extinct. Looks like that's fundamentally wrong."

"They must have migrated," Damien said. "But how did we not know they were here?"

I glanced at the carefully constructed room, the gaps between the saplings neatly filled with mud or daub. This place hadn't been built yesterday; the elves had been here for some time. Which made me also wonder how the shifters had missed them.

"Magic?" I suggested, but that didn't seem to satisfy Damien, who shook his head.

"Do you know what they want?" Jeff asked me.

"They said they were attacked."

"By the harpies?"

I shook my head. "The ones that jumped me said harpies were imaginary. They thought I was lying."

Sounds rose outside—shrieks and pounding feet. Instinctively, I pulled at my chains, seeking freedom.

Sentinel?

My head darted up, searching for the sound of his voice in my head. *Ethan? Are you here? We're chained.*

Working on it, he told me. *I've brought your army.*

"Something's up," Damien said, glancing at the noise that was beginning to shake the walls of our prison.

"Ethan's here. He said he's brought an army."

Before I could answer, a door on the other side of the room was shoved open. Three elves, the man from before and two new men, walked in. Without speaking or acknowledging our existence, they unlinked the chains that bound us to the floor. But they didn't unchain our bound hands and feet.

They yanked us to our feet and pushed us outside.

It was dark, the bits of sky visible through the canopy of limbs still indigo. But that was the only thing that made sense. We were in a wood, the trees stripped bare by winter.

We were also in a village.

Structures, cylindrical like the one we'd just stepped out of, filled every clearing in the woods around us, white smoke puffing from the openings in the conical roofs. Footholds had been cut into the tree trunks, and smaller structures hung from the trees. The structures looked old. Comfortable and lived in, with rough-hewn tools hanging along the exteriors and green linens strung across lines that extended between the trees. This wasn't a camp; it was a neighborhood.

The elves were *everywhere*. Hundreds of men and women, all approximately middle-aged, trim and fit in the same tunics, either running toward the sounds of battle with slicked bows in hand, or battening down their simple homesteads. Untying lines of laundry, carrying steaming cooking pots into their homes.

There was an entire city of elves tucked into the woods outside Chicago and no one had seen it? No one had discovered them? How was that possible?

"And I didn't even have time to welcome them to the neighborhood with muffins," Jeff murmured beside me.

"I didn't get muffins, either," I pointed out, trying to keep some levity.

"I didn't know you then. We get out of this, I'll get you a muffin." He tried for a smile, so I tried back.

"Deal," I said.

"This way," said the man from the shopping center, pulling my katana from the scabbard he'd belted around his waist.

I generally preferred not to be poked with my own sword, and certainly not by the very person who'd taken it from me. He yanked my arm, pulling me forward. Since we were moving toward the sounds, I didn't fight back. They were taking me precisely where I wanted to go.

With Damien and Jeff stumbling behind us, we walked the narrow path through the trees and up a low rise, which gave way to a snowy field, still dotted with the remains of last year's cornstalks . . . and marked by the columns of the invading army.

They'd found us.

CHAPTER NINE

THE SPOILS OF WAR

There were hundreds of shifters, some in NAC jackets, some in animal form. All behind the front line—which consisted of the Keenes, Nick, Ethan, Catcher, and Mallory—and waiting for orders.

Ethan searched the marching bulk, body stilling when he finally saw me, as he took in the chains on my ankles and whatever concoction of blood and dirt had stiffened on my face. His body went rigid, his eyes hot with fury, and I feared he'd begin the charge himself, ripping through elves in order to punish them for my injuries.

I'm fine, I assured him, hoping to delay First Blood, and glad he couldn't hear the hoarseness in my voice.

Sentinel, he crisply said. *You've managed to get yourself into trouble again.*

They nabbed me as I was walking down the sidewalk, I assured him. *And I think the* Canon *needs updating.*

Evidently, he responded, and there was a gravelly edge to his voice.

How did you find us?

Damien sent an alert before he was taken. The shifters scented out the rest of it.

The elf's fingers still wrapped tightly around my arm, we marched forward, creating another line of troops. Behind us echoed the muted and rhythmic *thud* of boots on soil. The elves had their own army, and quarters had been called.

They stretched out beside us, shifting their short rows to form three long lines with Rockette-level precision. They raised their bows and tucked arrows into the strings, the silver arrowheads glinting in the moonlight, the air thick with tension and magic.

Our escort pushed us to our knees, where we knelt on hard, frozen ground in front of our colleagues and loved ones, enemies at our backs, weapons in their hands.

Ethan looked calmly at the elves, his body stiff and hiding the fear and anger that I knew ripped at him. But fear was a nasty motivator, and we didn't need another supernatural war brewing outside Chicago. Not when events there were tense enough.

They were attacked, I told Ethan. *And they think we—the Pack and vampires—were the culprits. They followed us, took us in. They must have been waiting for an opportunity to get us alone.*

Ethan murmured to Gabriel beside him, probably offering the intel.

"You have breached our peace," said the elf. "You shed First Blood."

"We have shed no blood," Gabriel said. "We were attacked last night without provocation. Several members of our Pack were injured. Four are dead."

That didn't seem to register with the elf. "One of ours is gone. We seek retribution in equal kind."

As if those words were enough to justify murder, he lifted the sword ominously.

I braced to move, to fight back, but Ethan beat me to it. He unsheathed his katana, catching the moonlight like Excalibur might have. And he was Arthur, blond and strong and proud, willing to destroy a kingdom for his Guinevere.

"You make one move with that sword," Ethan said, stepping forward, eyes furiously green, "and you'll have every vampire in the world hunting you down. Beginning with me."

The elf's eyes narrowed with keen pleasure, as if the thought of taking on a vampire—or a world of them—was a prize, not a threat.

But Gabriel wasn't keen on the destruction of his kingdom, his Pack, or his allies. He put a calming hand on Ethan's arm.

"If you commit violence," Gabriel said to the elf, "you will breach the contract between us."

Ethan's eyes narrowed, and while he didn't speak to me, it was easy to guess the line of his thought. The Pack had a contract with a species that wasn't supposed to exist—which had apparently created a village just outside Chicago—and no one had bothered to tell us about it.

"You breached the pact *first*," the elf said again, his voice growing irritable and sounding not unlike an ornery child. "We claim the right of retribution."

Gabriel watched him for a moment, considered. "Support your claim." And when Ethan began to protest, Gabriel held up a hand. "I would hear precisely how the elves believe we wronged them."

"It was glamour," the elf said, damning me with a look. Glamour was the particular magic of vampires—the mythical ability to seduce and control others. But the ability to glamour varied significantly from vampire to vampire. Ironically, I couldn't glamour worth a damn.

"We were together for our midday meal," the elf continued. "We'd just taken our mead when the fog began to thicken."

That was a strong defense for me and Ethan. Fog or not, midday meant sunlight.

"What kind of fog?" Gabriel asked.

"Mist," the elf said, looking up, posing the word as a half question. It was a guess, and one about which he still had doubts. "Thick. And there was magic in it."

The elf's eyes went slightly out of focus, as if he was remembering precisely what he'd seen—and how it had felt. "Magic that swayed. Magic that seduced. It invited," he said, eyes focusing on me again. "It propositioned."

"You were propositioned by magic mist?" Gabriel mildly asked.

The elf looked back at him, glared, and ignored the question, continuing with his story. "We were overpowered by the magic, by the glamour. Like the undead, without control of ourselves or our bodies. We were drunk with magic and made senseless by it. Some lost awareness of the world. Some fought."

He swallowed visibly and clearly was uncomfortable. "Some copulated, there in the middle of the feast, rutting like animals. We are not prudes," he said. "But this was not about mating, about strengthening the clan. There was no lust in their eyes. No love. Only death."

I slid Jeff a quick glance, and he acknowledged with a small nod. We'd seen those flat eyes before, in the harpies who'd attacked the first night of Lupercalia.

This time, sympathy slid through my irritation. However incorrect the elf's conclusions about the cause of the trauma, there was no doubt his people had been violated.

"I do not remember all of it; most of us do not. But we recognized its insidiousness. It was glamour."

"And the First Blood?" Gabriel asked.

"Niera," the elf said. "One of the mothers of our clan. We awoke some hours later when the sun was nearly set, half naked, violated. She was gone. Her house was empty."

Gabriel frowned. "If she is missing, how do you know First Blood was shed?"

"Elves do not leave the clan," the elf insisted. "*Mothers* do not leave the clan." He smoothed a hand down the front of his tunic, seemed to soothe himself. "Because she would not leave us, First Blood was shed. Thereby, our claim is justified."

"Not against us," I said. My throat was still raw, the words hoarse, but the sound carried on the wind well enough.

"You have a claim against those who attacked you. We were not those people, and you're in the wrong."

The elf reached out to slap me for the second time, but I'd grown tired of the show. I was a vampire and, more important, a woman who'd rather go down with steel than with cowardice.

I reached up, punched his forearm to force him to release my katana. My hands were still bound, but I stretched the manacles as far as I could and just managed to snatch the dropping katana with my other hand. I jumped to my feet, spun the sword in hand, and waited.

I heard Ethan's warning in my head—*Sentinel!*—but it was too late for that. Spurred by my audacity, the elves formed a tight circle around me and Jeff and Damien, a thousand arrows pointed in our direction.

I ignored the welling fear and considered my odds, estimating I had a forty percent chance of taking out an elf or two before they took me out. I gave myself a four percent chance of surviving the fight.

"Steady now," Damien murmured.

"Do you see?" the elf said, gesturing at us. "Do you see the violence?"

"I see a woman attempting to protect herself against false allegations," Gabriel said. "All due respect, you're wrong. If the attack happened midday, vampires could not be responsible. They cannot face the sun."

"The fog—," the elf said, but Gabriel stopped him with a hand.

"It is irrelevant. A little moisture does not protect a vampire from sun. Besides—they were in our facility during the day under lock and key."

"You are also Other," the elf said with a sneer.

"Other and mourning our dead," Gabriel said. "We were attacked and put four of our own in the ground. Whatever happened here, we had nothing to do with it."

The elf looked at Gabriel and considered the evidence. Wrong or not, he was in a bad spot. If he backed down, he looked like a coward. If he authorized his elves to let fly their arrows, he'd truly break the contract with the Pack.

"Perhaps a truce," Gabriel offered.

The elf looked suspicious. "Of what manner?"

"Both our clans have been attacked by magic. Those attacks might be related. We are part of the human world, and we are investigating the attack. We will continue to do so. If Niera cannot be found, there is nothing we can do. But if she did not leave by choice, if she was taken, we will find her, and we will bring her home to you. And that will resolve the perceived breach."

The elf glanced back across his army. I didn't know if they could communicate telepathically, but he seemed to seek their input.

"We accede to your request," he said, turning to Gabriel again. "You will send a messenger under flag, and we will meet you here again and receive our mother. If this matter is resolved to our satisfaction, the clan will fade into the canopy again.

"But if it is not—if you protect murderers or engage in more treachery—the détente between our clans will be nullified. We will not fade, nor will we share this land that we inhabited before the rest set foot upon the soil. All of our clans will come forth. All of our villages will be visible once again. And humanity will pay for the transgressions that have accumulated in the meantime."

The elves closest to us unlocked our chains with small keys they pulled from leather cords around their necks. Damien and Jeff stood again, grimacing as they rubbed the spots on their wrists where the shackles had chafed. Even in the dark, it was easy to see the skin beneath was mottled and red, irritated by the silver.

The rest of the army released the tension from their bowstrings and dropped the arrows back into the leather quivers strapped to their backs. They all stood straight again, turned on their heels, and disappeared into the woods.

Their departure left the three of us, wounded and exhausted, looking back at the army who'd come to save us.

Ignoring the shifters around him, Ethan stalked toward me, lifted me up, and buried his face in my neck, releasing the tension he'd been holding while an army of elves surrounded his girlfriend.

"Thank Christ, Sentinel."

I didn't generally object to public displays of affection, but we were surrounded by hard-bitten shifters, and embarrassment bloomed in my cheeks.

Ethan pressed a hard kiss to my lips, leaving little doubt of the ravishment he intended at a more appropriate time. He released me, saw the pink in my cheeks, and smiled. "Let them see, Sentinel. I've no interest in hiding my affections."

We weren't the only sups in the mood for reunion. Tanya checked Damien's wounds while her sister stood shyly beside her, clearly not sure if she should step forward or if her attentions would be welcome. But Damien had eyes only for her. His dark brow was furrowed, his dark gaze focused on the girl's face, his expression intense and needy. I guessed the prospect of battle had sped his blood.

Jeff and Fallon talked quietly nearby. She pushed his hair behind his ears and inspected his face, the movements equally efficient and tender. As the second oldest in the Keene family, I guessed she'd taken care of her share of scrapes.

"Healing begins with loved ones," Ethan whispered.

"So it seems," I said, squeezing his hand.

Gabriel walked to us.

"Is Lupercalia usually this exciting?" I asked.

"Only when vampires are about. You two have a unique way of inciting trouble."

I smiled a little at the attempt at humor, but Ethan's gaze was heavy and accusing. Gabriel had withheld information, and Ethan wasn't happy about it.

"I'd like to speak with you," Ethan murmured, low and threatening.

"When the opportunity permits," Gabriel said. He turned to walk toward Damien, but Ethan grabbed his arm. The look in Gabe's eyes was deadly. He cast a glance at Ethan's hand like it was an alien thing, as if no one had ever attempted to grab him bodily.

"Careful, Sullivan," Gabriel said.

"Careful?" Ethan gritted out, jaw clenched and anger radiating off his body like heat off asphalt in summer. "My Sentinel was accosted, beaten, marched, and nearly beheaded in front of your shifters. She was held at arrow point—kidnapped from a public place—because you failed to mention the elves were alive and living in our backyard."

Since I'd held my own, I silently objected to "nearly beheaded" but found the rest of it accurate enough.

Gabriel's jaw twitched, his eyes swirling like a warming brandy. "Now is not the time or place to discuss these matters," he said, which made me wonder how much he'd kept from the rest of the Pack.

I took the opportunity to glance around, check the faces of the shifters, who still looked shell-shocked that an army of elves shared their territory. Whatever Gabe had known, he hadn't shared it with the rest of the Pack. And I guessed that omission was going to require some reckoning.

Ethan swallowed down irritation and released Gabriel's arm. The tension eased, just a bit.

"When," Ethan bit out, "would be an opportune time to discuss what just happened, and the fact that my Sentinel was kidnapped by elves?"

Gabriel watched him for a moment, his face offering nothing. "I need to speak to my people. Wait for me at the house."

He didn't wait for Ethan to respond.

Gabriel arranged for Damien and Jeff to get the car—and Boo—which still waited at the restaurant. The rest of us drove back to the estate in the variety of vehicles the Pack had used to get to the wood.

This time, neither the Brecks nor anyone else stopped us when we walked into the kitchen. The house was silent, the staff hiding or otherwise occupied.

Without waiting for permission, Ethan sat me bodily on a stool at the island while he searched the enormous, glass-doored refrigerator for sustenance. He pulled out two bottles of Blood4You, popped the tops on the edge of the counter like a frat boy at a mixer, and handed one to me.

"Drink," he said, putting the other bottle down.

"I don't need blood," I protested, but only weakly, as my stomach began to rumble from need. I wasn't exactly hungry—my nerves were still too shot for that—but my body was attempting to heal from the elves' abuse, and it wanted sustenance.

"Drink it," Ethan said again, staring down at me until I lifted the bottle to my lips.

It was gone in seconds, and I replaced it with the second before he could argue.

Mallory and Catcher walked into the kitchen, and Mallory rushed over. "You're all right?" she asked, scanning me for injuries.

"A little bumped and bruised, but I'll heal."

"Where were you taken?" Catcher asked.

"Shopping center in Loring Park. Four of them jumped me, bows and arrows right there in public view. They knocked me out—a choke hold," I explained, touching my neck. The skin was no longer tender, but the muscle beneath still ached.

A wash of shifter magic flushed through the room like a moody tsunami, angry and tense. It left an uncomfortable prickle on my skin and made my clothes feel uncomfortably tight.

I rubbed my goosefleshed arms. "What do you think's going on out there?"

Ethan made a sympathetic sound. "I imagine Gabriel is explaining to his Pack why he didn't mention the elves before to-night. Why he didn't mention the wolves at their door, no pun intended."

I finished the second bottle of blood, placed it on the counter beside the first. "How did they not notice it? The humans? The Brecks? A hunter, a farmer, a utility crew? Someone had to have seen them."

"Magic," Catcher said with a shrug. "A mechanism that allowed them to blend into the trees, or which obscured them completely."

"A village of hundreds in Illinois," Ethan said. "And that's one clan. If they came west from Ireland and Scotland, how many more clans might be sprinkled between here and the Atlantic?"

"Very many," Catcher guessed. "But perhaps the better question—how many of them have arrangements with the rest of the American Packs?"

"Probably too goddamned many," Ethan said grimly.

"Fuck you, too, Sullivan." Gabriel walked in alone, moved to a cabinet, and grabbed a bottle of whiskey with a plaid ribbon around its neck. He loosened the lid and took a slug directly from the bottle, throat moving as he swallowed. Maybe shifters had a different metabolism, as the quarter bottle he ingested would have put me on the floor. And maybe he was stressed enough to need it.

He put the bottle back in the cabinet, then braced his hands on the countertop and dropped his head. It was the second time in as many days he'd let his guard down in front of us. I both appreciated the trust—and regretted the need. Even with his back turned, it was obvious he was exhausted. His Pack had come to the Brecks' estate for camaraderie and fun. And they'd met only threats, violence, and death.

We waited until Gabe stood straight again, running his hands through his hair and turning back to us.

"The contract was negotiated by my father. He told Papa Breck when the Brecks bought the property, thought it was only fair Papa Breck know who was living nearby. When my father passed, Papa Breck told me. I've never even seen the elves until tonight."

"I'm not certain that's an excuse," Ethan said. "Not for what my people and yours have been through."

"The elves' interest is in keeping quiet, in staying underground. They were nearly eradicated. They wanted to live peacefully, and they have done so."

"Until tonight," Ethan emphasized, voice firm. "They are barbarians. They protect their lands without regret, kill without remorse. They do not believe in weakness, and they don't overlook it. They don't believe in pity. They kill children they don't believe will flourish, men and women past their prime. They do not live peacefully. They *wait*."

The reference to children and the elderly made me think—I hadn't seen either at the village. Everyone appeared to be in the prime of middle age. Maybe twenty-five to forty-five in human years. Anyone outside that group could have been indoors or hidden. Or perhaps they'd been culled.

"We have no fight with them," Gabriel said.

"Because you have not seen them fight," Ethan insisted. There was hard experience in his eyes. He'd been born in Sweden, had served his time as a soldier, and had nearly been killed because of it. He'd also apparently been in Europe long enough to have seen elves there on the ground and know their practices.

"I have seen battlefields littered with women and children. Ground they stained with blood. They attack without mercy, and they allow no survivors. That Merit, Jeff, and Damien were allowed to live today was a miracle."

"Or it is proof that this clan is different from those which lived in Europe," Gabriel said. "Humans are different now, too. Humans fight differently, battle differently."

"Humans battle with and through machines," Ethan said. "But that does not absolve them of their atrocities."

Mallory moved closer, catching both of their gazes. "Let's pause," she said, and I felt a gentle nudge of calming magic. It was a nice thought, but considering the story the elves had told about nonconsensual magic, it just left me feeling uncomfortable.

"The elves are clearly here," she said. "If, for some reason, we can't figure out what's going on here in the larger sense, how bad could this get?"

"They could seek revenge for the wrongs they think have been done to them throughout history," Ethan said. "The elves release their magic, show their societies to the world, and there's human panic and genocide. What we saw tonight was only posturing," he softly added. "Do not mistake their bows and arrows for a lack of savvy."

I rubbed my face, trying to soothe the headache that was beginning to build there, then glanced at Gabriel. I didn't think he was the type to feel guilty, but there was obvious regret in his eyes. It was time for a little optimism—or at least a little strategy.

"Then we need to ensure it doesn't get that bad," I said, meeting Gabriel's gaze. "If we do as they've agreed—find Niera and bring her back—will they go back into the woods again?"

He shared my gaze for a moment, then glanced at Ethan. "Sullivan?"

The question was an obvious concession—he was recognizing Ethan's expertise, looking to him for information.

"I don't know how honorable they are," Ethan said. "Fear tends to make new enemies. But we'll assume they'll hold to his deal."

"Go team!" I said with false cheer. As no one seemed moved by the faux enthusiasm, I waved it away. "So that's our solution. We find Niera. We have two attacks here—one on shifters, one on elves. The first attack by harpies, which weren't supposed to exist in the first place. The second against elves, which weren't supposed to exist."

"Is that a coincidence?" Mallory asked, face scrunched with the question.

"I don't know. But it seems significant. Harpies aren't an obvious weapon, and elves aren't an obvious target. So the person—or people—behind this have good information about supernaturals."

"So probably not a human," Ethan said.

"Not unless they have better knowledge than even you," I said. "And you believe yourself to be quite knowledgeable."

Ethan arched an eyebrow. "I resemble that remark."

"She has a point," Catcher said, crossing his arms and leaning back into his stance, preparing for some serious consideration and analysis. "Knowledge of supernaturals, and very serious intent. This isn't just a nymph pissed off because they ran a rubber-duck parade through the Chicago River without her approval."

"That didn't really happen," I said. But Catcher's flat look said different.

"Could and did. And cost me a week's worth of time."

"And a slew of gift cards for the stores on State Street," Mallory said with a smile. *I know what nymphs like,*" she added, in a singsong voice.

"The point is," Catcher said, sliding her a glance, "this isn't a run-of-the-mill issue, a minor grudge between sups."

"It's a full-out attack in the first instance," Ethan said. "And something else in the second. The glamour the elves mentioned—does it ring any bells?" He glanced at Mallory, Catcher, Gabriel.

Gabe leaned against the island. "Not for me. All due respect, it sounded like typical vampire mojo. Elves acting like zombies? Doing what someone telepathically directed them to do? Fighting? Fucking? Passing out?"

"Glamour doesn't work that way," Ethan flatly said. "It doesn't work over distance."

"And you're sure no vampire was nearby the elves when the attack occurred?"

At Gabe's question, Ethan opened his mouth, closed it again. "I am not," he finally admitted. "But glamour doesn't make zombies of anyone. It is suggestive, not unlike what Mallory tried a moment ago to calm us down."

Mal blushed prettily. "Just trying to help."

Catcher put an arm around her shoulder, squeezed.

But they'd given me an idea. "Maybe that's part of it—both times, the attacker mimicked some other kind of magic. In the first attack, the magic mimicked harpies. In the second, the magic mimicked vampire glamour. The attacker wasn't actually a harpy or a vampire—he was someone with magic enough to pretend to be *both*."

"That's powerful magic," Catcher said. "And magic with range."

"Range," Gabriel said, standing straight again. "How close would someone have to be to work magic that powerful?"

Catcher's brows lifted. "I'd actually meant the other kind of range—the ability to imitate different kinds of sups—but that's a good point."

I drummed my fingers on the countertop. "So someone is using a lot of magic—variable magic—relatively nearby to attack two groups of sups."

"Groups," Ethan said, tapping a finger against my hand. "Both were in groups—the shifters were gathered together for Lupercalia. The elves were together in their village."

Mallory reached out to a crock on the island that held spoons and spatulas and plucked out a rubberized whisk. "So they attacked when they could do the most damage?" she asked, as she toyed absently with the bent wires of the utensil.

"Maybe," I said. "But why? If this was a political thing, a grudge thing, wouldn't we know it? Wouldn't there have been a statement? Overt blame? They aren't even really framing someone, because they've used different magic both times. There's no obvious motive."

"Perhaps it comes back to the victims," Ethan said. "To the shifters who passed."

I glanced at Gabe. "The shifters you lost. Is there anything controversial in their histories? Anything that suggests they were targeted?"

Gabe leaned over the counter again, propping his elbows on it and linking his hands together again. "Not that I'm aware of. They weren't related, weren't friends. One was from Memphis— young guy who I think had some leadership ambitions. Messy childhood. Woman from New Orleans. Lawyer who went to Tulane. Excellent cook, and a very spicy woman."

Ethan and Catcher grunted in some kind of vague male agreement. Mallory and I shared a dubious look.

"Third was a man from Chicago. Assimilated. Lived with a human family, although the wife knew what he was." Gabe shook his head ruefully. "That phone call *sucked*. And you know about Rowan."

I reached out, touched his arm. "I'm sorry," I said, using the two words that were always woefully inadequate to ease anyone's grief, but still seemed the only appropriate thing to say.

Gabe nodded, patted my hand. "Appreciate it, Kitten."

"Then perhaps the key isn't the deceased," Ethan said, "but the missing."

We'd seen vampire disappearances before, and they hadn't been coincidental. They'd been the work of an assassin hungry for revenge, and he'd be difficult to catch and stop. But in that case, the key was the killings—the vampires were killed as warnings to the rest of us to leave Chicago. The bodies had been left for us to find.

"So we're back to Aline and the elf," Mallory said. "What was her name again?"

"Niera," Catcher said.

"Aline is definitely gone," I said, realizing I hadn't had a chance to report what we'd found at her house. The kidnapping and threats had interrupted our investigation.

"She's a hoarder—there was stuff everywhere in her house, but nothing really helpful until we found her computer. Jeff found a receipt for a plane ticket to Anchorage. She also has a storage locker, but the only thing in there was a box of ephemera. We haven't had a chance to look through it yet."

"Did the flight to Alaska look legit?" Catcher wondered. "Or planted?"

"It looked legit to me, but if you've got the ability to create winged monsters from thin air and turn elves into zombies, who knows?"

"Could they have something in common?" Mallory wondered. "Aline and Niera?" Apparently bored of the whisk, she stuck it back in the canister again to mingle with its colleagues.

"How could they, if Aline didn't know the elves existed?" But then I looked at Gabriel. Aline did seem like the conspiracy type, and God knew she hated the Keene family. "Did she?"

"Not that I'm aware of."

There had to be some connection. This many attacks—large-scale attacks—in two days couldn't be a coincidence. I looked at Ethan. "Have you talked to Luc?"

"Not yet," he said. "Seeing you safe was first on my list."

I nodded. "When you call him, you might see if Paige and the librarian are back from their rendezvous. The librarian has stores of microfiche and, you know, Internet access. If there's a con- nection between Aline and Niera, they'd be the ones to find it."

"A good idea." Ethan pulled out his phone.

"I'm full of them," I said, glancing at a clock on one of the Brecks' sleek appliances. "We only have a few hours until dawn. I'll check the box when it gets here, talk to Jeff or Damien about whatever I find. Maybe they can provide some context." I glanced at Catcher and Mallory. "Can you follow up again with Baumgart- ner, see if this new glamoury magic rings any bells? And check again on Simon if you still haven't reached him?"

"We'll do both," Catcher said, "but neither is likely to lead to much."

"Better to check and come up empty than miss a lead," I said.

Ethan looked at me with obvious amusement. "You're be- coming quite the investigator."

I searched my memory for a good quip about cops, maybe something from a film noir about private detectives that would have made him laugh, but came up empty.

"Book 'em, Danno?" Catcher offered.

"Close enough."

Jeff, Damien, and Nick walked into the kitchen together. Jeff and Damien looked significantly better than they had when I'd seen them before. They'd changed clothes and their superficial wounds were gone, probably because they'd shifted and let their magic do its work.

Nick walked to the refrigerator and took out a bottle of water.

Jeff carried Aline's box, which he set on the counter, then smiled at me. "You all right?"

"Fine. You?"

"Feel like I lost another life or two, but I'm okay." He nudged Damien collegially, but Damien just offered back a mild blink.

"Nothing?" Jeff said and, when Damien continued to stare, turned to me with a crooked smile. "Alrighty."

"Boo's okay?" I asked.

"Boo?" Ethan asked.

"Damien's babysitting a kitten we found at Aline's," I explained.

Damien nodded. "Was sleeping in the car. Now sleeping in a box in the living room. Any developments here?"

"Ethan's calling Paige and the librarian to check for any connections between Aline and Niera."

"That seems unlikely," Damien said.

"Agreed. But it's also unlikely that harpies attack shifters, and hours later someone pulls mojo on the elves."

"You're thinking they come from the same source?"

"We don't have any evidence either way, yet. But I'm thinking two major magical attacks in a five-mile radius in the span of twenty-four hours cannot be a coincidence."

"Put that way," Damien said, "I can hardly argue with the conclusion."

I rose, picked up the box. "We had a to-do list," I said, re-minding Damien and Jeff. "This part was my assignment."

Jeff nodded. "I'll see what I can do with her hard drive."

We looked expectantly at Damien. "I suppose I'm going to make some phone calls."

I glanced back at Nick, who stood quietly beside the refrig-erator, bottle in hand. "Can I borrow a room to look through this?"

Ethan looked worried. "Don't you want to rest?"

I shook my head. "Too much adrenaline. And irritation. I need to work. I'll be fine," I added, when the line between his eyes didn't disappear.

"Use the drawing room," Nick said, as if it would be obvious to everyone which room that would be. It was to me, as it turned out, because I'd been there a thousand times.

If Papa Breck's office was one of my favorite rooms in the Breck house, the drawing room was one of my least favorite. The office was a place of adventures and hidden secrets. The drawing room was a place of manners and sitting quietly. It was where Julia, Papa Breck's wife and the Breck family matriarch, would spend a quiet afternoon with a book and a cup of tea, or where she'd make me and the boys endure a time-out if we'd been too noisy in the hallways. "Your father did not make his money by letting out the bought air," she'd tell us, and demand we spend an interminable half hour sitting on hard, uncomfortable furniture until she was satisfied that we'd calmed down.

I was hardly "just a girl he knew in high school."

I carried the box into the drawing room. It was prettily arranged—lighter and more delicate than Papa Breck's study—with butter yellow walls and tailored furniture. A round pedestal table sat on one side of the room, with several hard wooden chairs (learned from experience) and a leather case that held two decks of cards. Both decks were missing their one-eyed kings, because we'd decided the cards held secret codes and deserved saving.

I put the box on the table, walked to the shelves that lined the other end of the room, tracing my fingers over the linen-covered hardbacks that were placed in groups amid bud vases and family pictures.

I found the copy of Ian Fleming's *Casino Royale*—because a book about James Bond with a casino in the title obviously had to relate to our one-eyed kings, and slid it from its home.

Tucked inside, back to back, were two aging kings of spades.

So many memories in this house. Each time I came back, I built new ones, even if they weren't always pleasant. I tucked the cards back into the book, slid the book back onto the shelf, and moved back to the table. I shoved the leather box of cards aside and made space on the table while I opened the box.

Just as the house had demonstrated, Aline wasn't one to throw things away. Anything. Receipts. Greeting cards. Lists. The paper wrappers that held silverware inside restaurant napkins. I assumed every scrap of paper and receipt in the box had meaning for her, some emotional weight that kept her from throwing them away, that bound them to her as the years went on.

I looked through the piles, separated them into groups, and when that didn't reveal any universal truths, put them into chronological order.

By the time Jeff knocked on the door, I had several tidy piles of paper and absolutely no clues whatsoever. Maybe he'd had more luck.

"Hey," I said. "What did you find?"

"Nada." He pulled out a chair and took a seat. "She plays a lot of solitaire, which just seems extra-sad."

"Travel plans?"

"The ticket looked completely legitimate. But there was nothing in her Web history that indicated she booked it on that computer." He shrugged. "Could be someone else booked it; could be she used a faster computer."

"So that doesn't really help us narrow anything down."

"It does not," Jeff agreed.

I frowned down at the box. "Honestly, I don't know anything at all so far. I've looked through everything in this box, stacked and reordered it, looking for a pattern." I gestured at the receipts I'd organized. "These piles are geographical. I was hoping something would hit. But I'm not seeing anything." I glanced at him. "Do you want to take a look? Maybe there's shifter significance I don't see."

"I doubt that," he said, but settled in to peruse.

CHAPTER TEN

PAPER MOON

We worked quietly, deliberately, searching through the only potential bit of evidence we had. And it wasn't much.

"I think keeping all this stuff would weigh me down," I said, pulling out a grocery receipt for utterly innocuous items: milk, eggs, cookies, paper towels.

"Yeah," he said, flipping through a stack of greeting cards. "But you have Ethan, a family, friends. You have connections." He flipped open a card, grimaced at whatever he found there, and closed it again. He put the card in the pile and looked at me. "I don't think she does. I mean"—he spread his hands over the stack—"all this stuff would be relatively meaningless to us. Cards from people who don't sound like they know her at all, bills, receipts. Photographs of other people's kids. It's almost like she was trying to build a life from paper, from the stacks of stuff that she kept in the house."

That was both poetic and sad, and it made more sense than I preferred to admit. If Jeff was right, Aline led a sad and lonely life that had been capped by a potentially sad and lonely end. We just weren't sure yet.

"So where does that get us?"

He pushed his hair behind his ears. "I'm not sure."

I stood up, getting a fresh perspective on the piles we'd made on the dark wood table. "Okay. So she's missing. The question right now is whether she's missing on purpose, or because she's a victim of the mattacker."

"The 'mattacker'?" Jeff asked, blinking.

"The magical attacker. I shortened it a little."

Jeff chuckled. "Shorten it all you want. But nobody else in the house is going to refer to the perp as a 'mattacker.'"

"You're probably right. But they aren't in the room right now. So—we know a flight was purchased for Aline—whether or not by her." I looked back at Jeff. "I don't suppose you know anyone with an airline connection?"

"No," he said, frowning. "Why?" But before I could answer, his brows lifted in understanding. "Because if she got on the plane, she probably wasn't kidnapped. I don't know anybody offhand, and I'd prefer not to hack into transpo databases. That kind of stuff gets you flagged."

"I think that's a legit reason," I assured him. "So she gets a storage locker, buys a flight, comes to Lupercalia. Leaves right before or right after the attack."

"There's just nothing here that touches on any of that," Jeff said. "At least, not that I can see. But that's part of the problem—it could all be relevant, and we wouldn't even know it because we don't really know what's going on here." He picked up a faded and water-stained receipt. "She got gas." He picked up a strip of three yellow tickets. "She went to the carnival." He picked up a small wax paper bag with a logo on one side. "She bought cookies at Fran's Delights of Loring Park. That has got to be the most pretentious name for a cookie joint I've ever heard, but I'm getting off track."

I was proud he realized that. He didn't always.

"None of this stuff means anything without context, and shifter context isn't helping much. None of it, as far as I can see, is shifter related. She lived like a human. Bought things like a human."

"Could that be the reason she's gone? She pretended to be a little too human?"

Jeff shrugged. "I don't think we can rule it out. It might be time to call your team."

I smiled at him. "I think we can arrange that." I pulled out my phone and started up the program Luc had created for the House's guards. It had timers, alarms, alerts, and, according to him, a "slick" little videoconferencing setup.

I set up the phone on the table and turned on the app, selecting the option to connect with the Ops Room.

An animated clip of Luc filled the screen. His animated cowboy hat bobbed back and forth as he screeched "Show me the Ops Room!" over and over again.

"Is that supposed to be a play on 'Show me the money'?" Jeff wondered.

"God only knows," I said, smiling with relief when the real Luc replaced the faux one.

He smiled brightly at Jeff and me. "Sentinel, I'm glad to see you're taking advantage of the technological resources we've provided for you. And that you're alive. Ethan said things got hairy. And for you, too, Jeff."

"Being a hostage is always a bummer," Jeff said. "But we came out all right."

"Have you heard anything about Scott?"

"Scott?" Jeff asked with alarm.

"Kowalcyzk's interviewing him today," Luc explained. "Jonah said the lawyers are negotiating with the mayor's office, the police commissioner, the feds. No other news yet."

"At least he's got advocates," Jeff said.

"And loud ones. The lawyers are all over TV, the Web, talking about how poorly their client is being treated, how it's baldly unconstitutional. They'll get him out, or set him up for a civil suit later."

"Sometimes you play by the rules they give you," I said. "I assume Ethan gave you the rundown about everything here?"

"He did. He's talking to the librarian. And good timing there; he just got back to the House an hour or two ago. What can I do you for, Sentinel?"

"We need to borrow your brain."

Ethan had given Luc the overview, heavy on the elves and their apparent existence. We stuck to the facts of the attack, walked him through what we knew, and brainstormed about the potential cause.

Luc wasn't convinced they were related at all. "Two different methods," he said. "One much more violent than the other. One kills, the other—what would you say—violates? One attack during the day. The other at night."

"On the other hand," I said, "it's two attacks on supernatural groups in Illinois within twenty-four hours. The methods may not have much in common, but they have to be connected."

"We need to know if she got on that plane."

"That's exactly what Jeff and I were saying. I don't suppose you know someone?"

He was quiet for a moment. "I might, you know, know someone." His cheekbones glowed faintly pink, and there was a bashful look in his eyes.

"Former girlfriend?" I asked with a grin.

Luc hunched over a little, as if shielding the camera and his answer from the other people in the room. From the topic, I assumed Lindsey was one of those people.

"Briefly," he said. "And I can't stress that enough. We haven't talked in a while, but I could maybe make a phone call. I wouldn't, of course, want it to become a thing."

"I'm *empathic*," we heard Lindsey call out offscreen. "And you're hardly whispering. I can hear you, Merit and Jeff."

We waved weakly back at Luc, whose face had turned a mottled shade of crimson.

A flounce of blond hair popped into view. "'S'up?" Lindsey asked with a grin. "Jeffrey. Merit."

"Will you please give your boyfriend permission to call his ex-girlfriend and ask if our victim-slash-perpetrator boarded her flight?"

"She hardly qualified as an ex-girlfriend," Lindsey said. "They may have bounced around together a smidge, but that's it. It barely counts."

I'd have much preferred to dive into Lindsey's scale of what did and did not "count" for purposes of "bouncing," but this wasn't the time.

"Excellent," I said. "I'm going to assume that means you have no objection to Luc calling Bouncy so we can continue our supernatural investigation and get the shifters and elves off our backs."

"Roger that," she said, before Luc nudged his way on-screen again. He no longer looked especially amused.

"So you'll let us know?" I asked cheerily.

He grumbled something, and the screen went blank. I scratched absently at an itch on my shoulder, glanced at Jeff.

"That was pretty awkward."

"Vampires," Jeff said with a shrug, as if that explained everything.

I yawned hugely, stretching back in the chair. I was still residually sore from being dragged around and bound. It was nothing that a little sleep wouldn't fix, but I was getting achy from sitting.

"It looks like bedtime for you, Sentinel."

I looked back, found Ethan in the doorway, hands in his pockets, lips curled in amusement. "Having any luck here?"

"Not a damn bit," I said. "We can't find anything that gives us a motive for Aline, or indicates she was a target of the attack. What about you? Any luck with Paige and the librarian?"

"They're looking through the archives," he said. "I was advised my request was substantial and it would take them some time."

Ethan's voice was flat, and I could easily imagine the librarian giving him a very pointed speech about the time he'd need to complete an assignment. Like most of the vampires of Cadogan House, the librarian was particular.

Another yawn racked me, and I raised the back of my hand to my mouth. I was too tired to hold it in.

"You've had a bit of an evening," Ethan said. "I think it's time to head back to the carriage house."

I nodded and stood up, regretting that the end of the evening hadn't been more productive.

"I'll get this cleaned up," Jeff said. "And check in with Damien." He glanced at Ethan, smiled. "Merit held her own. Had those elves shaking in their boots."

"I'm sure she did. And it probably didn't hurt to have a tiger in her corner."

Jeff smiled shyly. "I'm just glad we got everyone out of there okay. Hopefully, we'll find Aline tucked away on holiday, and Niera on a jaunt, and everything can go back to normal."

I didn't disagree with the hope, but I was beginning to think crisis was the new normal.

We had an hour until sunrise, but my body was already shutting down. Ethan all but carried me back to the carriage house, where Mallory and Catcher had showered and were lying on the couch, a predictable Lifetime movie on the television. Some men golfed; some wrenched. Catcher Lifetime'd.

I headed straight for the bedroom, stripped down to bare skin, and blistered myself in the shower. My body ached like I was awaiting the onset of the flu. I could only assume the elves had thrown me around like a sack of potatoes in the process of getting me into the village.

When I'd risked using all the hot water, I flipped off the faucet and wrapped myself in a fluffy towel. They had their prejudices, but you couldn't fault their taste in linens.

I pulled on a Cadogan T-shirt and plaid pajama bottoms, and then took care of the other necessary bit of business—sword care. I'd managed to snatch my sword back from the elves, but it hadn't come away unscathed. The steel was filthy, dotted with mud and probably worse, little clumps of dirt clinging to the scabbard. I placed both carefully on the floor, then grabbed the small kit Catcher had given me from my duffel bag. Rice paper. Oil. A whetstone to hone the surface.

I hadn't yet used the whetstone. The katana had been made by hands significantly more experienced and learned than mine; I'd long ago decided to leave sharpening to the experts. But I was good with oil and rice paper, which would clean the steel to a sheen and protect it from nicks during the next battle.

After removing the gunk with a soft cloth, I dotted oil onto a square of rice paper and folded the small sheet around the blade. With a smooth, swift motion, I wiped the oil from one end of the katana to the other, then repeated the process until the blade gleamed. The blade had been tempered with blood and magic, and with each pass of the paper I felt the answering shiver of satisfaction, as if the sword appreciated the care.

When I was done, I slid it back into the sheath with a *zing* of sound, and placed it on the top of the bureau beside Ethan's sword, already scabbarded. They made a beautiful pair, artisanal weapons of death, handcrafted protectors of honor.

As I patted myself on the back for my mental poetry, a knock sounded at the front door.

I opened the bedroom door and peeked into the living room.

For the first time tonight, it wasn't bad news. A teenager with pink cheeks stood in the doorway wearing a Loring Park Pizza cap, and the siren's call of roasted meat spilled into the air from the four steaming pizza boxes he carried. The scent was nearly tangible; I could practically see the wavy lines of meat smoke rising off the box.

A victim to my hunger, I marched into the living room.

"What's this?" Catcher asked.

"Dinner, I guess." The kid shrugged. "Guy at the house paid for it, sent me out here with it." He grinned. "Said you should tip me really well."

"I'll just bet he did," Catcher mumbled, pulling his wallet out of his back jeans pocket. He snatched out bills, then exchanged the cash for pizza and watched the kid head back down the driveway—as if there was a threat the pizza delivery boy might change his mind and attack.

After a moment, Catcher closed the door and put the pizza on the table. "I guess the Pack felt bad about last night's grub."

"Or tonight's hostage situation," Ethan said, throwing open a box and grabbing a steaming slice. Without napkin, fork, or plate, he dove into the slice, earning openmouthed stares from Mallory, Catcher, and me.

"I'm not that pretentious," he said over a mouthful of a pizza that looked like a butcher-shop special. I recognized pepperoni; the rest of it was a hearty, delicious mystery.

"You are," the three of us said together, but we were smiling when we said it. We all grabbed slices and took seats on the sofas.

"You find anything in your magic box?" Mallory asked.

"Receipts and ephemera. In other words, a big, fat nothing. You get anything else about Baumgartner or Simon?"

Catcher chewed, shook his head. "Simon is in South America. Decided a change of scenery was a good idea. I'm not crying that he's on a different continent. I told Baumgartner what we saw. He denied they were really elves—probably fairies or humans dressing up like elves—and said the magic sounded like vampires."

"Baumgartner is a royal sack of crap," Mallory said.

"And still prefers to keep his head in the sand," I suggested, then glanced at Ethan.

He'd opted for the forkless slice and was now swabbing his hands with napkins. I predicted fork in his future.

"The pizza's good," Mallory said. "It's not Saul's, of course, but it's not bad."

"You're a pizza snob," Catcher said.

She elbowed him. "No, I was raised right. Don't deny a Chicagoan the right to pick her favorite slice. It's un-American."

I was inching into my second when my phone beeped. The slice went back to the plate, and I scrubbed grease from my hands before pulling it out of my pocket. I checked the screen . . . and my stomach curled with icy-cold nerves.

It was Lakshmi.

She was reminding me—as if I'd somehow forgotten—of the favor I owed and the message she wanted me to pass along. And she'd carefully drafted her message to ensure I recalled her larger point.

THE HOUSES DESERVE A MASTER WHO CAN TRULY LEAD THEM, she texted. DO NOT LET SELFISHNESS DEPRIVE THEM OF THAT.

Was it so selfish to want him close? To keep on the same continent the man I'd come to love, to need, to depend on? Or was it selfish of her to ask, to demand sacrifice of others instead of putting herself forward as a candidate, taking her own stand against tyranny?

"Sentinel?"

At the sound of his voice, I remembered I was sitting in mixed company—and with him. I plastered on a smile I didn't feel and tucked the phone away again.

"It's nothing," I said, and grabbed a piece of pizza as if hunger was my only concern.

But of course it wasn't nothing, and the curiosity didn't disappear from Ethan's gaze.

Sunrise found us tucked into the bedroom. The house was locked, the guards outside, Mallory and Catcher curled up in the living room. While Ethan showered, I plumped pillows and folded back the covers, climbed into cool sheets.

And then I obsessed about the GP.

My phone was in hand, Ethan on my mind, Lakshmi's text under my squinty gaze. Jonah had tattoos on each arm—a devil on one side, an angel on the other. I thought of both, miniature devils and angels sitting on my shoulders, offering contradictory advice. But in my case, the angel looked like Seth Tate, Chicago's former mayor, a former angel of peace who'd become magically linked to his identical twin, Dominic. Dominic had been an angel of judgment, a devil, and was as fallen as they came.

The devil derided me for even considering giving in to Lakshmi, a member of the GP, which had caused so much trouble for Cadogan House we'd been forced to quit it.

The angel shared Lakshmi's fire, promising that I would be doing the right thing.

And all the while, as they debated, I still had to keep Ethan out of prison.

The bathroom door opened. Ethan, wearing only a towel, looked out. He'd brushed his hair, which was water-slicked back from his face.

Guilty and torn, I stuffed the phone hastily under the covers. But not so quickly he didn't see me do it.

I'd never been a good liar, and this wasn't an exception. "Arranging a secret rendezvous, are you, Sentinel?"

"No. Just checking in."

He arched an eyebrow. "You're a miserable liar."

"Actually, I can usually bluff pretty well. But apparently not to you."

"Is this about the message you got during dinner?"

"It is."

"And would you like to tell me about it?"

There were things I could have said. *You'd be the best GP leader. You should run. Take your position as the sire of vampires. Challenge Darius.* But seconds passed and the sun inched higher toward the horizon, robbing me of the ability to debate. And I wasn't going to take on something this serious when I wasn't at full capacity.

"Nothing big," I drowsily said. "Just a personal concern."

"A personal concern?" he asked, a spark of green fire in his eyes that I recognized as jealousy. He probably imagined the personal concern involved Jonah and the RG, as that was the only thing I normally wouldn't discuss with him in detail. But Ethan was the only man on my mind.

Apparently intent on guaranteeing that fact, he flicked a finger, and the towel fell to the ground, heaping at his feet. Ethan stood there, still damp, golden hair around his shoulders, hands on his hips and a less-than-modest expression on his face. Considering his impressive erection, modesty would have been wasted on me anyway.

I ignored my body's undeniable twinge of interest and dragged my gaze to his face. "Not that kind of personal concern."

He cocked an eyebrow. "You're certain?"

"That you'll be the only man on my mind?" Especially with the image of him standing there seared into my retinas and memory. "Yes. I'm quite certain. Positive, you could say."

He smiled a little. "Sentinel, you're mumbling."

"I'm tired. And your nakedness is distracting."

But I moved to him anyway. Because sometimes distraction was just the thing you needed.

Some hours later, darkness fell without a knock at our bedroom door or any other. But alarms weren't always raised with fists.

CHAPTER ELEVEN

—◦━◦◦━◦—

LOOK AT LITTLE SISTER

We were dressed the next evening and preparing to emerge from the bedroom when our phones rang simultaneously. I reached for mine, but Ethan found his first.

"Sullivan," he said, answering it through the speakerphone.

"It's Luc. Turn on the television. NBC affiliate. *Now.*"

Dread ran cold along my spine like a spill of ice water.

We ran for the door, pulled it open, found Mallory on the couch, yawning as she flipped through a magazine. Catcher was gone, but there was shuffling in the kitchen.

Ethan reached the television first, switched it on, and found the channel.

"What's the emergency?" Mallory asked.

A newscaster's solemn voice began to ring through the air, drawing my attention back to the television. And there on the screen was Scott Grey, his lip bruised and bleeding, one eye swollen, his arm in a make-do sling. He limped as he walked, two men in black suits escorting him from the police station. The man on his left whispered to him, close and confidential.

"Catcher," Mallory said, the same look of mortification in her eyes, "you need to see this."

Catcher emerged from the kitchen, a mug in hand and wearing only boxers. He nodded at me and Ethan, then fixed his eyes on the screen.

"Scott Grey, the quote-unquote Master of Chicago's Grey House of vampires, was led away from the precinct tonight by his lawyers after a day of intense questioning. Police spokesmen say they spoke with Grey about the recent murders and riots that have racked the city."

"Bastards," Ethan gritted out with obvious temper, needles of magic spilling into the air. "They've beaten him like he's a goddamned animal."

"Police say Grey is not a suspect in those events, but he may have information which could lead to the arrest of those suspected. John Haymer has more live from the precinct steps."

The shot switched to a young man with dark skin, sharp gray eyes, and a very serious expression. "Thank you, Linda. I'm here with Terry Fowler, a resident of Hyde Park, with commentary."

Haymer tipped a black microphone toward Fowler, a man with bony shoulders and a gleaming pate.

"It's about time," Fowler said, with a thick Chicago accent and a waggling finger, "that the mayor took some action on the hooligans that are running loose in our streets."

"Those *hooligans*," Ethan bit out, "are not vampires."

"And what do you think about the charges the city used inappropriate force against Mr. Grey?"

"Inappropriate force? He's a predator. They all are. Rioting, plucking victims here and there, probably grab you right off the street if they had a mind to. 'Bout damn time, if you ask me." He smiled with gusto at the camera, clearly happy about his forty seconds of fame.

There would never be a moment's peace, I realized. Not as long as human civilization had its own problems, not when vampires made such an easy target. Not when blaming us was easier than addressing deeply rooted social ills.

This was Celina's doing, the result of her outing vampires, the mess she'd made by announcing their existence to the public. It had been more than a year since she'd made the decision, held a press conference, brought vampires into a light they hadn't asked for. And now we were paying the price. This wasn't the age of the Inquisition or the Salem witch trials, but it was proving to be different only by mechanism and degree. Technology didn't make humans less blind; it only made it easier for hate and ignorance to spread.

"The mayor maintains the city's supernaturals are little better than domestic terrorists. What are your thoughts?"

"They're violent," Fowler said. "Creating chaos. Making good people afraid to go out at night. Isn't that terrorism? She should put 'em away or take 'em out."

"You mean the death penalty?"

"If that's what it takes, yeah. If it's good enough for humans, ain't it good enough for vampires?"

My blood chilled. His voice stayed casual, like it was nothing at all to suggest our deaths.

"Thank you, Mr. Fowler," said the reporter, looking straight into the camera again. "I've spoken with a number of individuals here outside the precinct. Although not all of them support the mayor's actions, it's clear they are concerned about the presence of vampires in their community."

The shot switched back to the studio, where the anchor, every strand of platinum blond hair in place, nodded. "Thank you, John, for that report. The mayor has not issued a statement respecting Mr. Grey's release. The mayor also has not yet identified a replacement for the head of the Office of Human Liaisons, who was arrested a few days ago for his role in the riots that have racked the city this week."

The camera shifted to the man who sat beside her, a brunette with thick eyebrows and a long, straight nose. "Thank you, Patrice. And now to sports."

Ethan flicked off the television.

"They actually think we're threats to the public welfare?" I asked.

"The mayor thinks *I'm* a threat to the public welfare," Ethan said. "And Scott is the bait they're using. And they're using him, well and thoroughly, after all we've done for the city. The times we've pulled it back from the brink. Assimilation didn't work. Living in public doesn't work. I'm not sure what our remaining options might be."

"Disappearing," Catcher said. "Just like the elves." He glanced at me. "Have you heard from Jonah?"

"I haven't even had time to look." I went back to the bedroom and grabbed my phone, found three missed calls from Jonah, and sent a message.

WE'RE WATCHING THE REPORTS, I sent. I'M SORRY GREY HAS GOTTEN DRAGGED INTO THIS.

He didn't immediately respond, so I kept the phone in my hand, went back to the living room, and wished him strength.

Ethan glanced back at me, the line of worry between his eyes. "I can't let them be punished on my behalf. Seeking shelter here to avoid a fight with the CPD was one thing. But others being targeted in my stead is something completely different. This isn't Scott's fault."

"It's not his fault," I agreed. "But he was at the House when Monmonth was killed. They'd have seen that on video." When rioters firebombed Grey House, we sheltered the Grey House vampires, a direct violation of the GP's blacklist. Monmonth had come to Cadogan House to enforce it, to force Scott and the rest out of their sanctuary, when he attacked.

"He's a witness," Catcher said, "because you did him a favor and let him into your House. But it hardly matters. Whether or not you're there wouldn't matter. If she thinks she can beat a witness with impunity, there's no act on your part that would stop her."

"And it would be dangerous," Mallory said, fear in her eyes. "She's willing to do all this when you clearly acted in self-defense. She's not operating within the bounds of the law."

"I'm not sure that matters to her," Ethan said, putting his hands on his hips. "The law applies to humans, which we are not. I'm sure she has advisers, lawyers on staff who are promising her that she's doing nothing illegal, nothing that's not sanctioned by vague and antiquated laws. Add in her argument that we're domestic terrorists, and she has a license to abuse her powers. Goddamn her." Furious magic buzzed around Ethan, filled the room. "Goddamn her and her narcissism."

My phone buzzed; it was Jonah again.

WE'RE MANAGING, he said. RG HELPING. LAWYERS TALKING TO SCOTT. ALL GUARD CAPTAINS COMMO'ING.

That was something, at least. The Houses would never be as strong apart as they would be together.

But Jonah had one more message to share: BEWARE—KOWALCYZK MEANS TO MAKE AN EXAMPLE OF ETHAN.

I could face down a harpy or an elf. But the thought of Ethan in trouble curled my stomach with fear.

"Ethan," I said, passing the phone to him when he glanced back at me.

"What am I supposed to do?" he slowly asked, handing it back. "Sit here twiddling my goddamn thumbs while they take the punishment she means to give me?"

"You'll stay here," Catcher said, "and keep the situation from getting worse. Scott has lawyers, and he's immortal just like you. And frankly, it's time the other Houses get beat up instead of Cadogan."

When Ethan opened his mouth to argue—probably with cursing—Catcher lifted his hands. "Stop. Just wait a minute. Let me play the asshole, and you can be pissed at me if you want. We go back a long way, Ethan. You know I don't bullshit you. Not on purpose anyway," he said, slanting a glance at Mallory. "For once, take my advice—let the others do the heavy lifting. If you go back, she'll crucify you. That won't do you, Merit, Malik, or anyone else any good. So Scott got a little bruised; he'll heal. This is not the first time or the last time authorities in Chicago have roughed up a witness or a suspect. Christ, how many times have you both been injured?"

He sucked in air, let it out again, looked between us. "What's happening in Chicago isn't great. But you knew when you came here that 'not great' was a pretty strong possibility. And in the meantime, an entirely new crisis has dropped into your life. Let's deal with that crisis first, before we run back to the arms of the other one."

The room went silent for a moment with the weight of Catcher's words.

"Been saving up that monologue for a while, have you?" Ethan asked, a hint of a smile at one corner of his mouth.

Catcher humphed. "Longer than I should have. We all have

improvements to make." He looked at Mallory. "I'm trying to make mine."

I caught Mallory swiping tears from under her eyes, love flooding between them. I looked back at Ethan, and the look he gave me was similarly deep. And surprising, as it often was. The fact that this four-hundred-year-old immortal, this Master of vampires and men, needed me was still occasionally bewildering. And awesome.

"Sentinel?" Ethan asked.

"You stay," I agreed. "Let our people do their thing in Chicago. And in the meantime, we try to fix what's broken here." I stepped forward and took his hands, knowing now the time was right. "We have to find the person who's attacking supernaturals. Because if we don't finish this now, there's a pretty good chance the Houses will be on their radar."

He pressed a kiss to my brow. "You're wise beyond your years." He glanced at Catcher and Mallory. "I wasn't certain I would ever have an opportunity to say this—but I'm glad you're here. I'm glad you're part of the team again."

Mallory grinned, a smile breaking like sunrise across her classically pretty face, now framed by blue waves.

"I'm glad you stopped being a pain in my ass," Catcher said.

"Well," Mallory said, pulling back her hair. "Now that we're temporarily hunky-dory, maybe we should get some work done."

"And coffee," Catcher said, walking back to the kitchen.

"You might also want to find some pants," I helpfully added.

Considering the one-finger gesture he offered, he didn't much appreciate the suggestion.

Luc agreed with our plan, as did Ethan's lawyers, who assured him Scott was fine and would have a glorious civil suit against Mayor Kowalcyzk when the time came. The lawyers had very particular concerns about Ethan's welfare should he fall into Kowalcyzk's hands, and weren't willing to turn him over. In the meantime, they promised to check with their contacts in Washington, alert the Justice Department to the mayor's acts, and, in the interest of clearing the air, invite the Homeland Security folks to come to Chicago and interview Ethan themselves.

I wasn't entirely comfortable with that course of action—it seemed to me like inviting the wolves into the henhouse—but we didn't have to worry about it now. We had larger concerns.

Ethan directed Luc to give Grey House anything they needed and asked Malik to make his own diplomatic phone call. We waited while he made the communication and reported back that Scott, too, agreed that Ethan should stay away.

"According to Scott," Malik said, calling back from the Ops Room, "Kowalcyzk is on the hunt."

"Does she know where I am?" Ethan asked as we sat together on the couch, mugs of coffee Catcher had distributed in hand.

"She does. Her goon squad told Scott she received an anonymous tip."

Ethan glanced at me, eyebrow arched. "Any bets on Michael Breckenridge?"

"He's the most likely candidate," I agreed. "But every shifter out there knows we're here."

"She hasn't moved on the information," Ethan said. "At least not directly. Pulling in Scott reads to me like a ploy. As we predicted, she doesn't want to move on the Brecks, so she's trying to lure me back to Chicago."

"If she had any cause at all, she wouldn't need the lure," Malik said. "She'd head down there and arrest you. But she doesn't have evidence of anything but self-defense, which isn't enough to arrest you in Chicago, much less cross jurisdictional bounds and convince the officers of Loring Park to go up against the city's biggest taxpayer."

"Still," Ethan said. "I don't like it. I don't like the game playing, and I certainly don't like her using others to get to me. She knows she has no case. Why not drop it?"

"Because riots," Luc said blandly. "The city's still reeling, and her popularity is in the toilet. She's got to come across as being hard on crime—and the perceived root of that crime—if she wants to survive a real election. Seth Tate being thrown out of office was a once-in-a-lifetime opportunity, and I imagine she knows it."

"And so we are the playthings of the fates once again," Ethan quietly said. "But we carry on and nobly endure. Thank you for the reports," he added, then glanced at me. "Oh, and Merit's grandfather?"

"Doing well," Luc said. "They're working on managing his pain, getting him prepped for rehab. Long road ahead, but his spirits are good. I debated what to tell him about your current shenanigans but opted for the truth."

"I'm sure he appreciated that," I said. "What did he say?"

"He was surprised—said he didn't know of any conflicts between the Pack and other groups. Was stunned about the harpies and the elves."

"Did you tell him about my heroism? Laud my bravery? Extol my fighting virtues?"

"I told him you fainted at the first sight of blood."

"That would be an obvious stretch considering the fangs."

"He knows you did well," Luc assured. "Oh, and your father called, Merit. He wanted to offer whatever assistance he could in the troubles facing the House."

"How . . . noble," Ethan said, flicking me a glance. I simply rolled my eyes. My father might very well have wanted, on some level, to help the House. But that desire would have been significantly dwarfed by the financial and political hay he thought he could make of it. He was an opportunist, and he'd already expressed an interest in becoming a financial sponsor of Cadogan House. There was no denying his power or money—being the city's chief real estate mogul had its advantages—but the cost of cashing in that chit would be much too great. And I already owed favors to too many bloodsuckers.

"I thought you'd think so," Luc said. "We'll keep you apprised of any developments."

"Do that," Ethan requested, and ended the call. He looked at me, humor in his eyes. "If I had a dollar for every time your father sought to buy his way into our favor—"

"Then you'd be as rich as my father," I said with a smile.

"Just so," Ethan agreed, then nodded at the door. "Let's get out there and see what the night brings."

The guards were gone when we opened the door, apparently satisfied that we weren't going to run and that we could care for ourselves now that the sun was down again. We walked to the house, found the front part of the house completely empty of shifters or staff.

Ethan put his hands on his hips, surveying the empty parlor and kitchen, then glanced back at us, brow raised. "Thoughts?"

I could sense the flow of magic from other parts of the house, moving toward us. "Follow the magic," I said, pointing to the hallway.

I led the way, the others falling into step behind me. The magic grew in intensity as we neared the eastern wing of the house.

"Ballroom," I murmured, pointing to the double doors up ahead. One door was closed, the other open a few inches. I moved toward it to peek inside.

Gabriel, wearing a long-sleeved Henley-style shirt and jeans, stood at one end of the ballroom, hands tucked casually into his pockets. He stood alone, the rest of the Pack standing before him, watching him speak. I didn't see any other Keenes but assumed they were part of the crowd. Their mood was grim, the magic strong but banked, like a thousand hummingbirds in place, but wings in motion, waiting for the call to move.

I pushed open the door just wide enough so we could slip inside. We lined up in the back, where Damien offered a mirthless smile.

"Normally," Gabriel said, looking across the members of his Pack, "we would cast our votes. You would speak, and as Apex of the Pack, I would be your voice."

He looked down for a moment, considering, then up again. "Tonight, I am also the words. Lupercalia is hereby canceled."

That was the call to arms they needed.

Sound erupted—shifters hissing and screaming out, accusing Gabe of cowardice, of giving in to intimidation, of lacking certain portions of the male genitalia. Magic filled the air: angry, peppery, biting. No longer banked, but swirling around the room like whirlpools and eddies in a river.

Considering what he'd faced down this week, they undoubtedly knew there was no basis to call the Apex a coward. But this wasn't about truth. This was about anger and frustration. The Pack had been wronged by someone—and they were taking it out on Gabriel.

He let them rant for a full minute, his expression blank, his shoulders square. He stared ahead as if their jeers couldn't touch him, were utterly meaningless, and couldn't change his mind. His body language told the tale: The decision had been made, and anyone with a mind to the contrary could go fuck themselves.

It took me a moment to realize his play, to figure out why Gabriel Keene, usually so attuned to what the Pack did and did not want, was suddenly playing dictator.

He was giving them an excuse.

They were shifters—their senses of self built upon the notion that they were braver than everyone else, with fuck-it attitudes and the power to back up the attitudes with action. If they'd voted to cancel Lupercalia, they'd have taken another psychic blow. Not just two showdowns, but three, the last a clear defeat. Gabe didn't want them to feel they'd taken an easy out, given in to fear. By making the decision, by being dictatorial, he put the weight of that decision on himself and himself alone.

It was, to them, an act of cowardice.

It was, in fact, the ultimate bravery. He would sacrifice himself for the good of the Pack, for their safety and longevity. But he would do it with cost.

He glanced at Berna, and she whistled, quieting the crowd immediately. I really needed to learn how to do that.

"I'm the Apex of this Pack," he said. "If any of you want to challenge me for that position, you know where I'll be. Until that time, the decision stands." With that, he turned and walked forward, the crowd dividing to let him through. He walked toward the door, a slant of his eyes the only indication that he'd seen us. If the rest of his family had been there, they didn't follow him now. Maybe this was part of his larger plan—to let the Pack have its moment to vent, and keep them out of the argument.

"Difficult to be the Master of any house?" I quietly murmured to Ethan.

"Indeed, Sentinel. One quickly learns the meaning of sacrifice." He glanced at the crowd, still unsure whether it should revolt or walk away and let the battle lie. "And the costs of it."

With Gabriel gone, we looked at each other, not entirely sure where to go. Should we follow Gabriel out of the room or stay here and keep watch?

"We all know this is bullshit," said one of the shifters—a hard-bitten, meaty man with long, braided hair that glinted with age. He wore an NAC jacket, with LETHAL stitched onto the front, and his eyes looked bloodshot and haggard.

"What have we become? Pussies? Humans? Canceling a party because things might get rough? We do not cancel Lup. The entire point of fucking Lup is to show off our cojones." He grabbed his crotch, smiled at the crowd. I presume he meant to show himself a virile shifter, but he only succeeded, at least in my mind, in looking like an entirely different kind of predator.

"What a moron," Damien whispered, his voice mild and faintly disgusted, which raised him even more in my estimation.

"And this harpy and elf bullshit? You know who attacks us when we're strong? Nobody. We were attacked because Keene can't hold our shit together. His old man was a fucking shifter. A fucking wolf. And now? We're cavorting with vampires, with sorcerers. The Packs don't cavort! We are shifters!" He beat a fist against his chest. "We eat. We ride. We fuck. We fight."

The magic in the crowd began to rise, buzzing louder. He was ramping them up, riling them up, preparing them for something.

Ethan firmly believed we needed the Pack as allies in this volatile time, but frankly I couldn't think of a group more volatile than shifters. We shifted from allies to enemies in the span of days, and sometimes over the course of a single day. They couldn't seem to make their mind up about us, and their fair-weather friendship was beginning to grate on me.

Lethal scanned the crowd, locked his gaze on Mallory.

"And then there's the fucking sorcerers," he said. "Was Gabe a pussy before he started playing with girls and their magic? Would he send us all home like whelps, tails between our legs? The elves show their faces, kidnap two of our own, and we don't fight them? We don't stand and deliver?" He barked out a laugh. "That's bullshit. Part of that hippie nonsense he's always spouting. 'We're all part of the universe,'" he said in a mocking voice. "She's making him soft."

Gabriel did have a holistic view of shifters, seeing the Pack as a crucial part of the natural world. It wasn't unlike the sorcerers' belief that they funneled magic through their bodies, although he hadn't voiced it that way. Regardless, he'd been talking about nature before Mallory went bad, and certainly before he became her tutor.

But Lethal wouldn't have cared about that. He was pissed and looking for an excuse to do some damage. And as he stared down at Mallory, a disturbing glint in his eyes, it seemed clear whom he'd picked as a target.

He began to stalk toward us, the rest of the shifters moving out of his way just as they had when Gabriel passed. I wasn't impressed that they stood by while a bully attempted to cower a guest, especially someone he could easily overpower—at least in terms of pure physicality.

Wordlessly, Ethan and I moved together and formed a barrier around Mallory and Catcher. Damien did the same.

My heart began to race with the possibility of a fight, and I let my irritation shine in my eyes.

Lethal emerged through the crowd in front of us, maybe ten feet away. The shifters closest to us—all in NAC jackets and with the look of bikers who'd been riding hard for a few days—looked between us, not entirely sure which side they'd bet on, but happy to see some action either way.

I'd been a victim yesterday; I preferred to be a perp today.

I stepped in front of all of them, flipped off the thumb guard on my katana, and lifted the handle just a bit, letting them know that I'd be happy to roll if that's how they wanted to play it.

"Did you need something?" I asked.

But it wasn't a big, burly shifter who wanted to talk.

"What the hell is wrong with you?" Emma, Tanya's petite sister, stepped out of the crowd on the other side of the room, drawing everyone's attention. She looked the opposite of Lethal in nearly every way—petite and fragile, wearing a simple cotton top and jeans, her eyes wide and face flushed with anger.

"We are facing crises—several, at once—and the only thing you can think to do is blame other supernaturals for our issues?"

There were mumbles in the crowd.

Any pretense of shyness was gone now. However quiet she might have seemed, she'd found her voice.

She looked at Lethal and made a sarcastic noise. "You want to challenge Gabriel? Then do it, you cowardly asshole. Don't stand up in here and cause trouble for the rest of us, and for these people, who've done nothing but try to help. I'm pretty sure you spent yesterday sleeping off a hangover."

The crowd snorted with laughter. I bit back a grin, deciding conclusively that I liked Emma. I also cast a glance at Damien, saw pride shine in his eyes.

But Lethal wanted his bit of infamy, and he wasn't about to give that up to Emma. "And who are you to talk about it? Are you even old enough to drink?"

Emma's expression didn't change, but she did put her hands on her hips. "Plenty. And I bet I can hold my liquor better than you can, Mervin."

It wasn't a very shiftery name, which was probably why Mervin preferred to go by "Lethal." But he wasn't happy about Emma pointing that out. His face went beet red.

"You think your sister's being married to a Keene's gonna save you? You think I won't hit you because you're one of them? Or because you're a girl?"

"No, I think you won't hit me because you're a bully who talks a lot and doesn't do shit about it."

"Come over here and say that to my face."

Her courage bobbled, and for a moment there was nothing but fear in her face. But she pushed it back, squared her shoulders, and met his gaze. And then she moved toward us, hands fisted at her sides as if courage were a bird and if she didn't hold tight enough it would fly away and out of sight.

She stopped a few feet from him. Together, we formed a triangle of dissension. Or a game of rock, paper, vampires.

Ethan? I silently whispered, thinking she looked small and frail staring down Lethal and his buddies. But I didn't want to step forward if that would weaken her position.

This is her fight, he confirmed.

"All right," Lethal said. "You wanna play?" He walked forward, shoved her.

I saw Damien jerk beside me, his eyes lined with concern, but before he could even think about moving, Emma moved.

He must have had a foot in height and eighty pounds on her, but she didn't seem to notice. Emma reached out, grabbed one of his wrists to hold him, then rotated her other elbow and brought it hard against the side of his head. She released him, and he stumbled backward.

"Fucking bitch," he murmured, rotating his jaw, setting himself, and lunging again.

He came at her like a bull, head down and forward, apparently intent on tackling her to the ground. But she was lighter, faster, more spritely. She turned to the side, neatly dodging his dive, and lifted a knee to catch him in the gut.

Magic rose in the room again, and the rest of the shifters began shuffling, obviously eager to join the fun.

The shifter in front of me—a tall woman with a long blond braid—grinned wolfishly. She wore the same leather jacket as the others, and ROSIE was embroidered into the front.

I dipped my chin, pursed my lips, and grinned at her. "Shall we, Rosie?"

The silver in my eyes spooked her; she swallowed hard and clenched her fingers, clearly rethinking her plan.

A *boom* on the other side of the room drew our attention away.

Lethal hit the hardwood floor on his back, then slid ten feet backward. His eyes were closed.

We looked at Emma, who shook her right hand, the knuckles split and dotted with blood. A hank of brown fair fell over her eyes, and she blew it up and out of her face.

I was in absolute awe, and a little bit in love.

Emma looked around at the crowd. "We've lost four people, have one missing, and you still want to fight? How stupid and stubborn do you have to be to think going forward with Lup is a good idea? So we haven't finished it this year. Who cares? Since when are we defined by whether or not we have a party?"

"Lup isn't just a party!" called a smart-ass from somewhere in the crowd.

"It's not just," she agreed. "And neither are we. We are the shifters of the North American Central Pack. And we've chosen Gabriel Keene to lead us. Until one of you has teeth enough to step forward and take it from him, then shut the hell up about it."

Without another word, she stepped forward and marched out of the room with a dignified tilt to her chin.

"I really like her," Ethan murmured.

"I seriously want to be her best friend," Mallory said, glancing at me. "No offense."

I smiled at her. "I thought the exact same thing."

Curious, I glanced at Damien. By the avaricious glint in his eyes, I guessed Damien liked her, too.

Damien lifted his head, glanced around the room, daring the shifters to step forward. "I think we're done here."

Magic hovered for a moment but dissipated, and shifters began filing out of the room.

"Crisis number three?" I wondered, as we watched them leave.

Catcher laughed mirthlessly. "If we start counting crises, we won't have time to do anything else."

And thus was the state of supernaturals in Chicago.

◆━◆═◆═◆━◆

CHAPTER TWELVE

COME ON, ALINE

We found Gabriel in Papa Breck's office, sitting on the floor with Tanya and Connor, who sat on a colorful mat and gnawed on the ear of a plastic giraffe. He wore a long-sleeved baby-sized NAC shirt and baby jeans, which were stupidly adorable. I had an urge—the first, as far as I'm aware—to nibble his little sausage toes. I decided the urge would not necessarily be welcome from someone with fangs, and kept my place.

Gabriel looked up, scanned us. "Good evening."

"You left a mess back there," Ethan said. "I presume that was intentional?"

"Intentional enough," Gabriel allowed. "We had to cancel Lup. There's no sense in continuing to risk the Pack to whatever's out there—or whatever presumptively extinct group of supernatural assholes decide to show up on our doorstep tonight."

"They weren't happy about the decision," Ethan carefully said, considering Gabriel.

"Of course they aren't. They're shifters. They don't give up, and they don't give in."

"Which is why you made the decision for them," I said.

Gabriel nodded, pleased. "Well done, Kitten. If the Pack can't make the hard choices, I do it for them. If they decide the choice was wrong, they can confirm someone else as Apex."

We'd seen that before, when Adam Keene challenged Gabriel for control of the NAC. The fight hadn't been successful, and we hadn't seen or heard from Adam since.

"It's the way of our world," Gabriel said. "Out of curiosity, who threw the fit?"

"A delicate flower named Lethal," Ethan said. "I presume the moniker was well earned."

Gabriel acknowledged that with a nod and didn't look surprised at the identity of the troublemaker.

"Emma stood up for your family, for the Pack," I said, smiling at Tanya. "And did a good job of it."

"She's got a good head on her shoulders. Entire family does, of course," Gabriel added, smiling at Tanya. He brushed fingers across her cheek.

"She's also got a great right hook," Ethan said.

"I taught her that," Tanya said, smiling up at Ethan. "We only look delicate."

"That is truth if I've ever heard it," Gabriel said, tickling Connor until the baby hiccupped with delight. "Any leads?"

"Not yet," Ethan said. "But we have a plan. Just need to touch base with the House. It would be helpful to get Pack feedback on anything we do find."

Nick stepped into the room, acknowledged us with a nod. "No one's put forth a challenge yet," he told Gabriel.

"It will happen or it won't," Gabriel said. He bobbed his head toward us. "They need to talk to their team in Chicago. I think you can oblige them with the technology?"

It was posed as a question, but his tone made the order obvious. Nick nodded obediently.

We followed him down a long, window-lined corridor to the western wing of the house, which had never been occupied, as far as I knew. This part of the house was utterly silent, and it was easy to imagine ghosts lurking in the darkened ends of corridors and inside wardrobes.

Ethan looked at me, and I shrugged. Whatever Nick had planned was a mystery to me.

He finally came to a stop in front of a nondescript door. On the wall beside it was a small wooden plaque with a brass plate. But the plaque was a ruse. He lifted it, revealing a digital screen recessed into the wall. He pressed his palm to it, and a red line of light passed back and forth along its surface, scanning for a signature.

When the scan was finished, there was a heavy metallic click within the doorframe. Several locks disengaging, I guessed.

"A biometric lock," I said, impressed by the tech. "Does Jeff know about this?"

"He should," Nick answered, pushing open the door. "He designed it. And the rest of this."

It was like we'd stepped into a time machine.

There, in the *Jane Eyre*–esque hallways of the Breckenridge mansion, was a room that held the highest tech I'd ever seen in real life. The floors were of the same hardwood as other parts of the house, but that was where the similarities ended. The room was dark, the better to view the massive screens that covered the three facing walls. There were no visible computers, but glass panels were placed around the room, their surfaces spinning with text and images, including the travel receipt we'd seen on Aline's computer. A long, gleaming white conference table and chairs sat in the middle of the room, and Aline's cardboard box was propped upon it, an anachronism amid modern technology.

Jeff and Fallon stood in front of the closest screen, on which two horses and riders in full armor galloped across a plain toward a huge stone tower.

This was Jakob's Quest, Jeff's favorite video game. And it seemed he'd found a partner in Fallon.

"Having fun?" Nick asked.

Jeff and Fallon turned back to us, both wearing headsets.

"Oh, hey," Jeff said with a smile. "Figured you'd make your way in here eventually. Thought we'd kill some time while you did."

I smiled at Fallon. "He's convinced you to join him?"

She grinned. "Other way around, I'm afraid. I introduced him to Jakob's Quest."

"She did," Jeff said with a smile, pulling off his headset.

I bobbed my head toward the screen. "I assume Jakob's the male rider. Who's the chick?"

The female character was impressively dressed in a jointed suit of armor much like Jakob's, but shaped for her curvier and more petite form. Her hair was long and golden, pulled into a complicated braid down her back, and her eyes were blue. A tattoo on her left cheek looked like a Celtic knot.

"That's Adriel," Fallon said. "She's the kingdom's crown princess, but she gave the throne to her twin brother and sister so she could keep the land safe."

Jeff reached out his hand and she took it, and they shared a look of such intimacy and love that I turned away, not wanting to intrude on it.

Ethan touched the back of my neck, acknowledging the love that swirled in the room.

"Now that we've covered the software," Ethan said lightly, "the hardware looks equally impressive."

"That's what she said," Jeff muttered. Love or not, he was still Jeff. I bit back a smile at Fallon's eye roll.

"We put it in a few months ago," Nick said. "After the incident involving Jamie."

The incident had been an unfortunate attempt at blackmail that Papa Breck believed was our fault. That was at least some of the reason for the strained relationship between us.

Nick walked to a freestanding screen, swirled a hand across the glass and, when a keyboard prompt filled the screen, typed in a password. The screen shifted, throwing up images of the house, the grounds on the right side. The left side showed news channels, newspaper headlines.

"It's impressive," Ethan said. "Have you had much cause to use it?"

"Not until this weekend," Nick said. "And unfortunately, not until after the fact."

I heard the guilt in his voice, the regret they hadn't been able to stop the harpies or elves ahead of time.

"Security cameras do not afford the gift of premonition," Ethan kindly said, hands behind his back as he stepped forward to review the screen. "You've heard about Scott Grey?"

"We have," Nick said. "The mayor doesn't seem eager to let up on you."

"No," Ethan agreed, sliding his hands into his pockets. "She does not, although I suppose that's not entirely surprising considering her past actions."

Jeff swiped the screen again, and Jakob and his trusty steed disappeared, replaced by a mock-up of the dry-erase board from the House's Ops Room.

"You made a whiteboard for us?" I asked with a grin.

Jeff shrugged adorably. "We've kind of become a team. It seemed like the thing to do."

"And with that," Nick said, moving toward the door, "I'll let you get to work."

He disappeared, closing the door behind him.

"The Brecks have a house of pissed-off Pack members," Jeff explained. "They'll be packing up, heading out, and he wants to make sure they remain calm until they do."

"Entirely understandable," I said. "Let's talk business."

Maybe I was becoming a private eye. I really needed to learn more of the lingo.

"The receipt," Jeff said, enlarging it on the screen. "Showing a flight to Anchorage. I talked to Luc, who talked to his connection at the airlines."

"Ex-girlfriend," I murmured, and Ethan whistled low, apparently recognizing the potential drama that would cause.

"Yeah. So she confirmed Aline was on the passenger manifest for the Anchorage flight, but she didn't show up or call to cancel."

"The ticket could have been a plant," Mallory suggested, but Jeff shook his head.

"Damien called the Meadows," Jeff said. "She reserved a room but didn't show."

"The Meadows is where shifters stay when they're in Aurora," I explained. "So she didn't get on her flight. And, more important, she didn't actually arrive."

"So she changed her plans?" Ethan asked.

"Or she met with foul play on the way to the airport," Jeff said. "But I haven't seen anything in the news along those lines. The receipts in the storage box were dated up to three days before

Lupercalia," Jeff said, showing a spreadsheet that itemized each and every one of them. He'd been busy. "And since we didn't find anything else in the locker, I'm thinking it's a red herring. She buys the storage locker because, literally, she's running out of space in her house."

"It was that bad?" Mallory wondered.

"It was that bad," Jeff and I simultaneously agreed.

"It's also possible she was never going to get onto that plane, and someone went to a lot of trouble to fake us out," Ethan said.

"That's a lot of trouble to go to for a Pack outcast," Catcher said, crossing his arms with a frown.

"Or it's exactly the right kind of trouble," Mallory said. "If you're gonna take out a shifter, why not make it a troublemaker no one's likely to miss?"

"Or both," I said. "She's a troublemaker. She planned to defect back to Alaska. But she didn't make it to the airport because someone intercepted her."

"But if you're going to intercept her, why do it with harpies and a full-on attack? Why not just grab her at home?" Mallory asked.

I shrugged. "For fun and profit?"

"She's still a shifter," Jeff said quietly. "She may be a pain in the ass, but she's still a shifter. She'd put up a fight if she knew they were coming. And if they don't have power of their own—if they're using magic and other species to do the fighting for them—maybe they thought the fight was necessary."

"The elves managed to grab you and Damien," Catcher pointed out.

"An *army* of elves," Jeff said. "With threats and promises to kill Merit if we didn't cooperate."

Ethan nodded. "So the harpies were a cover, or a way to completely throw the Pack off balance and sneak Aline away. We talked to her right before the ceremony began, so she didn't leave long before the attack." He glanced at Jeff. "I don't suppose there are cameras in the woods?"

"There are not," Jeff said. "Just around the house. I've run facial recognition, but there's no footage of her returning from the woods to the house."

Catcher nodded. "So she didn't sneak back in when the fight was under way, grab a bag, leave."

"Let's play this out from the beginning," I said, walking closer to the screen and glancing at the timeline. "She was living in her house, running errands, saving stuff. She comes to the Brecks' house. We meet her in the woods; the ceremony begins. The harpies attack." I glanced back at the group. "Does anybody remember seeing her during the attack or afterward?"

There was only telling silence.

"Truthfully," Jeff said, rubbing the back of his neck, "I wasn't looking for her. But no, I didn't see her."

Ethan stepped behind me, pressed his lips to my neck. "I love it when you play detective."

"I'm working," I said, but I said it with a smile.

"What's next?" Jeff asked.

"Niera," I said. "An elf and a mother. She was taken during or after the glamoury magic was used on the elves. And that attack happened during the day after the harpy attack."

"If we're assuming these are kidnappings, what could Aline and Niera possibly have in common? What's the motivation for taking them both?"

"They're both sups," Mallory pointed out. "There are plenty of people out there who hate us. Maybe the motivation's political."

But Catcher shook his head. "Political means proving a point. There's no evidence of murder here, nobody claiming responsibility. By all accounts, the attacks were by two completely different groups."

"Which we've decided is technically impossible, since vampires were the second group. If one group was doing this—or one person—who could it be?" I glanced at Catcher, Mallory. "This is old-fashioned magic, right? The kind you do, or make. So that's sorcerer territory."

"Yeah," Catcher said, shifting uncomfortably. "But it couldn't be anyone we actually know. Baumgartner, Mallory, Simon, Paige, me. That's the entire crew within the tristate area. And you'd have to be closer than that."

"Then we're missing someone, or ignoring them. Are there any other sups who could do this, who may or may not be extinct, or who we think are just mythological creatures?"

No one answered, so I took that as a no. Frustration building, I looked back at Catcher and Mallory. "Okay. So you guys can funnel the power of the universe, right?"

They shared a glance that was intimate enough to make me uncomfortable.

"I'll take that as a yes. Are there sups who can, I don't know, work spells or magic that might seem like the good sorcerer stuff?"

"They'd be sorcerers," Catcher flatly said.

I took that as a no.

Ethan's phone beeped, and my heart jumped nervously. He glanced at the screen, nodded, looked at Jeff. "It's the librarian. Can we conference him in?"

Jeff took Ethan's phone, and when Jeff tapped a few keys, the librarian appeared on-screen, his dark, wavy hair sticking up in disheveled locks, as it usually did. He wore a polo shirt and a new pair of black-rimmed glasses that, however unnecessary, added to his debonair-scholar appeal.

Beside him sat Paige, a woman who was almost ridiculously attractive. Vibrant, short red hair with a Marilyn-esque wave, pale skin, green eyes. She wore a heather gray Cadogan House sweatshirt that somehow, on her, looked elegant.

We'd found Paige keeping a lock on the Order's archives in Nebraska until Dominic Tate burned the place down. And then we brought her home, with the last few books she'd managed to pull from the flames.

"Librarian. Paige," Ethan said in greeting.

Paige offered a small wave.

"Liege," the librarian said.

"Have you identified any connection between Aline and Niera?" Ethan asked.

"Directly? No," he said. "No information on Niera beyond what you've provided, for obvious reasons. Basic biographical information for Aline, but nothing terribly interesting there. No, the key here isn't Niera and Aline; it's their disappearances. Long story short, they aren't the only ones who are gone."

If the librarian hadn't yet gotten everyone's attention, he got it now. Even the low hum of the computers seemed to drop another decibel.

"They didn't have anything in common except for the fact that they're supernaturals and they've disappeared. So we dug through newspapers and missing persons bulletins in Illinois, Indiana, Iowa, Michigan, Ohio, Wisconsin, and . . ." He fumbled through a stack of papers on the table in front of him.

"Minnesota," Paige politely finished, sliding him a smile. "You always forget Minnesota."

"I always forget Minnesota," he agreed. "We looked over those records for the last three years and cross-referenced the records with the North American Vampire Registry, friends in the community, anyone else we could think of to identify whether any of those missing persons were supernaturals."

"We talked to Merit's grandfather," Paige said. "He seemed very eager to offer his thoughts."

I smiled. "He's probably ready to jump out of his skin and appreciated the distraction."

"That he was," she agreed. "He's looking forward to seeing you. I told him I'd pass along his love."

"Consider it passed."

The librarian cleared his throat. He wasn't much for chitchat. "We took those missing supernaturals and looked for an associated supernatural event."

"An attack," I said, and he nodded.

"No harpies," he said, "but there are instances of magical attacks with some of those kidnappings. One involved a sudden bout of bloodlust—set off a bar brawl. Another was an indoor pixie attack. Nothing at the scale of the harpies or elf glamour, though."

"And how many did you find?" Ethan asked.

"That we can confirm, six."

Ethan blinked at the screen. "Six missing sups with attacks? How has no one noticed this before? Realized this was going on?"

The librarian frowned. "Why would they? Supernaturals didn't used to talk to each other. Most of this happened before we were out of the closet. Some group attacks you, you lose a member, you probably aren't going to publicize it."

Ethan nodded. "What groups did you find?"

"That's the unusual thing," the librarian said, crossing his arms on the table and leaning forward. "It's a veritable Noah's ark: troll of the non-River variety, sylph, doppelgänger, giantess, a suspected but unconfirmed leprechaun, and an incubus."

There was a buzz of recognition in my bones. "What about shifters and elves?"

"Neither," he said. The librarian read the names of the missing in chronological order, and Jeff added them to the growing "Victims" list on our electronic whiteboard, which already included Niera and Aline.

I scanned the list and looked back at Ethan, dread growing cold and heavy in my stomach. "How many of these species live together?"

"Together?" the librarian asked, lifting his gaze to me. "In families?"

"Families, clans, houses, whatever. How many?"

"Incubi tend to live alone. Ditto doppelgängers, trolls. The rest live in small bands—usually family-based structures. But that would be maybe five or six together at most. Nothing even approaching the size of a Pack or elf clan."

"Or the ferocity," Paige said, scanning a paper in front of her. "Most of the creatures on the missing list are relatively peaceful, keep to themselves. Incubi and leprechauns can be trouble-makers."

"It *is* Noah's ark," I said, walking to the board and pointing at the top of the list of victims we'd assembled chronologically. The first on the list? An incubus.

"You start with the solitary species," I said. "One supernatural at a time. Sups who live alone, who assimilate. They're easier to trap, to catch. And their human friends just think they've moved along, or they've been the victim of some traditional human violence."

"And then you ramp up," Jeff said, moving beside me to get a full view of the screen. "You target the sups who only band to-gether in small groups. The ones less likely to put up a fight, or the ones you can easily overcome in size."

"And once you've built up your confidence, you move to the trooping animals," I said. "Elves and shifters are harder to grab, their magic stronger, their groups significantly larger. So you employ big magic—full-on attacks to keep the groups distracted while you happily sneak away with one of their own. Perhaps you kill a few in the process, but who cares?"

"Okay," Catcher said, "but they could have snatched Aline at home or alone. Why make it complicated?"

"I don't know," I said with a frown.

"Let's say Merit's right," Mallory said, crossing her arms. "What's the real motive? So you have a bunch of different super-naturals. A checklist of some kind, and you're marking them off one by one. Why? What's the reason for something like that?"

"Hatred of supernaturals," Ethan suggested. "Taking them out one by one."

"But we haven't found any bodies," I said. "If this was po-litical, like something McKetrick would have done, there'd be some sign."

"Maybe research?" Paige suggested. "Could be a group looking for tissue samples, scans, X-rays."

"That kind of thing would probably be governmental," Catcher said, "but this doesn't really smell governmental. The feds prefer black helicopters to harpies. They might be interested in researching magic, but they aren't the types to use it."

"Could be ego," I suggested. "Someone working their way through the supernatural catalogue to prove that they can. To prove they're equipped and knowledgeable enough to best all kinds?"

"Like an MMA fighter working his way up the ranks?" Catcher wondered. "That's weird, but we've seen weirder."

"What kind of person has that much ego?" Mallory asked. "Would feel a need to work over, to serially kidnap, supernaturals?"

"And if he or she isn't killing them," I wondered, "if these are actual kidnappings—then where are they?"

"That's the next question," Ethan said, and lifted his gaze to the librarian. "Suggestions?"

As it happened, he did have suggestions. The librarian pulled dossiers from the missing sups with whatever background information he'd been able to find, and microfiche copies of local newspapers from the days of the disappearances. He sent the electronic files to Jeff, who directed them to video screens that were inset in the large conference table.

We updated Luc with what we'd found, then read and scanned the materials for two solid hours, perusing coupons for white sales and new car deals, stories about sports championships of every make and model, and the local dramas that played out across the pages. And we still came up empty.

Jeff's whiteboard was littered with potential links between the disappearances, connections we hoped would lead us to the actual responsible parties. Two of the sups had disappeared on holidays— Fourth of July and Labor Day—but only two. The rest were scattered across the calendar like confetti. Most were taken in summer and fall, but we decided that was probably because the sups were more active, more visible, when the weather wasn't miserable. Who wanted to traipse through four feet of Minnesota snow to kidnap a giantess?

At the end of our two hours, we paused and stretched, and Jeff ordered drinks from the Brecks' staff, who seemed more than happy to deliver them to a shifter of his repute. But the man who brought them still managed to give the rest of us dour looks on the way out.

We sipped coffee and nibbled the edges of the shortbread cookies, walking around the table to scan the others' screens, just in case a fresh pair of eyes would help tag something useful.

Turns out, it was a good strategy.

Mallory, who was across the room's conference table from me, nibbled on a shortbread biscuit and scanned the screen in front of her. She smiled, looked up. "You know what I haven't done in forever?"

"Sat still for ten minutes without distraction?"

She gave Catcher a childish face, then tapped at the screen. "The carnival. I haven't been to the carnival in forever."

Connections tripped and triggered in my brain, and I looked up at her. "What did you say?"

She smiled. "The carnival. I haven't been in years. I love a good corn dog. The deep-fried kind, not the fake ones you can bake at home. If it hasn't been swimming in oil, it's not a real corn dog. Who's with me on that?" She lifted her hand and glanced around the room, looking for support.

But my mind was forming a connection. I held up a hand. "Wait—what made you say that about the carnival?"

"Oh." She pointed to the screen. "There's an article about this carnival that was in"—she scrolled to the top of the page—"Clear Lake, Minnesota."

"Jeff," I said, and without needing additional direction, he was up and moving the data on Mallory's screen to the overhead.

The wonders of the Sidusky & Sons Carnival were spread in glorious color across two facing pages of the *Clear Lake Anthem*, advertising miraculous sights, thrilling rides, and midway games to test the strongest and cleverest of men.

"Sorry—why does the carnival matter?" Ethan asked with a frown.

Jeff and I looked at each other, nodded.

"There's a carnival right now in Loring Park," I said.

Jeff gestured to the box. "Aline went to it. We found tickets from the midway in her box."

"The carnival was here when Aline disappeared. The carnival was in Clear Lake when the giantess disappeared."

Catcher looked at Jeff. "Can you scan the rest of the newspapers for carnival ads or stories?"

"On it," Jeff said, and he was sweeping his hands across the screen, arranging files so the newspapers formed a neat grid across the screen. He entered a query into the search box. Almost instantly, matches began popping up across the screen, highlighting articles about the carnival that had visited so many midwestern towns.

The carnivals changed with every pass. Sidusky & Sons. The Bollero Bros. William's Amazing Traveling Wondershow. But the stories were essentially the same, as were the photographs of the Tunnel of Horrors.

"That's the same carnival as the one in Loring Park," I said, excitement building. "I recognize the ride."

"So what are we looking at?" Catcher asked. "A carnie with a hatred of sups?"

"Or a carnie who loves them a little too much?" I wondered.

Ethan slid me a glance. "Sentinel?"

"Maybe we're looking at a collector of supernaturals," I said. "Incubus, doppelgänger, troll, sylph, giantess, leprechaun, shifter, elf. And if they really are being kidnapped, being held, maybe they're doing it for a reason. Maybe they're being displayed somehow."

"A supernatural freak show?" Ethan asked. "Perhaps. Did you see an attraction like that?"

"No," I admitted. "And it was a pretty small carnival."

"That makes it easy to unload," Catcher said. "Easy to pack up and leave again."

"Which they clearly are doing, considering how much they move around." Ethan frowned, worried his bottom lip while he mulled the information on-screen. "Unfortunately, we aren't entirely sure who we're looking for. Is the entire carnival at fault? An errant employee? If they're holding the sups, then where? Jeff, can you see what you can find about the carnival, the owners?"

"On it," Jeff said. Normally, I'd have heard the clack of keys in the background. But since he'd upgraded his tech, his work was silent. I didn't realize I missed the sound—a comforting reminder that Jeff was there and his magic fingers were engaged—until it was gone.

It didn't take him long to cringe. "This is going to take a while," he said, pointing at the screen, where he'd opened a search engine but had gotten no results.

"First run on the carnival isn't pulling up anything other than the articles we've already seen. Not a Better Business Bureau complaint, a business filing, a single online review."

Ethan frowned. "That's unusual."

"Try impossible," Jeff said. "For a business that's been around this long, to this many states, there should at least be a review, a social media mention, if not the hard copy articles we've already found. But there's a complete blackout."

"So they're careful about what goes online," I said.

"Very," Jeff said.

"Okay," I said. "Let us know if you find anything." I glanced at Ethan. "We can make this trip just informational. Spy on the carnival for a bit?"

Ethan frowned at the screen again, propping his hands on his hips, mulling his options.

"No," he finally decided. "There's too much at stake to risk an opportunity like this." He looked at me. "I can't leave the estate, but you can. Go to the carnival. And quickly. Find an employee to interview, peacefully, quietly, and with no collateral damage. We need information before they move on, or we're going to be out of luck. Especially if they're so careful about their electronic trail. If Aline and Niera were their quarry, they may already be preparing to move."

He looked up at the screen, where Paige and the librarian still watched our discussion after their own break for snacks. "Try to identify friends, colleagues, of the missing sups. See what they remember about the carnival. Perhaps their missing friends mentioned it, made an acquaintance there, anything. Perhaps we'll get lucky. I'll stay here and get Luc up to speed."

He didn't sound thrilled about the possibility, but leaving the Brecks' house wasn't an option for him right now.

"Catcher, Mallory, Jeff, could you please accompany Merit on a field trip?"

"I think we can find the time," Catcher said.

Jeff and Catcher began discussing transportation options while Mallory slipped an arm through mine. "Is this seriously what you guys do all night? Make like Veronica Mars and solve crimes?"

I frowned, nodded. "As it turns out, yeah."

"It's fun." She pulled her hair back and into a ponytail, using an elastic she'd kept around her wrist. "Although I feel like we need embroidered jackets. Like the satin ones? We could be just like the Pink Ladies."

"I'll talk to the boss," I said. My voice was sarcastic, my but heart thudded with excitement I'd never admit aloud. I'd always wanted to be a Pink Lady.

CHAPTER THIRTEEN

BARNSTORMING

Catcher drove his sedan. Jeff sat shotgun, while Mallory and I shared the back.

The night was dark, the country roads essentially empty and thankfully clear of elven armies. Still, every time we neared a streetlight or floodlight, my stomach clenched with fear that we'd see the outline of a battalion of soldiers cresting a hill, bows in hand and arrows ready to strike.

Catcher had dialed in Luc and Ethan. "Ladies and gents," came Luc's voice through the speakers. "Once again, you're enjoying an adventure without me."

"We don't time them that way." Ethan's voice followed Luc's. "And I'm not there, either."

"As it should be," Luc said. "At least you had sense enough not to attempt to lead this particular away team."

"*Star Trek*," I murmured, picking out one of Luc's ubiquitous movie and television references.

"I have trained you well, Padawan."

"You're mixing your *Wars* and *Treks*," Jeff pointed out.

"They're interchangeable," Luc said, earning a horrified look from Jeff. "Why don't you give us the rundown on the carnival?"

I closed my eyes, trying to remember the layout. "It's in the corner of the shopping center parking lot. A small carnival—five or six rides, a midway."

"Semis or trucks?" Catcher asked. "I presume that's how they've moved the carnival from town to town?"

"Not that I saw."

"They probably park the trucks off-site," Luc said. "Keep them out of the public eye. Merit, what else?"

"There's a low fence—a gate—around it. Like a crowd-control barrier. Otherwise it's open. The rides are mostly along the out-sides, with the games and food in the middle. The attendants were pretty well dressed. They wore full outfits—costumes."

As we neared the shopping center, my nerves began to light, my blood running faster, anticipating the coming confrontation. When a rock bounced off the windshield, I nearly fell to the floor-board, my heart palpitating with tangible fear. Post-elven stress disorder was no laughing matter.

But when Catcher turned the car into the shopping center, the parking lot was empty.

"What the hell?" he murmured.

"What's wrong?" Ethan asked.

"They're gone," I said, hope deflating, and barely waiting for the car to stop before I opened the door and hopped out.

Everything was gone—the rides, the ticket booth, the games. The tourists and the carnies. Only the detritus of the carnival re-mained. The scents of fried food and exhaust, puddles of dirty water, scabs of black tape where cords had been adhered to the asphalt.

"We couldn't have been that far behind," I said, turning back to the group, who'd joined me in the lot. "You can still smell it."

"Maybe they thought their luck was running out," Mallory said, "so they decided to pick up camp and go."

"Or maybe they accomplished their goals and they're moving on to the next spot," I said, blue that we'd missed our targets. Utterly.

Catcher turned back to the car. "Let's get back to the Brecks'. Maybe Ethan can get Paige and the librarian started on where it might have gone next."

I nodded, then glanced up at the shopping center. The grocery store was closest to the carnival, and it was the only shop still open. A few people milled around inside, visible between the stems and serifs of the giant gilded letters that advised passersby of sales and specials.

I gestured toward the store. "Why don't I check out the grocery store? I'll ask when the carnival left, if they know where it's going next."

"Don't get kidnapped this time," Catcher said. "Ethan gets irritable when you get kidnapped."

"That's only one of the many reasons he gets irritable," I pointed out. "And I'll do my best. But I make no promises."

Considering the crimes we were investigating, that seemed best.

It was late, but the grocery store glowed with light and welcome heat. Disco played on the store's sound system, and the cashier nearest the door smiled when I entered.

She couldn't have been more than twenty, and she didn't seem to mind the late hour or the dearth of customers. She filed her nails and hummed along with the music, a headband with fuzzy cat's ears poking from her otherwise straight jet-black hair. She looked up at me and took in the katana when I walked over. Her eyes widened.

"Nice sword," she said in a whisper when I moved closer. "That's a katana, right?"

"It is, yeah," I said with a smile. I'd forgotten I'd worn it, and appreciated that she didn't feel the urge to signal the manager.

"Cool."

"Thanks. Question for you." I hitched a thumb toward the window. "The carnival that was here—when did it pack up?"

"I don't know. Why? Were you hoping to win a goldfish?"

"Not exactly." My prey was significantly larger, but I didn't mention that aloud. "I don't suppose you know where they were headed next?"

The front doors *shush*ed open. A woman with short blond hair walked into the grocery store. She wore snug jeans and a short red cape with a hood. It barely reached her waist and was perfectly cut, the type of garment you'd see on a New York runway. A very expensive leather handbag—the kind my sister, Charlotte, might have bought in the stores on Oak Street—was tucked on her arm. She looked, I thought with a smile, like a very chic Little Red Riding Hood.

"No clue," said the cashier, drawing my gaze again. "I'm not really into kiddie carnivals, you know?"

I took in the cat's ears, the Rainbow Brite T-shirt. "You'll appreciate them when you're older. Thanks for the help."

She shrugged and went back to her nails.

I walked toward the door but caught another glimpse of the girl who'd come in. She grabbed a red basket from a stack near the door and headed to the pharmacy aisle.

She looked familiar. I squinted, trying to remember the face and where I might have seen her. She wasn't a shifter. Not an elf, certainly, with that haircut or fashion sense. And she was down a bow and sense of entitlement.

I walked quietly closer, pretending to be interested in hot cocoa mix, dandruff shampoo, frozen chicken dinners. She pulled supplies—bandages, rubbing alcohol, gauze—into her basket.

A clerk stepped in front of me, blocking my view. He was another teenager, this time with dark skin, short braids, and suspicious eyes. "Can I help you?"

I grabbed a box of soda crackers from the Willis Tower–shaped display in front of me. "Are these, you know, on special?"

He looked at me for a moment, gestured toward the display. "The sign says they're two ninety-nine."

"Awesome!" I perkily said. I turned to a nearby shelf and pretended to be very, very interested in wasabi-flavored popcorn. Actually, I didn't have to try that hard. It was wasabi-flavored popcorn. I was already intrigued.

I waited a beat. Apparently satisfied that I'd only been nosy, and not pre-felonious, he disappeared. When the sound of his footsteps dissipated, I peeked around the end of the aisle again. The girl inspected the medical tape, and when a clerk approached and offered help, she waved him off with a smile, dimples at the sides of her cheeks. She turned just slightly, and I caught sight of her singularly gray eyes.

That's when I knew where I'd seen her.

Her hair was different now, and her clothes. She was no longer a brunette, no longer wearing her uniform, no longer enticing customers into the Tunnel of Horrors. But there was no denying the smile.

She was the carnival barker.

Like a deer scenting a predator, her head popped up, her eyes scanning for trouble.

She caught my gaze, and there was a hint of a smile on her face. But she turned back to the tape, fingers skimming the boxes.

I walked around the corner, checked out a rack of plastic sunglasses while Lionel Richie crooned on the store's music system.

The girl moved forward, disappearing into an aisle that, according to the sign hanging above it, held chips and soda.

Ever so quietly, I shifted closer, and when I reached the aisle, looked around the corner.

She was gone, but the thick rubber flaps that covered the entrance to the back room were swinging, and her basket was on the floor, the contents strewn about. She'd definitely made me.

And that wasn't my only problem.

In her wake were scents much too familiar—sulfur and smoke. Dominic Tate, Seth Tate's vanquished worse half, had smelled the same. But Dominic was dead; I'd seen Seth destroy him. Seth had left Chicago, and his scent had been different—lemon and sugar, like freshly baked cookies.

We hadn't known any other Messengers, as the dueling angels had once been called. And yet, here I was, standing in a grocery store that smelled like the devil's front porch.

I muttered a curse and took off, following her through the flaps and into a cold room that stank of overripe produce and cardboard. The room was large, with a polished concrete floor and office built into a corner. I ran to the office. A man in a collared short-sleeved shirt sat at the desk, munching on a sandwich. Roast beef, by the smell of it.

"You can't be back here!" he yelled, over a mouthful of beef and bread.

"Just passing through," I promised, then hurried down a narrow hallway to a storage area. This one held ten-foot-high stacks of boxes and wooden pallets. There was a back door across the room, but no one in sight.

"Can we just talk?" I asked, peering around a mountain of soda cartons, and caught a glance of blond hair hurrying away when a skyscraper of pallets rocked like a children's block-stacking game. As always, gravity won.

I jumped aside and missed the falling tower, tripped over a box behind me, and ended up on my ass one way or the other.

Footsteps echoed through the room.

"What the hell is going on here?" asked the meaty voice behind me. The back door clanged shut as the woman slipped through it.

I rose, ignoring the manager and his threats of police calls and litigation, but decided to send a little thank-you to Papa Breck in consideration for all the kindness he'd shown us.

"The Breckenridges will be happy to pay for any damages," I said, jumping over the messy pile of pallets and vaulting toward the back door. I slammed through it only to see her dart across the drive that ran behind the shopping center to the chain-link fence that separated it from the next property. A scrubby and empty lot, by the look of it.

I ran to the fence, jumped up a few feet, and began to climb. There was nothing remotely movielike about it, or elegant. The chain link wasn't securely attached, and it bobbed beneath my feet like I was climbing a rope ladder. I hit the top, felt skin slice as my palm caught one of the bare prongs of chain link. Ignoring the pain, I threw my body over the top and hit the ground.

Only then did I recall the fact that I could have simply jumped over the damn thing. Maybe the House library was the place for me.

The girl was already running full out across the lot, which was pockmarked with piles of dirty snow, frozen hillocks of dirt, and construction debris. Something had been planned for this space, but considering the cracked and peeling WILL BUILD TO SUIT sign that lay abandoned on the ground, it wasn't going to be finished anytime soon.

She ran with the long-legged grace of a marathon runner. I had vampiric speed and enhanced bone and muscle, but she was the running type, with a long stride and smooth motion that made it look completely effortless.

She reached a large concrete pad, hopped onto it, glanced back, searching the darkness to see if I was still behind her.

Because I was busy watching her, and not the ground in front of me, I didn't see the ditch until it was too late.

I fell down into the three-foot-deep depression, hit my knees on the ice and inches of muddy water that had accumulated in the bottom. The fall jarred me, and it took a moment to get my brain unscrambled. I got back onto my feet and toed up a knobby dirt incline until I was at ground level again.

I spat out a curse that would have raised even my liberal grandfather's hackles, and put my hands on my knees to catch my breath.

She was gone.

"She couldn't have just disappeared," Catcher said.

We stood on the edge of the lot, surveying the darkness, eyes straining for any sign or scent of the girl who'd so handily eluded me.

"She disappeared," I assured him, trying my best to squeegee mud from my leather pants. "I hit a ditch, wasn't down for more than a few seconds. When I looked up, she was gone. And she's fast. I never got closer than ten feet, and that was in the building. Out here, she was like a rocket."

"Supernatural?" Jeff asked.

"Actually, yeah." I glanced at Mallory, worried how she'd react. "She smelled like smoke and sulfur."

Jeff frowned. "Smoke and sulfur?"

He might not have understood the connection, but Mallory clearly did. She paled. "Like Dominic Tate. It's what the fallen smell like."

"Oh, damn," Jeff murmured, clearly understanding.

"Dominic's dead," Catcher said.

"Seth said there could be more Messengers out there."

"But not the fallen ones," Mallory said. "They were magically bound together into the *Maleficium*. Seth and Dominic only separated because Claudia kept Dominic safe all those years ago."

Or so we thought. This, I feared, was not going to help Mallory's recovery—having the Messengers and *Maleficium* thrown back in her face again.

"I'm sorry," Mallory said. "If this has anything to do with me, I'm sorry."

Catcher rubbed her back. "Let's not worry about what she is right now. Let's think about *who* she is and how we can find her." He looked at me. "Did she have any other physical characteristics we can search on? Piercings? Tattoos?"

"Nothing. Clothes looked expensive. Hair was blond, short. She had darker hair on the midway. It must have been a wig." I glanced at Catcher and Mallory. "Can you do some kind of searching spell and find her?"

"Locating spells are actually pretty complicated," Mallory said. "They don't work like bloodhounds. Otherwise we'd just use that box of stuff from the storage locker to find Aline. We'd have to have something substantial—something marked by her magical signature."

If only she'd whipped that expensive purse at me.

"Maybe the grocery store had security cameras," I suggested, looking at Jeff. "Could you do something with facial recognition?"

"I'll ask," he said, already thumbing his phone.

"What was she buying?" Catcher asked.

"Medical supplies—bandages, gauze. That kind of thing."

"So either she's a conscientious employer or a zookeeper with wounded animals," Catcher suggested.

I nodded. "If she's still here getting supplies, the carnival can't be too far away."

"The trucks pulled out about half an hour ago," Mallory said with a smile. "I followed up with the store. Pretended I had no clue why a woman had wreaked havoc in the back room. Made a few pithy comments about the state of the world, and the cashier opened right up."

"Cat's ears?" I wondered.

Mallory frowned. "What?"

She clearly hadn't spoken to the same cashier. "Never mind. Continue."

"So, Rhoda—that was her name, Rhoda—said the carnies kept to themselves, but before and after shift they'd come into the store for provisions. Snacks, drinks, deli food, booze, depending on the mood. She likes to travel—she and her husband have a camper—so she tried to make conversation about their route, but they wouldn't talk about it. Paid for their gear and left again."

"Even if the cashier had known where they were going next," I said, "there's a good chance they'll change their schedule. She knew we'd found her. Took one look at me and bolted."

"So where do we think they'll go next?" Mallory asked.

I smiled mirthlessly. "You're looking to add to your collection of sups, and you're an hour from the Windy City, which has the largest proportion of vampire Houses in the nation, not to mention nymphs, trolls, and God knows what else. I'll give you one guess: You aren't going to Disneyland."

We drove sullenly back to the Breckenridge house, none of us thrilled that we'd been so easily thwarted.

As we neared the house, we began to pass cars. A single car here and there, and then groups of four or five in succession. It was more traffic than I'd ever seen on the rural road that led to the estate.

"The shifters are going home," Catcher said, as we pulled into the driveway. There was something sad about that—it was morose that they'd departed under such unfortunate circumstances. Or maybe it was just the magic in the air, or the growing absence of it.

Gabriel met us at the door, Ethan beside him. We migrated into the front parlor, now empty of shifters, and out of the cold.

"Nothing?" Gabriel asked.

I shook my head. "They're gone."

"The entire carnival was packed up, moved out," Catcher said. "Merit found one of them in the grocery store, chased her down, but wasn't able to nab her."

Gabriel lifted slightly amused eyes to me. "That true, Kitten? Did you actually miss your prey?"

I decided not to tell him that I missed her because I fell in a ditch, as that would only add a thick layer of humiliation to the existing regret. I settled for glum.

"I missed her," I confirmed.

"And I might have found her," Jeff said, rocking proudly on his heels. "I was busy on the ride back."

I thought the backseat had been quiet. "Grocery store footage?"

"Yes, ma'am." He pulled out a sleek square of glass that looked like a miniature version of the screens in the Brecks' operations room, began to skim his fingers across it. The glass went smoky and nearly opaque, and images and text began to scroll across the front.

"Another new toy?" I asked. I wasn't much for gadgets, but it looked so deliciously tactile.

He kept his eyes on the screen, but a corner of his mouth perked up. "A portable to match the rest of the hardware. And here we are." He held up the glass, swiveling it so the rest of us could see.

"That's her," I said immediately, recognizing the light hair, dark eyes, dimpled cheeks. The shot, remarkably clear, was taken at the front entrance of the grocery store.

"The grocery store was robbed about a year ago, and they invested in some quality hardware. I told them we were investigating the dark-haired girl with the leather jacket"—that was me—"and the manager was more than happy to pass the photo along." He lifted his gaze, grinned full out. "He also asked about billing Papa Breck for the damages. Said they'd agreed to pay."

Gabriel flicked a glance my way.

"Technically, we were there on Pack business."

"We'll pay the store," Gabriel dourly said. "And we'll remember this incident the next time we hire vampires to do our dirty work."

"Do that," Ethan said. "And consider paying us next time instead of extortion. But back to the girl?"

"Her name," Jeff said, flipping the screen back and typing furiously, "is Regan, and I only found that because she'd been interviewed in one of the older articles about the carnival we uploaded. No last name, no date of birth, no last known address."

"Much like the carnival," Ethan said, "her history has been wiped."

"Indeed," Jeff said. "She's now a ghost. Except for the grocery store footage, anyway."

"Ghost may not be too far off," I said. "She smelled like Dominic Tate."

Gabe's and Ethan's reactions were pretty much the same as ours had been—surprise, doubt, concern.

"Dominic Tate is dead," Ethan said.

"He is. And there shouldn't be any other fallen angels out there. But I know what I smelled." I'd been held by Dominic Tate in a prison of sunlight; I wasn't likely to forget the smoky stink of it.

Gabriel crossed his arms over his chest. "Ethan's told me about this menagerie theory, if that's what we're calling it. But Merit said she didn't see an attraction like that at the carnival. What's the point of having a menagerie if you aren't going to show it off?"

Mallory raised a hand. "I've actually been thinking about that. It's like an invitation-only sample sale."

I got the comparison immediately, but the men just blinked with obvious befuddlement.

"Is this a food thing?" Catcher asked, earning a dramatic eye roll from Mallory.

"It's a fashion thing," she said. "It's when designers sell their samples for a very large discount. Very exclusive."

Understanding dawned in Ethan's eyes. "You're suggesting the public who attend the carnivals are not the target audience."

She smiled. "Exactly. So maybe the menagerie is also exclusive. They bring the carnival to town but you don't get in without an invitation."

"And they also bring the sups," Gabriel said with a nod. "Not as a carnival attraction, but a traveling menagerie. Same town, but separate location. Secret location, available only to certain well-heeled clientele."

Ethan nodded. "That could fit. The motive, perhaps, isn't

about the sups. It's about the ego, or perhaps the money. Impressing the hard to impress with an attraction they can't see anywhere else in the world."

Puzzle pieces fell into place. "And with every attack."

They looked at me.

"Sentinel?" Ethan asked.

"Having a menagerie is one thing. But when you've got powerful magic, it's not exactly a great story to just pluck someone off the street using it."

"Like they might have done with Aline," Ethan said.

I nodded. "Exactly. But if, to get the supernaturals, you have to fight for them? You set up an attack, claim your prey that way? Much more interesting story."

"It's a supernatural safari," Ethan said.

"And it demands a higher ticket price," Catcher said.

I nodded. "It would make sense, based on what we know."

"So if you're right, we'd be looking for someone insecure, or someone with a desire to impress," Jeff said.

"Someone who needs to be needed," Mallory added, "but doesn't feel any obligation to follow the rules in doing it. Being popular is better than being good."

"And yet," Ethan said, "someone who believes they'll find that fame or fortune in this fashion."

We stood there silently for a moment, contemplating that somewhat pathetic, but entirely believable, profile.

Gabe looked at me. "I assume you haven't yet determined where in Chicago the carnival might set up next?"

"Not yet. Catcher suggested we get the House on it. Maybe we can look at the carnival's previous stops? See if there's a pattern?"

Ethan nodded. "I'll talk to Luc."

Jeff nodded. "I'll dig further into Regan's ID, see if I can shake something loose there." He looked to Catcher. "I'll send you the photo. Maybe you can send it to Baumgartner, any other contacts you have, see if she looks familiar?"

"Will do."

The fierce wail of a frustrated infant rang through the house. Gabriel smiled.

"Kid's got some lungs."

Ethan smiled. "So he does."

"And I believe that's probably my cue to exit stage right. What's on your agenda?"

"Actually," Mallory said, sharing a glance with Catcher, who nodded, "we'd like to go home."

Gabriel's brows lifted. "Oh?"

"If there's a chance the carnival is headed back to Chicago," Catcher said, "I'd like to be there, on the ground, and get the word out to sups, the Houses."

"We came for Lup," Mallory said, "and unfortunately that's over. But considering what went down, we didn't want to leave without checking with you first. We don't want to make things worse."

He was quiet for a moment. "Go home," he said. "And thank you for your service. You did good out there. You stuck to your guts, to your heart, and you did that thing you do."

She beamed with obvious delight at the praise. "Thank you, Gabe," she said, laying a hand on his arm. "I suppose I'll see you at the bar when you get back?"

"That you will," Gabriel said.

Mallory and I exchanged hugs. "I'll call you," she said, rubbing my back before she released me again.

Catcher did the manly head-bob thing with the guys. "I'll

keep an eye and ear out in the Windy City. Talk to the supernatural community, see what I can find out. I'm going to have to
give them a warning—tell them, at a minimum, to stay away from
the carnival. We don't know that's how they do their targeting, but
it's all we've got. We can't exactly tell them to avoid harpies and
elves."

"Although that's also good advice," Jeff said.

"Truth," Catcher agreed. "I'll let you know if I hear anything
in the ether. And keep us posted."

Ethan nodded. "Safe travels," he said, and they walked to the
door.

"How much longer will she work for you?" I asked Gabriel.

"Not much," he said. "But she's not quite there yet. She will
be tested again."

I slanted him a glance. "Is that prophecy or guesswork?"

He made a throaty laugh. "Is there a difference?"

You tell me, I thought. Gabriel had prophesied there was another set of "green eyes" in my future, eyes that looked much like
Ethan's. It seemed like a reference to a child, but since no vampire
had successfully carried a child to term, that wasn't actually a possibility.

But still.

"Two down, two to go," Gabriel said, glancing at Ethan, a grin
pulling up a corner of his mouth. "As you two have not yet solved
this particular mystery, I presume you'll be staying here."

"We're staying," Ethan flatly said, "because the mayor still
wants my hide and the Brecks have offered us shelter. In the
meantime we'll continue to investigate the menagerie."

He glanced at his watch. "But at the moment, I think we'll
return to the carriage house. I need to check in, and we need to
get the House started on research." He glanced at my muddy

pants and jacket. "And I presume my Sentinel would appreciate a change of clothes."

"Cadogan's Sentinel, if that's what you meant to say, would appreciate a change of clothes. And a shower."

Gabriel grinned. "She has your number, Sullivan."

"And my heart, for better or worse." He looked at me and smiled, ignoring the mixed company, and sent blood rushing to my cheeks.

Jeff cleared his throat. "So, I'm going to head to the Brecks' ops room," he said, tucking away his toy again. "Faster processors in there."

"For searching, or for Jakob's Quest?" I wondered.

It was Jeff's turn to blush. "A little work, a little play, makes Jack a happy boy."

Gabriel held up a hand. "I don't need the details of how you and my sister spend your playtime, whelp."

"And I don't want to give them to you," Jeff assured him. "Talk to you all later."

Ethan and I said our good-byes, but before I could turn to follow Ethan to the door, Gabriel took my arm. I looked up, found his eyes intense and swirling.

"The future I once shared with you, Kitten. Do you think that's prophecy or guesswork?"

I presumed he meant his green-eyes prediction, and my heart thudded against my chest.

I shook my head. "I don't know." My voice was barely a whisper. "You tell me."

"It's exactly what you think," he said. "But there will be tests for you, as well."

And with those words hanging in the air like so much ripe fruit, he disappeared, leaving me, heart pounding, standing in the hallway.

A child, with Ethan.

Gabriel had as much as confirmed it, even if he hadn't said the words aloud. My heart blossomed with hope and love and possibility . . . and also fear. What had he meant by "tests"? I'd been attacked, seen my city nearly destroyed and my grandfather nearly killed, and I'd watched Ethan die to save my life. Was it the GP? Was it Ethan's challenging Darius, or some injury he'd have to endure? And if a child was in our future, was our being together an inevitability? Or was Gabriel's prophecy the shifter version of a devil's bargain? Would I get exactly what I wanted, but with some horribly ironic twist?

"Are you all right?" Ethan asked as we walked back to the carriage house. "You seem tense."

He was right. Gabriel's words hung thick around my neck; once again, I was too unnerved to voice them to Ethan. I'd kept secrets from him before. Secrets I thought weren't mine to tell, like my membership in the RG. Revealing that fact had put Jonah at risk as much as it did me.

"I'm fine," I said as we stepped to the threshold and he turned the key, opened the door. The carriage house was empty, the pillows on the sofa bed tidy again. They'd already gone, leaving the two of us alone.

Ethan closed the door, locked it.

"No, I'm not fine," I said, the words bursting out of me like air from a pricked balloon. "We need to talk."

CHAPTER FOURTEEN

JUST A BITE

He looked at me, face carefully neutral, his hands tucked casually into his pockets. It was an expression of mild attention, or would have been if his gaze hadn't been crystalline, his shoulders set. He was a Master vampire, and he was prepared for bad news.

"It's not bad news."

He quirked an eyebrow.

"It isn't," I insisted. "But I think we should sit down."

"Now I'm definitely worried." But he moved to the sofa and sat, leaning forward, elbows on his knees, as I took a spot across from him. I wanted to see his face, his eyes.

It all went together—the green eyes and the prophecy and the GP. It was about us, about vampires, about shifters. It was tangled together in my head like a ball of twisted wire. And that made it hard to get out.

"The RG has friends," I said. "Powerful friends. Including one who did something that helped the House. And to whom I now owe a favor."

His eyes went flat. He didn't care to be reminded of my RG membership, and especially not when he thought I'd be confessing something he didn't want to hear.

"That friend has come to collect. That friend has asked that I convince you to do something that would be dangerous. Potentially deadly, and potentially magnificent."

Ethan blinked, sat back, crossed one leg over the other. But his eyes stayed cool and on me. "And you didn't tell me this because?"

"Because of the deadly and dangerous parts." I dropped the bravado and put it out there. "Because it would pull you away from me. Inevitably."

His expression softened, just a bit. "I see."

We were quiet for a moment, magic—fearful and tentative— swirling in the air around us.

"And do you want to tell me what the dangerous and deadly parts are?"

Only if I could make you swear that you wouldn't do it, I thought. *And swear that you would.*

And that, at its heart, was the dilemma I faced. That he would do, and would not do, the thing that I anticipated as much as I feared it.

That was when I realized the truth: Either way, I would win. And either way, I would lose. Telling him didn't matter. Telling him wasn't the point.

Trusting him with the telling of it—that was the point.

And so I trusted in him, and in us. "There are members of the GP who want you to challenge Darius for his position. Who want you to be their king."

Ethan's lips parted, and his eyes widened in shock, but he didn't make a sound. I wasn't sure if he was surprised by the idea or that I had connections powerful enough that I could give him information about the GP, instead of the other way around.

"I don't know what to say."

I nodded, gave him time to process it.

"I've certainly thought about it—what it might be like to hold that position if Darius resigned. The good that could be done. God knows there's sufficient room to maneuver there. But to challenge a living member? That decision could be deadly."

"I'm supposed to encourage you," I told him. "To convince you to do it."

"Because the person who told you this wants me to hold the position—or they want me out of the way?"

The blood drained from my face. It hadn't even occurred to me that Lakshmi's motives might not be pure. I considered our conversation, thought about the hope in her eyes, and dismissed the possibility she was being less than earnest. She was honest that Ethan's challenge might not be successful. But that didn't mean she wished him dead.

"I believe the friend wants you to hold the position," I said. "They respect you and your alliances."

"But you don't want me to do it. Why? If I was successful, it would be a profound opportunity for vampires."

"You may not be successful. You have powerful enemies. And even if you were—I've already lost you once. I don't want to lose you again."

His expression softened. "You think I would have to choose."

"Wouldn't you? And wouldn't I?"

"What, precisely, would you be choosing between, Sentinel?" His expression was still mild, but there was a bite in his words.

"Between London and Chicago. Between you and the House? Between you and the RG? Being part of the RG while you're Master is one thing. Being part of it while you're the king of all goddamned vampires is something entirely different." Theoretically, an honorable GP meant a quiet RG. But just because I believed in Ethan didn't mean the rest of the RG wouldn't want to keep an eye on him. Absolute power, after all, corrupted absolutely.

His eyes narrowed dangerously. "You cannot shake me loose, Sentinel."

"I'm not trying to shake you loose," I assured him. I was just trying to be practical.

Hell, I thought. If we'd already gotten the GP bit out there, I figured I might as well tell him the rest.

"Have you ever talked to Gabriel about prophecies?"

He'd been staring at the floor, but he suddenly lifted his gaze to me. "Prophecies? No. Why?"

I imagined voicing the words would be like confessing you'd found a guy's secret engagement ring. It was a confession of intimacy I hadn't yet earned.

"He said in my future—there would be someone with green eyes. Like yours. But not yours. A child." I cleared my throat. "Our child. Because of some favor I'd do for Gabriel."

The color drained from his face, even more than you'd expect from a four-hundred-year-old vampire.

Part of me found it gratifying that he'd have the chance to enjoy the same kind of shock I'd been carrying around for months. Part of me found it terrifying, that he'd regret the possibility he'd be permanently attached without having made the choice on his own.

He stood up, paced to the other end of the room.

"Could you maybe say something?" I asked and, as my stomach roiled with nerves, braced myself for the worst. That was part of who I was, part of how I'd been raised. There was always a punishment to bear, a condition attached to the love I was granted.

But when he turned, his eyes were green fire. "He said . . . you'd carry a child?"

I swallowed, nodded.

"My child? *Our* child?"

Another nod, as I contemplated what I thought wasn't fear, but awe, in his eyes. He strode back to me, pulled me up from the couch, and kissed me brutally.

His lips were firm, his tongue insistent, sending my blood racing even as my body and mind slipped down and into the kiss.

He pulled back and cupped my face in his hands, rested his forehead against mine. "A child. A *child*." It was easy to hear the miracle in his voice, and even when he pulled back, my face still in his hands, there was doubt in his eyes. "Tell me precisely what he said."

And I did. Twice, and about the prediction that I'd be tested first. But none of it dulled the wonderment in Ethan's eyes. He put his hand on my stomach like I was already in the full blossom of pregnancy.

"A child. The first vampire child. Do you know what a miracle that would be? Or what a strength? What a boon to the North American Houses?"

It was my turn to take a step back, as a frisson of anger turned up my temper. "Or to the GP, if you were to lead it."

He apparently missed the tone in my voice, or he ignored it. "Frankly, yes."

"Is that why you're excited about this? Because it would give you a political advantage? Can we put aside strategy for the purposes of this conversation?"

"Sentinel," he said, and I caught a warning tone in his voice.

I marched over and stuck a finger into his chest. "Don't you dare call me 'Sentinel.' I am not your Novitiate right now, not when we're talking about this."

"We're talking about a unique event in vampire history."

"We're talking about bringing a child into the world." My head began to spin. Saying the words aloud actually made me light-headed, and I groped for the closest chair, then planted myself in it before my vision went completely black.

"Breathe, Sentinel," Ethan said, with a hint of amusement in his voice.

I was not amused. Not at all. Not by the realization that I'd be gestating the only vampire child in history. That we'd be the only vampire parents in history.

Ethan bent to one knee in front of me. "Are you having a panic attack about a child?"

"No," I said, head swimming. "That would be cowardly and ridiculous. I want to have kids. Kids are great. But I would be the first and only vampire mother. Every other vampire in the world would be armchair-mothering me."

He pushed the hair from my face. "Did Gabriel say this miraculous event was going to happen tomorrow?"

"Well, no. There's the testing first."

"Then I presume you have a bit of time to prepare," he flatly said. "As do I." He looked up at me, one knee on the ground, one knee propped up. The perfect position for that certain pre-matrimonial deed. A slow smile began to cross his face.

"Don't you dare do it," I warned him with a pointed finger. "Don't you dare fake propose to me again."

"Who says it would be fake?"

I rolled my eyes. "Like you just happen to have a ring in your jacket pocket."

Much to my surprise, and terror, he didn't answer with a joke.

His eyes sparkled, which made my stomach roll with nerves. Surely he didn't actually have a ring in his pocket. We hadn't known each other long enough. Hadn't been together long enough.

"Jesus, Ethan." I punched him on the arm. "*No.* You do *not* have a ring in your pocket."

"Poor, worried Sentinel." He pulled me to my feet, embraced me. "The weight of the world on her shoulders."

"That weight is entirely on my uterus," I corrected. "Or will be, after the test."

"Yes, you may have mentioned that," he dryly said. "And he gave you no indication of what, precisely, that meant?"

I shook my head, put my hands on his chest, looked up at him. "What if it's you? What if you decide to challenge the GP and you're injured? Or killed? Or what if you win and you end up in London?"

"Then either you're scheduled for an immaculate conception, or we'll still see each other occasionally." That sparkle was back in his eyes. He was really and truly enjoying this.

"You're not helping. Seriously—what are we going to do?"

"About the possible child? I can think of several things, Sentinel. Most of them require nudity. Several are illegal in the more conservative states."

I elbowed him in the ribs. "About the GP."

His expression sobered. "I don't know. I don't know." He ran his hands through his hair. "How solid is the support?"

"Solid," I said. "Enough to guarantee GP votes. Not enough to guarantee a win or a bloodless coup."

He nodded. "That's true of most things worth doing, I've found. They're rarely guaranteed."

Then he looked at me with a slanted gaze. "Sentinel, exactly how long have you been holding all of this in?"

"For too damn long. On both counts."

He chuckled and, with a hand at the back of my neck, pulled me forward again. "I love you, Caroline Evelyn Merit," he said, pressing his lips to mine.

He kissed me gently, his mouth needy and insistent, tongue tangling with mine and lips nipping gently as he pressed his body against mine. His hand slid along my rib cage, cupped a breast, and thumbed my nipple, inciting and arousing. My body sang with desire, blood humming with the need he was creating, the blinding want that began to demand action.

He moved forward, pushing me against the back of the couch, his erection solid between us. "You won't shake me," he said, his lips against my neck, trailing kisses over the spots he'd bitten me before, a promise of things to come.

"The carnival?" I managed to murmur, thinking of the work we needed to do.

"We are allowed to live," he said. "To take a moment for us." He took that moment, unzipped my muddy jacket and tossed it to the floor, then did the same with the shirt I'd worn beneath it. His gaze found my breasts. His hands followed, and all rational thought exited my premises. With impressive speed.

I hummed, equally revved and drowsy from the movement of his hands and the cant of his hips against mine. There was little doubt what he wanted, or what he'd take.

His mouth still on mine, the intensity near brutal, as if he might simply devour me, he stripped the fabric from my breasts and covered them with his hands, tongue tangling with mine, a hint of what he had in mind. He moved my hand to his erection, ground his body against me, releasing my mouth to heave out breaths, arching his back to watch my hand move against him.

He made a sound as much growl as word, then pulled off his shirt and the rest of my clothes, leaving me naked before him.

His eyes were silver, his fangs needle sharp, his body nearly quaking with anticipation and desire.

Without taking his eyes from me, he unzipped his jeans, dropped them to the floor. The silken boxers offered little guard against his impressive erection, and he dropped those, too, leaving nothing but his naked form before me, his eyes swirling with magic, his body obviously ready.

He took his arousal in hand, wetting his lips as he stared down at me. Eyes narrowed and glinting, his body taut and golden skinned and there for the taking, he stroked, toying with me, daring me not just to touch him, but to brave the intimacy.

Dare, I would.

I pushed him backward, steering him toward the low French chair in the corner of the room. He sat down, his hand still busy, his eyes on my breasts.

I straddled him, and his lips found my breasts, toying and nipping until my blood burned with need.

He offered no more preliminaries, which would have been wasted. I was ready, my body eager for him. With a grunt and a brutal curse, he plunged upward, filling me, bowing my body and leaving no boundaries, tangible or otherwise, between us. His hands found my waist and he held me against him, forcing me down with each plundering stroke.

He put his hand on my face, holding my chin, forcing my gaze to his as he pumped. I wasn't sure if he was committing my face to memory or ensuring that I committed his face to mine. The act was brutally intimate, allowing neither of us to hide behind closed eyes.

"Merit," he said, his voice ragged. "I need you. I love you."

"I love you."

Forever, he silently said. *Regardless.*

Forever, I said to him.

He lifted me, rose with me in his arms, and stalked toward the bedroom like a pirate with his treasure. He placed me on the bed like I was delicate, fine boned or porcelain, and immediately covered my body with his. With the force of a man long denied, he plunged between my thighs, his strokes as hard and fast as they'd been before.

Before, he'd sought to relieve his own ache, to find his own release. This time, his demands were all for me. Every muscle in his toned body worked for my pleasure, to send me over the edge, to send my mind and body and soul reeling. He found my mouth and plundered it as well, his tongue hot and welcoming, teeth at my lips as ferocious as his body.

And then he flipped my body over, and I moaned with pleasure, fistfuls of sheets in hand as he thrust without hesitation, filling me, devouring me. Ethan took without quarter, gave without pretension. He moved with a harsh rhythm, demanding, insistent, daring me to take my own pleasure, and doing his damnedest to send me there.

I screamed out his name, felt the building shudder from the release of magic, pushed any embarrassment that might have caused to the back of my mind.

I paused for breath, wet my parched lips, then rolled over and looked at him. His eyes quicksilver, his body hard, quivering with want.

I cupped my breasts, offered myself to him again.

His lips curled in animal pleasure and he pushed between my thighs again, my body offering no resistance.

"Teeth," he demanded when he was inside me. "I want your teeth on me."

Drunk with passion, I obeyed the command, sinking my teeth

into the skin at his neck, the rush of blood—hot and powerful—
sending my body into immediate overdrive. Ethan growled out
my name as my body shook with the force of the pleasure, and he
gripped the headboard with white knuckles, straining to hold
back as pleasure rocked him, too.

Now, I demanded, forcing him to drop his own barriers, to hold
back nothing from me, not the man, not the soldier, not the
vampire, not the Master.

"Merit," Ethan groaned out, pushing upward with a final
thrust, emptying himself with a cry that sounded equally an-
guished and fulfilled at the same time my body arched with
pulsing pleasure.

Minutes later, we stood together beneath the spray in the room-
sized shower in the carriage house bathroom, his body behind
mine.

It was such a simple thing for him to massage shampoo into
my hair, to slick soap across my back. And it was probably the
most intimate thing we'd ever done.

"Switch," I told him when my hair was squeaky clean. He
dunked his head beneath the spray, pushed his fingers through it
while water slipped down the arch of his back and across his very
bitable ass.

I felt my body stir to life again but ignored it. I'd had my fun
for the evening. We were getting clean, and then we were getting
back to work.

I squeezed shampoo into my hand, rolled it in my palms, and
reached up to run it through the golden locks of his hair. He
dropped his head back, braced his arms on the sides of the shower,
and let me care for him.

And when the shower was done, when we pulled on the thick

white robes that hung in the bathroom, I sent the message that, I hoped, satisfied my favor to Lakshmi:

I'VE TOLD HIM. THE DECISION IS IN HIS HANDS.

I hoped it would be enough and, when our phones began to simultaneously ring, thought she was so pissed by the response that she'd called me and Ethan both. But the communications weren't from Lakshmi.

I grabbed mine first, scanned the screen, found a message from Luc: NAVARRE 911. RAID. MAYOR'S THUGS. INJURIES.

"Merit," Ethan said, and I glanced back, found his phone in hand, as well.

"Domestic terrorism?"

He nodded and called Luc, got an answer on the first ring.

"I'm outside Navarre with Lindsey," Luc said, the wind howling behind him. It was Chicago, after all. "We're out of sight but keeping an eye on things. Jonah's got a few Grey House folks around, too."

Probably not just Grey House, I thought, but members of the RG keeping an eye on things, ready to step in if the need arose. I wasn't taking all their work.

"What happened?"

"We aren't entirely sure. We only got a little from Will." Will was Navarre House's very green guard captain. "Apparently the mayor's thugs showed up to take Morgan in to interview, and he refused. They surrounded the House, went inside. They're still in there. The vampires are all outside."

"Considering where we are, and the fact that we ran, I can't exactly blame Morgan for refusing the interview. How's Malik?"

"On full alert," Luc said. "We pulled all the temps onto duty, have them outside. We've also offered asylum to any Navarre vamps who need a place to go."

"Good," Ethan said. "Good. Keep an eye on things, and make contact with Jonah. Offer whatever assistance you can provide. And in the meantime, call the lawyers. We're coming home."

Fear bloomed cold in my chest. Ethan hung up the phone, tossed it on the bed.

"You want to go back so you can be Kowalcyzk's next victim?"

"Better me than them in my place," Ethan said. "I can't let any more vampires take my punishment. I've stood by too long."

"She's baiting you. Escalating to scare you back to Chicago."

Ethan began to get dressed, pulling a shirt over his head, his hair still damp and tucked behind his ears. "Quite possibly." He zipped up his jeans. "And I did as everyone asked. I waited her out. But no more."

I hadn't made Kowalcyzk's decisions, but I still felt like I'd failed. If Harold Monmonth hadn't made it so far into Cadogan House, if I'd taken him out first, if the GP had been more afraid of the House's Sentinel, Ethan might be out of danger.

"I'm sorry," I said. "I'm so sorry for this."

Ethan looked at me, danger in his eyes. "Are you under the impression this has something to do with you, Sentinel?"

"I was supposed to protect you, protect the House. And look where that's gotten us. The mayor thinks we're enemies of the state, and she's not above beating a Master vampire. I should have killed Harold Monmonth when I'd had the chance."

He strode to me, took my chin in hand, forced my gaze to his.

"That woman's personal failures are not your responsibility. Nor would the death of Harold Monmonth by your hand have changed anything. Except that it would be you heading to prison, rather than me."

"My father could have kept me out."

Ethan's eyes cooled. "Perhaps. Perhaps he would have. Perhaps he'd have bribed Kowalcyzk to keep you out. And if he had? And assuming she'd actually accept it, he'd consider the bribe a loan, and he'd exact payback, come hell or high water. You've owed a favor to a very powerful individual, Merit. You know how oppressive that feels."

He was right, but that only made it worse. There was no knight in shining armor who could rescue him, no trick of Chicago politics—and there were a lot of tricks in that particular bag—that would keep him out of prison. We'd already used the chit in our possession, the fact that Detective Jacobs didn't blindly follow the mayor's dictates, and the reprieve had been only temporary.

I nodded. "I know you're right. I just want things to be different."

He put his forehead against mine. "We cannot change the world, Merit. We do what we can in our small corner, and we act with honor. We rise to the occasion, and we do our best."

He kissed me. "That is what we will do for now. Our best. Get dressed. Message Catcher and make sure he knows what's going on. Message Jonah and let him know we're coming back. I'll talk to Gabriel. This is going to require some finessing."

I nodded. "I'll pack, get our stuff together."

He looked at me, considered. "Actually, I think I'd prefer you go with me. You are his kitten, after all."

I humphed. I was nobody's kitten.

We found him in the kitchen with Tanya and Connor, who sat in a high chair with bright orange goo smeared across his face. He gargled happily when we walked in.

"Vampires," Gabe said, offering Connor another spoonful of orange goo. "What brings you by?"

"Are you hungry?" Tanya asked, gesturing toward the kitchen. "The staff's asleep, but we could find you something."

"We're good, thank you. We actually wanted to talk to you about leaving. Things have come to a head in Chicago—and we believe the carnival is headed there anyway. We'd like to return, as well."

"A head?" Gabe asked.

"The mayor had roughed up Scott Grey. Tonight, they raided Navarre House."

"She's not playing around to get you back."

"No, she is not. And others have taken the brunt of this particular experiment long enough."

Gabriel chuckled. "Yeah, running isn't really your style." He smiled at Connor, who mawed the mouthful of goo with bright and happy eyes. "Kid loves carrots. Craziest thing. Tanya and I both hate them."

He used the rubber edge of the spoon to clean up Connor's mouth, then passed the utensil to Tanya and wiped his hands on a kitchen towel.

"The Pack is gone," he said. "You upheld your deal to investigate while they were here. And when the elves were attacked in daylight, they knew it wasn't your doing. The Brecks haven't left, obviously, but solving a mystery isn't going to change their minds about you."

"No," Ethan said. "I imagine it will not."

"And you still have the elves to sate," Gabriel said. "You owe them Niera, or we'll all have hell to pay."

I imagined Chicago overrun with androgynous bow-and-arrow-wielding elves. Considering the state of their technology, couldn't the military handle them easily?

Ethan looked at me. "I know what you're thinking, Sentinel. That they'd be no match for black helicopters. But locusts do not need weapons to constitute a plague. They only have to be themselves."

A potent metaphor.

"Safe travels and good luck," Gabriel said, standing and offering each of us a hand. "You do your species proud."

"Call me the next time you're in the city," Ethan said, then slid his gaze to me. "I believe we have some things to discuss."

Gabriel smiled wolfishly. "So we do, Sullivan. So we do."

I let Ethan drive back to Chicago. Considering his looming incarceration, it seemed only fair.

I also let him select the channel, and he found a station playing hard-driving Chicago- and Delta-style blues. The songs were grim, their lyrics telling tales of love and love lost, of heartache and adversity. He kept his hands on the steering wheel and his gaze on the road, but he seemed buoyed by the music, by the reminders that hard times were universal, but time always marched on. Usually in twelve bars.

Ethan pulled directly into the House garage and parked the car in the spot he'd given me—but solely for the protection of Moneypenny. Ethan keyed us into the House but paused before ascending the stairway to the first floor, clearly contemplating what he was about to do.

"Maybe we should take the back stairway," I suggested. "We can put down our bags, and you can have a few minutes to collect yourself."

He looked back at me, smiled. I caught a brief flicker of gratitude in his eyes, as if he'd had the same thought but wasn't sure how to broach the subject without appearing cowardly.

We walked to the other end of the basement and the service stairway, climbed to the third floor, and then walked down the hallway to our apartments. The House smelled faintly like cinnamon and flowers, and none of the faint animal tang that permeated the Brecks'.

We found the apartments just as we'd left them. Cool, dark, beautifully appointed. The furniture was European, the ceilings high, the walls painted in warm colors. A vase of hothouse peonies sat on a side table, filling the room with the smell of flowers and the spring that would soon be approaching.

Ethan put his bag on the bed and walked to one of the windows, then pulled back the lush silk and velvet drapes that covered it. I dropped my bag and followed him, let him gather me into his arms as he stared out into the night. Unlike at the Brecks' estate, there was light aplenty in Chicago. We were in the middle of a residential neighborhood, with the lights of downtown in the distance. Snow still covered the grounds that surrounded the House, giving it an ethereal glow.

Ethan sighed, embraced me tighter.

"She can't hold you forever. There's no evidence."

"She *shouldn't*," he agreed. "But that doesn't mean she won't try. Especially if she's squawking about domestic terrorism and ignoring the city's other problems in the meantime."

"As long as she doesn't mess up your pretty face."

Ethan leaned back and peered at me. "My pretty face?"

"I'm dating you because you make good arm candy."

He made a dubious sound, squeezed me one more time, and then let me go. "We have the city's best lawyers," he said. "We'll hope that will be enough."

I hoped he was right, but hope wasn't going to bring him home again.

CHAPTER FIFTEEN

PARTING IS SUCH (BITTER)SWEET SORROW

Ethan changed from his jeans and shirt into a button-down shirt, black pants, and a suit jacket with modern lines and a fashionably snug fit. He pulled back his hair, then glanced at me.

"You're incredibly handsome for a felon and terrorist," I told him, hoping to get a smile. I got an arched eyebrow, which was good enough.

We descended the stairs together, fingers linked. The foyer was full of vampires, and I had a sudden sympathy for the wives of discredited politicians who'd made similar appearances, trying to maintain a pleasant smile while lawyers and vampires mingled at the bottom of the stairs like sharks preparing to feed.

The magic in the air was frazzled and nervous, flitting about the room like stinging bolts of lightning. Ethan's vampires were nervous, and understandably so.

"Andrew," Ethan said, extending a hand to the man in the very well-cut black suit who stood beside Malik and Luc. He had dark skin, short hair, and a French-cut goatee that joined the moustache above his lip. His eyes were dark and set beneath a dark brow. His expression was serious.

"Ethan," he said, and they shook hands heartily. "You're ready?"

Ethan nodded, put a hand at the small of my back. "Andrew, my significant other. Merit. She stands Sentinel for the House. Merit, this is Andrew Bailey of Fitzhugh and Meyers."

Andrew and I shook hands as he gave me an efficient appraisal. "A pleasure to meet you, although I'm sorry it's under these circumstances."

"Same here," I said.

He glanced at Ethan. "Why don't we talk for a few minutes? I'd like to explain how this will proceed."

"My office," Ethan said, then glanced back at the other vampires in the foyer, who'd gathered a second time in just a few days to ensure his safety and see him off.

"I won't leave without saying good-bye," Ethan said with a smile, which made them chuckle in relief. "We'll discuss the details and be back shortly."

Ethan shined in times of crisis. He knew when others needed him to be strong, and he filled that role with aplomb.

I followed Ethan, Andrew, Luc, and Malik to the office, squeezing Lindsey's hand as we passed her on the way.

"Glad you got home safely," she whispered, and I nodded.

The décor in Ethan's office matched the rest of the House. European furniture, careful accessories, built-in shelves of beautiful wood, and vases of flowers. His desk filled the front right side of the room, a conversation area the left. There was a conference table across the back.

Luc headed directly for the bar tucked into the built-in bookshelves on the far side and poured amber liquor into a short glass. He downed it immediately.

"Rough week, Lucas?" Ethan asked with a smirk.

"Yes," Luc said, drinking another finger of Scotch before putting the bottle away again.

"Navarre's status?" Ethan asked.

"The vampires are back in the House, but they're basically under House arrest. Grey took in six vampires—folks who were away when the raid happened and didn't want to go back."

Ethan looked at Andrew. "They'll release Navarre House if I go in? And please take a seat, or have a drink if you'd like. The bar is open."

"I'm fine, and I'd rather stand if you don't mind."

Ethan nodded, and we all stayed standing. This didn't seem like the time to get comfy on the couch. I certainly wasn't in the mood to relax.

"To your question, yes: Kowalcyzk's representatives have advised the units will have no further interest in Navarre if you go in."

I guess that confirmed Kowalcyzk's extortion.

"We're communicating with Navarre's lawyers, so we can ensure she actually keeps her promise. They're relieved that you're here."

"Understandable," Ethan said. "And when I go in?"

"You'll be interviewed about the death of Harold Monmouth," Andrew said. "But not by the CPD. They still have a warrant for your arrest, but the mayor is using her domestic terrorism task force to conduct these interviews. That takes them outside the purview of the CPD, which is unfortunate, as I understand you have allies there."

"Some," Ethan said. "Although likely enemies as well."

Andrew nodded. "The firm has contacts in Homeland Security, and I've contacted them, requested they make contact with the mayor's office, provide some oversight. I don't know how far that will go, but I prefer to have the protections in place rather than leaving an ambitious politician with no evidence and less foresight in charge."

"Our opinions align," Ethan said.

"The interview will take place at the Daley Center," Andrew continued. That building held the city and county offices. "I won't be in the interview room with you—no right to a lawyer as a suspected domestic terrorist—but I've arranged for the room to have two-way glass. I'll be outside. They'll keep you there until they're satisfied they've gotten the answers they want, even if it means the sun's in the sky."

"They have a dark room?" Malik asked.

"They do. They understand you're essentially unconscious, not by choice, when the sun comes up. They've arranged for a room without windows so you can bed down. And the interview room doesn't have windows, either, just in case they decide to get creative around sunrise."

We were capable of being conscious during the day, but it wasn't a pleasant experience. I'd been kept forcibly awake once and preferred not to repeat it.

I started to speak, found my voice trembled, and started again. "And if they assault Ethan?"

Andrew leveled dark eyes at me. "Then we take the city for everything they're worth, and we have evidence to expose Chicago for the tragedy that's occurring here."

We looked at each other for a moment. He was giving me, I realized, time to consider him, to evaluate him, to trust that he would care for Ethan as I did. I wasn't eager to give Ethan up to anyone, but I was immediately glad he had this man in his corner.

I nodded, breaking the spell and offering my trust. "How long will they hold him?"

"Under current law, until they're satisfied he isn't a threat. There's an obvious self-defense argument here, especially considering Monmonth's violence against the humans before he even got inside the gate. And we have the security video of all the above, although Kowalcyzk's office has rejected it." The flat tone of his voice left little doubt about how much he respected that particular decision.

"We'll push to get him released after twenty-four hours," he said. "And the entire firm is on call, so if the House needs anything, wants an update, they can contact us. I think that's everything for now, unless you have other questions?"

Ethan blew out a breath, shook his head, stiffened his shoulders. "I believe that's it." He looked at Malik. "Lakshmi?"

"Still standing by," Malik said. "Considering her willingness to delay presenting the GP's demands, I'm beginning to wonder if they've actually made any."

I worked studiously to avoid looking at Ethan, afraid my expression would give something away. I hadn't actually told him that Lakshmi was the vampire to whom I'd owed a favor, or the one who supported him, but it probably wouldn't be difficult for him to ferret that out. Especially if he could read it in my face.

"I've no doubt she has her own agenda," Ethan said. "But there seems little doubt she's also here as an envoy. If they hadn't sent her, they'd have sent someone else." He frowned, scratched his temple absently, glanced at Malik.

"If she gets impatient, meet with her. Better to give her a meeting of some type than have her declaring war."

"Of course."

"Anything else?" Ethan asked, glancing around, but no one said anything. "In that case, Malik, you have the House," he said. As often happened, something quiet passed between them, a ceremonial transfer of power, or perhaps a quick, silent prayer for the safety of themselves, the House, and the Novitiates who dwelled within it.

Ethan buttoned his suit jacket, adjusted his pocket square. "I believe we're ready."

Ethan emerged from the room as he had three days ago, to nervous looks of vampires waiting outside his office. Last time he was running from the very thing he'd committed to do tonight.

He took my hand in his, and together we walked down the hallway, Cadogan's vampires sharing their support.

"We love you, Liege," they said as we passed.

"You'll get through this."

"The House will get through this, Liege."

They patted his back, touched his arm. Two offered embraces, then quickly stepped back into line. They'd lost him a few months ago and had miraculously gotten him back. They weren't eager to give him up again.

When we reached the foyer, the crowd thinned to give him access to the front door. He squeezed my hand, and I couldn't hold back the tears that filled my eyes.

"You're ready?" Andrew asked, opening the door to escort him out.

"A moment," Ethan said.

And there in the foyer, with half the House's vampires looking on, he put his hands on my face, and he kissed me. The kiss was soft but insistent. Ethan Sullivan did not hesitate to demonstrate to the House exactly how he felt about me.

The magic in the room transmuted, became less about fear than hope. Somehow, because they'd seen Ethan kiss me, they calmed. Perhaps because of the reminder that he had every incentive to come back healthy and whole.

After a moment he pulled back, his hand on my cheek, his thumb stroking my jaw.

Be careful, Sentinel, he silently said. The kiss had been for the House; the words were just for us. *Guard Malik, the House, yourself.*

You be careful, too.

I've every intention of it, he said with a smile. He pressed another kiss to my lips—softer, sweeter—before releasing me and walking toward the door.

There, with his hand on the frame, he turned back and faced his vampires.

"What happens outside these doors is not relevant," he said. "It is how you respond to them, how you move forward, that reveals your character.

"You are Cadogan vampires. You are honorable, brave . . . and more stylish than most." He got the chuckle he'd undoubtedly wanted. "To that end, and to remind you who you are, we have something to share."

Malik walked forward with a box in hand, one that I recognized from our apartments. He opened it, pulled out a silver pendant on a chain, which gleamed like quicksilver beneath the foyer chandelier. Our previous House medals, circular disks inscribed with our positions and the House's GP registration number, were outdated since we'd ditched the GP. These pendants, silver droplets with the House's name and our positions etched into the back, would be the new reminders of our vampiric family.

There were sparks of excitement in the hallway.

"We'd hoped our provision of these medals would be in a slightly more formal occasion," Ethan said. "But it is the symbol that matters, not the pomp and circumstance."

Ethan leaned forward, and Malik clasped the first pendant around Ethan's neck, which shined like a droplet of silver blood at the base of his throat. There was something nearly sensuous about the curve of it and the way it settled perfectly there.

Helen, the House's den mother, appeared at Ethan's side in her typical tweed suit, a basket of small crimson jewelry boxes on her arm. She began handing out the boxes to the Novitiates in the foyer.

"Be strong," Ethan said, glancing across the room and meeting my gaze with a short and decisive nod. "I'll be back soon enough." He stepped outside and pulled the door closed, disappearing from view.

Fear tightened my chest.

Lindsey stepped beside me, put an arm around my waist. Luc took point at my other side.

"He'll come through this," Luc assured me. "He's a soldier. He is trained and can endure much."

"I don't want him to endure anything. I don't want his life, his well-being, to be fodder for someone else's political career." *Keep him safe*, I thought, pleading to the universe and whatever gods inhabited it. *Please keep him safe.*

"We know you don't," Luc said, patting my back tenderly and a little awkwardly. "But he is Master of this House, and he does what he must to protect it. It's the life he chose to lead."

"Because he can handle it," Lindsey said.

"He definitely can. There are stories I could tell you."

"Your stories are always disgusting," Lindsey said, reaching around me to poke him in the shoulder. "And they usually involve bordellos. I don't think that's really going to help Merit."

It actually did help Merit, and I chuckled a little in spite of myself. "Bordellos? Really?"

"Chicago had its share once upon a time," Luc said with a shit-eating grin that earned an eye roll from Lindsey. "There was this one, Ruby Red's. Every single girl was a redhead, natural or otherwise."

I held up a hand. "I don't need the specifics. I just want Ethan to be okay."

Luc looked earnestly at me. "Merit, of all the vampires in the world, who else is stubborn and pretentious enough to stand up to a self-righteous prig like Diane Kowalcyzk?"

He had a point there.

Since there was no use in spending the hours of Ethan's incarceration staring at the door like loyal hounds waiting for him to return, we received our House medals, clasped them on, and walked back downstairs to the basement, where the Ops Room was located. Much like the Brecks', Cadogan's Ops Room was where Luc and his guards held court and monitored security. It was also, appropriately enough, where we planned operations against House enemies, and it was home to the whiteboard we used to work through our investigations.

Like the ops room in the Breck house, it was all about tech. A conference room where we could plan, a large screen on the back wall for videos, monitoring, considering evidence. Computer stations lined the walls, where vampires could keep an eye on the House's security cameras or do research.

I walked to the conference table, prepared to take a seat, but stopped, trying to make sense of what I saw on the tabletop.

A bag of kettle-style salt-and-vinegar potato chips had been slit down the middle and lay in the middle of the table. The chips had been pushed to one side, and the other bore a puddle of ketchup. I had, as I assumed did most people, a love-hate relationship with salt-and-vinegar potato chips. But the ketchup was new. And, frankly, a blasphemy.

"What's this?" I asked, swirling a finger in the air above what I assumed was intended to be a "snack."

"That," Luc said, "is a bit of a miracle. Brody introduced us. Say hi, Brody."

Brody, blond, thin, and as tall as a skyscraper, sat at one of the computer stations that lined the room. He was one of the Noviates Luc had temporarily hired to help with House security since we were down a couple of full-time guards. He'd been a member of Cadogan House for fourteen years, a Yale graduate and former Olympic swimmer whose athletic career had been ended by a drunk driver. He'd applied for House membership in the hopes of finding a new kind of team.

Brody turned and waved with a charming smile. " 'S'up."

"We're thinking about bringing him on board full-time," Luc said, gesturing toward the snacks. "He shared this little nugget in his interview."

"It's pretty good," Brody said. He stood up—I nearly winced at the possibility he'd knock his head on the ceiling—then walked over and dipped two chips in the ketchup, popped the concoction in his mouth. "You're missing out."

I was an adventurous eater, but pairing potato chips and ketchup was going to require a paradigm shift I wasn't currently prepared to entertain.

I sat down at the conference table, put my hands flat on the tabletop. "Let's talk about the carnival."

Luc and Lindsey joined me. Luc dipped a chip into the ketchup, ate it with a grin while I looked on. "Mmm," he said, earning an elbow from Lindsey.

"Maybe you'll want to skip the noshing and ask the rest of the gang to join us?"

"You're no fun, Sentinel," he said, but pushed the dials on the phone and conferenced them in.

"This is Luc in the Cadogan Ops Room," he said with faux gravity, "dialing you in to discuss the carnival investigation by direct order from the Sentinel of Cadogan House."

I glanced mildly at Lindsey. "Did you spike his blood with caffeine?"

"*Die Hard* marathon was on TV last night," she said. "He's been weaponized since then."

Jeff, Catcher, and Paige offered their hellos through the conference phone.

"No librarian?" Jeff asked, when he didn't say hello.

"He's back in the stacks looking through newspapers," Paige said with amusement. "And not to be disturbed."

"You're a better woman than I am, Paige," Luc said, earning curious glances from all of us. Thankfully, he moved on. "Let's talk carnival, folks."

As if optimism and preparation would be enough to make developments happen, I moved to the whiteboard, marker in hand.

"We've identified not so much a pattern, but a path," Paige said. "The carnival basically treks back and forth across the upper Midwest once a season. They go out as far as Montana, then come back as far east as Ohio. They ignore the seasons—hold carnivals year-round."

"I suppose the hunt for supernaturals doesn't have a season," Luc grimly said.

"That's what it looks like," Paige agreed.

"What about Chicago?" I asked.

"They hit it once every season, and it's always after Loring Park."

"Good," Luc said. "Good find. Where do they go?"

"We've identified four possible spots so far. Two of them don't exist anymore. They were parking lots, but they've been built over. They also camped near Prospect Park and the grounds of St.

Athenogenus—it's a Catholic school in West Town. Arthur's looking for any additional stops in Chicago. But since they aren't online, he has to go through the actual papers and microfiche."

I held up a hand. "I'm sorry—Arthur?"

There was silence for a moment as we all leaned eagerly toward the phone, awaiting confirmation that the librarian actually had a name.

"Oh, crap," Paige said, and I could imagine her wince through the phone. "I was not supposed to say that. He prefers to go by his title, for the respect, you know. He's 'the librarian.' But I've gotten so used to calling him Arthur."

"We'll stick with 'librarian,'" Luc said, smiling at the rest of us. We'd all heard the name; there'd be no unringing that particular bell.

I added Prospect Park and St. Athenogenus to the whiteboard. "We need to get folks out there right now to check those locations," I said.

"Don't need people," Jeff said. "Got satellites." The familiar *clack* of keys echoed through the receiver. He must have been back with his computers, although it occurred to me I wasn't exactly sure where that was. The Frankensteinian computer he'd used at my grandfather's house had been torched in the fire.

"Where are you working?" I asked.

"Home," Jeff said. "My own equipment. Which makes for a change. Differently tactile than the Brecks' stuff."

It occurred to me that I had no idea where Jeff actually lived. "And where is home?"

He cleared his throat. "I have a condo in the Loop."

"Oh?" I asked. "Where?"

"Um, it's in the Fortified Steel building."

He said it so quietly the words were garbled, and it took my brain a moment to unscramble them. Fortified Steel was one of Chicago's most historic buildings, built when the city was a commodities powerhouse. It sat beside the Chicago River, a tall, square column of symmetrical windows with a famous copper dome on top. It was one of the many prestigious addresses in the Loop.

I'd had no idea Jeff had those kinds of resources. And since he'd barely mumbled the address, he apparently didn't want to discuss it.

"All right," he said, changing the subject. "I'm pulling satellite images for those locations, popping them up to you."

The screen behind us turned on with a glow and hum, and two photographs filled it. One was a parking lot, the other a park field still covered in snow. Neither held a hint of a carnival.

"Crap," Luc said. "That's a strikeout."

"Could be they haven't set up yet," Brody said. "They only left Loring Park a few hours ago."

"Good thought from the new guy," Luc agreed, scanning the photos. "But the equipment has to go somewhere, even if they aren't open to the public yet. Jeff, can you zoom out? Maybe there are semis parked in a lot nearby."

Jeff zoomed out both images, giving me an odd sense of vertigo. And it didn't help substantively, either. Neither image showed anything more than we'd seen before.

"They could be at a different location, or they broke pattern," Luc said. "Maybe they realized they'd been tagged, decided to go somewhere else. Or maybe they're lying low for a few days until the heat's off."

"Or maybe they're lying low for a few days because they're planning the next kidnapping," I said.

"We'll keep looking," Paige said. "And let you know if we find anything."

"That brings us to the next point," Luc said. "Catcher, have you had a chance to talk to sups?"

Silence.

"Catcher?"

"Sorry. Sorry. I'm here. I was being bugged by a sorceress."

"I wasn't bugging anyone," Mallory, the aforementioned sorceress, said in the background. "I just want you to keep your damn feet off the coffee table. And I don't care that I don't sleep here right now. That's not an excuse."

"Ah, supernatural love," Luc said, giving Lindsey a baleful look, which made her roll her eyes. But she still smiled a little.

"Sups," Catcher said. "Talked to Grey House, asked Jonah to get a message to Navarre, considering. Called the nymphs, River trolls. They haven't been invited by anyone to a carnival. They didn't even know one would be going on, especially in February. They're also on the lookout for unusual magic. They know to call us if anything happens."

"What about Regan?" I asked. "Jeff, any luck there?"

"I haven't found anything else," Jeff said. "Not even a couple of levels down. She's completely off the radar, or at least under her current name."

"I might have something," Catcher said. "Baumgartner recognized the photograph. He didn't have a name, but he thought she looked like a woman who'd come to the Order four or five years ago looking for membership. Said she had magic, wanted to join up. He did some initial testing, determined she wasn't a sorceress, and rejected her."

Luc whistled. "And that, my friends, is what we call a motive. She gets rejected by the Order, decides to start targeting sups."

"Not all of the people rejected by the Order become serial kidnappers," Catcher dryly said.

"You weren't rejected," Luc said. "You got kicked out for bad behavior."

"So she's definitely not a sorceress." I'd half hoped the sulfuric smell of her had been a coincidence, or malfunctioning HVAC at the grocery story. I guess that was not to be. "That means we have to consider the possibility she's connected to the Messengers." And given her skills, the presumptive ringleader of these particular shenanigans.

"That's impossible," Mallory said.

"Only in the traditional sense," Luc said. "Maybe she's not one of them per se. But she could be a student, a pretender—a kid with magic who wants us to believe that magic is ancient and prestigious. Hell, as little as we know, she could be Seth Tate's kid, for Christ's sake."

Catcher snorted. "In this day and age, any kid of Seth Tate's would have announced it to the world already."

"And he'd have told us," I said. "Maybe not pre-*Maleficium*, but after it, certainly. If he'd known he had a kid—or a fourth cousin—who could cause trouble for us, he'd have told us."

Or so I hoped.

Still, I added the possibilities to the whiteboard. "We have to find her," I said. "Or both of them—Regan and the carnival—before she targets someone else." And we needed to do that while finding a way to get Ethan out of lockdown before Mayor Kowalcyzk decided to make an example of him.

Luc checked his watch. "We'll need to do that," he agreed. "But we're nearing sunrise, so it's not going to happen tonight. Let's pack it in for now, touch base at sunset. Paige, let us know if the librarian finds anything else."

"Roger that," she said, and there was a *click* as she dropped from the call.

We said good-bye to the others, and they dropped off the call as well. Luc's personal phone rang almost immediately.

"Luc," he said, lifting it to his ear.

He nodded, listened, spoke quietly with the caller, and after a moment, hung up the phone and looked at us. "That was Will, the guard captain at Navarre. The terrorism squad is packing up at Navarre House."

That meant Ethan was officially in interview, or in custody, depending on how the mayor's office was spinning it.

"That's good news," Lindsey earnestly said, catching my gaze. "It means she's sticking to her word. That's exactly what we want."

I nodded, but the clenched ball of worry in my stomach didn't unknot much.

"Why don't you take some personal time tomorrow at sunset?" Luc said. "You haven't had a chance to see your grandfather yet. Take an hour—go say hello."

It was a good idea. I hadn't had a chance to visit the hospital since he'd been admitted. We'd gotten home too late tonight, but if I went after sunset tomorrow, I could probably catch him during visiting hours. Still, we were in the middle of an investigation.

"Is that a good idea right now? Considering?"

"You need a break," he said. "And you need to visit your grandfather. Run the carnival bit past him. See if he has any ideas."

I nodded.

"How about a movie tonight?" Lindsey asked. "We don't have time for a full run before sunup, but we could fit in half a show, maybe some snacks?"

I thought about the offer. While I wasn't thrilled about the idea of going back to the apartments alone and spending the entire evening obsessing about Ethan, I also wasn't up for another night of entertainment. A bottle of Blood4You, roaring fire, and good book seemed like a much better option.

"Thanks, but I think I'll pass. I've been surrounded by sups for a few days now. I need a little quiet time."

Luc chuckled, fingered the new pendant around his neck. "Sentinel, you live in a literal house of vampires. You're going to be surrounded by sups regardless."

For better or worse.

I added what we'd discovered to the whiteboard, said my good nights, and headed upstairs to the first floor. I heard sounds coming from the front parlor and walked toward it.

A dozen Cadogan vampires stood around the television mounted above the fireplace. The TV was tuned to a news station and the coverage of Ethan's arrival at the Daley Center.

Ethan climbed out of a town car and then walked, Andrew at his side and four officers surrounding him, into what looked like an underground entrance. Reporters who'd staked out the door yelled questions and accusations, wondering why Ethan had killed Harold Monmonth, where he'd been for the last three days, and why he'd finally come back to Chicago. He kept his eyes clear and stared straight ahead, ignoring the questions. But the line between his eyes tightened with each new volley, and it was clear he had plenty of things to say to them.

After a moment, Andrew directed him to stop and faced the camera. With his broad shoulders and intense expression, Andrew looked more like a soldier or bodyguard than a lawyer. But either way, and whatever the reason, he commanded their attention. They quieted immediately.

"Ethan Sullivan is innocent of the various accusations—political, criminal, and otherwise—that have been leveled against him. He is being targeted because he is a vampire, and the mayor's office, respectfully, is targeting him because she's looking for a scapegoat. The citizens of Chicago know better, and I'll be glad when we can put this entire matter to rest."

The tension in my chest eased just a little. Thinking I'd seen as much as I needed to, I turned to walk away, but the sudden gasps behind me had my heart pounding, and I turned back to look.

"Altercation at Daley Center," read the screen now, and the footage showed Ethan being escorted into a small room, a table and chairs visible through the door. But there was a bright bruise blooming across his left cheekbone.

Sometime between his arrival at the building and his reaching the interview room, he'd been assaulted. Punishment, maybe, for his refusal to come in earlier, to acquiesce to Kowalcyzk's request that he sacrifice himself for her political agenda. And if they were knocking him around before he even got into the room, what more did they have planned?

Fear bubbled and spilled over, and I strode from the room before the tears tracked down my face. I made it as far as the stairway, stopping to knuckle away the tears, hoping no one had seen my quick exit or the reason for it. The last thing they needed was to see their Sentinel bawling in fear. There was a place for tears; it wasn't here, when the House needed its officers to be strong.

An arm wrapped around my shoulder. I looked up, surprised, into Malik's eyes.

"Are you all right?"

He was so quiet, so reserved, I wouldn't have expected him to offer physical solace, which made the fact that he had offered it even more meaningful. I had, over the last year, gathered up an assemblage of weird and wonderful friendships. They all had their ups and down, and some of the downs were pretty miserable. But sometimes, times like this, I could just be grateful.

"I'm fine," I said with a half smile, still swiping at tears. "Long night."

"No argument there," he said, but his eyes continued to track my face, as if he wasn't quite sure I was telling him the entire truth.

"How are you?" I asked. "This can't be easy, this back-and-forth Masterdom."

He chuckled, his green eyes crinkled with amusement. "Musical chairs aren't my preferred method of serving this House."

"At least you get to keep your rooms," I said. "And don't have to move in and out of the Master's suite."

"That is some consolation," he agreed. "Although you have better closets."

I hadn't actually seen Malik's closet, but as Ethan's was the size of a room in itself and outfitted with lush wood and thick carpet, he was probably right.

"Ethan would be lost without his suits."

"He would," Malik agreed, and patted my arm. "He would be lost without many things, including you. Go upstairs. Get a good day's sleep. This will be over tomorrow, and you and Ethan can enjoy a reunion."

I thanked him, walked upstairs, and hoped he was right. But I feared in my heart of hearts that we were all underestimating the depth of Kowalcyzk's ignorance.

I kept to the plan I'd laid out for Lindsey, snagging a bottle of blood from the tray Margot had left in the apartments and both of the cellophane-wrapped Mallocakes, my favorite processed snack.

Chocolate and blood didn't sound appealing, but it might have been the pinnacle of vampire comfort foods.

I changed into pajamas, nabbing one of Ethan's button-up shirts, the trace of his cologne lingering even after a wash, and buttoning it on. I turned on the fire in the onyx fireplace with the flick of a switch, and sat down on the rug in front of it, the bottle in hand.

My phone beeped, and I snatched it up greedily, hoping for good news about Ethan. It was Lakshmi, with another favor to ask.

KEEP HIM SAFE, she messaged.

I wanted to call her back, rail at her for standing by while Ethan bore the blame for acts by her colleagues. But vitriol would do no better now than tears. I put the phone aside, but the sting of her words stayed with me.

Wasn't I trying to keep him safe?

I stared at the fire until the sun rose, watching the forks and tendrils rise and shift and move, letting it blank my mind and send me to sleep.

CHAPTER SIXTEEN

THIS MAGIC MOMENT

The sun set again, and I awoke on the floor beside the fire, curled into a ball with the crook of my elbow as a pillow, the fireplace still crackling, the empty bottle beside me. I sat up and stretched, working out the kinks of spending ten hours asleep on a hardwood floor, then flipped off the fire and put the bottle on the tray the kitchen staff would eventually collect.

"Another night in paradise," I mused, and turned to the shower.

As part of the miracle that was Cadogan House, I found my leathers clean and shiny and ready to wear again. I dressed for war, belting on my katana, my hair in a ponytail, and the new Cadogan pendant around my neck. It felt differently than the last one had, the medal colder and thicker. But no less meaningful, and I was glad the tradition was under way again.

Now that I was back in Chicago and back on the clock, I grabbed my phone, texted Jonah. ALL WELL AT GREY HOUSE?

SO FAR, SO GOOD. MORGAN ON A TEAR ABOUT NAVARRE RAID.

That thought actually made me smile. Although Navarre was

the origin of most of our troubles, the House rarely had to deal with the unpleasant consequences. Maybe now Morgan would appreciate the spot Celina had put us in all those months ago by announcing our existence to the world.

WORD ON ETHAN? he asked.

NOT YET. I'M ABOUT TO HEAD DOWNSTAIRS. ALSO GOING TO VISIT GRANDFATHER. MAY NEED YOU ON MISSING SUP CASE.

ROGER, Jonah responded. KEEP ME POSTED.

Taking Luc's advice, I called the hospital, confirmed visiting hours, and prepared to head out. But I had two quick stops to make before I left.

The first was to the Ops Room. It seemed only fair that I'd check in with Luc before leaving campus, even though he'd given me permission the night before.

I made my way downstairs, and Helen stopped me on the first floor, a scrap of paper in hand. She extended it with perfectly manicured fingers, a silver charm bracelet dangling from her wrist.

"What's this?" I wondered.

"Your garage code," she said, smiling mirthlessly. I guessed she wasn't thrilled that a peon so far down the chain of command had won access to the garage. Helen was adept and capable at her job. But she was the growly sort, and she had very specific opinions about who deserved the spoils of Cadogan House... and who did not.

But I wasn't going to look a gift Helen in the mouth. I glanced at the code, memorized the numbers, and tucked the paper into my pocket.

"Thank you," I said. "I appreciate it."

She grumbled something about "waiting list" but headed down the hallway at a brisk clip.

I walked downstairs to the Ops Room, found Lindsey, Luc,

and Kelley, another permanent House guard, at the conference table. Juliet, the last of the permanent guard crew, was gone, still taking it easy after her run-in with McKetrick.

The television wasn't on, but the mood was as grim as it had been in the parlor last night.

My stomach flipped. "What's wrong?"

"Oh, nothing in particular, Sentinel. Just the usual bullshit. City's on our case. Shifters are on our case. GP's on our case. I'm knee-deep in complaints and I'm running out of fucks to give."

I glanced at Lindsey.

"That's not from *Die Hard*," she said. "He's just improvising."

I smiled, took a seat at the table.

"Why are you so chipper this morning?" Luc asked.

"Oh, I'm not. But I had my first day of sleep in three days without sups pounding on my door or alarms ringing me awake. It made a nice change. Did you see Ethan's bruise last night?"

"On his cheek? Yeah," Luc said. "Wasn't thrilled with it, but he's in Andrew's hands now." He smiled. "I've seen him in action. And trust me—*Law & Order* has nothing on this guy. I will guarantee you he's making a note of every time Kowalcyzk's people so much as look at Ethan the wrong way. And he'll nail them for it."

"He might have a long list by the time Ethan gets released. Did he give you an update on when that might be?"

"He did not. Said they put him in the dark room during the day, but they kept him up after sunrise and roused him before the sun set again. Rendition tactics—they're trying to make him slip up, change his story, give them some doubt to pin an arraignment on."

Grim as that sounded, it made me smile. As Luc had noted yesterday, there were few as stubborn as Ethan Sullivan. And while he did his unenviable job as Master, I had to do mine.

"Do we have anything on the carnival?"

"Nothing else so far." He took in my zipped-up jacket, my belted sword. "You going to the hospital?"

"I am. I have my phone if you need me. And I checked in with Jonah—he said things are calm at Grey and Navarre, all things considered."

Luc nodded. "So we have a momentary lull, at least until we come up with something."

I took that as a dismissal. "Do me a solid," I said, heading for the door. "Find me a carnival."

The amount of grinning I did at the basement door as I typed in my code, heard the hearty *click* of the tumblers shifting, was probably inappropriate. But I was from Chicago, and I had not only an off-street parking spot, but a heated, indoor parking spot. It was a luxury few of us even bothered to imagine. Like Money-penny, it was another silver lining from the rioters' beating of my poor, departed Volvo.

Moneypenny sat, sleek and silver, in her appointed spot. The "Visitor" designation had been painted over, and "Sentinel" sten-ciled over the white rectangle in vibrant blue.

"This does not suck," I murmured, and pulled Moneypenny into the cold Chicago night.

The Ops Room had been my first stop en route to visit my grandfather, but I had one more errand before heading south. My grandfather had a sweet tooth and a favorite cookie, and I could only imagine that the food he was served by the hospital didn't offer much in the way of sugary treats. I grabbed a bag of Oreos from a quick shop along the way and drove to the south side hos-pital where he was being treated.

I was half surprised my father hadn't yet transferred my grand-father to their home in Oak Park, the neighborhood where my parents lived. That's where he'd recuperate when he was discharged. But they hadn't moved him yet, so I pulled into a visitor's spot in the garage and followed the stream of families with balloons and flowers into the hospital.

The hospital smelled the same as it had when he'd been admitted a few days ago: like disinfectants and flowers.

My grandfather was muttering when I stepped into the doorway, a remote control in his hand, his eyes on the small television that hung on the opposite wall. He looked like I expected many grandfathers did—caterpillar eyebrows and a halo of hair that didn't quite cover the bald spot on the top of his head. He usually preferred plaid shirts and thickly soled shoes, but tonight he wore a blue hospital gown.

At the sound of my knock, he glanced up and smiled, then held out his arms. "Come on over, rover."

I did, offering him a gentle hug. "I'm glad to see you're up and awake."

"Awake, anyways," he said. "Up's going to take a little longer. My gams aren't going to be the same."

I nodded. "Probably no stilettos for you for a while. But you'll manage."

"I will," he agreed.

I sat down on the edge of the bed, atop white sheets, and put a hand over his. His skin was thin and bruised, although I wasn't sure if that was from his injuries or the tubes and wires that still ran from his body to machines at his sides.

"I brought a present." I presented the bag of Oreos and loved the sudden, wide pitch of his eyes.

He slid open the drawer on the nightstand beside the bed. "Hide 'em," he said at the sound of footsteps in the hallway. "Nurse'll be in here to check in, in a few minutes."

Sure enough, a nurse peeked in—ponytailed, fresh faced, and wearing blue scrubs.

"You all right, Chuck?"

"Good, Stella. Thanks," he said, with a little wave.

She smiled and wandered off, and my grandfather sighed.

"She seems nice," I offered.

"They're all nice. But they're nice constantly. Every hour when they check in, every time they open the door in the middle of the night and let the light in. And I'm a cop. Former, maybe, but still a cop. I don't need to be checked on like a child." His tone was growly and irritable, and it made me feel infinitely better. Growly and irritable seemed like a stop on the journey toward healing.

"I'm looking forward to a night's sleep in a dark and quiet room."

Noise erupted from the television set, drawing our gazes.

"News," he said. "I was hoping to catch the Blackhawks score."

I didn't know much about hockey; the only time I'd been to a game was when Grandpa had gotten tickets from the family of a grateful citizen. He'd been a fan ever since.

"Did they win?" I asked.

He used the bedside remote to turn the volume down. "Not even close. Three to one."

That seemed close enough for me, but hockey was its own weird world, and I didn't feel qualified to point out the difference.

"How are you feeling?"

"Today, a little achy." He shifted uncomfortably.

"Do you need something for the pain? I could call Stella."

He gestured to the electronic drip at the side of the bed. "Got it," he said. "But I don't like to use it. Dulls the mind."

And a cop, former or otherwise, would not want a dulled mind.

"How long are you going to have to stay here?"

"Doc thinks forty-eight more hours. They want to make sure everything's in the right place—and going to stay there—before they send me to Oak Park. Your father has hired a slew of nurses and doctors."

"You sound resigned," I said with a smile.

"They're being very generous," my grandfather said, very diplomatically. He might not have agreed with the decisions my father had made, but he wasn't much for criticizing.

"Have you thought about where you'll live when you're up and running again? Will you stay on the south side?"

Chicago wasn't a city without problems or violence, and the south side bore much of the weight of those issues. As a cop, Grandpa decided the south side needed him more than the north, so that's where he and my grandmother had made their home. That was undoubtedly part of the reason for my father's lifetime quest for money and power.

"I haven't quite gotten that far," he said. "Although I'm thinking I'm done with stairs for a bit." He put a hand on mine. "Catcher told me about Ethan. How are you?"

"I've been better."

He nodded. "You've been dealing with a lot lately. The riots, now the mayor. I didn't think she'd actually resort to violence. If I didn't think *another* demonically possessed mayor was seriously unlikely, I'd say she was under the control of darker forces."

"Yeah. It was odd enough when the first mayor split into two. I'm not sure she's got enough brains to make two."

"I wish there was something I could do. A call I can make. But she's pulled this one away from the police department, probably because she knows they have sense and pay attention to rules of evidence. But these terrorism folks?" He shook his head. "They have to justify their existence. Vampires are a new threat? Great. They now have a basis to request a budget for next year."

"Unfortunately, we don't have a lot of pieces to play in this one. We can't use magic against her. She'll just call us enemies of the state, and we'll never see the light of day again. Figuratively," I added. We already were biologically barred.

"You could always ask your father," my grandfather carefully said, which earned him a look.

I certainly could ask my father to put in a word, to use his significant capital to convince Kowalcyzk to back off. I was sure it wouldn't be the first time a bribe was offered or taken in Chicago. But I didn't trust my father's motives, and I certainly wouldn't want to owe him a debt.

But my father was still my grandfather's son, and I actually respected him. So I answered politely. "I don't think that's the best option."

"Well, I'll tell you one thing," my grandfather said. "I don't really care to be in here when this city is falling down around us."

Unfortunately, being out there wasn't proving all that helpful, either.

"Is it time for you to think about slowing down?" I asked the question out of obligation, even though I knew the answer—and predicted the flatness of his expression.

"Caroline Merit. You know better than that. I'm a cop. Always was, always will be." He looked down at his blanket-covered legs. "And it's going to take more than a bump to make daytime television look good by comparison. Especially when you're out there. You're still mine to protect, baby girl."

I leaned over, pressed a kiss to his forehead. "I love you, Grandpa."

"I love you, too, Merit. And now that you've cleared your conscience," he said with a grin, "what did you really want to talk about?"

I smiled. He read me better than nearly anyone. "Aline and Niera," I said, and he nodded.

The librarian and Paige had given him the details. So when he nodded, I gave him an update, telling him about Regan's involvement, the other disappearances, and the magical attacks.

"We haven't been able to find her or the carnival."

"You think there's a link between her and Dominic Tate?"

"I don't know. It doesn't really fit what we know about the Messengers and the breakup of the *Maleficium*."

He looked at me for a moment. "You're thinking about finding Tate."

I blushed. I hadn't actually considered it as a tactic—why invite trouble?—but I was running out of options. Chicago's vampires were potential targets, and the longer it took to find Niera, the higher the risk the elves would consider the truce breached. And that was unacceptable to me.

"It's an idea," I admitted. "He'd know better than anyone what she is—and how to stop her. What do you think?"

He whistled. "His history was, as you know, inconsistent. I know he's fashioned himself as a different man after the *Maleficium*. Do you believe him?"

"Yeah," I said. "I know Seth Tate, and I knew Dominic Tate. Seth was a different man after the split. Not just personality-wise. He's still a politician," I said with a smile. "But magically. Psychically, I guess. You could tell he was different. And he's the key to this. I'm just not sure how."

"Sometimes you have to follow your gut." He smiled a little.

"And in this particular case, I'd check with chain of command. Follow your gut, but cover your ass."

Advice didn't get any better than that.

I didn't want to end on such a dark note, so I turned the conversation to something lighter and we chatted a little while longer, sneaking Oreos from the drawer after ensuring the coast—and hallway—was clear. We apparently hadn't been in Loring Park long enough to miss any important family events. My brother's wife was still very pregnant, and my father still had money coming out of his ears.

Supernatural events were slightly more interesting. Four of the city's petite and busty River nymphs had visited my grandfather, bringing jars of "healing" River water that were confiscated and emptied by my grandfather's nurses—and bringing a fight over which segment of the River had the most beautiful architecture. Apparently there wasn't much to do during the frozen winter months.

When my grandfather yawned and barely managed to hide it, I decided it was time to go. I gave him a kiss, left the rest of the embargoed cookies in the drawer, and promised to keep him updated if anything interesting happened.

Traffic was an ugly snarl, and Moneypenny and I practically crawled our way north again. The House was quiet when I walked in, the energy tense and subdued. I'd have expected to get a call if Ethan had been released, but the tension in the air was sign enough.

I found Luc, Lindsey, Brody, and Kelley around the table in the Ops Room. Kelley twirled a lock of her straight black hair while staring at the overhead screen, which was once again tuned to an all-news channel.

What would it have been like, I wondered, to have been a

vampire in an age before the Internet, twenty-four-hour news channels, social media, text messages? Before technology provided a constant assault of drama, bad news, and Things You Should Be Worrying About.

Tonight, the news showed Diane Kowalcyzk posing in front of a poster propped on an easel. Shots of Ethan, Scott, Morgan, the Masters of the three Chicago Houses, were pictured beneath a headline that read ENEMIES OF CHICAGO?

The question mark, probably the brainchild of some lawyer who thought it would protect the city against a libel charge, was laughable. Who'd see the photographs, read the headline, and think she was posing a question?

"You have got to be fucking *kidding* me!" Luc said, pushing back from the table with enough force to rattle the entire twelve feet of it.

"She's made a Wanted poster," Lindsey said, eyes wide as she stared at the screen. "People will want his blood. All of their blood."

"Kelley, get in touch with Jonah and Will," Luc ordered, eyes still on the screen. "Make sure they're seeing this." Kelley nodded, plucked up her phone from the table, started dialing.

"We have to do something," Lindsey said, looking back at Luc with obvious fear in her eyes. "We can't just let this go on."

"We are doing something," Luc said, but he didn't sound convinced. "We've hired lawyers, and we've connected with reporters. That's what we can do right now."

"The lawyers and reporters aren't helping," I said. "We can't leave him in there. He's an enemy of the state and he's surrounded by law enforcement officers and felons."

"And what, exactly, would you like me to do, Merit? Beg the mayor to release your boyfriend because you're afraid for him?"

I flinched from the heat of his words; Luc wiped a hand over his face. "I'm sorry. That was uncalled for. I apologize."

"It's okay," I said. "Unfortunately, you're right. They think he's an enemy of the state; there's no begging we can do that will release him."

"What about your father?" Brody asked me, drawing groans from the rest of the room.

"Not an option," Luc said. "So don't even consider it." He blew out a breath, ran his hands through his hair. "We have to let Andrew do his job." But he sounded just as frustrated as I felt.

I put my head on my folded arms. "Why does my father have to be such an asshole?"

"Because we all have our burdens to bear. And if you're even thinking about making that call," Luc said, pointing a warning finger at me, "put that thought out of your head immediately. Ethan would lose his shit if he thought you asked your father for help."

"I know," I said, lifting my head. "And I know I can't run in there with a sword or two. But I sure would like to." I thought of what my grandfather had said about magic, about the darker forces that had affected the last mayor. "Maybe she's got her own Dominic. A little evil twin who lives in her helmet hair and makes her do evil, dirty things."

Luc laughed. "That is both perfectly absurd and perfectly appropriate."

Speaking of evil twins, it was time to offer up the plan I'd been considering.

"I'd like to find Seth Tate."

He just stared at me. "Sentinel, have you lost your damn mind?"

"No," I said, and since the tone didn't sound convincing, I said it again with feeling. "*No.* I have not lost my mind, damned or otherwise. Look—Regan's either a Messenger or she's got a connection to Dominic Tate. Either way, Seth's the only person we can ask about it. He can help us identify her—and tell us how to take her down.

"And, while I'm there, maybe I can talk to him about the mayor. Maybe he has an idea about how we can bring her around."

That, he looked interested in.

"I don't think he's dangerous," I offered. "Before he left, he told us he was looking for contrition. He sounded earnest and Ethan trusted him."

"Respectfully, Sentinel, Ethan isn't here, and I'm not one to invite trouble while he's gone. Tate's demonic half was stripped from his body, so sure, he shouldn't be evil. But he's still powerful. And we can't exactly account for that."

"Actually, I think she'd be okay," Lindsey said. "Seth Tate has the hots for her."

"He does not," I protested, but I could feel the burn skimming up my cheeks. We had a history, yes, but it wasn't romantic. At least not from my end.

"All right," I said. "So you all think this is a bad idea."

"It's not the *worst* idea I've ever heard. It's at least one or two up from the very bottom." He scratched his head. "But I'm not thrilled about sending you to play with Seth Tate while Ethan's incarcerated."

"Ethan will live."

"Easy for you to say. If you're hurt, he'll come after me."

"Seth is our best option to figure out what Regan is—*how* she exists."

Luc's jaw worked. "Even if I said yes, you still have to find him."

"Actually," I said, "I have an idea about that."

"He may not want to come back."

"He probably won't want to. It's my job to convince him."

Luc's phone began to ring, and he glanced at the screen. "It's Jonah. Grey's seen the ad." He lifted it to his ear, glanced at me. "Find him first. Then we'll talk."

I called Mallory first to confirm her location. She was still in Wicker Park, didn't plan to head back to Little Red until Gabe returned to the city.

I didn't show up empty-handed. Just as Mallory had brought me raspberry donuts, I showed up with a pint of Ben & Jerry's, which had been legal tender for much of our relationship.

Catcher opened the door, looked down at the goods and then up at me again. "I suppose you're friends again?"

Normally, he'd have accompanied that statement with a solid dose of sarcasm. But this time, there was a kind of softness. Hope, instead of derision.

"I think we're trying," I said. "She said she was here?"

"In the basement."

That made me cringe a bit, and then immediately regret it. The basement was where she'd "studied" for her magical exams—and where she'd prepared the magic that led her to Nebraska.

Once again, Catcher's smile was understanding. Maybe he was evolving, too. "Checks and balances," he said. "I've warded the basement, and alarms go off if the magic she works reaches a certain threshold. I've also put a baby monitor down there."

He must have seen the shock on my face, as he snorted gleefully. "She's not pregnant. It helps me keep track when I'm busy."

I peeked into the living room, saw a half-empty bowl of cashews and a bottle of 312 on the coffee table, and a Lifetime movie on the television.

"Busy?" I asked.

He smiled lazily. "We all have our hobbies. Now, come in or not. You're letting in the cold air."

Catcher Bell. Twenty-nine going on sixty-five.

I walked inside, and Catcher closed the door behind me and immediately went for the couch. I moved through the living room and dining room to the kitchen, where the basement door was located. I stuck the ice cream in the freezer and headed downstairs.

And then I goggled.

What before could have been the setting for a horror movie—all dark corners, cobwebs, jars of questionable substances, and magical miscellany—had become Martha Stewart's own bright and shiny craft studio. The walls has been painted cheery white, and the floor had been covered in long planks of honey-gold wood. The ceiling had been finished, and recessed lighting installed. The space was now lined with white cabinets and bookshelves, and the bookshelves were lined with matching glass jars with hanging labels. Foxglove, wolfsbane, St.-John's-wort, and hundreds of others.

In the middle of the room there was a giant white island, the countertop balanced on shelves covered in old-fashioned books. Mal, wearing a T-shirt and long, feathered earrings, her hair in a messy blue bun, sat on a stool behind the island, crushing something green and fragrant with a marble mortar and pestle that rested beside the baby monitor Catcher mentioned. Mal smiled and whistled as she worked, earbuds in her ears, occasionally glancing at a sleek tablet while she mixed ingredients. It was very suburban, which wasn't a term I associated with Mallory. And yet, somehow, it seemed to suit her perfectly.

Finally realizing she wasn't alone, she glanced up and pulled the earbuds from her ears, dusting her hands on a gingham apron tied around her waist.

"Hey," she said with a smile. "Welcome to the new abode."

I twirled a hand in the air to indicate the space. "What the hell happened down here?"

"Catcher happened," she said conspiratorially. "He didn't feel like he'd done a very good job mentoring me during, you know, the unfortunate period. So he did this. Isn't it phenomenal?"

"It's astounding. It looks like a completely different place."

"I think that was the point. Clean beginnings and all that. But that's not even the best part." She rose and leaned over the table, picking up a clipboard that had been decoupaged with magazine clippings. A piece of paper was stuck beneath the aluminum clip. "Good deeds," read the title, with bullet points for a list not yet filled in.

"Good deeds?" I asked.

"It's my to-do list," she said. "It was Tanya's suggestion, actually. That I learn to use magic—this time for real—with a charitable aim."

I had a momentary stab of jealousy that Mallory and Tanya had become friends. Not that I begrudged her friendships, or the empathy that undoubtedly came with her exposing herself to other supernaturals in the world. I guess I was, as Ethan often accused, more human than most.

"What kind of good deeds?"

She put the clipboard back on the table. "That's what we're currently trying to figure out. I'm thinking I'm going to offer my services up to Chuck when he's one hundred percent. Maybe the nymphs could use help? Or the River trolls? I don't know. This is all very early in the planning stage. The point is, though, if I have this power, I should be doing something with it. Something good." She shrugged. "We just have to work out the mechanics."

"I think that's a great idea," I said. "Let me know how I can help."

She smiled. "I had this sudden memory of that yard sale you offered to help with a few years ago."

"What you call a 'yard sale' was two ponchos and a pair of worn Birkenstocks from your hippie phase."

"And a Bob Marley rug."

"And a Bob Marley rug," I allowed with a grin. "You didn't need my help. Besides, you had your crusty boyfriend. What was his name?"

"Akron."

I snapped my fingers and pointed at her. "Right! Akron, named because he considered Akron the jewel of American cities."

"Fun as this walk down memory lane is, it's not why you're here," she said, smiling curiously. "You said something about a favor?"

"I did. I need to find someone. Magically."

She frowned. "We talked about that. Decided it wouldn't work for Regan or Aline."

"I know. But I think the—what did you call it? magical signature?—will be different here. I have something you can use. Something good, I think."

I pulled the velvet pouch from my pocket and emptied it onto the table. The gold glinted in the light, and Mallory's smile slowly faded.

Silently, she looked at the medal for a moment, as if she could sense its magic and it scared her. I immediately regretted that I'd brought it. I reached out a hand to snatch it up again, but she shook her head.

"I just need to get Catcher."

The baby monitor crackled. "I'm on my way," he said. Seconds later, he trotted down the basement stairs. He really was paying attention.

"What's going on?" he asked, looking back and forth at us in search of the trouble he expected had brought him downstairs.

Mallory pointed to the medal. Catcher looked momentarily confused, but the magical signature must have been enough for him, too, to understand the gist. He looked at Mallory, then at me.

"Why is Tate's magic all over this?"

"When he was imprisoned, I gave him my medal—used it to pay for information. He didn't give it back until he left. By then, I'd already gotten a new House medal. And when we left the GP and turned our medals in, I kept this one. I just had a feeling about it." I looked at both of them. "I'm sorry. I didn't think it would have that much magic left in it."

"It doesn't have much," Catcher said. "Just memories, yes?" he asked, turning to Mallory.

She blew out a breath, clearly trying to compose herself, then nodded. "Memories. Very clear ones. Very"—she rubbed her hands over her arms, where goose bumps had lifted—"tangible memories."

"And why is it here?" he asked me.

"Merit wants to find him," Mallory said. "Although we hadn't gotten to the why of it."

"He's our best bet to learn about Regan—to figure out what she is and what to do with her. And I was also hoping he might be able to talk some sense into Mayor Kowalcyzk."

"You think he'll play along?" Catcher asked.

I shrugged. "He was contrite when he left. Wanted to redeem himself. I'm hoping he still does and that he'll consider this a favor to the city of Chicago. And me."

"Do you really think he'd be able to change her mind?" Catcher asked.

"I don't know," I said. "But Ethan's not exactly accessible. And even if we wanted to owe my father, I don't think Kowalcyzk would roll over for a bribe. Not when she thinks she's making political hay. I can't fight him out, or the city will destroy us. As long as she calls him an enemy of the state, the evidence is irrelevant. And God knows she isn't going to listen to me. I was hoping she'd listen to Tate."

Catcher looked back at the medal, blinked. "It's not a *horrible* idea."

For the first time, I felt a sliver of hope. "I can take 'not horrible.' But not if it will hurt either one of you or endanger Mal's recovery. He's alive." I looked at her. "I won't trade his life for yours. If you can't safely do this, then you don't do it. The risk isn't worth it."

She looked at me for a long time, then Catcher.

"Your call," he said. "These decisions have to be yours."

She nodded, then put her hands flat on the table on either side of the medal and looked down, her eyes scanning back and forth as if she was reading a magical text. And maybe she was.

"Both of them are in there. A bit of Seth, a bit of Dominic." She looked at me. "He sees you as his, in a way."

I started. "He—what?"

She looked up. "Seth, not Dominic. He's been part of your life for a very long time, and that's meaningful to him."

"Like, romantically?"

"No, Mary Sue. Not romantically. You're just . . . there. Like an achievement, maybe because he was searching for something. Fame. Power. Popularity. In reality, of course, he probably wanted to rid himself of the parasitic demon that he didn't know was attached to his soul. But, you know, details."

"You got all that from my medal?"

She gestured offhandedly toward it. "It's a piece of jewelry, not a memoir. But I can get a little. The issue will be the mechanism. We'll have to link the medal to a map if we want to get anywhere with this."

She spun on the stool and looked at Catcher, arms crossed. "What do you think? Compass in water? Map on a dart board? Google Maps?"

Catcher's eyes shined. "Damn, I love it when you talk shop."

"Especially when destroying the world isn't the side dish," Mallory murmured.

"That helps," Catcher admitted.

They decided on their tools, and Catcher cleaned off the table while Mallory prepared the magic and the spell.

It was both more and less complex than I'd imagined it would be.

Less, because it involved such mundane materials. A map of the U.S. torn from a road atlas, the front cover of which bore a smiling insurance agent with perfectly coiffed brown hair. A large glass baking dish of water, which held a sliver of cork, the House medal stuck to the top with a thin sewing needle. The map was submerged in the water, the make-do magical compass bobbing above it.

Humble materials, but the magic was profound.

When her station was prepared, Mallory stretched and shook out her wrists and arms, rolled her shoulders like a swimmer preparing for a sprint. She was surprisingly calm, her movements reverential. Instead of making her anxious or manic, the preparations seemed to soothe her. Her hands, once chapped from the aftereffects of black magic, looked healthy again, although they were still marked by faint, crisscrossing lines from the damage she'd already done.

She looked up at me, smiled. "It's different now. I mean, not the magic per se. But the preparations. They remind me why I'm doing what I'm doing, force me to calm myself, to approach it logically."

I smiled a little. "Kind of like doing dishes?"

She chuckled. "Exactly like doing dishes. The North American Central Pack isn't perfect, any more than the Keenes are perfect. But they know magic. A healthy kind of magic. A useful kind of magic. I couldn't have gotten better without him. Not really."

"This will be kind of like dousing," Mallory said. "Water witching. Except we aren't looking *for* water. We're looking *through* it."

She pulled her legs up, sitting cross-legged on a stool too small for it, which made her look a little like she was floating like a meditating yogi. She put her hands flat on the table and looked down at the water and the cork that bobbed inside it.

"And away we go," she quietly said.

The buildup was so slow, so smooth, that I didn't realize she'd begun spooling magic until the other objects on the table began to vibrate. The room had warmed, just a bit, not uncomfortably, but like I'd just moved a little closer to a roaring fire on a chilly day. I didn't know I'd be able to tell the difference, but this was obviously good magic. There was no uncomfortable edge, no angry itch. It was calmer. Smoother, rippling the air in smooth waves that rolled across us instead of crashing into us like Mallory's magic had once done.

By the expression on Catcher's face, he was feeling it, too. He generally had three moods—bleak, pissed, and sardonic. (He might have been three of Snow White's rejected dwarves.) But here, in this rehabbed basement with his rehabbed girlfriend, he actually looked . . . content. Proud and thoughtful, a little bit smitten, and generally satisfied with his lot.

Good for him. And her. They could use a little smitten and content.

Mallory drew the magic to a crescendo and pointed her index finger at my House medal. A blue spark sizzled from her finger to the cork. The medal heated, the edges glowing orange at first, then heating to white-hot, the metal warm enough to boil the water around it. The cork shivered and began to spin, whirling like a top in the middle of the water, then zigging across the surface like a bug, back and forth as it tried to find its target.

"Go on," Mallory whispered encouragingly. As if in answer, like a child itching to please its mother, it dove and disappeared.

As fast as it had begun, the magic dissipated again.

"That's a good girl," Mallory said, standing to peer over the water.

"Did it work?" I asked, stepping carefully closer.

"It picked a spot," Mallory said, wincing as she dipped her fingers into the edges of the dish.

"Hot, hot, hot," she murmured, almost to herself, carefully lifting the map from the bottom of the dish.

The cork, still quivering, was neatly pinned to the near center of the map. Mallory let the rest of the water drain, then placed the map on the table.

Catcher stepped forward, peered over Mallory's shoulder. "Portville, Indiana," he said. "I guess that's where you'll find your man."

CHAPTER SEVENTEEN

THE BANKER

Portville, Indiana, was gritty, a hard-bitten industrial town on the southern tip of Lake Michigan, just across the Indiana border. Portville had a reputation as a crumbling, blue-collar city abandoned by industry, its remaining vacuum filled by gangs, poverty, and violence.

Seth Tate, a fallen angel with contrition on his mind, had taken up residence there. If he'd really been serious about making amends for his past bad acts, the location was entirely appropriate. It definitely seemed like a city that needed help. On the other hand, during his less angelic days, when he'd been under Dominic's influence, he'd been a drug kingpin and a befouler of vampires. A dirty city was just the type of place for him to work some dirty magic.

Either way, I had nothing more than the town's name, which the Internet told me had nearly one hundred thousand residents. Not an address, a workplace, a church, or a precinct—but a name. This was going to be a challenge.

This was a big task, and I was going to need a partner. Unfortunately, both my official partners were under wraps. Ethan was in custody, and Jonah was captain of a House whose Master had been called an enemy of Chicago. He was going to have his hands full keeping his people safe.

That meant I needed to look elsewhere. So when I was in the car again, I pulled out my phone and called Jeff.

"Hey, Merit."

"Hey." I got to the point, and quickly. "Can you get away for a little while?"

"You planning a trip?"

"I am, actually. What do you know about Portville, Indiana?"

"Not a thing. Should I?"

"It's where Seth Tate's currently living."

"Ah," he said. "Sulfur and smoke?"

"Actually, yeah. If she's connected to the Messengers, he's the best person to tell us how. I still have to check with Luc and Malik, but I think they'll say yes."

"And Ethan?"

"He won't mind as much if you go with me."

"I know when I've been beat. Where should I meet you?"

Since I was already on the south side, I gave him the address of the convenience store I'd pulled into to make my calls. "I've got to cover my bases. I'll let you know as soon as it's a go."

"I'm leaving now," he said, apparently convinced I'd get the okay.

I was glad Jeff was on my side. Now I had to make sure the rest of the pieces aligned.

That alignment took phone calls. Plural.

I called Luc, told him Mallory and Catcher had found Tate, and Jeff had agreed to go with me to see him.

Luc hung up, and while I blasted Moneypenny's heat and sipped the soda I'd grabbed at the convenience store—heavy on the ice and cherry flavoring, 'cause I was in that kind of mood—I waited.

Ten minutes later, I got a call back. My stomach buzzed with nerves.

"It's Malik," said the temporary Master of the House.

"*Liege,*" I acknowledged, a word I'd gotten used to during Ethan's demise.

"Visiting him is a risk."

"It is. And so is waiting for Regan to strike again, risking the elves attacking, and pissing off the Keenes. I was in Dominic's prison, Malik. I know what he was capable of. But Seth Tate is not Dominic. The man we saw after the split was a good man, an earnest man, and he meant to make amends for the things he'd done. He stayed at the House, for God's sake."

"Ethan authorized him to say at the House," Malik quietly said, his tone making clear that he hadn't agreed with that decision.

"I don't know if he'll live up to that in the long run. But who else can we ask?"

Although I wasn't entirely sure talking to Tate was a great idea, I was willing to stand behind it—and take the fall if necessary. I tried to pour that confidence and bravado into my voice.

"The idea is not without risk," I admitted. "But I'm happy to take that risk on. We don't have a lot of good options right now, and we're stalled on Regan. I think it's time to use the alliances we've created. He's within driving distance, and he owes us a pretty big favor. Let me and Jeff drive down there. One conversation with him, and we see how far we get."

Silence, while I gnawed the edge of my thumb.

"You go down tonight, you come back in one piece," Malik said. "If he seems even remotely unstable, you abort the plan. If the situation seems dangerous, you abort the plan. If anything happens to you, you'll have Ethan and me on your ass, and you don't want that, Sentinel."

"No, Liege," I agreed. "I definitely do not."

I did a happy dance. Not because I was thrilled to see Tate, but because I was thrilled to be doing something. Standing around the House and watching more footage of Ethan in trouble wasn't going to help me at all.

"We'll keep looking for Regan and the carnival," Malik said. "Find us a guardian angel."

It was my primary goal.

At first, I waited for Jeff outside the car, leaning against it like I was the baddest vampire in the modern age. Or certainly the vampire with the sweetest ride.

But it was February—in Chicago—and I quickly rejected that idea, climbed inside, and turned up the heater.

Jeff arrived a few minutes later, parked his car at the edge of the parking lot, and climbed in. "This is a damn fine automobile," he said.

"Tell me about it." I gestured toward the forty-four-ounce Mountain Dew in the cup holder, and the sticks of beef jerky I'd wedged between his cup and mine.

"What's this?"

"Provisions. And a thank-you gift. That's what gamers use for fuel, right?"

He looked at me with a mix of pity and adoration and my heart melted a little. "That was really nice, Merit." He opened a stick of jerky, dug into it. "But don't tell Fallon. She's not a fan of processed food."

"It's just between us," I promised, and we headed south.

The city lined up along the edge of Lake Michigan, with industrial ports and brick smokestacks reaching into the sky on the lake side, and dilapidated buildings on the other.

The main street was flat-out depressing, half the shops—still marked by their antique cursive signs—boarded up and closed. When manufacturing moved out, it took time for anything else to move back in. The Midwest and Rust Belt had dozens if not hundreds of towns proving that very point.

I found a cluster of new businesses close to the freeway, and pulled into the lot of a store that carried animal feed and farming supplies. You didn't have to go very far outside Chicago to reach farmland.

"Need a snack?" Jeff asked with amusement.

"Need recon," I said, pulling the photograph of Tate from my pocket. "We know he's in the city. We don't know much more than that."

He gestured toward the photograph. "This is your big plan? You're going to wander from store to store asking if anyone has seen him?"

In fairness, it sounded much more logical in my head. "He was the mayor of Chicago, and he's looking for redemption. I don't think he's going to lay low. I think he's going to get out there. Mix it up. Mingle."

"He can't still look like that," Jeff said, pointing at the photo. "He'd be recognized. We're not that far from the city."

"I didn't think of that," I admitted. But we had to start somewhere. "I'll try this. In the meantime, work some of your computer magic and see what you can find in the ether. I'll be right back.

"No backup?"

"We don't want to scare them," I said. "If I go in alone, I'm asking questions. If both of us go in, we're ganging up."

When he finally nodded his agreement, I walked inside, a bell ringing on the door to signal my entry. The store smelled of leather and grains, and I lingered in the doorway for a moment, enjoying the fragrance. It smelled earnest, like hard work and chores.

The store was empty of people at this late hour, and a man, probably in his forties, stood behind the counter in a collared shirt and pants and a bright green vest with a name tag that read CARL.

He looked up at me, smiled. "Evening. Help you?"

"Yeah, actually, although I have kind of a strange request." I walked toward the checkout line and pulled the photograph from my pocket. "I'm looking for this man."

I held out the picture. He glanced at it for a moment, then back at me.

"Sorry. He doesn't look familiar." His eyes narrowed with interest. "Did he do something wrong?"

"No." I frowned, realizing I hadn't come up with a cover story, and opted for the truth. "He's a friend of the family who disappeared. We're trying to find him."

As if sympathetic, he looked at the photograph again, shook his head. "Sorry. But good luck."

I thanked him, tucked the photograph away again, and climbed back into the car. Jeff had pulled out that slick little square of glass, and he was tapping the screen busily.

"Let me guess—you've already found his address and favorite Chinese place?"

"No. But I just increased my mage to level forty-seven."

"Gaming has a lot of math, doesn't it?"

"You have no idea." He put the screen away again. "I found nothing, but of course I'm using mobile equipment, which isn't quite as nice as the box I had at home when you called me and I could have looked it up."

"You rehearsed that speech for a while, didn't you?"

Jeff grinned. "I take it you weren't successful, either?"

"Not even a little. He didn't recognize the picture."

The next guy and the girl that followed also couldn't give me anything. In the end, it was the fourth stop and floppy-haired shifter who got it done.

"Let me take this one," he said, climbing out of the car with me as we walked inside a twenty-four-hour diner that had seen better days—and cleaner linoleum.

He scoped out the waitstaff, spied a pretty, delicate-looking blonde behind the cash register, and walked up. Her hair was pulled into a dank ponytail, and there were bags of exhaustion beneath her eyes.

"Hey," he said. "I'm sorry to interrupt your night, but could I maybe ask you for a favor?" His eyes were bright and blue, his smile completely guileless. I'd have done a favor for him. As long as it wouldn't have gotten me in trouble with Fallon.

"A favor?" she asked, blinking. "From me?"

"Yeah." Jeff winced, all apologies. He held out the photograph he'd borrowed from me in the car. "We're trying to find this man. I don't suppose you've seen him?"

Her eyes widened. "Father Paul? Is he in some kind of trouble?"

So Tate hadn't just shed his identity; he'd changed his name and apparently taken on religion. Although I guess that wasn't hard to believe. He was an angel, after all.

Jeff smiled almost foolishly. "Oh, not at all. We've actually just been trying to find him. We heard him speak—and really liked what he had to say. But we haven't been able to find his Web site or anything."

She laughed. "Father Paul's not one for technology." She checked her watch. "You can probably find him at the food pantry. He works late nights sometimes, helping stock shelves."

"And that's near here?" Jeff asked with a beaming smile.

"Half a mile up the road. And tell him Lynnette said hello."

Jeff smiled. "We absolutely will. Thanks a lot for the help."

Lynnette waved a little, and we walked outside again.

"You were tremendous," I said, stealing a glance at him. "And a damn good actor."

"You grow up around sups," Jeff cryptically said, "you learn to finesse the truth."

According to the gospel of Lynnette, Seth Tate, former mayor of Chicago, was now Father Paul, and he worked at a food pantry in Portville, Indiana. Considering the havoc he'd wreaked in Chicago, I wasn't sure if it was incredibly ironic or perfectly appropriate that he'd apparently dedicated his life to service.

The food pantry was unmistakable, several large steel buildings up the road, a pretty green, leafed logo painted along one side of the largest. I parked Moneypenny in a visitor's spot and glanced at Jeff.

"You ready?"

He nodded. "Let's do this."

We walked inside and found a pretty woman with curly hair at the front desk, typing on a computer keyboard. She looked up and smiled when we entered. "Hello. Can I help you?"

"Hi," Jeff said. "Sorry to bother you, but we're looking for Father Paul. I understand I can find him here?"

The phone rang, and she picked it up with one hand, pointed down the hallway with the other. "He's in the warehouse. Down the hall, to the left."

"Thank you," Jeff said with a smile, punctuating his appreciation with a chipper tap on the counter as we walked down the hallway. It was a clean and happy place, the walls covered in children's drawings and signs for previous holiday canned-food drives. The hallway led directly into the warehouse, which was impressive.

The space was huge, with a polished concrete floor, and was filled with twenty-foot-tall shelves of food in boxes, some wrapped in cellophane to keep them together. Smiling employees and volunteers walked the aisles with clipboards and moved pallets with forklifts into trucks that waited in three open bays.

A man with a scruffy beard and plaid shirt walked up to us, befuddlement in his expression. "Are you Laurie? The new volunteer? With a friend, maybe? We could use someone in the sorting room."

"Sorry, no. We're actually looking for Father Paul. The front desk said I could find him in here."

"Oh, sure. He's in diapers." The man gestured toward the other end of the warehouse, and I stifled an immature laugh at his inadvertent joke.

The warehouse was chilly, cold air blowing in through the open bays. But the staff looked happy to be at work, buoyed, maybe, by the fact that they were helping others.

We did, indeed, find Seth Tate in diapers. But not literally.

He was tall and handsome, with blue eyes and wavy black hair. His hair was neatly trimmed, but a tidy black beard covered his face. If you hadn't known Seth Tate, hadn't been looking for him, you wouldn't have seen the resemblance. It helped the disguise that he also wore a neck-to-ankle black cassock, the type of garment worn by priests. Seth Tate was hiding in plain sight, only thirty miles from Chicago.

He had a box of newborn diapers in hand but glanced up suddenly and met my gaze. His eyes widened with pleasant surprise, which calmed my nerves a bit. I'd been afraid he'd see our arrival as an unpleasant reminder of what he'd done in Chicago.

"Could I have a minute?" I whispered to Jeff.

"Take your time," he said. "I'll be here"—he scanned the shelves—"in toilet paper."

Seth put the box on a nearby table, and we walked toward each other, meeting in the middle. I could see he wanted to reach out, to greet me with an embrace, a kiss on the cheek, and a whispered "Hello, Ballerina," as he'd greeted me as a teenager. I'd been a dancer, and I'd been photographed meeting Tate, a friend of my father's, in a tutu.

But he held himself back, stopping three feet away. He clasped his hands behind his back as if he wouldn't be able to resist the temptation of human contact. Still, I caught the smells of lemon and sugar.

"Merit."

"Father Paul," I said, with a knowing glance. "You're looking well." I gestured toward the rest of the warehouse. "This is an impressive operation."

He nodded, his gaze scanning the shelves and boxes. "It is a temple to generosity. All of this is donated to those in need."

"Have you been here long?"

"Since I left Chicago. It's my current mission, I think." He tilted his head at me. "And I think I'm not the only one on a mission. What brings you here, Merit?"

"A mystery. And politics."

"Always," he said. He looked at me for a moment without even so much as a breath. "Perhaps we should speak somewhere more private?"

I nodded, and Jeff and I both followed as he walked toward the door, the cassock's thick fabric *swish*ing as he moved.

People offered greetings and shook his hand as they passed, apparently unaware of his history or the fact that he was an angel and could sprout wings large enough to carry us both out of the building.

We headed out into the chilly night and toward a picnic table that had seen better days, its wood faded and cracked.

Tate sat down on the bench, back to the table, skirt swirling as he moved. Jeff and I stood by, watching as Tate stared silently at the men and women coming from and going to the warehouse's busy shipping bays.

"What can I do for you, Merit?"

I gave him Regan's history, detailed the kidnappings and attacks, explained that we'd yet to find her and were risking a truce with the elves. And then I got to the point.

"I chased her in Loring Park. She smelled like sulfur and smoke."

His expression stayed the same, but I saw the tiny hitch in his eyes. "I'm not sure I understand."

"She has power—a lot of it. She's not a sorceress. And she smells like Dominic did. We thought no other twins had separated when the *Maleficium* was destroyed."

"They didn't. Or shouldn't have. I was the only one touching it."

"Is there a chance you have children?"

His eyes went wide. "Do I have children who are kidnapping supernaturals, you mean?"

Irritation was beginning to rise. "We've come to you because we need help. Because you're the expert in this area. That's not an insult—it's a magical fact. You know more about Messengers—fallen or otherwise—than anyone else we know. We need you."

He sighed, rubbed his temples. And then he looked at me, apology in his eyes, and I felt lost. "I'm sorry, Merit. But I truly don't know anything that could help."

I glanced at Jeff, who shrugged.

"All right," I said. "In that case, maybe there's something else you can help with. Long story short, Mayor Kowalcyzk's off her rocker. She's arrested Ethan for a death he committed in self-defense, beaten Scott, raided Navarre, and put together a goon squad because she thinks we're domestic terrorists."

"And what do you want me to do about that?"

I bit back cross words. "I don't know. Can you talk to her? Explain to her that supernaturals aren't her enemies?"

"She wouldn't listen to me, Merit."

I felt hope draining. "You know that for a fact?"

"Fact enough. She thinks I'm a felon. And even if she listened to me, she doesn't appear that willing to use reason or logic."

"I'm just asking you to try."

He looked away, worrying the inside of his cheek. "I can't return to that life, Merit. Not when there's so much to do here. So much good I could do. So much good I am doing."

"There's good to be done everywhere," I said. "But the good in Chicago is the kind only you can do. I don't know where else to turn."

"Chicago isn't my home anymore. It is lovely to see you, though. Would you like to stay? Work for a while? I think you'll find it feeds the soul."

I looked at him, mystified by the naive cheer in his voice. He couldn't have missed the panic and fear in mine.

"This isn't my town," I pointed out. "And it isn't really yours."

His gaze snapped back to mine, and I saw the spark in his cold blue eyes. He wasn't unaware of my panic.

He was in denial.

"Chicago is troubled," he said.

"It's not perfect. But it moves forward, and it fights. Its people and its vampires fight."

He made a sarcastic sound. "For what? There will always be another monster around the corner, Merit. And I know. I was one of them. People will always be afraid of the monster. And that fear will win every time."

"Courage has nothing to do with winning," I quietly said. "Courage is about fighting the good fight. Stepping forward, even when stepping forward is the crappiest of all possible options."

I looked at Jeff, saw the appreciation in his eyes, and smiled. "It's taken me a long time to understand that," I said. "But I do now."

I glanced at the people who moved behind us, hauling pallets, reviewing clipboards, and preparing shipments.

I looked back at Tate, the furrow of his brow as he looked at them, and the distance that I saw there. He wanted to be part of what they were—of lives that were simpler than his own. I understood that perspective; I'd shared it for some of my nights as a vampire. But like me, he knew it wasn't to be. He just wasn't ready to admit it yet.

"I don't begrudge anyone their recovery," I said, thinking of Mallory. "But there's something to be said for redemption. And right now, you have a perfect opportunity."

I kept my gaze on his, hoping against hope that he'd change his mind, spring up, go with us back to Chicago.

But he didn't speak a word, and my chest tightened with fear and frustration.

"If you change your mind, you know where to reach me." I turned my back on him, began to walk with Jeff toward the parking lot again.

"Merit," Tate said, filling me with hope.

But when I looked back, there was nothing but regret in his face.

"I'm sorry."

The apology made me feel even worse.

I didn't text the House that I'd been unsuccessful. I wasn't ready to admit how utterly useless our trip had been or how resistant Tate had been to helping us. I wasn't ready to face the degree of his denial about how he'd shaped the city, helping make it what it was today, for better or worse.

Of course, I still hoped he'd come to his senses and appear outside Cadogan House, holding a radio above his head, contrition in his eyes and stern words for Diane Kowalcyzk on his lips.

Unfortunately, and much to Luc's chagrin, life wasn't a movie, and Seth Tate wasn't interested in our concerns. I empathized with him. It was undoubtedly easier to make good for your past bad acts in a tidy, cheery warehouse miles away from the mess you'd made, than on the ground in Chicago and in the middle of the trouble. In Chicago, he was the defrocked mayor, the man with the nasty past. In Portville, he was Father Paul. A man with a mission to help others.

Maybe that was what irritated me most—that he'd gotten a clean slate, free and clear. Tate hadn't stayed in Chicago to face the consequences, to tell his tale, or to pick up the pieces. I had to give Mallory props for sticking around, fessing up, and trying to make it right.

"What are you going to do now?" Jeff asked as I focused on the road ahead of us, which was marked by billboards for outlet malls, chiropractors, attorneys.

"I don't know. But it's making me irritable."

"I wish I had some advice to offer," he said, glancing out the window. "Or some strings to pull."

"Yeah. Me, too."

My phone beeped. I was a careful driver, so at my nod, Jeff checked the screen.

"Well, well, well," he said.

"Ethan's free?" It was easy to tell what was on my mind.

"I doubt it, because there are a hundred supernaturals picketing in front of the Daley Center demanding his release."

CHAPTER EIGHTEEN

OCCUPY CHICAGO

I dropped Jeff off at his car and raced back to Cadogan House. Car keys still in hand, I joined Malik, Luc, and a dozen other Cadogan vampires in the front parlor, where the television had been tuned again to the drama at the Daley Center.

In the time it had taken me to get back to the House, the crowd of protestors had grown to several hundred, many of them carrying FREE ETHAN! and SUPERNATURAL JUSTICE signs. I didn't see anyone I recognized, but most were bundled up against the frigid night air.

"Any luck?" Luc asked, when I sidled next to him in the crowd of vampires whose gazes were trained on the screen.

"In finding him, yes. In convincing him to talk to the mayor, no. He's started a new life, and he wants to stay that course. He's working at a food bank. Noble work, but not exactly helpful here. Any news from Andrew?"

The question made his brow furrow, which made my stomach turn uncomfortably. Luc was usually unflappable. If he was concerned now, we had problems.

"They haven't released Ethan, and they haven't allowed Andrew to speak with him. He hasn't had blood since he arrived. Just water. They're saying they think blood will turn him into some kind of supervampire."

"That's ridiculous." It was also worrisome. A blood deficit would weaken him, and eventually that need would drive him to find blood wherever—and however—he could.

"That's bureaucracy. And never mind that you can buy Blood4You at every supermarket in town."

"What about the feds? Andrew thought he might have some luck there."

"They've declined on jurisdictional grounds," he mockingly said. "They'll send in troops if there's a 'legit' threat to public safety, but they don't feel that's happened yet." He turned back to the screen. "That might change, now that Ethan's fan club has taken the stage."

"See anyone you know?" I asked Luc, who squinted at the screen.

"Not that I can tell."

"How'd it get started?"

"We aren't sure. Rogue vampires seem like the best bet, but we haven't heard anything from Noah suggesting this was going on or asking us to participate."

Noah was the unofficial leader of Chicago's Rogue vampires. "And are we participating?" I wondered.

Before he could answer, a crowd of vampires in jeans and parkas tromped down the stairs and paused in the foyer, checking in on us. I recognized the ringleader, a sable-haired vampire named Christine, whose father was a famous Chicago criminal defense attorney. Not Ethan's attorney, but it wouldn't surprise me to learn they'd been in contact.

She pulled down the hood, revealing sharp cheekbones, sharper eyes, and a lovely face. "We're going to the protest," she said, meeting Malik's gaze. He stood on the other side of the arc of vampires in the parlor and watched her mildly.

"Speak now or forever hold your peace?"

"What you do on your time, including supporting our woe-begone Master, is your business. But don't get yourselves arrested."

She grinned, nodded. "Liege," she said, and her troops left the House.

"I hope that doesn't make more trouble," I murmured. Christine had always been the boisterous sort.

"They want to support their Master," Luc said, "and unlike you, they don't get many chances to do it."

He had a point there. How many times had I had the opportunity to wield steel for Ethan and the House? Too many, by my count.

"It warms the cockles of my heart to see all those sups stepping out in support of our Master. And probably some of that support is legit, and not just because they want to sleep with him."

I goggled, stared at him. "They what?"

Luc snorted. "He's not my type, but there are plenty of folks out there who appreciate your vampire boyfriend for more than his strategic mind." He tapped a finger against his temple.

I blinked. "And where is this coming from?"

He pointed to the screen and the gaggle of teenage girls who grinned and smiled at the camera, holding signs bearing glittery hearts and professions of love for one Ethan Sullivan. The girls, who had pink cheeks and infatuated smiles, couldn't have been more than fourteen or fifteen.

"Where are their *parents*?" I murmured, thinking I wasn't thrilled that my "vampire boyfriend" had a fan club.

On the other hand, they had excellent taste.

"Anything new on the carnival?" I asked him, lest we forget about the other supernaturals potentially in danger.

"Actually, yes," he said. "The librarian found one more location—Paul Revere Park. Carnival was there last year. But it's empty again. They appear to be laying low."

Which meant we had no other leads on where Regan, the carnival, or the missing sups might actually be—assuming our theory was correct and they were still alive. It was beginning to look like we'd have to wait for them to make a move, which didn't thrill me. A harpy attack in the woods beside Loring Park was one thing; a harpy attack at Soldier Field would be something altogether different.

My phone beeped, a message from Jonah. NEED BODIES AT PROTEST. WEARING MIDNIGHT HIGH SHIRT?

It was an RG assignment, signaled by the reference to the Midnight High School T-shirt. The school was fake, but the T-shirts were real, worn by RG members to secretly signal their membership.

I glanced at Luc and the others. I could get away, but I was going to have to explain to him why I was leaving and where I was going. The odds I'd end up arrested or on television by the end of the night were too high otherwise.

I tucked the phone away again, leaned toward Luc. "Can I talk to you outside for a minute?"

Luc's brows lifted, but he nodded and followed me to the foyer.

We stopped in a quiet spot beyond the staircase, where he crossed his arms, looked down at me with chin tipped down. "What's on your mind, Sentinel?"

I moistened my lips nervously. "I have to go to the protest. For reasons I'm not at liberty to discuss. But I didn't want to sneak out of here without telling you I was leaving."

He looked at me for a moment, then leaned closer. "This have something to do with that secret project Ethan has you working on?"

I opened my mouth, closed it again. I wasn't working with Ethan on a secret project, at least to my knowledge. I was only aware of two real secrets: Lakshmi's GP challenge invitation, and my RG membership. Maybe Ethan had prepared Luc for the inevitable fallout of one or both of those things.

"Yes?" I offered.

That must have been the right answer, because he nodded. "Be careful, and keep your phone on."

I messaged Jonah, arranging a meeting place, a spot two blocks north of the Daley Center, where we could find each other before we reached the chaos of the plaza and protestors.

Even from two blocks away, the sound was deafening. Much like during the human riots that had plagued the city last week, there were chants of protest, supernaturals demanding Ethan's release, demanding rights for the city's preternatural population. And like the humans, they weren't especially subtle about what they'd do if their demands weren't met. "No justice, no peace," was a common refrain.

But unlike the human demonstrations, this protest carried the signature sensation of magic. A lot of it—chaotic and unfocused, like eddies of water swirling in the rapids of a rocky stream.

Jonah rounded the corner, walked toward me. There was no denying it: The Grey House guard captain was a looker.

Tall and trim, with shoulder-length auburn hair that framed clear blue eyes. He'd gotten his fangs in Kansas City, but he looked more like a warrior from a windswept cliff in Ireland, with his honed cheekbones and chiseled chin. Tonight he wore jeans and a navy pea coat, which only added to the effect. I half expected him to speak with a lilting accent but probably would have enjoyed it too much if he had.

"Hey," I said, a little shyly. I hadn't seen Jonah in a few days, and I spent so much time dealing with drama on behalf of Cadogan House that I didn't have much time to serve as his partner in the RG.

"Hey," he said. "How's the House?"

"Nervous. They don't like Ethan being out of reach. How's Scott?"

"Fine. Pissed. There are a few Grey House vamps out there tonight. He didn't want them to come but didn't bar them outright."

"Ditto at Cadogan."

Jonah nodded. "Let's get moving."

We walked down the street and toward the plaza, each step bringing us closer to the noise and magic.

"Who organized this?" I asked.

"Don't know," he said. "Word of mouth, I assume."

It was a completely rational assumption, but that didn't make me feel any better about walking into it.

"Plan?" I asked him, now forced to raise my voice to account for the noise.

"We're monitoring. We're here as peacekeepers, and we'll stay on the perimeter. Help anyone who looks like they're in trouble, or help disperse the crowd if things get dangerous."

I'd left my katana in the car—all the better to keep the CPD from harassing me about it—but the dagger was tucked into my boot. It was the only weapon I'd have if things got ugly. On the other hand, if things got ugly here, even a sword might not have helped.

Daley Plaza was open on three sides, bounded by Clark, Dearborn, and Washington streets and the Daley Center. It was a large expanse of concrete, punctuated by an insectlike metal Picasso sculpture reaching fifty feet into the air and a square fountain currently closed for the winter.

The plaza was packed with people, the crowd thick and heavy like deep water, so that each person was leaned or shoved into his or her neighbors, sending the wave forward.

Cops in black gear were visible on the edges, as were a few journalists with video cameras on their shoulders, and a few vampires standing in pairs outside the main crush. RG members, I thought, trying to keep the city's supernaturals safe.

"There are a lot of people here," he said.

"There are. And a lot of magic." It was rising and falling like the movement of a symphony, raising uncomfortable prickles on my arms. "Itchy magic," I said, scratching absently at the back of one hand.

It occurred to me that I was probably within telepathic distance of Ethan, and I called out to him silently but could practically feel the words bouncing back to me. Too much magical interference, perhaps.

"Let's walk the perimeter," he said, and I nodded, fell into step beside him. The night was cold, but the crush of bodies in front of us worked like a furnace to push heat in our direction.

The crowd was diverse, from obviously smitten teenagers who grinned with excitement at the cause to vampires and shifters I didn't recognize, wearing bleak expressions and repeating their pleas for Ethan's relief over and over and over again.

"Your man has a lot of support," Jonah said.

"The cause has support," I corrected, stopping short when two twentysomethings in coats and scarves bounded out of a cab and into the fray with neon posters demanding supernatural rights and Ethan's release. "I can't believe how many of them know who Ethan is."

"He has fan sites, Merit."

I stopped, looked at him, and found a bemused expression on his face. "He does not."

"Next time you're online, look up EthanSullivanIsMyMaster-dot-net. It has fan fiction. You're not doing a very good job of keeping up with Ethan's many admirers."

"There is no such place, and there is no such fan fiction."

This time, he stopped and looked at me, his expression flat.

My mind whirled at the possibility of hordes of human women lusting over my very vampiric boyfriend. I decided I found it endearing, since I wasn't worried about his fidelity. Although my Internet research was clearly lacking. I made a mental note to catch up when I had some free time.

Still, the reminder of Ethan dimmed my mood. "Do you think they'll release him?"

"In his lifetime? Yes. Unfortunately, that lifetime may last an eternity."

Not exactly the most inspiring of thoughts.

We passed a man and woman who wore Midnight High T-shirts beneath unbuttoned coats. The man was tall and gaunt, with pale skin and thick sideburns; the woman was petite, with dark skin and curls. He was Horace, a Civil War volunteer and member of the Red Guard. I hadn't yet learned her name.

Horace exchanged the slightest of nods with Jonah as we passed. An acknowledgment of our membership, our partnership, our vampiric fence around the plaza.

We edged around the perimeter and turned to the other side of the crowd just as a woman, petite and dark haired, walked up the sidewalk in a satin coat and four-inch platform shoes, a red dress visible beneath and a cloak of magic flowing around her.

She was barely five feet tall, but with each step, another man or woman in her vicinity trained their eyes on her, awestruck. Like all nymphs, she had the big-eyed beauty of an anime character.

I glanced at Jonah, saw the same glazed expression on his face.

"River nymph approaching," I warned, a little late. "Although I forget which part of the river she controls."

"North Branch," he said, then cleared his throat. "Her name's Cassie."

Cassie looked up, discovered us standing there, and rushed over in her platform heels, her coat swirling behind her.

"You're Chuck's granddaughter!" she said as she batted her lashes. But when she looked at Jonah, her smile turned pouty. "Where's Jeff?"

I winced sympathetically for Jonah and for any other man in Chicago who was not Jeff Christopher. Geek or not, he had a way with the nymphs.

"He's not here tonight. I'm sorry."

Tears bloomed in her large eyes, and her lower lip quivered.

I did not have time for a nymph on a crying jag. "Jeff mentioned you," I said. "Just last night. Said he thought you were terribly pretty."

She clasped her hands together with obvious glee. "Did he?"

"He did," I assured her, then glanced cautiously at the roaring crowd. I wasn't sure that was exactly River nymph territory. "Are you here for the protest?"

"I am," she said brightly. "There's a party tonight. I got a gorgeous invitation!"

I wouldn't have called it a party, but before I could protest, she launched forward and slipped into the crowd.

I glanced at Jonah. "A 'gorgeous invitation'? To a protest?"

That sounded suspicious. And manipulative.

"Regan?" I wondered.

"I think we should keep an eye on her," Jonah said.

I nodded. "Stay close. If we get separated, meet at the fountain."

"Roger," he said, and I moved into the crowd.

Cassie was small, but the crowd parted to let her move forward, as if they were the river she controlled. I kept my gaze on her spot in the crowd as she moved deeper.

"You got her?" Jonah yelled out behind me, the crowd growing thicker and tighter as we advanced, the decibels higher.

"I see her!" I yelled back, holding out my hand behind me so he might grab it and keep us connected in the crowd.

Our fingers brushed just as shoving erupted to my right side, elbows pointing into my back and hips. I pulled back my arm, keeping my gaze on the divot Cassie had made in the crowd, and pressed my feet into the asphalt, trying to gain purchase. But the shoving grew stronger.

My irritation began to rise.

I pushed in the direction I thought she'd gone, panicking when I couldn't see the shine of her satin jacket or feel the bubble of magic around her.

"Crap," I murmured, wincing as a foot stomped on mine. The crowd tightened, contracted like a heartbeat. I breathed out slowly through pursed lips as bodies snugged against me, magic and smells and sounds crowding me on all sides.

After a moment, the press of bodies moved in the other direction, freeing me up enough to stand on tiptoes, scan the crowd for Cassie.

I found her, ten or twelve feet away, her arm on a man's shoulder as she smiled and strained to see over the crowd.

I had only an instant of relief.

She turned around to look, her expression pained, as if she'd been surprised. And her eyes, wide and innocent, went blank. I'd seen those eyes before. The same dead expression, the absence of will. The harpies had worn it well.

Things were about to get very, very bad.

"Cassie!" I called out over the crowd. "Cassie! Are you all right?"

She didn't turn, but her eyes rolled back, and her head began to loll. And there, only feet away from her, was a girl in a red cape.

I swore, began pushing through the crowd. Regan had found a perfect spot to disappear another supernatural, and she was doing it right before my eyes.

"Cassie!" I screamed out, wedging my body in an effort to push through the crowd, but the people around me were wedged in tight and looked around in irritation as I used elbows and knees to shove through them.

"Get out of the way!" I pled, looking over the top of the crowd for her hair or the barker's, trying to trace where they'd gone. "Stop! Stop those girls!"

The man beside me threw out an arm, catching me in the stomach. I sucked in breath and swore out a curse that widened his eyes and had him moving back.

"Back off," I told him, and the sight of my silvered eyes had him raising his hands and giving me what little room he could.

I scanned the crowd but saw nothing. No dark hair, no nymph and captor sliding quickly through the crowd to make their getaway.

"Damn it!" I yelled, loud enough that the people around me gave me nasty looks. I ignored them, just as they ignored my panic and pleas for assistance.

I needed higher ground, so I ran to the Picasso and scrambled up the incline that marked its base, then jumped onto the next ridge of metal, which put me just above the crowd. I surveyed the bodies, looking for Regan.

After a moment I found her, the cape's hood still lifted, slithering through the crowd, dragging the nymph behind her. They were headed toward Dearborn. If they got clear of the crowd or jumped in a cab, I'd lose them. I didn't have time to find Jonah. I only had time to haul ass.

I jumped down, hit the ground in a crouch, and took off.

This ended tonight.

She got to the edge of the protestors before I did and slowed her jog to a walk, Cassie walking awkwardly behind her, her wrist in Regan's hand. To anyone paying attention, it would have looked like Cassie'd had a little too much fun at the protest. But not many were paying attention. The crowd was growing, their calls for Ethan's release louder with each round.

I reached the perimeter just as she reached the street and took off to the north, toward the River. Appropriate location for a nymph, but not when the nymph was being dragged while under the influence of drugs or magic.

I spied a woman in a red T-shirt as I ran to the sidewalk and yelled, "Find Jonah!" as I passed her, hoping she was an RG member and actually knew who Jonah was.

Regan and Cassie were nearly a block ahead. They dodged

the entrance to the Daley Center's underground parking lot and crossed the street, Cassie jogging along awkwardly behind.

"Regan!" I yelled out, dodging a speeding cab and the curses of the driver, who lowered his window to make sure I'd heard them. "Stop right now!"

She ignored the demand and darted across Dearborn, barely missing the front end of a CTA bus. She hopped the curb but lost her balance in the frozen mountain of ice on the other side and hit the ground, Cassie behind her.

Regan glanced behind, then took off, leaving Cassie in the snow.

I'd gained half a block but stopped at Cassie's side, taking in her dilated pupils and vague expression.

"I'll take care of her, Merit!" Jonah said, running across the street and signaling me onward. "Go get the girl!"

I took his word for it and took off. Regan kept running north, dodging people and disappearing into the shadows of an El track that covered Lake Street. I quickened my pace as she began to climb one of the vertical supports that kept the train tracks in the air.

She climbed clumsily, was five feet in the air when I reached her, jumped up, and grabbed her ankle. She kicked it off, catching me in the shoulder. I ignored the shot of pain and grabbed again.

Arms pinwheeling in the air, she fell, pushing me down behind her and landing on top of me with enough verve to leave me momentarily breathless.

She turned, began pummeling me with her fists. A train rushed by overhead, the roar blocking the dull thud of her fist against my breastbone, the crack of her knuckles against concrete when I dodged a second blow.

I reared back, pulled up my legs, and made contact with her

abdomen. With a *whoop* of air, she fell backward, hit the ground, and skidded a few feet behind her.

I climbed to my feet, hobbled toward her, and reached down to pull back the cape's hood.

The girl who blinked back at me was definitely not Regan.

⊶ ⊰⊱ ⊷

CHAPTER NINETEEN

REDEMPTION SONG

The girl also wasn't entirely in our plane of existence.
She sat on a chair we'd placed in the middle of the Cadogan training room, completely unmoving. She was approximately Regan's height and build but had short, dark curls in place of Regan's shock of platinum hair. Her eyes were deeply brown, and at the moment, open and blank.

She hadn't spoken at all, hadn't even acknowledged where we were or how we'd gotten there. I'd driven Moneypenny home; she'd been in the back of Jonah's car.

Cassie had snapped out of her trance and was upstairs in the foyer, where Lindsey had volunteered to entertain her with fashion magazines while they awaited Jeff's calming presence.

The training room door opened, and Paige walked inside, her vibrantly red hair set off by jeans and a long-sleeved, pale blue shirt with a V-neck. Even in jeans, she had a smoldering sensuality, like a magical, rusty-haired version of Marilyn Monroe.

Eyes mild, she surveyed the room, nodding at me and Luc

before her gaze fell onto the girl. She stared at her for a moment, tilting her head at the girl with obvious fascination.

"She hasn't spoken?"

"Not a word," I said. "Not the entire time."

"You said she tried to grab a nymph?"

"Did grab her," I said. "But we grabbed her back before she could make it to wherever she was going."

Paige dropped to one knee, looking into the girl's eyes, then leaned forward and sniffed delicately at the cape. Sniffing out magic wasn't unusual among sups; it had, actually, been the way Malik had first figured out Mallory's sorcery.

Her nose wrinkled and she jerked back, looked at me. "Sulfur, as we suspected."

"Her?" I wondered.

"No, not this girl," Paige said. She took to her feet again, fisted her hands on her hips. "It's in the fabric. The girl's been ensorcelled, but I use that term loosely. This isn't Order magic. It's"—she frowned, pursed her lips—"something else."

"Can you bring her out of whatever this is so we can ask her some questions?" Luc asked.

"I can certainly try." She glanced at us, wiggled her fingers. "Move back, please. Behind me."

We did as she directed without objection. I knew what magic sorcerers could make—and the balls of light and fire that usually accompanied it—and I didn't want to be downwind of it.

Paige stood, shimmied her hair from her shoulders, and looked down at the girl. "On three, you'll awaken. Refreshed, perhaps a bit confused, and ready to talk." She lifted curled fingers in front of the girl's face. "One, two, and three." Paige snapped her fingers.

Like she'd flicked a switch, the girl looked up, around, and blinked back confusion.

"That was it?" I asked, not disappointed exactly, but certainly surprised by the lack of flash and magic.

"Recall," Paige patiently said, "that you don't see everything. Every sorcerer has their own style. In situations like this, I try to keep the physical manifestations as mild as possible. She'll remember what she saw; it'll be better for her if it wasn't traumatic."

The girl focused glazed eyes on Paige, then us. There was fear in her eyes; if she'd had a run-in with Regan, I didn't find that surprising. On the other hand, she could be an accomplice. Just as guilty, but a very good actor.

"Are you all right?" Paige asked.

She swallowed thickly, nodded, her eyes still darting around the room, hesitating as she took in the antique weapons that hung on the walls. "I didn't do anything. It wasn't me. It was her."

"Let's hold on," Paige said, voice smooth and calm like a supernatural therapist. "One step at a time. What's your name?"

"I'm Harley. Harley Cutler. Harley Elizabeth Cutler." With each repetition of her name, her focus became sharper. "Where am I?"

"You're in Chicago, with vampires. Allies," Paige said, lest she not think better of us. "You're at Cadogan House."

"Regan," she said, glancing nervously around. "Where's Regan?"

Luc stepped forward, crouched in front of her. "We were hoping you could tell us that. Do you remember what happened tonight?"

"Remember?" She looked down at her body, her clothes, seemed to realize she was wearing the cape. She began clawing at it, peeling it off.

"It's Regan's," she said, voice suddenly frantic. "This is Regan's." She managed to get it off, threw it to the floor.

"Where is she?" I asked.

Harley looked up at me, and the fear in her eyes transmuted to anger. "I don't know." Recognition dawned in her eyes. "You chased me—at the plaza. You saw me grab the girl, and you chased me down the street."

I nodded. "That was me. You were going to take her back to Regan?"

"Not because I wanted to!" Her eyes went frantic, scanning each of us as if she had to prove to us she was innocent. I'd seen her eyes; I believed her.

"She set it up," Harley insisted. "Made me wear the cape. Said you'd seen her in it."

"Why did she want to make you look like her?"

She shrugged. "She didn't want to get caught. She didn't think you'd consider the plaza a target. But just in case . . ."

Regan had been right. We hadn't considered it a target until we'd seen that damn Little Red Riding Hood getup. But it fit her MO—create a chaotic, magical situation and use it as a distraction to lure out a sup.

"The protesters weren't real," Harley said. "Not all of them, anyway."

"They certainly looked real," Jonah said, glancing at me. "The magic felt real."

He was right, but he hadn't seen the harpies. Didn't know the extent of Regan's ability to mold magic.

"The magic was real," I said, getting a nod from Harley. "But the bodies were magic. Solidified magic, but still magic." I turned back to Luc and Jonah. "There were at least three hundred sups at the Daley Center, all makes and models. Getting sups to do anything together is like herding cats, and suddenly hundreds of them show up at the Daley Center?" I shook my head. "There's no way that's real."

"They were like the harpies," Harley confirmed. "She knew she only needed to seed the plaza—get enough fake bodies in there to make it seem like a real protest, and folks would join in."

And they had, I thought. Vampires. Nymphs. Even human teenagers.

"You were one of her victims?"

She nodded. "I'm a sylph. And a waitress—I was a waitress—in Madison. Most sylphs stick to their trees, but I was curious. Wanted something more, you know? I went to college, which nobody did, got a crappy job. Tried to save up some money. My parents haven't talked to me in a really long time. Because I was trying to pass."

Pass as human, she meant. Pretending to be human instead of a supernatural. If she'd been separated from her family, it would have been that much easier for Regan to take her without commotion.

"She's been kidnapping supernatural creatures? Keeping them together?" I asked.

Harley nodded. "She calls it the collection. I was part of it."

"She has an elf and a shifter now?"

Harley nodded. "Yeah. They're new."

Relief flooded me—not that Regan had taken Niera and Aline, but that we'd confirmed their kidnapper. One step closer to solving our elven problem.

"We were with the Pack when the harpies attacked," I explained. "And the elves kidnapped us, thinking we'd hurt them. We learned about Regan after that."

"Harley, where's the carnival?" Luc asked.

"Humboldt Park. But that's not where she keeps the collection—always somewhere else. It would be too easy for the
regular humans to find otherwise. And she doesn't want the regular
humans to find it. That's what she calls them—the regular humans.
She only caters to the fancy ones. Good names, old money."

Guess that ruled out using my father to help find her. His
money was substantial but new. Likely too gauche for Regan.

"That's what she says. She has a network—people that come
to see the collection year after year."

"And where will we find it?"

"I don't know. I never know. It's two train cars—big ones. The
carnival travels by train, and then semis pick up the cars and
transport them to the locations. We stay in the cars. And even
when we're allowed out, we don't get to go far. We never know
precisely where we are unless we happen to see a sign."

"All the supernaturals are in two cars?" I asked.

Harley nodded. "They're not much more than cages. She
keeps them sedated with magic."

"How many supernaturals does she have?" Jonah asked.

"Right now? I think eighteen," she said, eliciting a low whistle
from Luc. "The nymph would have been nineteen." Harley
smiled nervously. "She was really excited about getting closer to
twenty. She thinks it's a milestone."

For a woman who collected supernaturals, twenty would have
been a nice, big number. Unfortunately, it was nearly twenty kidnappings in the span of three years, of supernaturals whose friends,
lovers, and parents still had no answers.

"We can help you get back to your tree, your family," Luc said.
"If that's what you'd like to do. But we'd appreciate any help you
can give us to find the rest of them, so we can reunite them with
their families, as well."

Harley nodded, her eyes filling with tears, which she knuckled away. "I'll help however I can. I would like to see my mom and dad. I don't know if they missed me, but . . ."

She trailed off, and I put a hand on her arm. "I'm sure they missed you and will be thrilled to know that you're safe."

"Why don't we move to the Ops Room?" Luc asked, apparently no longer believing Harley a threat. "We can get comfortable, maybe get you something to eat?"

Harley nodded shyly.

"Good," Luc said with a nod. "And we'll see what else we can figure out about where Regan might be. I'm going to just check in with Malik. Merit, you want to get her settled?"

Harley stood, glancing around the room. "What is this place? Like, some kind of vampire fraternity house?"

"If you only knew," I said.

According to Harley Cutler, the cars used to transport and hold the supernaturals were long and silver, like old-fashioned trains or Airstream trailers. The edges were round, the surfaces shiny and reflective. Unfortunately, they did not have KIDNAPPER or ILLEGAL SUP COLLECTION screened atop them in screaming red paint that would have made them visible from the ground.

Still, as Harley ate a sandwich from a tray Margot had pulled together, we passed the information along to Jeff, who'd popped down after calming Cassie and helping her get situated at her home along the River.

"I can check yesterday's satellite images of the city," Jeff said, "but a silver train car's not exactly going to stand out. It could take time—if we're able to find it at all."

"Do what you can," Luc said, then glanced at Harley, who stuffed Cheetos into her mouth like she hadn't eaten in a month.

She covered her mouth as she chewed. "She fed us," she said. "But organic stuff. Gave us lunch boxes like we were kids. I miss Cheetos."

I imagined I'd have felt the same.

"Assuming we do find her," Luc said. "And speaking of which—and I apologize for interrupting your meal, Harley—but can you tell us anything else about Regan that might help us find her? Where she's from? Her last name?"

"I don't know," Harley said. "I didn't know her name. She just went by Regan. And I didn't know her history. One of the other sups told me Regan's mother was dead, and she didn't know her dad. But she had this sense, you know, that she knew she was special. That she had a lot to share." Harley shook her head nervously. "Sorry, that probably doesn't make much sense."

"It makes perfect sense," he said. "And it's very helpful. Please—keep going."

"Um, well." Harley pushed a tight curl behind her ear. "She had some insecurities, I think. Issues about the fact that her dad left. I mean, she didn't talk about that stuff with me."

"She made all the magic?"

Harley nodded, crossing her arms, more comfortable now. "Did it all herself. Not with us—she has a separate place where she stays, sleeps. Most of the carnies just stayed in cheap hotels, but that wasn't for her." She nodded again, leaning forward. "She thought of us as family. And I think the collection was a family for her. A way to say, 'Look at this amazing thing I built, this family I made from scratch. Look at me, world.'"

Luc nodded, put a hand on Harley's. "That's very helpful. We appreciate it."

"Sure," she said, but her eyes clouded again. "I guess I should think about going home or something."

"You can stay here for a day or two if you'd like to get settled," Luc said. "We've already gotten permission from the boss. Or we can get you back to Wisconsin now."

Harley considered, looked up at us. "I think I want to go home. How many chances do you get to start over, right?"

That, I thought, depended entirely on whether you were a vampire.

Jonah, Luc, and I stepped into the hallway, where Luc closed the door behind us, looked at me.

"Go to Humboldt Park. Check it out, just in case. Could be Harley's right, and there's absolutely nothing there relating to the collection. But I don't get the sense Regan trusted her quarry with the details, so you might find something Harley doesn't even know about."

"Or we might find Regan," I said. "She was a barker at the first carnival. Pimping the Tunnel of Horrors."

He glanced at Jonah. "You got time for a ride along?"

"If Scott clears it, sure."

"The magic that Mallory used to find Tate," Luc said. "We have Regan's cape. Can't we go that route again?"

I shook my head. "It's not that specific. It got us to a city, but not an address. We still had to find him on our own." And in a city as big as Chicago, that was going to take time, even with satellite images and a description.

"What about the protest?" I asked Luc.

Luc nodded. "Catcher's keeping an eye on it. He still has your grandfather's contacts at the CPD, and they've reached out to him for advice on the sup angle. Fortunately, the CPD still has domain outside the halls of the Daley Center."

"And Ethan?" Jonah asked.

"Andrew's calling with updates. He's got a libel and slander complaint against the city ready for filing based on the public enemy list. He's just waiting for Scott's lawyers to look it over. No word from Morgan, of course, but that's not unusual. He prefers to ignore problems while we deal with them.

"Still no word on a release time, but Andrew says they let him visit Ethan a couple of hours ago. He's looking worse for wear—the terrorism hounds are apparently using this unique opportunity to test the boundaries of the Eighth Amendment."

Since that one, I remembered from a lone history class in college, involved cruel and unusual punishment, it didn't make me feel any better.

I braced myself. "How bad is it?"

"Bruising, broken cheekbone. The goons believe they're saving the world. In many cases, they might be correct. But not in this one." Luc patted my arm. "I'll let you know if anything happens. Go check out the park. We take this one step at a time."

Humboldt Park was a large, slightly L-shaped expanse of grass, trees, walking paths, and baseball fields between the Humboldt Park and Ukrainian Village neighborhoods. The grass was still covered with snow, except in the bottom corner of the park, where Jack Frost's Winter Wonderland had set up shop. Regan had changed the name again, but the rest of the carnival looked and smelled the same.

Jonah parked along the street. "Katana?" he asked as we climbed out of the car and over the hillock of snow that still marked the curb.

"I think not tonight. Too suspicious. I have a dagger. You?"

"Same. Plus a couple of extra toys."

It was generally considered déclassé for vampires to carry concealed weapons. The katana, roughly three feet of honed steel, was difficult to hide, which made its use more honorable among the vamps who actually cared about such things. I understood the sensibility, but in twenty-first-century Chicago, one needed to be a little more practical.

"And what toys are those?" I wondered, stuffing my hands into my jacket pockets to protect against the chill, as we walked toward the carnival entrance.

"*Shuriken,*" he said. "Ninja stars, in American parlance."

I nodded. "Sure. I look forward to seeing those in action." It was late, and there weren't many humans around. But the occasional couple wandered past us, so this probably wasn't the best time for *shuriken.*

We walked inside, started at the midway. We could buy tickets for the ring toss, duck shoot, baseball throw, or water gun game, or funnel cakes with any number of toppings.

My stomach began to growl. I couldn't remember the last time I'd eaten.

"Need dinner?" Jonah asked.

"Not from here." And not now, when there was a chance we'd end up pushing and shoving an unidentified sup around. "But I wouldn't object to a drive-through on the way home."

"Duly noted. Hey," he said, brightening as he saw the pirate-ship ride, the boat swinging back and forth while a few brave humans raised their arms victoriously. "I've always wanted to ride one of those."

"Need a ticket?" I slyly asked.

Jonah humphed, and while he watched the ride's pendulum motion, I checked out the man working the controls. Thin, dark skin, bored expression. Human, with a giant wad of gum in his mouth. Not obviously a part of any magical scheme, which meant we needed to move on.

Regan, not surprisingly, was nowhere in sight. She'd probably have known by now that Harley wasn't coming back, and she'd lost her nymph. The rest of the ride and game operators were human, and there was no other scent or feel of magic in the air.

We made a full circle around the block and were about to start a second pass, when I caught a pop of red through the trees.

"Jonah," I said, stepping off the path and onto the snow beyond it. He stepped beside me, peered into the darkness.

"What is that?"

"I'm not sure." I pulled the dagger from my boot and, when I caught the glint of silver in his hand, moved forward.

It sat beneath the bare and stretching branches of an ancient tree, a wooden wagon atop large wooden wheels. The wheels, spokes radiating from a center hub, were probably three feet across. The wagon itself was a long, rectangular base with a tall, rounded top, nearly circular, painted vibrantly red. The back end had two small windows, covered by curtains, with a short, narrow door between. A yellow scalloped ladder ran down to the ground. There wasn't a single sign of life.

I'd seen pictures of tinkers and travelers, of families who lived in wagons outside the strictures of normal society. This was nearly too picture-perfect to seem real.

"A vardo," Jonah quietly said.

I glanced over at him. "What?"

"A traveling wagon. Often used by the Romani in Europe. Not often seen in Chicago."

I closed my eyes, dropping the defenses that kept my sensitive vampire senses from overwhelming me, and listened for any sign of life. I heard nothing, felt nothing, magical or otherwise.

I opened my eyes again, glanced at him. His eyes were focused on the wagon, gaze intense. I wouldn't have to worry about Jonah.

"I don't think anyone's in there."

"Me, either," he said. "Let's go."

I climbed the short wooden staircase, which squeaked beneath my feet, and peeked inside. It was dark and silent, with no sign of life. I tried the doorknob, found it unlocked, and glanced back at Jonah, ensuring he was ready.

When he nodded, I pushed it open.

Light spilled into the small space from the open door behind us. It was a single room, cozy and luxurious, with a small velvet settee and blankets and rugs on nearly every surface. Candles were scattered here and there, and a wooden trunk with brass strapping sat in front of the settee like a coffee table.

There was a hanging bar of clothes in one corner, and I recognized the ensemble I'd seen in Loring Park. The tiny hat she'd worn hung atop a small antique bureau topped by an oval mirror. Pots and bottles of makeup littered the surface.

And under it all were the scents of smoke and sulfur.

"She lives here," I said, and Jonah nodded his agreement. "Harley said she stayed in her own place. Although it's odd that she doesn't stay with the collection."

"Maybe she goes back and forth," Jonah suggested. "Stays here when the carnival's open, goes there when it's closed. This gives her an office, a home base.

"Papers," he said, moving toward a small folding table with X-shaped legs on the other side of the room. Two neat stacks of paper sat atop it.

While he checked out the table, I moved farther inside, running delicate fingers over the knickknacks and trinkets. A small Limoges box in the shape of a Scottish terrier. Foreign coins. And atop the trunk, inside a beautiful gilt frame, a photograph of a woman. She had hauntingly pale eyes and curls in perfect, thick spirals that framed her pretty face. MOTHER was printed in gold script across the bottom corner of the frame.

"Regan's mom?" Jonah asked, stepping behind me.

"I don't know. But it's something."

I pulled out my phone, took a picture of the photo, sent it to Jeff with a request: PHOTO MAY BE REGAN'S MOM. SCAN AND MATCH?

ON IT, he immediately messaged back.

I figured I might as well take the opportunity to check on her whereabouts. We were already out and about, after all. ANY REGAN UPDATE?

CHICAGO IS BIG.

I took that as a mild rebuke and put my phone away again, then propped the picture on the trunk again. "What about the papers? Anything there?"

"Nothing. It's just maintenance logs for the rides. She might have another agenda, but it looks like she takes care of the day-to-day stuff."

"That's something. I just hope she takes care of her sups."

Neither the wagon nor the carnival offered us anything more. While Jeff continued his search for Regan, her collection, and the woman in the photograph, we drove back to Cadogan House. Jonah, thankfully, made good on his promise of food, driving through a local burger joint and springing for a cheese-and-bacon-laden burger greasy enough to require a handful of napkins, and utterly delicious.

We returned to Cadogan to find Harley gone, Luc, Lindsey, and the temps in the Ops Room.

"Anything?" Luc asked, looking up.

"Just the photograph," I said, skipping the explanation since Jeff sat at the table beside him. I sat down, too, and Jonah took the seat beside me.

"She has a wagon," he said, "a vardo, but she wasn't there."

"No other sign of magic or Regan. That's a dead end for now." I glanced at Jeff, who was busily scanning images on his tablet. "Anything new on your end?"

"Nothing in the city, or with the picture," he said. "I've found an image-comparison algorithm, and I've applied it to satellite images of Chicago, but every reflective set of windows on a skyscraper looks like the top of a silver truck trailer. Ditto the photograph. But I'm pushing it along. Moving as quickly as possible."

He sounded as tired as Luc looked. It had been a long week, with political and supernatural drama, and it looked like we were all beginning to feel the fatigue.

My phone rang, and I pulled it out. The number was unfamiliar, although the caller had a Chicago area code.

"Hello?" I asked.

"Hello, Ballerina."

I sat up so quickly the chair knocked the edge of the table. "Seth. It's good to hear from you."

All eyes in the room turned to me. Luc gestured toward the speakerphone, but I shook my head. I wasn't entirely sure what this would involve, and it seemed better to handle it quietly.

"I've been thinking about our conversation."

I was immortal, and a predator, and Sentinel of my House. And I still crossed my fingers under the table.

"I want to talk to you about Diane Kowalcyzk."

My heart began to thud against my chest. "I'm listening."

"I recruited her, Merit. She was a young alderman, fit right into my team. She worked hard, put in a lot of long hours. I'm not saying she's taken the right path since then, but she was loyal."

"I don't understand. Why are you defending her?"

"Because I feel guilty for not coming clean earlier. It's occurring to me, a little late, that doing good deeds isn't going to be enough for me to wipe the slate clean. I still have a lot of baggage to unload."

I understood his need to confess, but I'd latched on to the first thing he'd said. I leaned forward, gestured for pen and paper. "Come clean about what?"

He was silent for a moment. "Diane Kowalcyzk's real name is Tammy Morelli."

I blinked. "The mayor of Chicago has an alias?"

"She does. And if you employ your tech-savvy friend, I believe you'll find plenty of information to provide leverage for you and the other sups to use."

I wrote down the name, slid it to Luc, who immediately handed it off to Jeff. But that didn't ease the greasy feeling in my stomach.

"Blackmail's a little off-color for an angel, isn't it?"

He didn't bother with denial. "It is. And it's easy for me to stand on a pedestal and talk about doing the right thing. But sometimes doing the right thing means getting your hands dirty."

"Truer words," I muttered, thinking of all the times I'd fudged the truth to keep my people safe and happy, including recently. "Thank you, Seth."

"You're welcome, Ballerina. Oh, and about the girl—I've racked my brain, but I can't think of anything helpful. I'm sorry."

It took me a moment to switch mental gears. "Actually, I have something specific for you there. Hold on—I'm going to send you a photograph." I forwarded the picture we'd found in the vardo. "Do you recognize the woman?"

There was a long silence, long enough that my blood began to hum in anticipation.

"Jesus," he finally said, his voice hoarse with emotion.

That hum turned to a full-on roar.

"Her name was Annalissa Purdey. He met her years ago."

I scribbled that name, too, and passed it to Jeff. "He?" I asked Seth.

"Dominic."

I blinked, confused. "I don't understand. What do you mean *he* met her?"

"We shared a body," he said. "I didn't know it at the time, of course. But looking back now, I realize there were times when he ... when he was in control, with all his ego and self-righteousness. He was stronger at some moments than others."

"And he was stronger with Annalissa Purdey?"

"They had a romance. It must have lasted five months, or perhaps six? I only vaguely remember. She was a young lawyer. A litigator. Smart. Bright. Very driven, and her ethics were, let's say, flexible." He chuckled mirthlessly. "She was right up his alley.

"He was driven by the attraction—strengthened by it—and he used that to push past me. It's been—what—nearly two decades?"

"I'd put Regan at twenty-three or twenty-four, so, yeah, about two decades. You'd have been so young."

Seth chuckled. "When one is immortal, age is negotiable. But what does Annalissa Purdey have to do with the girl you're seeking?"

I thought of the inscription on the photograph. "We think Annalissa Purdey is her mother."

He went stone silent, as did everyone else in the room. I could feel the weight of their stares, the tension as they waited for someone to voice the obvious implication.

"Regan is . . . Annalissa's daughter?" Seth asked. "But that means she's . . . Jesus," he said again, and I heard the shuffling of fabric. He was sitting down, I imagined, and deservedly so. I probably should have advised him to do that in the first place.

"Your daughter?" I asked. "Or Dominic's?"

"I don't—" He cleared his throat. "I don't know. Yes? I mean, we shared the body, but he was the one who had the affair. Is she his daughter? Is she my niece? I don't know. Does it even matter?"

"It matters if it helps us find her. And we need to find her, Seth."

"I'm sorry—I don't know how to help you do that." Frustration was clear in his voice. "Can you find her mother? Trace her that way?"

"We're looking," I said. "We'll let you know if we find anything."

"I have—he had—a daughter." This time, he sounded awed. "If you find her . . . ," he said.

"We'll let you know," I promised him. "Thank you for calling, Seth. It means a lot to us. To me."

"You may have given me a family," he said. "That means a lot, too."

We ended the call, and I rubbed my hands over my face. "I swear to God, the sups in this city could have their own reality show."

"Sex happens," Luc said. "With demons, too."

"I guess." I glanced at Jeff, who was squinting at his tablet, tongue peeking from the right side of his mouth.

"Annalissa Purdey is deceased," he said, sending a photograph of an obituary to the screen. The story used the photograph,

MOTHER still engraved at the bottom. They must have borrowed Regan's picture.

Luc grabbed his phone. "I'll ask the librarian to look into her background. Maybe something will help us locate Regan."

I nodded, glanced at Jeff. "Tammy Morelli?"

"Tammy Morelli," he said, swiping the screen, "is a con artist." Another photograph replaced Annalissa's, and the woman could hardly have been more different.

Tammy Morelli had a hard-bitten look. Her hair was permed, a curly halo around a face I didn't immediately recognize. Her nose was a little bit thicker, her chin a little bit smaller. But her eyes were the same.

"That's Diane Kowalcyzk," I said. "Who was she?"

"A grifter," Jeff said, tapping the tablet again and pulling up a series of newspaper articles. "Scam" figured prominently in most of the titles.

"It appears she had a fondness for art and insurance fraud," Jeff said.

Luc whistled, stretched back in his chair, and kicked his feet on the table. "Now, that, my friends, is something I can work with."

We had a wish list, and now we had information to bargain with. It was time to use it.

With Ethan out of pocket and Malik in charge of the House, Luc was designated as the official House negotiator. He coordinated with Andrew and left for the Daley Center with the hope of reaching a deal with the mayor.

However unethical that deal would be.

We didn't bother going back to the Ops Room. Jeff brought his screen upstairs, and vampires filled the rest of the parlors on the first floor to wait for news. Malik sat beside me on a couch, reading through a contract, one leg crossed over the other.

Lindsey paced the hallway, afraid Luc would get wrapped up in the city's political nonsense and he'd suffer Ethan's fate.

One hour and thirteen minutes later, I received a message from Luc.

WE'RE ON OUR WAY HOME.

I closed my eyes and breathed.

Everyone was excited. But most were smart enough to stay indoors and out of the cold, which sat heavy across the city.

I sat on the front stoop, my hands tucked between my knees to keep them a hairsbreadth from frostbite.

A car door slammed, and my head popped up like an animal sensing her mate. Slowly, I rose from the step.

He strode through the gate as if in slow motion, golden hair streaked with blood, a fading purple bruise across his cheekbone. His jacket was off and fisted in his hand, and his eyes burned like fiery emeralds.

Sentinel, he silently said. *You are a sight for sore eyes.*

I ran like the hounds of hell were behind me, jumping into his arms and wrapping my arms and legs around him. *Thank God,* I said. *Thank God.* I said it to the universe, to him, for him.

He embraced me with bone-crushing strength, buried his head in my neck.

I fisted my hands in his hair, tears flowing over. Tears of relief, of love, of grief. Tears of gratitude that I'd been granted yet another chance with him.

He'd told me once he wasn't certain how many of his lives he'd already given up, or how many he had yet to give. I didn't know, either, and didn't much care, as long as he still had one for me.

When clapping emerged from the front door, I dropped my legs and slid down his body, averting my eyes with embarrassment.

Ethan smiled, tucked a lock of hair behind my ear. "I believe they were applauding you, Sentinel."

"You're a liar," I said, dropping my hot cheek to his shirt. "But I'm okay with that."

Vampires came forward, embracing him, shaking his hand, and grinning with delight.

"It's good to be home," he told them. "And I don't believe I'll request those particular accommodations again."

There were good-natured chuckles from the vampires.

"If you'll excuse me, I need to sit. It's been a long night."

While Malik and Luc helped him inside, and the rest of the vampires followed, I pulled out my phone.

Ethan was home and safe, even though he'd stepped into danger to protect others from violence he believed was his responsibility to bear. He'd trusted his instincts and the skill of the people he'd gathered around him. It was time to set him free, to let him fly and hope that he returned again.

I texted Lakshmi. HE'S FREE AND HOME. HE SHOULD CONTROL OUR DESTINIES.

To the casual observer, the message would have read like I was asking her to do me a favor. But really, it was a receipt. An acknowledgment that Lakshmi had been correct, that Ethan was the right man for the job.

The rest of it was up to fate.

He made his rounds through the House, greeting his vampires, checking with Malik. By the time he found his way upstairs, I was in pajamas, in front of the fire, and his bruises were nearly healed.

He closed the apartment door, placed his suit jacket across the back of a desk chair.

"And here we are again, Sentinel." He walked forward, nearly stumbling with exhaustion, and grabbed the chair to steady himself.

I jumped to my feet. "Let me help."

"I don't need help," he quietly said, but he accepted the arm I put around his waist and let me guide him to the bed. He winced as he sat down, as if every part of his body was beaten and sore.

And from the look of it as I unfastened buttons and pulled the shirt from his shoulders, it was.

"They did a number on you," I quietly said, unsure whether I should be screaming or crying at the outrage.

"I'll heal," Ethan said, gaze on me as I dropped his shirt to the floor, flipped off his shoes, and helped him unbuckle his pants. Under any other circumstances, his gaze would have been demure and seductive. But tonight, he looked exhausted.

I turned off the fire, flipped off the lights, and climbed into the cool sheets beside him. The pain be damned, he pulled me against his body.

"Thank you for rescuing me, Ballerina," Ethan drowsily said. "And if he ever so much as lays a hand on you, I will break it."

I smiled against his chest, fell asleep to the sound of the slow and steady beating of his heart.

‒‒◄═►‒‒

CHAPTER TWENTY

THREE-RING CIRCUS

The sun fell, and my eyes snapped open. Ethan, golden and beautiful, stood beside his bureau, already dressed and pressing cuff links into place. He'd showered and cleaned up and looked perfectly healthy.

"Good morning, Sentinel."

"Good morning, Sullivan. Sleep well?"

"I slept," he said with a smile. "After the last twenty-four hours, that was glorious enough."

I grabbed my phone from the nightstand, hoping for a message or update from Jeff about Regan's position or the collection. But I found nothing.

"The kidnappings?" Ethan asked, and I nodded.

"Luc filled me in on the details last night. It was a good idea, calling Tate."

I felt a tingle of relief. "We weren't sure you'd see it that way."

"If he'd hurt you, I'd have killed him myself. Fortunately, all is well. And he has a family."

"That's what it seems."

"Chicago has become a very unusual world now that you're in it, Merit."

"I'd like it to become a smaller world. We still don't know where Regan is."

Ethan nodded. "Keep at it. You'll find her eventually, and when you do, I want to know about it. I'd also like to address the House before everyone begins their days."

A bolt of nerves shot through me. Discussions in the ballroom meant serious matters. "About?"

"The future of the House," he cryptically said. "Get dressed."

I gave him a salute and toddled to the shower.

I dressed in leathers and wore my katana, which made me the odd vampire out in Cadogan's lovely second-floor ballroom. Most everyone else wore their black standard-issue Cadogan suits, their new teardrop medals winking atop pale skin. Luc, who wore jeans, and Helen, who wore a pink tweed suit, were exceptions to the general rule. I moved to Luc, stood beside him and the rest of the guards.

The mood of the vampires who filled the room was nervous but excited. Those who'd missed Ethan's arrival were obviously glad to see him back, and I could hear the whispers about how their Liege had fared in custody, and if he was as healthy now as he'd been when he left.

Ethan stepped to the dais in the front of the room, Malik beside him. Thunderous applause filled the air. Ethan smiled, letting his gaze scan and catch the eyes of the Novitiates who stood before him.

Ethan allowed the applause to go on for a moment—he still had his ego—before lifting his hands. The room quieted instantly.

"It's nice to be home again," he said, which set off another round of hoots and applause.

"The city acted unfairly toward us, toward Grey House, toward Navarre. We have helped this city over the last few months with issues they were unable or unwilling to address, and they have done us no service by accusing us of wrongdoing."

His gaze narrowed. "I can affirm, for better or worse, that they believe they are doing the right thing for Chicago. This is no political ploy or attempt to win votes. They, the mayor included, have been advised by many—and wrongly—that supernatural creatures are the enemy. Frankly, much of the trouble we've seen in the last few months can be laid at the feet of supernaturals. That fact is undeniable. But we also are the solution. And the vast majority of us are trying to do right by the city that we love.

"I'm happy to announce the mayor has agreed to begin peace talks with the city's supernaturals. The mayor also has agreed to engage Merit's grandfather once again as supernatural liaison on a probationary basis."

There were happy cheers and several friendly pats on my back. I would, of course, have preferred my grandfather become a fan of daytime television instead of dealing with more supernatural drama. But he was who he was. And it wasn't my place to deny him that.

"But there is another issue we should discuss," he said. This time, my stomach curled into a tight knot.

"Lakshmi Rao has traveled to Chicago to meet with us as a representative of the Greenwich Presidium to set forth the GP's demand for retribution in the death of Harold Monmonth. As you may imagine, I don't believe their demands have any basis in reality. But the GP is what the GP is. We will hear her offer, and we will act accordingly."

He looked at me. "The world is changing. Our world is changing. We will do our best to meet the challenges we face with honor, with bravery, with respect for those around us. That," he said, looking across the sea of vampires again, "is what makes us Cadogan vampires." He raised his fist into the air. "To Cadogan House!"

"*To Cadogan House!*" shouted his vampires in unison.

I loved Ethan Sullivan. Lusted for him, in many instances. But I respected him most of all. And just like my grandfather, he was who he was.

It wasn't my place to deny Ethan, either.

Ethan excused the House, and the vampires filed out the door, heading off to their jobs or assignments. Ethan and Malik lingered in the front of the room.

I glanced at Luc. "I'll meet you in the Ops Room."

He nodded. "Do that, Sentinel. We'll be waiting for you."

I walked toward Ethan, nodded at Malik as he clasped Ethan's hand, then filed out with the rest of the vampires.

He still stood on the dais, a foot above me, looking down with hands on his hips. "Hello, Sentinel. I recall we've been in this position before."

"So we have. When you named me Sentinel."

He stepped down, touched a finger to the medal at my neck. "And much has passed since then."

I looked up at him, ignored my fear, and spilled out what was in my heart. "We need a change. Vampires need a change, solid leadership, and a new direction. You could provide all that. You should challenge Darius. Make the GP respectable again."

Shock and pleasure in his eyes, he stepped forward, wrapped his arms around me, and pressed his lips to my forehead. "There is much to be gained. And much to be lost."

My heart pounded with sudden fear that he'd included me in the latter category.

"The future of the House is uncertain," Ethan said, but he didn't seem worried. He kissed me again. "For now, Sentinel, get down to the Ops Room and see about its present."

I found Jeff tucked in with Luc and Lindsey at the conference room desk.

"How's the search going?" I asked, taking a seat on the other side of the table.

"It's not," Jeff said, with unusual irritation. "Do you know how long it takes to search every square block of the city looking for trailers one block at a time?" He winced, ran his hands through his hair. "Sorry. I'm just frustrated. This is taking for-freaking-ever." He looked up at me, and even Jeff—Jeff of boundless energy and good humor—looked tired. "And we don't have any basis to narrow this down. We have no bio information, no personal information. I even looked online to see if Regan might have sent invitations electronically, and found nothing."

I blew out a breath, looked at the whiteboard. The information about Regan was limited. Extremely limited. "She lost her mom," I said. "Didn't know her dad. Has some insecurities about that. Considers herself a kind of nomad, if the vardo is any indication. But what else?"

"You saw her at the grocery store," Luc said. "Did she buy anything that might provide a hint?"

I closed my eyes, imagined her standing across the room, a grocery basket in hand. She'd looked at medical supplies, but that was all I could remember.

"She had good fashion sense. Jeans, red cape." I glanced at Lindsey. "Come to think of it, it was an outfit you could have pulled off."

"Of course I could have."

"Designer handbag, too. If she likes fancy, maybe she likes fancy neighborhoods." I glanced at Jeff. "Can you search neighborhoods based on per capita income? Maybe we can narrow down the search that way?"

Jeff nodded, was already busy tapping on his portable.

Helen appeared in the doorway, looked at me. "There's someone here to see you," she said. "A man." With that announcement, she disappeared again.

I frowned, looked at Luc, who shrugged. "If she thought he was dangerous, she'd have kneed him in the balls. A fierce fighter, is Helen."

I wasn't sure about that, but I understood his larger point and trotted upstairs to the first floor.

Damien Garza—tall, dark, and sleek in his leather jacket— stood in the Cadogan House foyer.

"Damien," I said, ignoring the looks of interest from the vampires in the foyer. "What are you doing here?"

"Regan," he said. "I believe I can find her. But I need a team."

He looked uncomfortable at the conference room table, his head four inches higher than anyone else's. The fact that we were staring at him probably didn't help.

"How's Boo?" I asked, breaking the ice.

Damien broke into an endearing smile. "Good. Likes his kibble. Sleeps on an old T-shirt."

"That is adorable," I decided, and couldn't help but wonder if he was bare chested while the kitty borrowed his shirt.

Apparently wondering too loudly. Luc kicked my foot under the table, smiled at Damien. "Tell us what brings you into the city."

"I've got a cousin, a human, who lives in Lincoln Park. I've asked my friends, family, to keep an eye out for the carnival or anything else suspicious. She called me earlier tonight. There's a new development in Lincoln Park called Briarthorne. Gated community, very exclusive. She lives across the street. Said she saw two big silver trailers pull through the gate last night."

"Jesus," Luc said, eyes wide and excited. "Regan's trailers."

Damien smiled. "That's what it sounds like to me. And I want in on the op."

Luc reached out, offered Damien a hand. "Sir, that won't be a problem."

"I've scoped them out," Jeff said, the overhead screen zeroing in on Lincoln Park and the Briarthorne development. He ducked to street level so quickly my stomach flipped as if I'd actually been diving toward it, and then he began to scan the neighborhood.

The houses were luxe, with large pools and enormous garages, both rarities in Chicago. Jeff panned the shot through the gate and up the street, past one large lot after another. The neighborhood was huge; they must have razed a lot of real estate to fit it in. Streets gave way to a small park crisscrossed by sidewalks.

"There," Damien said, pointing at the two sleek trailers that sat at the end of the park.

"Ballsy of her to put down in the middle of the city," Lindsey said. "And in the middle of the money and power."

"Not all the money and power," Luc snarked. "Merit's parents live in Oak Park."

"Har-har," I said. "Not ballsy if it's a gated community," I added. "That gives her protection."

Luc nodded. "And the cost of admission gives her resources and makes them believe they're seeing an exciting and exclusive safari."

"I'll tell Malik and Ethan we've found her," Luc said, picking up his phone.

"I'll call Catcher and Mallory," I offered, opting to give Jonah the night off. After all, we had an extra shifter.

By the time the entire crew was assembled, the Ops Room buzzed with energy and magic. Several vampires, two sorcerers, and two shifters. Jeff called Gabe to advise the Pack we'd found Regan's menagerie, but they were still in Loring Park; waiting for them would have slowed us down. The longer we waited, the longer we risked she'd move again. And next time, we might not get so lucky.

The map of Briarthorne was still on-screen, giving everyone a sense of the location.

"Two trailers," Luc said, pointing to the screen. "North end of the park, end to end. Jeff, Damien, Catcher, Mallory, Ethan, and Merit will go. We'll stay here to keep an eye on the House just in case Regan decides she has a unique opportunity to test our security." The idea was undoubtedly a good one, but he didn't look thrilled about the idea of staying behind.

"Helen is preparing the ballroom for triage and shelter," Ethan said. "Any sups who wish to come to the House can do so. We'll have transportation at the park in order to get them here. We'll also assist in reuniting them with their friends and families, wherever that might be."

"And what about Regan?" Jeff asked. "At the risk of being grim, there are many, many people who will want a piece of her when all this is done."

"They will," Ethan agreed. "But our job is not to decide her fate."

"When we've secured the sups," Luc said, "we'll call Detective

Jacobs and advise she's a suspect in the kidnapping of several supernaturals. That will keep her behind bars long enough."

"She's got magic. He may not want the responsibility."

"The mayor created mechanisms to deal with Tate once upon a time," Ethan pointed out. "They'll deal with her, too."

"We have a deal with the elves," Damien said. "Taking Niera home, safe and sound. We'll deliver her when they're free."

Luc nodded. "You get in, you free the sups, you contain Regan. And when it's all done, you get a groovy sense of accomplishment, and we get Gabe and the elves off our backs. And probably dinner. I think Helen's ordering pizza."

Luc stood, braced his hands on the table, and looked us over one by one. "Be careful out there. And set phasers on awesome."

Crickets chirped in the silence.

Lindsey shook her head and patted Luc's hand. "Better luck next time, hon."

It was late, and the neighborhood was mostly dark. We parked on the side opposite the trailers and made our approach, quietly, in the dark. The gates were black wrought iron, cresting to a point between two stone pillars. The streets beyond were quiet, dotted with ornate streetlamps.

I looked up at the gate, which had to be twelve feet tall. I was better with down than with up and didn't want to fudge an ascent in front of my colleagues.

But a wrought-iron gate was no match for a Jeff Christopher. While we huddled in the darkness beside one of the pillars, Jeff pointed his magic tablet at the card reader notched into the stone until the light above flashed green and the gates swung open.

"Achievement unlocked," I said with awe, and caught his flashing grin.

"I knew you were a gamer at heart," he whispered.

We crept quietly through the gates and into the neighborhood.

"The park's up the street and around the curve," Jeff whispered, tucking the tablet away again. We stuck to the median that separated the parkway. The trees on the hillock were still empty of leaves, but they gave us a bit of a shield in case anyone bothered to look.

The road curved, and we followed it to a pretty park that took up a long ellipse between two sets of houses.

There, beneath the limbs of winter-bare trees, were two silver, gleaming trailers.

The faint vibration of magic hummed in the air.

"We do one trailer at a time," Ethan said. "Merit, Mallory, Catcher, and I will go inside. Jeff, Damien will wait here; keep an eye out."

When everyone nodded, we crept to the closest one, found the door at the end. Ethan hopped onto a step at the back of the truck, pulled down a giant silver handle, and pulled open the door.

Steps descended, and Catcher and I followed Ethan inside.

"Jesus," Ethan muttered, making a motion across his chest as if to ward off the evil.

The car was divided in half by a passageway, with fluorescent lights running above. It was clean and white and smelled faintly of pine-scented cleaner. Each side of the car had been divided into containers arranged like small sleeping pods. Each pod held a supernatural. I recognized a harpy, a leprechaun, his skin faintly green, a giantess sitting in the largest of them. They wore clean blue scrubs and looked to be in good health, but their eyes were blank and they stared absently.

Tears pricked at my eyes, but I pushed them back. Now wasn't the time to grieve for the years they'd lost. It was time to give them the rest of their lives.

I looked over the cases, realized who was missing. "Niera and Aline aren't here."

"There's another trailer yet," Catcher reminded me. "They could be in there."

"Then let's get started," I said. I moved to the first cage and put a hand on the lock—a long silver pin inside a complicated twisting mechanism—but Catcher slammed a hand against the door before I could open it.

I looked at him, bewildered. "We have to let them out."

"We will," he calmly said. "But unlocking the doors right now won't help. If they're charmed into this kind of oblivion, they aren't going to be able to run out of here when we open the doors. And they might be spelled to attack."

"What do we do?" I asked.

Catcher looked at Ethan. "I'll take this trailer. Mallory can take the other. We'll unwind the spells, get them ready for release." He looked at Mallory. "You remember how?"

"Yep," she said, crossing her arms to hide the tremble in her fingers. But I'd rather have her afraid than cocky and dangerous any day.

Ethan nodded and we walked outside again, explained what we'd seen.

"Damien, stay with Catcher. Jeff, stay with Mallory. Keep them safe while we find Regan."

"One thing," Catcher said, when Mallory and Jeff had left for the other train car. He pulled a set of connected silver hoops from his pocket. "Handcuffs, magically enhanced. It's what we used on Mallory. They should hold her." He tossed them into the air, and Ethan caught them neatly with one hand.

"Thank you," he said. "Get them free."

With a nod and a spark of magic, he got to work. Ethan and I surveyed the park.

"Odds are better if we separate," I told Ethan.

"I agree. I'll take the east side. You take the west."

I nodded, adjusted the tension on my belt. "Will do. I'll call if I find her."

"Do that." Before I could leave, he wrapped an arm around my waist, pulled my body against him, and pressed a hard kiss to my lips. "Do protect what's mine, Sentinel."

I made a sound at the possessive tone in his voice but still reveled in it. That I was strong enough to take down a foe didn't mean I didn't enjoy Ethan's alpha male attitude every once in a while.

"Same to you, Sullivan," I said, and headed off down the sidewalk.

The night was chilly, but this was Chicago, gated or not, and Chicagoans were used to the chill. A few people were out and about, walking dogs or returning late from work with quick steps around the edge of the park. Including one girl with platinum blond hair.

I've got her, I told Ethan. *East side of the park, moving south.*

I'll circle behind, he said. *You intercept, and carefully.*

Without killing civilians or myself, he meant. Not unreasonable advice.

I stepped off the path, watched while she moved closer. She wore a long black coat, nipped at the waist and buttoned up, and a large glossy shopping bag hung off her shoulder.

As she neared, I caught the unmistakable scents of smoke and sulfur.

When she was four feet away, I stepped in front of her. "Hello, Regan."

She stopped, eyed me curiously. "Merit, I presume. Sentinel of Cadogan House."

"That's me. I understand you have wings."

I'd hoped to catch her off guard with the reference to something I bet she showed very few people.

The ploy worked. Her eyes widened, and her hands whitened around her bag. "You don't know anything about me."

"I do, actually. At least, I think I do. Your mother told you your father was special."

Her jaw twitched, and her voice was controlled fury. "You don't know anything about my mother."

"Oh, I know a lot about Annalissa. And your father was special, as it turns out. Magical and talented and very unique. I'm sorry to say that he's no longer with us, but his twin brother is alive. Your uncle." At least, that was the relationship I'd decided on. We were in the fuzzy territory where magic and genetics collided, and I wasn't really sure of anything.

"Oh, and your uncle's an angel."

For the first time, she looked genuinely flummoxed. "What?"

"An angel, and a very good man, Regan. I can help you meet him, if you'd like."

She snorted. "You think I'm going to trust you? You want to put me in a cage."

She didn't seem to get the irony. "You've committed crimes in several states," I pointed out. "Kidnapping, primarily."

She looked disgusted by my ignorance. "They weren't kidnapped. They are my family."

"They are in cages. Drugged and stuffed inside cages like animals while you've been out shopping." She flinched, proving I was on the right track.

"Is that how you treat family? You keep them safely locked

away so they aren't gone when you return home? So they don't leave you like your father did?"

"You don't know anything about me or my family."

"I know too much," I said, the honest truth. "And I know you can't force a family with magic just because you're pissed off at the real one."

I'd pushed her over the edge. She let out a scream, whipped around the shopping bag, and slung it at me. I put up an arm to dodge it, wincing when the weight of it hit my arm. Using my hesitation, she took off across the park.

And so the chase began.

She's heading for the trailers, I told Ethan, running full out and trying to close the gap between us. She hurdled a bench and I followed, thrilled when the vault put me five feet closer to her.

I paused long enough to pluck the dagger from my boot and send it spiraling, end over end, in her direction.

Regan yelped when it bit into her shoulder, stumbled forward but caught herself, yanked it out with a scream.

The scents of smoke and sulfur grew stronger. When she turned back to me, the dagger glinting in her hand, there was murder in her eyes. "Do you know what I am?"

"I do," I assured her, unsheathing my katana and settling my fingers around the handle. I kept my gaze on hers, and my expression just as haughty.

"You're the daughter of Dominic Tate. The niece of Seth Tate, former mayor of Chicago, and an angel. You're also a spoiled brat. But that's just my opinion."

Regan launched herself forward, swiping the blade in a shot I neatly dodged.

I sliced horizontally, and she ducked to avoid the blow, bringing up the dagger with a clean shot that nicked my shin. A line of pain burned hot, but I ignored it, finished my spin, and attacked downward.

She rolled across the ground, popping up a few feet away. We circled each other, and as we turned, I caught movement from the corner of my eye—Ethan stood nearby, his sword still sheathed but his eyes cold and calculating.

Feel free to join in, I told him, jumping back to dodge her advance and the tip of the blade.

You seem to be managing fine on your own. The sups are unspelled and released. You might mention that to her.

"The gig's up, Regan. The sups are gone. It's just you and me."

She cursed, moved forward, dropping the blade and using the weight of her body to send me to the ground. My katana skidded away, and snow seeped into the gaps in my leather, sending wet trickles down hot skin.

"They're my *family*," she yelled, trying to pummel me into submission.

"They have . . . their own . . . families," I reminded her. I grabbed her fist, twisted, and pushed her over, pinning her to the ground.

I was faster, but she was stronger. Regan screamed, threw me off and away. I flew back six feet, skidding across the ground.

I believe now I might join you, Ethan said.

Too late, I told him, wiping blood from my eye. *She's mine.*

I put my hands behind me, flipped to my feet, and snatched my katana from the ground, spinning as I turned to face her again.

She flew out an arm and a crackle of magic that sent the tree behind us to the ground with an enormous *crack*. I jumped as it fell to the ground a foot away, branches swaying with the force of the movement, and a sizzling, chemical scent in the air.

"You're a little old for tantrum throwing, aren't you?" I asked, jumping atop a branch and rolling the katana in my fingers.

"I'll show you a tantrum," she said, holding out her palms, a fiery sword appearing between them. She immediately swung it at me, and I neatly dodged and sliced again.

"Of course she has a flaming sword," I murmured, dodging another slice. Regan didn't have the training—her movements made that obvious—but she had strength and magic enough to wield her flaming steel like a champion.

Sirens rose in the distance, and I caught my chance. I dodged, sliced, and moved gradually toward the sidewalk and the blue and red lights that were racing up the street.

She let out a low growl, my hair standing on end as she prepared to throw out another blade of magic.

I ducked and hit the ground as a sizzle lit the air. But it was Regan who crumpled, the sword in her hand disappearing with a puff of smoke.

We looked behind us, where Detective Jacobs stood beside a squad car, a Taser in hand. He smiled, his smile a deep crevice in his dark skin.

"Just thought I'd offer you a hand," he said with a wink.

I'd always liked him.

Ethan applied the cuffs, and Catcher helped transport Regan into the back of Detective Jacobs's vehicle.

When possession was transferred to him, they walked back to where Ethan and I stood by, just close enough to ensure she'd been taken into custody.

"That will hold her," Catcher said. "They're going to use the same dampening magic they used on Tate. Apparently the corrections departments across the U.S. have developed some pretty good skills in that area."

"I'll contact Gabriel," Damien said, nodding toward Niera and

Aline, who sat on opposite ends of a nearby bench. Even in crisis, there was no friendship between these particular clans.

Aline stood and walked toward us, looked at me and Ethan.

"I don't know that I trust you. But I know how to give thanks where thanks are due."

She held out a hand. Dumbfounded, I accepted it. The deed done, she turned and walked back to the bench, where she sat sullenly again.

"Well, that happened," I said. "I don't know if that moment of friendship will stick, but it's a start."

"Sometimes," Ethan said, "that's the best we can hope for."

"And speaking of hope," I said, glancing at Niera, "we have a truce to make good on."

They stood in long, precise columns that stretched across the field near their village. They'd traded their simple tunics for gleaming armor and open helms with thin guards that covered their noses, and each held a bow and arrow. There must have been thousands of them, and they stood with robotic precision, ready for action.

Perhaps not so unlike the metaphorical locusts.

We stood in front of them, a smaller group than the last time we'd met. The Brecks, the Keenes, Ethan, and me. More vulnerable to the elves without an army behind us, and trusting that they'd stand by their word.

But not so trusting that we didn't have our swords unsheathed and at the ready.

And at my side stood Niera. She made no sound, just as during the trip to the Brecks' estate. But she'd stared at the sights with a mix of wonderment and fear that sent magic through the car. It seemed the elves had avoided all contact with the metropolis that lay at the edge of their territory.

The elf who'd presented us after the kidnapping—or so I thought, as like the fairies, they looked fraternally similar—stepped forward, a standard-bearer at his side.

"A truce was called," he said, "pursuant to the terms of our pact. What say you now?"

Gabriel stepped forward. "Your clanswoman Niera was taken against her will, by a creature of immense power. We identified the creature. Tracked her. Obtained Niera's release. And we bring her back to you today."

He gestured toward Niera, who stepped forward.

The elf's expression stayed mild, controlled, but there was relief in his eyes.

Niera walked toward him and into his embrace. There were shouts of joy and relief from the elves, and a burst of fresh magic, until the army swallowed Niera into its ranks once again.

"The pact has been fulfilled," Gabriel said.

"For now," the elf agreed. "We will see what the future holds." They turned on their heels and began the silent march back to their wood.

We watched in silence until they'd disappeared completely, until the trees no longer shook from the army's intrusion.

"I don't know about you," Gabriel said, "but I think it's time for a drink."

CHAPTER TWENTY-ONE

ORANGE IS THE NEW BLACK

At dusk the next evening, Lakshmi arrived to discuss the GP and its variety of issues, looking gorgeous in a sleek black dress with an asymmetrical neckline and stiletto heels. I stood in the foyer with Luc, Malik, and Helen, nodding politely as she arrived, and then directing her to Ethan's office.

"And now, once again, we wait," Luc said with a grumble. "I swear to God, I spend half my time doing that."

I didn't disagree. But I'd already arranged a way to spend the time.

An hour later, I stood at the tall fence outside the former brick factory where the CPD had held Seth Tate once upon a time, and where they now held his niece.

And now, thanks to Detective Jacobs, Regan and her uncle were going to have their own reunion.

A taxi pulled up the long drive, and after exchanging bills, a man emerged. He had short sandy hair and a thick nose, and he wore khakis and a button-down shirt.

Seth Tate could have passed for an accountant, but he still smelled like freshly baked cookies.

"Nice disguise," I said.

He nodded. "They'll have the building warded, so I had to go old-school."

Headlights appeared in the darkness, and a golf cart pulled up to the gate. A young, fit woman in a black uniform climbed out and walked to the gate.

"Caroline Merit and John Smith?"

I waved a little bit. "That's us."

She nodded officially, unlocked the gate, and held it open for us.

"Mind the gap," she said, gesturing toward the bench on the back of the cart.

"John Smith?" Seth murmured as he took a seat beside me.

"The alias wasn't really the key component of the plan," I said, as the guard accelerated and we bobbled down the gravel road. The factory was actually a set of several large buildings used to mold and fire bricks during wartime. Seth had been held in a small stand-alone building, but we passed it as we headed toward a long single-story building on the other side of the compound.

"Are you nervous?" I quietly asked, as his gaze settled on his former prison cell.

"A little," he admitted. "I've never had a niece before. Or a relative of any kind other than Dominic. And I'm not sure he counted."

"More a supernatural parasite."

"And yet he was sentient enough to control me. To connect with a woman and father a child."

But Dominic had been a lover in his time. He'd seduced Claudia, the queen of the fairies. It had been her love that bound Dominic to Seth and kept him out of the *Maleficium*.

The guard stopped in front of the entrance and escorted us into the building. It was a large empty space but for the series of small square rooms that dotted the concrete floor. Guards were stationed here and there, and they had the look of well-seasoned military types.

The mayor wasn't taking any chances with Regan. And she now had a facility to hold a small supernatural army. Not a comforting thought.

"She's in the first one," the guard said, gesturing us forward. The rooms were made of concrete, with a window and door on the front side. "You can go ahead."

We walked toward the window, peered inside.

Regan sat at an aluminum table, and she'd exchanged her designer clothes for an orange jumpsuit. She moved nervously in her chair, kept nervously touching her hair. She might have been a badass in her element, but here she looked small and insecure.

I glanced at Seth.

He watched her, head angled, eyes wide, for a long moment. "There's more of him in her than I'd have imagined," he finally said.

"Is that good or bad?"

"I'm not certain."

"All things considered, I don't know if she's capable of contrition. But maybe you can give her peace. Maybe you can ensure she doesn't hurt anyone else."

Seth nodded. There weren't many times I'd seen him nervous. But here, facing the family he hadn't known he had, he looked absolutely bewildered.

"You can do this," I said. "And right now, I don't think you even have to be good at it. You just have to be there."

He squeezed my hand. "You are wise beyond your years, Ballerina."

"Immortality tends to do that," I murmured.

Seth blew out a breath, put a hand on the door, and walked inside.

Regan looked up as Seth walked in and sat down in the chair across from her.

"What's going on in there?" the guard asked, moving closer to the door.

"A family reunion."

Maybe a little family would do them both some good.

They talked for nearly an hour, which was all the time Jacobs could eke out of the mayor considering the multiple charges against Regan.

I stood by watching from the window with the guard until Seth's hour was up and the guard knocked on the door again.

Seth squeezed Regan's hand, rose, and came to the door.

When he stepped outside, his gaze found mine. There was a disconcertingly familiar intensity in his eyes that scared me to the bone. Had I made a mistake, bringing him here? Putting the two of them together?

"You're all right?"

He nodded, and a smile blossomed. "I can't thank you enough for this. For arranging this reunion after everything that's happened."

I hadn't expected thanks, and it flustered me. "You're welcome. It went okay?"

"It did," he said, scratching his head nervously. "She's got issues. Many of them involve Dominic; others, magic. But I think there's a chance for her, Merit."

I glanced back at Regan and thought about what Gabe had said at Lupercalia, there with Mallory in front of the totem before things had gone so wrong. About those brave enough to crawl back from their wrongs and try to make things better.

"The supernaturals in her menagerie were well cared for. She told me she thought of them as family. Maybe that's what she needs now. Maybe she is capable of contrition; maybe she isn't. But she's yours, and you deserve the chance to help her try."

"Oh, I intend to," he said, and before I could respond, he pulled off his wig and the plastic that had covered his nose. He ran a hand through his dark hair, smiled at the guard.

The guard, whom Tate had finally managed to shake, swallowed hard. "You're—you're the mayor."

"Former," Seth said with a soft smile. "Now I'm just a man, and I believe you'll find there are warrants out for my arrest. I've been avoiding my punishment. But I'll take it now."

The guard looked at him for a moment, then back at me, clearly unsure what to do. It couldn't have been every day that she was faced with a felon who offered himself up to incarceration.

"It's no trick," Seth said. "I'm just finally—after too long—doing the right thing. I'd like to serve my time honorably."

Another moment passed, but the guard relented. "All right, then," she said, gesturing two more guards forward. While they watched Tate with weapons drawn, she cuffed his wrists with zip strips she'd pulled from a pouch on her belt.

"You have a right to talk to a lawyer," she said, putting a hand on his arm.

"No need," he said. "But you might want to call the mayor."

When the guard gestured toward the second room, Seth looked back at me and smiled magnanimously.

"What are you doing?" I asked, still completely dumbfounded.

"Neither Dominic nor I protected her before. But if I'm here, I can protect her now. At least in some way."

And he let the guard lead him away.

The House cafeteria was located in the back of the first floor, the large windows looking out over the beautiful grounds that surrounded the House. Snow still glistened magically there. It was between meals, so the cafeteria was empty but for the bustle of staff who worked to prepare the next round of meals for the vampires.

Ethan wasn't yet done with Lakshmi, so I sat at a wooden table in a wooden chair beside one of the windows and stared out across the lawn at the banks of trees and hillocks of undisturbed snow. A rabbit darted into view, paused and looked around for predators, then dashed away to safety again.

At the sound of footsteps, I looked up. Ethan walked into the room, then over to a glass-doored cooler on the opposite wall. He grabbed two bottles of Blood4You, brought them to the table.

"You all right?" he asked, popping the tops on both and handing one to me.

"Having some quiet time. I don't get that often."

"No," he agreed. "You do not. Seth?"

"Incarcerated," I said. "Turned himself in so he'd be in prison with Regan."

Ethan's eyes widened. "He's made quite a turnaround."

I nodded. "That's an understatement. But it's also kind of perfect."

I made myself wait a beat, gave him an opportunity to take a drink, before asking him. "What did Lakshmi say? What is the GP demanding of the House?"

He took another drink, set the bottle on the table. "The GP believes, as we have killed one of their vampires, they have a right to the same."

My blood chilled. "They want to kill a member of Cadogan House?" The GP had made ignorant and thoughtless moves before, but none as heartless as that. None that were as conniving or, frankly, stupid.

"They're bluffing," I said, and Ethan smiled back faintly.

"Bluffing or not, that was their offer, delivered here by Lakshmi Rao. I understand you're well acquainted."

I kept my expression as neutral as possible, but I was sure he saw the hitch in my eyes. "Oh?" I innocently asked.

He gave me a dubious look. "She is supportive of the idea of challenging Darius for the GP. She suggested I should do it."

"Hmm. And are you?" I realized my hands had begun to shake, and I tucked them between my knees. Even if I accepted the notion that Ethan loved me unconditionally, that didn't mean I wouldn't fear for his safety if he decided to challenge Darius.

He looked at me for a long, quiet moment, took my hand. "I believe, Sentinel, that I am."

I felt like I'd been pushed off a cliff, suddenly dizzy, suddenly worried. "And the House? Chicago?"

"Will be protected," he said. "There is a long road before the leadership of the GP is settled. A potentially dangerous road," he admitted. "But a long road nonetheless. All things can be worked out."

"And London?" I asked. "Can it be worked out?"

"Come here," Ethan murmured, and before I could move, my hand was in his, and we were moving. He led me up and out of the cafeteria, down the hallway, and up the stairs.

"Where are we going?" I asked as we rounded the third-floor

landing and headed down the hallway to a room I knew was empty except for the pull-down ladder that led to the attic and the House's widow's walk.

"I'm showing you something," Ethan said, pulling down the ladder. He gestured toward it. "You first."

I knew when to obey without sarcasm. I climbed up and into the attic, which wasn't much to see. Mostly rafters and insulation. The window that led to the roof was closed. I unlatched it and pushed it open, assuming that was what Ethan had intended me to do. As he climbed the ladder behind me, I stepped outside.

The widow's walk was a narrow ledge around this part of the roof, marked by a short wrought-iron barrier. Lake Michigan was a dark stain to the east, and downtown Chicago shined to the north.

The roof creaked as Ethan stepped beside me. He put one hand around my waist and used the other to point at the blinking lights of the city.

"There," he said. "If I take power, that is the new seat of the Greenwich Presidium."

It took me a moment to understand what he'd said, the scope of the change he'd just proposed. "You want to move the GP to Chicago?"

"I *will* move the GP to Chicago," Ethan said, filling those words with every bit of pretention and egoism I knew him capable of.

He tilted my chin to meet his gaze. "You are my soul, Merit. But vampires are my body. To be whole, I must respect both. And the GP has held court too far from the American Houses for far too long. It's time the GP came home to roost."

"They'll fight to keep the seat in Europe," I said. "Danica and the others won't let you move it."

"If they do not control the GP, they will have no choice." He touched a fingertip to my lips. "I made my choice, Merit, many months ago. There is no turning back. Not now."

His lips so soft, yet so stern, he pressed his mouth to mine.

"I will have both of you," he said. "My Sentinel and my city. And the GP will learn exactly how stubborn we both can be."

Photo by Dana Damewood Photography

Chloe Neill was born and raised in the South but now makes her home in the Midwest—just close enough to Cadogan House and St. Sophia's to keep an eye on things. When not transcribing Merit's and Lily's adventures, she bakes, works, and scours the Internet for good recipes and great graphic design. Chloe also maintains her sanity by spending time with her boys—her favorite landscape photographer (her husband) and their dogs, Baxter and Scout. (Both she and the photographer understand the dogs are in charge.)

CONNECT ONLINE

www.chloeneill.com
facebook.com/authorchloeneill
twitter.com/chloeneill